D1521248

Sleight of Hand

Tech Billionaires book 3

A Novel

by:
Ainsley St Claire

Tech Billionaires: Sleight of Hand/Ainsley St Claire—1st edition

Dedication
&
Thank you

To my three boys. You are my reason for everything. Thank you so much for your love and support.

Thank you to my amazing editor Jessica Royer Ocken and my incredible typo hunting/beta reading team: Nancy, Linda, and Courtnay. All of you make my words beautiful. Thank you!!!

Thank you to my readers. For allowing me time in your busy schedule to share with you the crazy stories that are in my head. Without you, none of this would be possible.

GET THE NEWSLETTER

If you like to download a free copy of *Gifted* and sign up for Ainsley's Naughty Readers to receive the latest news on my upcoming novels, sign up for my free author newsletter at https://dl.bookfunnel.com/zi378x4ybx

CHAPTER 1

Tinsley

"Look at that man who just walked in the door, Tinsley. Holy guacamole, he's sex on a stick and hot, hot, hot."

I turn to look at my best friend, Chrissy Matthews, and follow her line of sight. The man she's looking at *is* something to behold: dark, messy hair that contrasts with pale skin, brooding blue eyes, and his body... I fan myself. His T-shirt is stretched over his arms and chest and his jeans are showing off, well, his massive package.

I lean over. "How much you want to bet he stuffed a sock in his pants?"

She looks him up and down. "No way is he that big."

He looks over at us and smiles. When he makes eye contact with me, I smile back.

It seems to encourage him, and he makes his way to us. "Hello, ladies."

"Hi," Chrissy offers.

"What are we celebrating?"

I look over at Chrissy and give her a careful shake, so hopefully, she understands not to go there.

"We're celebrating a Tuesday night," she says.

"I like that. May I celebrate with you?"

He looks at me, and how can I refuse?

I have to say, Chrissy and I look fantastic tonight. Not club-ready, but I'm not in my usual T-shirt, sweatshirt, and jeans. I have on a dark blue, strapless sundress and a pair of peep-toe stilettos. Chrissy's dark blond curls are piled high on her head, and she's in a pair of jeans and a wrap sweater that shows a tremendous amount of golden-toned cleavage.

He pulls up a stool between the two of us.

Chrissy picks up her almost-empty glass of wine and takes a big swig. "My name is Madeline, and this is Amanda."

I chuckle that she uses our fake bar names. She's out to tease this poor guy. I almost feel sorry for him. Maybe.

"Nice to meet you both. My name is Peter Landon." He leans toward my ear and whispers, "It's not a sock. Care to feel for yourself?"

I'm shocked that he heard me in a crowded bar on a busy weeknight. "Thanks," I manage. "But I don't typically feel men up until I've had at least a few drinks."

I'm out with Chrissy to celebrate the sale of the company I started, Translations, to a larger startup, which officially happens tomorrow afternoon. I sold to Disruptive Technologies in the hopes that together we can do something truly amazing.

Peter motions to the bartender. "Can we get a sloe comfortable screw, a sex on the beach, and a blowjob, please?"

Chrissy and I exchange looks. We may have met our match.

He takes out a black American Express card and hands it to the bartender. "Please open a tab for these beautiful women."

I roll my eyes. "Laying it on a little thick, don't you think?"

"Trust me, nothing is little, and you did say it would take a few drinks for you to verify that I don't stuff my pants with socks."

I shake my head and smile. My panties have officially melted. He puts his arm around me, and his hand rests on my back. I feel the electric charge shoot right to my core. The only thing that's been keeping me company lately is Bob — my battery-operated boyfriend — and while Peter's forwardness should have me throwing what's left of my drink in his face, instead I'm quite turned on.

"So, what do you both do for work?" he asks.

This is where Chrissy shines. Watching her spin a web of deceit is quite fun. "I teach fourth grade at St. Anthony Catholic School, and Amanda is a nurse."

"So, it's either hot for teacher or naughty nurse?"

Damn, he's good. That's our joke. I might actually like this guy.

Chrissy swears that men don't like smart women, so in situations like this, we downplay our brains. She has an MBA from Harvard and runs marketing for a major bank, and I went to Stanford and have a degree in electrical engineering and software development.

"Which is your preference?" I ask.

He gives me a salacious grin. "They all sound good to me."

The bartender places our drinks in front of us. Chrissy reaches for the shot glass and puts it down on the bar in front of her. Peter and I watch as she leans over and picks up the glass with her mouth, downing the shot in one gulp. When she puts the glass back on the bar, she wets her lips and makes a moaning noise as she licks the whipped cream away. Her act has caught the attention of several here in the bar.

"Thanks for the drink," she says.

"I'm happy to order you another round." Peter smiles at her while his arm remains wrapped around me.

She shakes her head.

He turns to me. "Which do you prefer? Sex on the beach or a sloe comfortable screw?"

I reach for the sloe comfortable screw and raise the glass to him. "To an evening of fun."

His eyes lock with mine. "I'll drink to that."

"Well, I need to go. I have a date with a beautiful blond pussy with an amazing tongue." Chrissy picks up her bag and winks at Peter. She's talking about her cat, but he doesn't need to know that. "Thanks for the blowjob."

"Any time, Maddy." He reaches for her hand and kisses her knuckles.

Chrissy turns and gives me a quick hug. "I want a text later tonight to verify if it's one sock or two." She steps back and stares at his package. "I'm guessing two."

As she heads for the door, I pick up the sloe comfortable screw and take a deep pull. I need to cool off.

"So, tell me more about you." Peter's whisper in my ear makes my nipples pebble.

Damn, this man is becoming my kryptonite.

I shrug. "There's not much to tell. I work at the hospital as a surgical nurse. What about you? What gets a man a black American Express card?"

He signals the bartender and points to our drinks, asking for a second round. "I suppose…" He doesn't look at me. "…a solid idea that someone is foolish enough to buy."

I'm not interested in his money, so I won't push. I can relate, given that my partially formed idea will be bought tomorrow for ten million dollars. But I'm not telling him that. He thinks I'm a naughty nurse.

"You must be thirsty to be ordering another round so quickly."

He leans in, and I can smell his pine scent. I like it. "I'm ready to show you that I don't stuff my pants with socks, and I, too, have a wicked tongue."

With over a million people living in less than seven square miles of this city, I have two choices: I can go home to Bob—again, or I can take this fine specimen of a man up on his offer. If he doesn't have a sock in his pants, he may be more than I can take.

"Then what are we waiting for?" I ask.

"There's a hotel just across the street."

"I was thinking the coatroom," I suggest. I don't want to spend the night with him. I just want a quick and thorough fuck.

He nuzzles my neck. "I like the way you're thinking."

The bar has a coatroom that's busy during colder seasons, but given that the early-June weather is perfect tonight, there's nothing going on. It's a large closet, with a bench and a mirror. It might be fun, and a bit adventurous.

I grab Peter by the hand and lead him to the closet, and the door isn't shut behind me before his lips are on mine. His tongue is aggressive as it probes my mouth.

I'm dizzy with desire. I can't be sure, but I think this man just kissed my lips off.

I step back and try to regain some composure. "I want to see your cock."

"I promise you will, but first, it's all about you." Turning me around to face the mirror, he bends me over the bench, pushes my skirt up, and looks at me as he caresses my ass. Then he bends down and licks the insides of my thighs, which are glistening wet already.

Yanking my panties down, he spreads my legs apart. I can see him behind me in the mirror. He's watching me, too, as he puts his fingers deep into my pussy, sliding them in, nice and easy. It feels good. I begin to breathe heavy, small moans escaping my mouth.

"You're so tight. Do you like that?"

I nod, enjoying his thumb strumming my clit while his fingers rub my g-spot.

He smacks my right ass cheek, and it stings. He's made me want this, and I'm powerless to stop my body from responding.

He's fucking me with his hands, and he pushes my hair off my neck, caressing the hollow of my throat with one thumb as he bangs me from behind. I press myself into his hand, my legs open, and my hands holding the bench and wall to keep me steady.

His tongue is everywhere, inside me, on my clit, licking my thighs. He winds his hand around in my hair and pulls. He arches my back and puts his fingers inside me again, not just banging, but more like he's feeling me from the inside. My orgasm hits quickly, and my legs quiver.

"That's it, sweetheart."

He licks up my cum as it leaks down my legs. "It's sweet nectar." He holds my head in one hand and puts the fingers of his other hand into my mouth so I can taste myself.

I comply and suck his fingers.

"You're so sexy," he rasps.

It's time to see if he's as big as I think he is. I get down in front of him on my knees, then reach up to unbutton his jeans, looking at him the whole time.

There's no sock; he's just big. I free the hard rod from his pants—the purple head glistening with pre-cum and the veins bulging. I've only seen cocks this big in adult toy stores. I didn't think they came like this in real life.

"Now that you know I don't stuff my pants with socks, what are you going to do with me?" he asks.

As he threads his fingers in my hair, I lick the tip, and I hear his sharp intake of air. I'm not sure how much of this I'll be able to swallow, but I need to find out. I wrap one hand around the base of his cock and guide him in. He walks toward me, filling my mouth, and I slide back to keep from gagging, until he has me shoved up against the wall.

He pulls out and yanks me back to my feet. He spins me around and throws me back over the bench again, bent forward at a ninety-degree angle with my legs apart.

He pulls out his wallet, and I watch as he sheaths his cock.

I shiver with excitement.

He rubs the shaft through my slit and pushes inside.

Little explosions happen across my vision as I reach another climax. The feeling, oh God, it's more orgasmic than I've ever felt.

Forget Bob. This is what real pleasure feels like.

I see stars, and I'm squirting, coming. He's pounding me, and it's all happening at once. I've never been so overwhelmed. It feels like honey dripping down my thighs. I can't stop myself, and I let out a long, screaming groan, my eyes squeezing shut as fireworks explode.

An hour later, I stumble out of the coatroom on a multi-orgasmic high.

We didn't exchange numbers or anything. It was just hot sex. Damn, that man was amazing. This is going to be a good week. Tomorrow I get a big, fat check and a bunch of stock options. Life is perfect.

I text Chrissy.

Me: No sock. I may have to replace Bob, though.

Chrissy: Did you exchange contact info?

Me: Nope. If it's meant to be, I'll see him again. But I'm not counting on it.

"Welcome, Ms. Pratt." The receptionist greets me the following afternoon as I walk in. "Would you like a cup of tea?"

It's pretty bad when the receptionist knows my name *and* my drink order. It's taken a long time to pull this deal together. "That would be wonderful. Thank you."

"Mr. Arnold will meet you in the large conference room shortly." She opens her arm to the all-glass room beyond reception with a stunning view of the bay and

Berkeley on the other side.

I can't sit down. I'm both nervous and excited. I've met with Claire Walsh several times, and we've hashed out our deal. I wish I could take the obscene amount of money they're paying me and go sit on a beach for a few months to decompress, but unfortunately, part of the contract requires that I remain with the company for the next five years for the first ten percent of the shares, and another five years for the next ten percent.

My phone rings, and it's my mother. "Hi, Mom."

"I just wanted to wish you luck today. Are you nervous?"

My mom is a high-powered attorney and partner in her law firm in Denver. I owe her everything. My dad left us when I was a baby, and it was always just the two of us. She's the reason I've worked so hard to do so well.

"A little nervous, but I now have a regular paycheck, and you can finally drop me from your health insurance."

She chortles, and I know she's smiling. I was coming off of her insurance in a few months when I turn twenty-six anyway. "We'll have to find some warm sand to celebrate on."

"Eventually I should be able to do that. Sounds good to me."

"Sweetheart, congratulations on a tremendous accomplishment. I'm extremely proud of you."

My mom has never been one to shower me with compliments, so I'm more than thrilled that she called. "Thanks, Mom. I'll talk to you later tonight."

I walk over to stand at the windows. I'm watching the barges make their way behind Treasure Island and underneath the Bay Bridge, headed for port, when I hear my lawyer enter the conference room behind me.

"Good afternoon, Tinsley. How are you today? Did you go out and celebrate last night?"

He has no idea. "I did. Thank you. I still can't believe the deal we got."

He nods. "Don't be fooled. *They're* getting a deal with your idea. Today you'll sign all the contracts and get a nice check."

I nod. I take a big breath as I watch Claire arrive with her lawyers. She's all perfect white teeth and dressed in expensive, pale pink pants and a white pressed shirt that shows off her light-almond skin and perfectly coiffed, dark brown hair.

Two more men fall in behind them, and as we make our way through the introductions, I freeze.

"Tinsley, this is my brother, Landon, head of development, and our chief investor, Mason Sullivan, with SHN."

He recognizes me at the same moment I realize it's Peter from last night.

Holy fucking shit.

"So nice to meet you, *Tinsley.* Claire has told me so much about you." He smiles, and my knees almost buckle.

I've committed the next ten years to working with the one man I never thought I'd see again.

CHAPTER 2

Tinsley

I falter. What is Peter, er, *Landon* doing here? Clearly, I was not the only one with a fake name last night. When he shakes my hand, a bolt of electricity goes through me as I think about what we were doing around fourteen hours ago. I'm sore from the fun we had in the coatroom yesterday. He was anonymous then, and now he's a business partner. *What did I do?* One moment of foolishness is going to crater my life.

After the introductions are complete, my attorney asks everyone to take a seat. My side of the table is just my attorney and me. Disruptive Technologies has Claire and Landon, an investor who apparently must sign off on the deal as a major shareholder, and three lawyers. It's rather intimidating.

As we take our seats, Claire removes two robin's egg blue Tiffany boxes with white satin bows from her bag, along with a bottle of champagne. She places them in front of me. "These are for you."

I look at Landon, and he smirks. Claire is almost

bouncing up and down in her chair. She and I hit it off immediately when we met. We were introduced by a mutual friend I'd gone to school with and Claire knew from a former business adventure. I'd known she *and her brother* owned the business—Claire is the brilliant business side and Landon knows the technology. How did I not Google the shit out of Landon since I hadn't met him through this entire process? I Google the men I *date*. Now I'm walking blind into a decade-long partnership.

Fuck!

I still would have sold my company to Disruptive. I just would have avoided fucking Landon, particularly in a coatroom.

I pull the ribbon on the long, narrow box and peek inside. My heart melts. It's a Tiffany fountain pen covered in ampersands. I can't believe how much this simple gesture makes me want to cry, or at the very least, jump across the table and hug her.

"It's for inking our deal today," she says. "It's your idea *and* ours together that will unite people from all over the world and change the way the world communicates."

I stare at the pen. It's almost too special to use. "I'm so touched. Thank you."

She grins broadly. "I think you'll like the other one, too." She claps her hands.

I carefully undo the ribbon and remove the lid of the second box. Inside is a Tiffany star keyring with a fob attached.

Claire shrugs. "We don't do keys anymore, but the fob will get you into the office."

"Should we get to those contracts?" Landon asks in what seems to be a misguided attempt to rein in his sister.

Her enthusiasm is a big part of why I'm joining this company.

One of their lawyers takes out a folder that looks like it contains a full ream of paper. He doles out an inch-deep portion to everyone at the table. Looking between my lawyer and me, he walks us through each paragraph, and my lawyer carefully reviews every document. It's everything we've agreed on. I will have twenty percent of the company if we sell or are acquired. Otherwise the first ten percent vests at five years and the second at ten.

When we get to the end, we all sign, and Landon pops the cork on the champagne and pours everyone a small glass.

"To new beginnings." His eyes smolder as he stares at me, and my core clenches. Working with Landon Walsh is going to be very interesting.

"I want a picture," Claire announces.

She hands Mason her phone and sticks Landon between us. He puts his arms around each of us, and his touch is searing. My nipples pebble. I'm grateful to be wearing a padded bra.

We spend the next half hour celebrating, and I talk to almost everyone but Landon. It's almost like we're working to avoid one another.

As our little party breaks up, Claire announces, "I need to do a quick errand. I'll catch up with you in a second."

Mason leaves, and the lawyers walk us out. Landon stands behind me in the elevator, and he rubs his hand lightly over my ass. I catch the reflection of his eyes in the doors and give him a scowl. He grins.

After we say goodbye to the lawyers, he looks at me. "I guess we have a few things to discuss. Your place or mine?"

My eyes widen. "Are you crazy?"

"Well, okay, we can start here. Amanda?"

"Peter?"

"My name is Peter Landon Walsh, the third. I go by Landon since my father goes by Peter."

I roll my eyes and cross my arms.

"You're the one who called yourself by a completely different name."

"No, that was Chrissy, actually."

"So, her name isn't Madeline? I guess she isn't an elementary school teacher?"

I chuckle. "Nope. She's the head of marketing at America Bank."

"I can see why *she* might want a less-intimidating job. But in this town, it's not intimidating to tell a guy you're a developer."

I roll my eyes again.

"You need to stop rolling your eyes, or I'm going to have to punish you."

My core responds again, but I won't give him the satisfaction of knowing that. "Are you fucking with me? If you'd known I was a developer, you wouldn't have been nearly as interested."

"Honey, with those tits, I promise you, it wasn't your coding skills that interested me last night."

"Well, you're not going to see them again."

He steps forward, and I think he's going to kiss my neck, but he just takes a big whiff. "You smell so fucking good. I bet I do get to see them again — maybe sooner rather than later."

"In your fucking dreams."

"Why are you so hostile? I just gave you ten million dollars, and I'm set to give you twenty percent of my company."

"Are you high?"

"No —"

"Tinsley!" Claire comes running up and links her arm with mine. "I see you two are getting to know one another. Let's grab dinner, and we can do some more talking. I'm so excited you've joined us. This is going to be an amazing partnership. We are so lucky to have you."

She leads me to a car at the curb, and a huge man I recognize from the signing opens the door to a Suburban. "Thank you, Greg," Claire says.

He shuts the door once the three of us are loaded.

"Where should we go?" Claire looks at Landon.

"My place," he replies.

I look at him through squinted eyes. "What's the plan?"

"We can get an early start on tomorrow." Landon looks at his sister expectantly.

While I may own twenty percent of the company, Claire and Landon together own fifty percent, the investor owns twenty percent, and the employees own ten percent. I don't have much sway. Right now, I just keep thinking I've made a colossal mistake, arranging things so I have to spend the next ten years with a man my body can't help but respond to. I need to talk to Chrissy and get her advice.

"Greg, can you take us to Landon's place?" Claire asks.

We drive toward Union Station, and I'm stunned when the car stops in front of The Adams. It's considered the most exclusive high rise in all of San Francisco—fifty stories of unimpeded views of the Bay Bridge, Twin Peaks, downtown, and the Marina District. The building takes up almost half a city block, and each floor has two apartments, except the penthouse, which has one.

I've dreamed of spending some of the money I just got to buy into this building. A unit recently went up for sale, but it's being kept quiet. I only know because I've been watching.

The doorman opens the car door. *Doorman? Who in San Francisco has a doorman?*

"Thanks, Mike," Landon says as he exits. He offers his hand to his sister and then to me to help us out of the back.

We follow him into the dramatic, black and white, two-story lobby. I've seen it in pictures on the *Architectural Digest* website, but the images pale in comparison to this. The second floor is lined with bookshelves, overflowing with beautiful books, and high-backed chairs with ottomans for reading. The palatial entrance is home to a full-time staff and doubles as a gallery for a curated art exhibit from the San Francisco Museum of Modern Art.

Landon stops at the Parisienne-style reception console,

which somehow manages to be antique and modern all at once. The woman behind the desk exclaims, "Welcome home, Mr. Walsh." She hands him his mail.

"Thank you, Dee." Turning to us, he asks, "What are we up for for dinner tonight? Thai? Chinese? Indian? Japanese? Italian? Vegan?"

I shrug. "I'm easygoing." I smile smugly. *Go ahead, Peter. Let's tell Claire what we did last night.*

I can see he wants to respond. His jaw flexes, and he looks like a wolf stalking its prey.

Claire seems entirely unaware of what's going on. "Let's go for Thai," she says. "I'm dying for some tom young goon. That spicy soup will clear out my sinuses."

"Thai it is. I'll have pad thai with shrimp," I say.

"Pad see ew for me, then," Landon informs the woman behind the console.

"I'll have that delivered shortly, and Jonah will bring it up." She takes some notes and sends us off with a smile.

"Hi, Landon." A perky redhead with a substantial bosom approaches in form-fitting yoga pants. "Where have you been?"

"This is part of his harem," Claire whispers. "Just watch. It's usually a great show."

"Hey, Tiff." He looks at us, and I see Peter from last night emerge. "I've been around."

She touches his arm. "Marla's coming back into town. She'd love a repeat."

Claire looks at me and rolls her eyes.

My insides revolt, and I think I need to vomit. He's a manwhore. *Of course he is.* He's a good-looking guy with a big bank account, very alpha and overly confident. *Why did I break my sex-fast with him?*

"We'll see." He winks at her, and she giggles.

I shake my head and Claire turns and walks to the elevator. "My brother is the stupidest man on Earth. I swear he's slept with all the single — and probably a few married —

women in this building."

The knife in my stomach twists. The next ten years are going to be painful.

"Do you live in the building, too?" I ask.

"Gawd, no! I lived with him growing up. It's bad enough that I *work* with my older brother now. I've been renovating one of the houses off of Lombard, on the most crooked part of the street. It had been converted into two flats, and I'm converting it back to one. The view out the front is the gardens and the trail of cars. The view out the back is Alcatraz and the North Bay."

"And, she's pissing off all her neighbors since she blocks the alley with her construction trucks," Landon adds as he rejoins us.

"I am not. When the crews get deliveries, it's typically during the day. The rest of the time, they're in my driveway and garage."

Landon flashes his key fob, and the elevator takes us up. Claire and Landon barb back and forth, but they're not antagonistic, which should make working with them fun.

When the elevator doors open, Landon takes four strides in. But I find myself still standing in place. I'm shocked. My eyes are riveted to the floor-to-ceiling windows, and it takes me a minute to realize he has the most coveted piece of property in San Francisco.

Landon steps back toward me and whispers in my ear. "You can close your mouth and stop drooling."

"I'm sorry. I didn't realize you had the penthouse apartment in The Adams."

"We went to high school with the architect, so he had an in." Claire looks at her brother through squinted eyes.

Landon walks over to a bar in the corner and begins to pour drinks. "Where do you live?"

"I have an apartment on Nob Hill."

He nods. "Mason, our investor, lives over on Nob Hill. You may have seen him walking his dog, Misty, at

Huntington Park."

"I knew I'd seen him before. He has a beautiful golden retriever. Is he dating Caroline Arnault? I see her with the same dog sometimes."

"Yes," Claire chimes in. "They're getting married next spring in Italy."

When dinner arrives, we sit at a beautiful table and talk. The conversation progresses from work and our plans to our personal lives.

"It's like you have two sisters to harass you now," Claire says to Landon.

"Just what I *didn't* need." He pretends to complain, but he has a grin smeared across his face.

Claire looks at her Apple watch. "Oh, crap! I promised Nick I'd meet him fifteen minutes ago. He's pissed. I'll see you both in the morning." She air kisses us and runs for the elevator.

When the doors close behind her, Landon looks at me. "Last night was thoroughly fun."

I slowly nod. "Totally out of character for me."

A grin emerges on his face. "We could do it again, properly."

I shake my head. "Not a good idea. We're stuck together for the next ten years."

"Who says we can't work together and fuck on occasion?"

"Me. I don't play with guys I work with."

"We've played once, and I thought we played well together. Where does that leave us?" He looks at me with his beautiful brown eyes. They're so dark, I can barely make out the irises.

My heart beats fast, and my body screams, *yes, yes, yes.* "In your rearview mirror." It's taking all my self-control to not kiss him.

He rubs his thumb across my thigh. "And if you change your mind?"

He stares at my lips, and I move away. He's like a magnet.

I gather all my strength. "I won't."

He stands up and looks out over the bridge. "I thought of you all night. You weren't interested in a hotel room. You didn't pry about my job or my black American Express card. We both had an itch that needed scratching, and we did it well." Landon turns and looks at me like I'm a glass of water and he's just crossed a desert. "Damn, we did it very well. I think we can keep it separate. It could be a lot of fun."

I stand and begin to pick up the discarded cartons and our dirty plates. I walk them into the kitchen. He *did* scratch an itch I hadn't scratched in a long time. It's still not a good idea to get involved with him. I'm the one who has the most to lose. I want to remain a partner and not fuck this all up.

"I should go," I tell him. "We have an early morning, and I want to make sure I get a workout in tonight."

His eyebrow rises, and I blush at the innuendo.

"See you in the morning."

I can already tell he's going to be mercurial. I look up and say a silent prayer for patience. I also consider drugs to suppress my sex drive.

As my rideshare crosses town, I text Chrissy.

Me: You will never believe this. Peter, no-sock boy, is actually Landon Walsh, my new business partner.

Chrissy: What. The. Fuck. Are you kidding me?

Me: I wish I was. Quite the surprise at the meeting this afternoon.

Chrissy: What are you going to do?

Me: Not him. And you know what's worse?

Chrissy: LOL! Tell me.

Me: He's the owner of the penthouse at The Adams.

Chrissy: What the hell? Your dream building? So now you have to deal with him all day at work, and you'll live in the same building?

Me: Work, yes. But, no, I won't be able to live in my dream building. And can I tell you how amazing it was today? Why did I have to fuck him in the coatroom? What must this guy think of me?

Chrissy: That you have an amazing pussy.

Me: He did offer me work with "benefits."

Chrissy: Is that a benefit for everyone at Disruptive, and is it in the employee handbook?

I have to laugh.

Me: It was tempting.

Chrissy: I hope you took him up on it.

Me: Nope. I'm just getting home. Talk to you tomorrow. Wish me luck.

I walk into my small, one-bedroom apartment and look around. I've worked out of this place for the last three years. It wasn't for nothing. I can't have an ongoing affair with my new business partner. That would be a huge mistake.

CHAPTER 3

Landon

I look down at the amber liquid in my glass. I need it to forget my disappointment. I had planned to look for Amanda again tonight, starting at the bar where we'd met—maybe celebrate with her in more than just the coatroom. I never expected to see her sitting across the table from me this afternoon. *Shit!*

I can't believe that amazing woman is now my business partner. She stopped me in my tracks last night, and I was telling her the truth—I haven't been able to get her off my mind since.

I've never had a problem mixing business with pleasure. And last night was not only physical pleasure but also an intellectual pleasure. I loved the back and forth. She's smart as fuck. And physically, she's a man's wet dream with honey blond hair and a smattering of freckles I want to lick up all over her perfect golden skin. *Damn.*

But she shut me down pretty hard tonight. Usually, I'd

call my sister and get her advice. She's my gateway into the often-confusing mind of women. But I can't tell Claire this time. If I do, she'll hang me up by my balls and make work miserable with her constant watching over me. No, I can't talk to Claire.

My phone rings.

"Hey, Mom," I answer.

"Landon, I saw in the news today that you and Claire closed on the new company." Leave it to my mother, who lives in Vancouver, to be reading tech news about California.

"We did. They're developing a language solution right out of Star Trek where you put a device in your ear, and it runs an immediate translation. Right now, it does six languages, and they're working on slang and regional idioms."

"That's huge for Disruptive," she responds.

"We think so. Claire bonded with the main developer, who's a smart woman."

"Do I detect a bit of admiration?"

"We've always known Claire is the smartest of all your children."

"I've never said that. Both my children have amazing talents."

I smile. My mom is always the diplomat. "How's the rain?" I ask.

"The weather is outstanding right now. We should be almost rain-free until October."

Vancouver, where I grew up, is stunning this time of year. It's lush and green—the best weather in Canada. But it also rains for nine months of the year, and the gray is depressing. I think that's why I've adjusted so easily to San Francisco. I do miss warm summers, though.

"It's beautiful here, too," I tell her. "When are you and Dad coming down?"

"We're looking at later this month. Your dad wants to look at a boat for sale in Marin."

Their timing couldn't be worse, as we'll be swamped with this merger, but I like having them here. "Sounds great. Will you stay with me? Claire's place may not be done by then."

"Whatever you two want to work out. We're fine. I'll send our itinerary to your assistant, and you just let us know."

"That'll be fun. You'll get to meet Tinsley, our new partner. Maybe we can all have dinner together."

"We'd love that."

I know she's being truthful. My parents always enjoy meeting our friends and the people we work with.

After we say our goodbyes, I text Claire to alert her of our parents' impending visit. This will stress her out, but I'm hoping to get ahead of it.

Me: Just talked to Mom. They're coming out at the end of the month. With your place under construction, they can stay with me.

Claire: That would be great. When I talked to her earlier today, she said they were thinking about it. I could use some of her design expertise with the new house.

Me: That's probably why she's coming — that and Dad's found a boat in Marin he wants to check out.

Claire: Great.

Claire: Are we ready for Tinsley's team tomorrow? I want it to be a good day for them.

Me: Agreed. And yes, I think we're ready. This is going to be a considerable change to have so many women in the office.

Claire: Worried about all the estrogen?

Me: Not at all. But you know some of our developers don't know the first thing about women. It'll be like middle school.

Claire: LOL! You're so right.

Me: See you in the morning.

I sit in my dark apartment and relive last night for the thousandth time. This morning when I woke up, I was excited. I was closing on a new acquisition that will make a difference with my company, and I'd met a girl who interested me.

Both those things are still true, but now they're all tangled up together, and that sucks. At some point, I pull myself out of my chair and head to bed.

The alarm goes off at five. Tinsley played center stage in my dreams last night, and my cock is as hard as a steel rod. A full decade is too long to wait to taste her again. I look at myself in the mirror, and along with the day-old growth on my face, my eyes have big, dark circles. I pull on some workout shorts and a long-sleeve tee and head to my workout room.

My customized Peloton bike sits in a room overlooking the Bay Bridge. Between the giant glass walls, which open, and the screen ahead, I can feel like I'm riding a bike outside — only much safer and with an instructor pushing me to ride hard. I often pretend I'm riding across the Bay Bridge. The weather this morning is brisk, but it gets my blood pumping. Forty-five minutes later, I'm covered in sweat and breathing hard, and the anxiousness that plagued me when I woke up has been pushed aside.

Now I'm ready to meet the day.

It's just after seven when I exit the elevator to meet Stan for my ride to the office.

Tiffany stops me in the lobby. "Hey, you. I missed you this morning. I don't see you in the gym anymore." She touches my arm, rubbing back and forth.

"I've been on my Peloton up in my apartment."

"Ohh, that sounds fun. I've never been up to your apartment. I'd love to see your Peloton."

She looks up at me through her eyelashes, and it's crystal clear she wants to see more than my exercise bike. She doesn't know which apartment is mine. She only knows it's above hers. Few people know I'm the one who lives in the penthouse. That's the advantage of an elevator that your fob signals — no light-up buttons.

I'm not interested in her. I had an okay time with Tiffany and that friend of hers once, but it was exhausting. It's hard enough to make sure one woman is satisfied, let alone two.

The car drops me at my building, and I'm sitting at my desk with a coffee from our expensive Italian coffee machine by seven thirty.

My pulse jumps when not fifteen minutes later, Tinsley walks in. She's carrying a box, and I hop up to offer my help. "You're nice and early."

"We didn't confirm a time, and I tend to be an early bird," she says. "Well, and a night owl sometimes, too."

She smiles the most glorious smile, and I remember her mouth around my cock. My stomach turns, and said cock stiffens. This woman is going to kill me.

"Here, let me take you to your new office," I tell her. "It's right next door." I lead her to where she'll be sitting.

We have a frosted-glass panel through the middle of the clear walls separating all the offices, though for a moment, I wish we didn't. But I saw Sean, the head of Disruptive's development team, scratch his balls too many times, making it necessary.

"You got a tour while I was out of town, right?" I ask.

She nods. "Yeah, Claire walked me around last week while I think she said you were playing in a poker tournament in Maui."

I nod. That was a great Memorial Day weekend. "I won the entire thing."

She looks me over carefully. "Of course you did; you're a math genius. Didn't you go to CalTech at something like fourteen?"

I'm impressed. She's done some checking on me. "I was sixteen. But I play poker with people like Nate Lancaster, Jackson Graham, Viviana Prentis, and the real math rock star, Mia Couture."

Her brows arch in surprise. "How is that any fun when you can all count cards and have three conversations going without missing a beat?"

I grin. She gets it. "It comes down to knowing how to bluff. You know your opponent has already figured out what cards you likely have in your hand. That's why we play *together*, in person—you have to be able to see their faces. This last tournament was at the estate Jackson Graham won from Viviana Prentis in a previous game."

She rests her elbows on the box I put on her desk. "Did he bet the Hawaiian estate while you were there?"

"No, he actually sold it to his fiancée, so it wasn't his to bet—which is probably why he did it," I grouse.

She shakes her head. "You all have too much money."

"You're not going to be in any food lines anytime soon," I remind her.

"I haven't seen an actual payment yet. Your check could bounce."

There's a sparkle in her eye. I know she's teasing.

I shake my head. "The money's already in your account. It was wired yesterday as soon as you signed. What's the first thing you're going to spend it on?"

She takes a deep breath. "I had my eye on one of the apartments at The Adams, but I don't think —"

I feel my eyes go wide. I know which unit is going up for sale. "You were looking at suite eight-fifty?" I can't wait to get rid of the bastard who lives there. He's being prosecuted for sexual assault in the workplace.

She nods, looking surprised.

But it's still not the spot for her. "That's a dump. It has only a partial view of the bay and mostly of Treasure Island. The majority of the windows look out on the alley and the building to the west. We need to find you a different unit. I'll keep my ears open. I may know of a few things opening up in the building."

The architect, Mike Spencer, and I both own six units we haven't put on the market yet. We were holding on to them as investments, but maybe I can talk him into selling one on the fifteenth floor. It has a great view, and I wouldn't mind if Tinsley was in my building.

"Don't worry about it," she says. "I'll find something. I'm not in any hurry. There are lots of options."

"You don't want to live in my building?" It's considered the most elite dwelling in San Francisco.

The line between her eyes deepens. She's so cute. "I didn't say that."

"Not in words, but I saw that look."

"I had no such look." She smiles, and I see all her teeth. They're beautiful — straight and white.

What the hell is wrong with me? Her teeth? Jesus, man. Step up your game!

"Did Claire show you where we set your team up?"

"She said right outside my office. Has that changed?"

"No, not at all."

I'm at a loss for words. I should leave her to unpack and get ready for her day, but I'm too preoccupied with her.

"When do you think they'll be here?" I ask.

Tinsley picks up her phone and checks the time.

"Within the hour."

"Great. Let's get you some caffeine, and we can sit in my office and talk."

She takes a deep breath. "I suppose that will work."

We walk into the break room. Like all Silicon Valley startups, the company supplies breakfast, lunch, and any and all kinds of snacks and beverages. Breakfast is just getting set up, and today is pancakes and fruit. Not my favorite.

We sit in my office. "This morning, our HR person will go through paperwork with you and your team while IT gets your computers set up on our system. Did Claire tell you about our team?"

"She did mention you had no female developers."

I nod. "Some of these guys are pretty awkward around women, so if any comments are off the mark, or they give anyone a hard time, please let me know. We can pull HR in and talk to them."

"We've all worked in tech for a while. We know the type."

"I swear, they're great guys."

She holds up her hand. "I get it." After a moment she adds, "I thought I would take my team out for lunch today."

"I think that's a great idea. Would you like Claire and me to join you?"

Her face scrunches up. "I think I'll do it on my own. I want to talk to them about how everyone feels about the move. Danica Meyer, our translator, prefers to work from her apartment, and this is going to be an adjustment for her."

"Because of the sensitive nature of our product, we typically require everyone to be on our network here in the office. But if you believe she needs to work from home, we can figure it out."

"I think she should work in the office, too. I thought I might sit in the bullpen with my team and leave my office for times when it's too loud for someone to work, and they can work there."

My eyes grow wide. I've never seen a partner willing to give up their office. "Are you sure? We have conference rooms."

"At least for now, I think it will help the transition."

There's a knock at the door, and I look up.

A beautiful woman — brown skin with dark freckles across her nose and cheeks — sticks her head in and looks at Tinsley. "Hi. Where do you want me to put my stuff?"

Tinsley stands. "Landon, this is Vanessa Brown, our industrial designer. She's going to take the translation software and put it into a small earpiece."

She smiles and steps forward with her hand extended. "Nice to meet you."

"Welcome to Disruptive Technologies," I tell her.

"We're happy to be here," she replies.

I help to get my team settled, we do our HR stuff, and before we know it, it's lunchtime. I was prepared for some off-color, sexist jokes from the Disruptive developers, but mostly we got averted eyes. These guys are *scared* of women.

As we walk through the lobby, a tall, leggy blonde is standing there, looking around expectantly.

"Have you been helped?" I ask.

She sighs. "No, I haven't, thank you. I'm looking for Landon Walsh. Is he in today?"

The hair on the back of my neck stands up. "I believe so. What's your name?"

She gives me a withering look. "Lori Laine."

It hits me who she is — a local newscaster and minor celebrity. "Let me see if he's still here. I'll be right back." Looking over at my team, I tell them, "I'll catch up with you guys downstairs. Save me a seat."

I walk back to Landon's office, and he's on the phone. I

write a quick note.

Lori Laine is here to see you. Are you available?

I hand it to him, he nods, and I walk back out front. "He's on a call, but he knows you're waiting."

Her face brightens, and I hear Landon behind me. "Lori? What brings you here?"

I turn to him and force a smile.

"I thought we might grab some lunch, if you're available." She rubs her tongue across her top lip. *Gross.*

She steps toward him, and I'm definitely a third wheel.

"Excuse me," I say, turning to go.

"Wait, um, Tinsley, meet Lori Laine. She's with the local news. Lori, Tinsley is our new partner and the developer of the software we'll integrate into our offering."

Her face says she's not interested in talking to me. I don't care. She's a bunch of empty space anyway.

"Oh, right." I nod. "I thought I recognized the name. I guess they're right. With the right makeup, the camera does hide your age."

She attempts to vaporize me with her eyes. I turn to Landon, who smiles.

"Ladies, why don't we all go to lunch together?"

I shake my head. "I'm good. I'm taking my team out to lunch. Thanks, though." I turn and push the button to call the elevator, praying it comes quickly.

As I step into the car, I hear her say, "She's just jealous of me — I have the brains, the beauty, *and* I have you." She talks in baby talk. *Bleck.* She giggles as the doors shut, and I roll my eyes. I'll never watch her newscast again.

I stalk out of the elevator and into the restaurant in the lobby of our building. I'm mad, and I don't know why. Landon and I aren't dating. We had a one-night stand — a one-hour mistake. I don't know why I'm letting some bimbo get to me.

I join my team at the table and try to put it out of my mind. That is until I look up and Landon and Baby Talk are strolling by, hand in hand.

"Oh, there's Landon. Isn't he dreamy?" Ginger Wang is my tester, and she's the most desperate of my team to be in love. She's wonderful, but I think she begins planning a wedding after every first date.

"Hey, look. He's with Lori Laine," Vanessa murmurs. "Figures he'd be with a celebrity."

"Damn, that man is absolutely fine. I wouldn't kick him out of bed for eating crackers," adds Danica, her brown eyes flashing. She smooths her copper hair flirtatiously, and I suppress my annoyance. She's our lead translator and speaks eight languages.

I can't take much more of this. "Okay, you three. Let's stop focusing on Landon and worry about how we move forward with our piece of the project. We'll be working with his team, so let's try to keep our tongues in our mouths."

"Oh, I could lick him right up," Ginger remarks dreamily.

CHAPTER 4

Landon

Lori couldn't have picked a more inopportune time to come here. She called last night while I was having dinner with Claire and Tinsley. I didn't call her back, because I don't want to see her anymore. I certainly didn't want her to show up unannounced and uninvited at the office.

I watch Tinsley get in the elevator. No matter what she said, I should have gone to lunch with her and her team. It's their first day. Claire is usually the one who won't take no and muscles her way into what's right — like taking the new employees to lunch and making them feel welcome on their first day — but she's gone to some girl-doctor thing. *Shit.*

"How about we go across the street?" I suggest to Lori.

There's a Paradise Bakery close by, which has good coffee and excellent baked goods, salads, and sandwiches. The line is long, but we take our place. Lori attracts attention wherever she goes — she loves it, but pretends to be annoyed. It's one of her many irritating faults. I'm beginning to wonder what I ever saw in her.

"What would you like?" I ask.

She leans in and runs her fingers up my chest. "You." She smiles, and I know she'd prefer to head to a hotel and have a nooner. We've done that before, but I'm not interested anymore.

I need to be honest with her. "About that... I've met someone."

She steps back and eyes me carefully. "What does that mean?"

"We shouldn't be together in private."

"Are you playing hard to get? Because, baby, you've got me, and I have this desire to make every one of your fantasies come true. I'm so wet right now..." She bats her eyelashes.

I study her. She's a Botox-addicted, surgically enhanced woman looking for a payday. That's not what I want. "I promise I'm not playing hard to get. I think we should take a break."

"I've never tied you down—although the idea does sound appealing." She laughs huskily.

My cock has no response. That's certainly telling.

"We don't have to tell anyone. I work evenings, and I'm always open to meeting you at the Fairmont. You can eat me for lunch."

She licks her lips, and I wonder if she realizes it's repulsive when she does that. "I don't think so."

A look of hurt crosses her face, and I regret being so direct.

"I'll be here when you tire of her," she says in baby talk, playing with the buttons on my shirt.

I give her a small smile. My regret for being direct is done. *Nope.* She doesn't understand that I'm not interested. I step up to the counter and motion for her to order.

"I'd like a green salad with no dressing and a black coffee."

She doesn't even eat real food. Ugh. Another massive peeve of mine.

"Just a drip coffee for me." I hand over my credit card.

"You're not eating?"

"No, I need to get back to the office."

Her hand wanders to my cock, and I step back. She giggles salaciously.

I definitely don't want this. "Enjoy your lunch."

I pick up my coffee and walk back to the office, leaving her waiting for her plain lettuce and caffeine. A huge weight is lifted from my shoulders.

The afternoon screams by, and the next thing I realize, the sun is setting. I look out across the office and notice Tinsley isn't sitting at her desk. Did she go home already?

I stand up and look around, and I find her and her team huddled over a computer, discussing something. The software she designed removes a final barrier to open communication with anyone, and our goal is to eventually include almost all sixty-five hundred languages. It's a fantastic complement to our platform, which gives personal devices the ability to communicate anywhere in the world—no more dead spots, even in the middle of the ocean or deep in a forest.

I wander out to hear what they're discussing. It's definitely all about the coding—fixing a variable that isn't working. I watch the way she and her team bounce from one thought to the next, and I'm blown away by how seamlessly they work together.

"How's it going?" I ask.

I get grins from most of the team, but Tinsley bristles. "We're good. We're just wrapping up for the day."

"Great. Can I take you all out for drinks?"

I get nods from the team, but a scowl from Tinsley.

She's upset, although I'm not sure why.

"I'll see who else is still here, and we can meet at the elevator bank in ten minutes," I tell them. "There's a great place just up the block we can walk to and get to know one another."

I look out across our bullpen and spot a few of my more senior staff still hanging around. "Anyone up for joining us for drinks at Whitley's?"

A few nod and seem interested.

"I'm taking the Translations team out, if you're interested. First round on me. We're meeting at the elevators in ten."

I get a few nods, and as I head back to my office, I send Claire a quick text.

Me: I'm taking the Translations team and a few of the guys out for drinks at Whitley's if you want to join us.

Claire: Have fun. Be sure to buy. I'm catching up with Nick tonight. See you in the morning.

We're a scraggly-looking group as we walk down the street to Whitley's. "I wonder if they have a coatroom?" I ask, trying to get a reaction out of Tinsley, but she doesn't even acknowledge my comment. *Great.* What could she be pissed about? This is going to be fun.

The happy hour crowd has dissipated, so we're able to get a good-size table that seats all of us. It's great to see my team and the former Translations team begin to integrate. The server arrives to take our drink order.

"First round is on me," I inform her.

She nods.

After she orders, Tinsley excuses herself and heads to the restrooms. I'd really like to know what's upsetting her.

I walk over to the old-fashioned jukebox and pretend to study the songs. When Tinsley walks out of the ladies room, I pull her in. "Pretend you're helping me pick some songs to play and tell me what's bothering you."

"Nothing."

"Are you sure? You didn't even glare at me when I asked if the bar had a coatroom."

She smiles. "I didn't hear you. I was in my own world. With today being our first day, we're still working out the kinks. We're having a problem with the software. I need to check it out on my home Wi-Fi and see if it's the office network connection."

I'm almost elated that it isn't something I said or did. "Let me know if I can help."

She nods. "Looking at our motley crew, I think you'd do well to go with the Village People and 'YMCA'." She points to the song on the list below.

I snicker. I love her sense of humor. "You're funny."

She curtsies. "Thank you."

I do as she suggests, and the team laughs and performs "YMCA" at our table.

As the song finishes, the server arrives with our drinks. She places a sloe comfortable screw in front of Tinsley and delivers a sex on the beach for me.

I wink at Tinsley. At least she's finding humor in our situation. I would have sworn she wanted the Earth to swallow her whole when she saw me at the contract signing.

My cell phone pings. I put Tinsley in my phone under the fake name she gave me when we met.

Amanda: You're incorrigible.

Me: We can check if they have a coatroom.

Amanda: No way.

Me: Repeats might be fun.

I watch as a beautiful blush covers her chest. I wouldn't mind seeing how low that blush goes.

A little while later, my phone pings again.

Amanda: Better run. I've got work to do.

Tinsley stands and gathers her belongings. "I need to get home. You guys have fun tonight."

Our teams are integrating well, and they barely look up at her as she waves goodbye.

She pulls her leather coat on over her T-shirt and throws her backpack on her shoulders before she heads out the door. As she walks away, I can't help but notice her heart-shaped ass in her jeans. I want to chase her down, but I also don't want to be obvious. *Patience.*

Me: You did great today, and we're glad you're part of the team.

CHAPTER 5

Tinsley

The next day, Claire and I sit outside for lunch, enjoying some of the rare sunshine before it becomes hot in the desert valley, which brings the fog in.

"I love this time of year," Claire says on a sigh, smoothing her dark hair, which is perfect as always.

I look up and shut my eyes, willing the sunshine to give me lots of vitamin D. "Me, too. I grew up in Denver, where we have more sunshine than San Diego. I miss the sun living here."

She nods. "I grew up in Vancouver, where the sun only shines in the summer. We covet the sun so much that I bought a place up in Napa last year for hot summers. You'll have to come. It's in St. Helena. It used to be a monastery and has a few hundred acres of grapes, but a giant vintner has leased them. I don't mind. The deal comes with several cases, and I don't have to do any of the work to maintain the land."

"Count me in. Sounds fantastic."

"Right? I should plan a girl's weekend."

"That sounds like a blast."

She claps her hands. "I'll work on that. How are things going in the office for you and your team?"

Our salads arrive, and we dig in. "Everything is going okay. It's just been a few days, but we're still having problems with the software and the office network connection."

"Is Mattis working on it?"

"He tells me he is. I'm the only one who's struggling. Everyone else is chugging along."

"Make sure Landon is aware."

I nod. "Who's this Nick you went to see the other night?"

"The guy I'm seeing. I'm dating outside our world."

I grin. "Alien, huh?"

Claire giggles. "Might as well be. Everything we do is foreign to him. He's a civil engineer down in Palo Alto."

"What does he know about you?"

"Nothing. He has no idea who I am. It's totally refreshing, actually."

"He hasn't Googled you? Do you use a fake name?"

"No sign that he's Googled me. He thinks I work in marketing for a start-up. Do *you* use a fake name?"

"My best friend, Chrissy, and I use them sometimes when we go out. She's the chief marketing officer for America Bank, and I hate telling guys I'm a developer and started my own company. They become condescending assholes. Suddenly they have to prove they're better than I am, and they go about it like they're in junior high."

Claire throws up her hands. "Men are so easily intimidated by smart and successful women."

"That's why Chrissy and I usually go with traditionally female jobs — bank teller, teacher, nurse, receptionist. Once a guy learns I'm not only good at writing Python code but can also take them out on Fortnite, it becomes exhausting. And if I don't want to sleep with them, they get angry."

Claire shakes her head. "Have you ever had someone figure out you're pranking them?"

Uh, yeah, your brother. But I can't tell her that. "I think so. We met a guy the night before the purchase who caught every curve ball Chrissy threw. It was actually a lot of fun."

"What happened with him?"

"Nothing." I shrug and look away. "We all had fun and left at the end of the night without exchanging any real information. It was refreshing."

"That sounds like someone you should try to find again."

I shrug. "Sounds more like too many nights of dealing with the typical assholes."

Claire laughs.

"Dating is hard work," I add. "And you have to put a lot of energy into it. I'm still looking for that person who doesn't care that I'm smart *and* got lucky, even if I'm not perfect—someone who'll accept me for who I am."

"I agree. I have some friends I think should join us up in Napa for our weekend. You'll like them. They're all successful women, and not everyone is in tech. You and Chrissy should join us."

"That'd be great. I'm sure she'd love that. Let me know."

"I'll work on it this afternoon and be in touch."

"Why the fuck can't my computer work on the network?"

I'm getting frustrated. It's been a week now, and I end up going home and working all night to keep up since I can't get my computer to connect in the office. I look over to Landon, who's had a parade of staff coming in and out of his office all morning. He's available. I quickly stand up and walk over.

I knock on the glass wall outside the door. "Hey. You got a minute?"

He looks up and smiles. My body tingles with the memory of what we did.

"Sure, what's up?" He points to a seat across from his desk.

"We've been working a week now, and I'm still unable to get on the network here to make additions or changes in my code."

"Have you told Mattis?"

It's difficult not to roll my eyes about how worthless Mattis Yung is. I've brought it up to him, and he blows me off. *WTF?* I paint a smile on my face. "I have. Every day. He tells me, 'I'm working on it,' but each night, after working all day here, I go home and program. It would be great to be able to do it here."

A small line appears between Landon's eyes, and his head tilts. "May I see your computer?"

I swear, if Landon mansplains to me about networks, I'll take my shoe off and hit him over the head with it. I stalk back to my cubicle, disconnect from all my monitors, and hand him the laptop.

He clicks around as he looks at things. "It shows you're connected."

I count to ten in my head. "Yes, it does. Now go into the Python coding screen and try to write a basic script."

"I don't actually know much Python."

"Just type the line above it. That's fine."

I watch his fingers fly over the keyboard. He knows Python. He's added an embedded line that says he'd like to lick my pussy again.

I cock my head to the side as if to say, *Really?*

He turns the computer toward me, proud of what he's done.

I already knew that part would work. Now I'm ready

to wipe that smug grin off his face. "Please set the code."

He does, and the computer goes to a black screen and begins the restart sequence.

"What did I do?" Landon's mouth opens, stunned by the black screen of death.

I shake my head. "That's the problem. It works for me on my home Wi-Fi, but since we've started working here, every time I complete my code and set it, the computer reboots. And, before you ask, nothing I've typed in is added when it comes back online."

He turns the computer toward me so I can enter my passwords to finish the startup sequence. As he looks over the lines of code I've written, his brow creases again.

"Obviously this won't work as we move into the next stage. I'll need to be able to code as we test to correct for translation delays."

"Does this happen every time?" he asks.

I nod.

"Your code is elegant, and while I'm no Python expert, it looks clean, so I can't see why this would be happening."

"I've scoured the code looking for something that might cause the reboot, but there's nothing. I keep going back to it being something in the network here."

He picks up his phone "Mattis, can you please come in here?"

Mattis walks in with a big smile on his face until he sees me. Then his face falls, and his nose flares in anger.

I don't know why he's surprised and angry. I waited a week to rat him out, and now my patience is out the window—along with my sleep for the last week.

"Mattis, where are you with Tinsley's computer on our network?"

"It's connected to the network. I can see it from the network desktop."

"Each line of code she writes in the office causes the computer to reboot. There's something going on."

He shakes his head and shrugs. "I can see her on the network. I don't know what else I can do."

Landon reclines into his chair and steeples his fingers as he scrutinizes Mattis, who squirms under his glare. He turns to me. "Tinsley, can you excuse us a minute?"

I stand and pick up my computer. "Of course." I'm vindicated. I wouldn't want to be Mattis right now.

As I go, Landon calls, "Can you shut the door on your way out?"

I nod and pull it closed behind me.

After that, I hear smothered conversation going back and forth in staccato bursts. Landon himself warned me his male employees might have trouble adapting to a workplace with women. If Mattis can't get on our train, sounds like he's going to get kicked off.

Using my time wisely, I hit the ladies room and talk to Ginger about how she's doing on the testing and reviewing of my code. I hear voices raised, but pretend I don't.

Eventually, Mattis walks out and glares at me before returning to his office.

Landon comes out a moment later. "You said you can write when you're not on the network?"

I nod.

"Grab your computer and your belongings. I want to take a trip."

My team knows what my issue is, so they understand. "I'm on my phone if you need me," I tell them as I pick up my purse and computer and wave goodbye.

Landon swipes his fob for the elevator, and we travel down until the doors open in the garage. He walks over to a black Lamborghini.

I save my comment until we're both inside. "What are you compensating for with this thing? I know it isn't a small dick."

He grins at me. "No, it's definitely not a small dick. Which, by the way, would love to revisit your pussy and mouth soon."

My heart races. "Is that where we're going? Because I was hoping for a bite to eat."

He shakes his head. "Actually, I almost fired Mattis. I don't know what his deal is, but he's convinced it's an issue with your program and not the network. I believe you, so I thought we'd run to my place and use the secure Wi-Fi to give it a try. And we can order some lunch."

"That's fine." I'd invite him to my place, but the foyer outside his elevator is bigger than my entire apartment.

We pull into the parking lot of his building, he waves his fob over the elevator panel, and it takes us to his apartment.

As we walk in, I'm immediately drawn to the opulent view. "What would you do if you had to go to the lobby from the garage?"

"I push the L button."

"Where's the L button? I only see a fob pad."

He grins at me. "There's a G button, too. I'll show you on the way down."

While I pull my laptop out and begin the startup sequence, I hear Landon on the phone.

"Bash, can you let Greg know I took the Lamborghini home today? I'm working from my apartment for the afternoon. I may need him to drive someone home later."

I shake my head. I realize he's talking to his security team. There's no way I'm letting them drive me home. Even though absolutely nothing is going to happen between Landon and me today, I'm not going to do that ride of shame. Probably countless women have been driven home by his security before. No.

A little while later, I snack on the pizza that's been delivered while I wait for Landon to get off the phone and give me the Wi-Fi password. Once he does, I begin tearing through the code. Each time I hit enter, the computer registers the new lines and adds them in — no restarting. *Success*. I keep going with Landon standing behind me.

"This makes no sense," he murmurs.

"I agree."

He picks up his phone from the table beside me. "Mattis, we're here in my apartment on the secure Wi-Fi, and it's working fine. It's an issue in the office. I want it fixed immediately." He's silent for a few moments, listening to Mattis. "Fix it, or I'll find someone who can."

His voice sends chills down my spine. He hangs up and puts the phone down, still standing behind me. "Let me know if my looking over your shoulder bothers you."

"You're fine. I'll ignore you." His smell of citrus and pine distracts me, though. Ignoring him is more difficult than I care to admit.

"I'll be back," he says.

I keep pushing through. I hear Landon on the phone and figure he's working from his home office. Before I realize it, the light from outside is diminished enough that I need some lighting to keep the strain off my eyes. I look around, but don't see a switch for the light above my head. I look at the time on my computer, and it's after seven. *Where did the day go?*

I save all my work and go in search of Landon. There's a light on in the living room, and I find him with two glasses. He's pouring wine.

"Are you done?" he asks.

I shake my head. "Not nearly, but I could go for a break."

"Good. I've ordered dinner." He hands me a glass of cold white wine.

Tasting the wine, I take a seat on the couch that faces the windows. "What a great view."

"I love it." He sits down and rests his arm behind me.

Heat emanates from him. I need to control my alcohol intake. I can't let too much reduce my defenses.

"It's pretty cool to sit here in a few months when the

fog rolls in. Sometimes it's below this floor, so it's like I'm sitting above the clouds."

"I'll bet that's beautiful."

I don't hear it ring, but Landon picks up his phone. "Hello, Dee." He's silent a few moments as he listens. "Yes, have Manuel bring it up. Thank you."

"Dinner has arrived. I hope you don't mind, but you had shrimp the other night when we ordered Thai, so I ordered cioppino and sourdough bread from Fog City Diner."

I'm stunned. Cioppino is a San Francisco specialty — fish stew. "It's my favorite. Thank you."

He smiles. "It's my favorite, too."

CHAPTER 6

Tinsley

I push my empty stew bowl away. "That was incredible. I didn't even know that was on Fog City's menu."

"On occasion." He smiles, and I know they made it specially for us.

"Thank you. Any word from Mattis on what's causing the issue with my computer and the network?"

"I'm afraid not. What would you think about meeting with your team in the morning, and then we can work here in the afternoon tomorrow so you can code?"

I've had two glasses of wine, and my filter is a little loose. "Are you going to proposition me?"

"Of course." He grins. "But also, I know my Wi-Fi is secure, so I prefer you here, rather than your apartment. I've spoken to my security group, and their cyber team is also going through our network. It may take a few days, but it's raised a red flag for them, so they're on it."

"I'm fine with that. Have you talked about the situation

with Claire?"

"I have. She's upset—mostly because you talked to Mattis about it several times, and he blew you off. She's convinced if you'd been a man, he would have paid more attention."

I twist the stem of my wine glass. "And what do you think?"

"She's probably right. I'm watching how Mattis is working with Jim Adelson's team. Their developer is a woman."

"That will be thoroughly telling. Is he purely a network guy, or is he a failed developer?"

"He came to us as a network guy. I don't remember his resume and whether he's done any development work."

We sit in silence, watching the lights flicker across the Bay Bridge.

"I had fun with you the night we met," Landon remarks in a low tone that revs my traitorous body.

I smile. "So did I. I never expected to see you again."

"I'd planned on going back to the bar to find you the next day."

Heat rushes through me, and I can't help but be pleased. "Really?"

"I figured you weren't a nurse, and unless Chrissy had a wealthy boyfriend or girlfriend, I was fairly certain she wasn't a teacher."

I turn crimson. "We do that a lot. Most guys don't notice." I pause a moment. "How did you know I wasn't a nurse?"

"You didn't want to talk about it. And I was pretty sure you weren't even looking for what you got."

Not in the least. "I'm not impulsive like that."

He shrugs. "It was a lot of fun. I liked you that night. But after watching you with your team and seeing the way your mind works with your code, I like you even more."

"I'm sure I'm one of many…" I deflect the compliment.

"No, you aren't. I'd like you to consider exploring something with me."

I shake my head. "As tempting as that may be, it has a neon sign that shouts, MISTAKE all over it. We're committed to working together for ten years, or until we sell Disruptive."

He's quiet. "I think if we don't explore what's going on between us, *that* would be the mistake."

I shut my eyes. I'm so tempted, but I don't usually keep guys around for long, and in this situation that would be a disaster. I open my eyes to find Landon looking at me. In the muted light, his eyes are begging. I take a deep breath. "How about a compromise? I don't have much of a long history with partners. I don't know you well enough to know if that's the case for you—"

"That's a fair statement," Landon offers.

"So how about we get to know one another better?" His face brightens. "We can hang out together—with our clothes on—for the next few months, including Claire on occasion, but for now we remain friends and co-workers. Then we'll see what we want after that."

Landon's shoulders fall. "That's probably the smart thing to do." He looks at me. "The longest I've been celibate since I was seventeen was two weeks."

My jaw drops. "I hadn't been with anyone before you that night in a long time."

He leans his head back and groans. "Do you know how tight you were? It was like a vice—incredible." He shakes his head. "I'm going to become overly familiar with my right hand."

"Bob and I will maintain our close relationship."

"Who is Bob? If I'm damn well going to be celibate, you are, too. You don't get to have someone while we figure this out."

His face is turning beet red. I can't stop my laugh. "Bob is my vibrator. Bob stands for battery-operated boyfriend."

He looks up. "Jesus, woman. You about gave me a

stroke."

"I see that." I'm still chuckling.

"I've never been much of a voyeur, but I wouldn't mind watching you and Bob together. Can we have FaceTime sex while we wait?"

I shake my head. "You're going to make the next six months hard, aren't you?"

"Six months? A couple means two." He rubs his hands on his thighs. "You're going to kill me."

I shake my head. "It's the only way. If we become friends first and *then* lovers, we might not ruin our work relationship."

"At least you didn't say, *we could make a go of getting married*."

"Married? No way. I don't believe in marriage."

Landon's eyes pop wide. "What?"

"Nope. It's a piece of paper. Why do you need a piece of paper to remain committed to someone?"

"Do you want kids?"

I shrug. "Probably with the right person, sure. But you don't need to be married to have kids either." I scrutinize him. "You want to marry and have kids?"

"I do. But not right away. I'm only thirty-one. I have time. Men can have babies into their seventies."

"True, but only with much younger women," I remind him.

"You're much younger."

"No, I'm not. Six years is nothing."

Landon has a twinkle in his eye. "Do you think we should have sex to seal the deal?"

I look at the ceiling. He's going to wear me down. I'm sure of it. I need to remain strong. "Absolutely not. We'd never stop."

"Well, at least we agree on that."

"We have amazing chemistry. But please look at it from my point of view: if it doesn't work out, I walk away with nothing. All the work I've done is out the window."

"I know, and honestly, Claire would castrate me if I did something that caused you to leave the company. As soon as she met you, she was all about you being part of Disruptive. And, trust me, there's no stopping her when she sets her mind to something."

"I like Claire a lot, and we have to consider that. I suggest that if after six months we decide to make a go of a personal relationship, she needs to be onboard with it, too."

"I've never asked my sister for that kind of permission before," Landon grumbles.

"She thinks you're a manwhore." I cringe. That was awfully direct, but he doesn't seem to mind.

"I'm not as bad as she thinks." Landon pours himself a third glass of wine and offers the bottle to me, but I put my hand over the top of my glass.

"Didn't Claire and I hear Tiffany talking about a threesome with you and her friend the other day?"

He looks sheepish. "Well, um, maybe. But it wasn't fun at all. I don't ever want to do that again. The movies make it seems so much easier."

I skip right over the porn reference, because those make a lot of things seem easy — a woman's orgasm, for example. "Anyway, we have to consider Claire if we decide to become more than friends."

He huffs. "Fine. Claire can have a say. What do we do if she says no?"

"We'll have to follow her lead and see if we can convince her. She can't feel like it's two against one."

"I want it clear that I hate this — not only asking my baby sister for permission but also waiting for hot, kinky sex with you."

Kinky? Aggghhhh, he makes this so hard. I close my eyes a moment.

I open them to look at the clock, and it's after ten. "I guess I should head home. I'm too tired to work anymore, and tomorrow morning is going to come quickly."

"I'll call Greg, and he can take you home."

"No, that's okay. That seems like a ride of shame. I'll call a rideshare."

"It's what I pay him for. He doesn't mind."

I make a few clicks on my phone. "I have a ride waiting for me outside." I gather my belongings and give Landon a hug. "Six months will go by in a blink of an eye."

"Not likely," he grumbles.

The elevator pings, and I step inside. "See you tomorrow."

He nods. "I'm going to have to use my hand now."

"It's good for you." I wink at him and grin as the elevator doors shut. Then I hold on to the wall to keep standing. That man makes me weak in the knees. While I know growing a friendship is what we need to do, it's not going to be easy.

I'm going to need Bob tonight.

On the ride home, I keep rehashing the conversation. My cell phone pings.

Landon: Be good to Bob tonight.

I snort-laugh.

Me: Don't get carpel tunnel syndrome. I'm going to need that right hand in six months.

Landon: Whenever you're ready to help, let me know.

Me: You're very naughty.

Landon: In six months, I plan on showing you how naughty I am.

A shiver rushes through me.

Me: I can't wait. It's not going to be easy for me either.

Landon: Sleep well, my friend. See you in the morning.

Me: Goodnight.

I wake in the morning before my alarm goes off. Bob took care of me before I went to sleep, but Landon was in my dreams last night. He was teasing me and not letting me finish.

This sucks.

I debate another round with Bob, but instead, I pull myself out of bed and head over to the YMCA to work out. I love the Y. It's a great cross-section of San Francisco — from billionaires to people barely making it — all hanging out together.

I spend forty-five minutes swimming laps. As I drink from my water bottle and try to cool down, I hear my name.

I turn and see a guy I dated at Stanford, Tomas Vigil. "Tomas, how are you?"

We're both wet from the pool.

"I'm great. How about you?"

"I sold my idea and my company to Disruptive Technologies last week. Life is good."

"No fucking way. That's fantastic."

"Thanks. Where are you?"

"I'm still working on the water-purifying software."

"When we depend on seawater for drinking, you'll be a wealthy man."

"That's what I tell myself." He rubs his towel over his

wet hair. He's a six-foot-two Adonis and has filled out quite nicely since college. "We should get together soon."

"I'm kind of seeing someone, but I'd love to catch up. The partners and I are talking about meeting up tonight at Chemistry Bar & Grill. You should join us. Claire and Landon Walsh are awesome and deeply connected in the Valley."

"You're working with the Walshes? That'd be great. My cell phone number hasn't changed. Do you still have it?"

"I do. My number hasn't changed either. I hope you can make it tonight."

The morning at the office with my team goes great. I assure them there are a variety of software and network experts diving into my issue. But Mattis is nowhere to be found today. I check with Landon, and he isn't sure where he is either.

As our meeting breaks up, I let my team know I'll be working from Landon's apartment in the afternoon.

"Does he work with his shirt off?" Ginger asks dreamily.

The girls all giggle.

"I hope not," I answer. "But even if he does, I work at the kitchen table, and he works from his home office."

"I'm married, and I'm not even into men, and I still think it would be hard to work with him closely." Vanessa looks at Ginger, shaking her head.

Danica leans in to the group. "I understand he's off the market. He told Lori Laine he wasn't interested in her anymore and had met someone."

My head snaps up. "Where did you hear that?"

"My best friend was behind them in line last week at Paradise Bakery," she says. "She couldn't believe it. Landon got coffee and left, but Lori made a scene after. That girl has had too much plastic surgery and uses too much bronzer."

I can't believe what I'm hearing. That was our first day in the office when she dropped by. "He's a great guy, but he's just my business partner," I assure them. *And right now, that's true*, I remind myself.

Landon appears a few minutes later, just as the clock hits noon. "Are you ready?"

I quickly finish up with the girls. "I'll be on my cell if you need me or anything comes up," I tell them.

"If Landon needs help *rising* to the occasion, be sure to give us a call."

My eyes widen at Ginger's comment. The others are nodding with salacious grins.

I roll my eyes. *And we think men are immature…* "I'll see you in the morning. You all know what you need to do."

Landon guides me to the elevator, and we begin our descent. "How's your team doing?"

"You've got some fans among them."

"That's good." He smiles.

"And I'm all caught up on the Landon gossip."

The elevator opens, and he guides me toward the curb, where Greg is standing with the door open.

"What's the Landon gossip?" he asks.

"I'm to call my team if I need help getting you up."

"What?"

I nod. "You've made quite an impression on them."

He reaches the Suburban before I do and pauses to allow me to enter first. "You do a fine job of getting me up, and I'd love for you to get it down."

I start to protest, but he holds his hand up to stop me.

"All that matters is that I've made quite an impression on *you*."

I pause a moment. I can't start the afternoon off flirting, or I may never get to work. "Who were you supposed to be meeting that afternoon in the bar when we first met?"

"A group of guys I went to college with. I saw them.

They're good guys."

"Oh, that reminds me. I ran into a guy I went to Stanford with. His name is Tomas Vigil. I invited him to meet us for drinks at Chemistry tonight. He might be someone for Claire."

Landon's brow furrows. "She's dating someone."

"He isn't right for her. He doesn't even know who she is."

He jumps back a bit. "What?"

"He hasn't Googled her."

"So what?"

"He thinks she works in marketing for a startup. He's not that into her if he hasn't looked her up."

Landon considers this. "I suppose you could be right. I'm reserving judgment, though."

"That's fine. I'll let them figure it all out." I turn and look at him. "I wanted you to know he's coming, and that I was clear with him about *my* status. I'm keeping my part of our deal."

"I appreciate that. I like that you told him you were seeing someone."

"I understand you told Lori Laine the same thing last week."

"How did you know?"

"Like I said, I'm up on the gossip. Danica's best friend was behind you in line at Paradise. She also said Lori had a fit after you left."

"I haven't seen it in the gossip pages, at least."

We pull up in front of his building. Dee greets us when we enter and hands Landon a large paper bag.

"What's for lunch?" I ask.

"You'll see." He holds the bag away from me.

I pretend I don't care, but once we get into the elevator, I try to be stealthy and look in the bag.

Landon shakes his head. "I'm learning a lot. Surprises are hard for you."

"You're part evil, you know that?"

"Wait until I have you naked and tied up. I'll show you evil." He winks.

"Claire may not allow that."

"I've already figured out a plan for Claire. Don't you worry."

The elevator doors open, and we walk into the kitchen. I set up my computer, and Landon takes our lunch out of the bag. "Vanessa said this is your favorite."

I grin. "It's a Chinese chicken salad from Pang Tom's?"

Landon smiles, and his eyes twinkle with mischief. "You play dirty."

"Just you wait. I've got lots of tricks up my sleeve. You'll be begging for it long before our six months is over."

"Who said I wasn't already?"

He puts the salad down and steps in. "Then why are we waiting?"

"You know exactly why." I stare him down a moment, and he finally steps back.

He hands me my salad. "I understand."

CHAPTER 7

Landon

I'm just a few days into this whole friendship-first thing with Tinsley, and Jesus, it's going to be near impossible.

Not having sex will be difficult, but being close to her and not being able to explore may be more than I can do. Her face when she orgasms is burned in my memory, and I want to see it again and again in person.

I can do this will be my mantra.

Still, for the last two days I've struggled to keep my focus on my work. We need to integrate the translation technology into our software. It's not working, and I'm not paying enough attention to see where the errors are. As the clock hits six, I stretch my legs and go check on Tinsley out at the kitchen table.

"How did it go today?"

"Great. A few more days of five hours of uninterrupted coding, and I may catch up."

"Tomorrow is Saturday. Let's plan some time

together."

She looks at me like a deer in the headlights.

"As *friends*. We can wander the Union Station Farmer's Market, and then we can come back here and work. How does that sound?"

She gathers her belongings and packs them into her bag. "I suppose that's okay." She eyes me skeptically. "What time do you want to meet?"

I shrug. "We can have breakfast together. Do you prefer breakfast in bed?"

She laughs. "You're going to make six months seem like six years, if you're not careful."

"I aim to please."

Her eyes dilate, and she bites her lower lip.

I put my arm around her and rest my hand on her hip. I drink in her smell, wanting so much to lick and bite her neck. "I'm all about pleasing and satisfying."

She regains her control and subtly moves away from me. "We could meet somewhere close to the market since it's in between our apartments. And typically, coffee is fine."

Her bag is packed, and she swings it over her shoulders. I gesture for her to lead the way to the elevators. As we ride down to the waiting car, the chemistry in the elevator sizzles. I need to stop thinking about what her breasts feel like pressed up against me — and her tongue sliding into my mouth.

I clear my throat. "Have you told Claire you've invited Tomas tonight?"

She looks at me, surprised. "No, I forgot, but this way it will seem like less of a fix-up."

Chemistry Bar & Grill is on the other side of my neighborhood, certainly within walking distance, but Jim Adelson, the head of Clear Security, has asked that Claire and I not wander the streets alone until he has something figured out. I know Jim well enough that I don't question.

The ride is short, and when Greg stops the car, we get

out. I watch Tinsley stretch her neck. Sitting and staring at a computer makes us all a little hunched over.

"You need a massage to work those knots out," I tell her.

"Are you volunteering?"

"I do have magic hands, but if we're going to stick to our plan, I can't do it." I lean down and whisper in her ear. "My hands won't stop at the knots in your shoulders, nor will they stop until you're shaking from multiple orgasms."

She yelps and steps away.

I look at my watch and then at Greg. "How about two hours, unless I call?"

He nods.

Inside, I spot Claire with a man, deep in conversation. We aren't actual twins, but we are incredibly close. I can tell she's flirting, but not overly interested.

Tinsley points to a tall, lanky man on the other side of the bar with a beer in hand, talking to a girl whose breasts are barely contained in a low-cut T-shirt. "There's Tomas."

Tinsley catches his eye, and he nods.

Claire stands and gives Tinsley a giant hug, and the guy talking to her seems to disappear. "How is working at Landon's place going?" she asks. "I hope he isn't annoying you too much."

I don't wait to hear her answer, instead walking over to the bar to order our drinks.

After a minute I place a sloe comfortable screw in front of Tinsley and wink. If nothing else, we can have our little secrets.

"What are you drinking?" Claire asks.

"It's sloe gin, Southern Comfort, and orange juice," Tinsley tells her. "Would you like to try it? We can get a glass and pour some in."

She shakes her head. "I don't have to taste it to believe it's good."

"It is."

Claire turns to me. "You're drinking a sex on the beach? What happened to your typical bourbon?"

I shrug. Nothing gets by my sister. I have no doubt she knows what Tinsley is drinking. "I felt like a fruity drink."

"You *cannot* take the bartender to a hotel tonight," Claire tells me. She looks over at Tinsley and rolls her eyes, as only a sister can do.

I kiss her on the temple. "Little sister, I will make you that promise."

Claire turns her focus back to Tinsley.

"Has Mattis figured out what's going on with your computer?"

Tinsley shakes her head. "He wasn't in this morning, so I don't know."

"I spoke to Jim and his team this afternoon," I tell them. "They can't figure out what's going on. He also insisted we need to travel with protection for now. No walking." I take a swig of my drink and watch Claire, making sure she understands.

"Yeah, I know," she says. "Has something changed?"

"He'll let me know tomorrow." I look at Tinsley. "They'll have someone meet you in the morning, too."

"I planned on going swimming first thing. Is that okay?"

Claire nods. "Oh yes, they'll go where you go."

"I'll let them know you want to hit the pool," I tell her. "What gym do you go to?"

"Just the Y."

"I'll alert them. They'd also like to look at your computer. I told them we might be able to drop it off tomorrow afternoon after you're done working."

Tinsley's face contorts. Like any good developer, the idea of having strangers look at her computer scares her. "How long do you think they'd keep it?"

"We'll stand there while they download it onto a secure portable drive, and you'll have it back immediately."

Her face relaxes. "That works then."

Tomas shows up and puts his arm around Tinsley. "Hey!"

No fucking way. The hair on the back of my neck stands up. I don't like how friendly this guy is at all.

She turns and smiles at him. "I can hug you now."

She gives him a quick squeeze. When they break, she turns toward us. "Tomas, please meet Claire and Landon, my business partners."

I don't like how familiar this "old college friend" is with Tinsley. I essentially growl at him, and Claire gives me a funny look.

"Don't mind him. I'm Claire, and grumpypants is my brother, Landon."

Tinsley maneuvers so Tomas stands next to Claire, and they begin to chat. She's asking him all about what he's working on — some water purifier thing. My radar is up, and I don't like this guy — not for my sister and definitely not for Tinsley.

"What's wrong," Tinsley asks quietly.

How does she not see that Tomas wants in her panties? She can't be that blind. I give her a look.

Her hand rests on my thigh as she leans into me. Under her breath, she whispers, "It was only a hug. I invited him so he could meet Claire."

"It's exciting to see so much enthusiasm for environmentally based companies," Tomas says.

Claire nods. "Our friend Jackson Graham's solar panels recently exploded."

"Aw man, that was awesome to watch. His plans were stolen by a Chinese competitor, and he was able to use what happened to his advantage? Amazing. It catapulted the company through the stratosphere."

This is bullshit. Who the hell thinks a water purifier is worth anything? "How are you making ends meet?" I ask.

"Well, I do some contract work in Python and Java

development, and when that dries up, I've had short-term gigs at Starbucks and a bakery in my neighborhood," Tomas says. "Gotta pay the bills, right?"

He seems a little too smooth. I don't trust this guy. Tinsley recently earned ten million dollars, and I would bet her alumni network has shared that tidbit. He's probably the first of many sharks she'll encounter. Claire and I will have to sit down with her and talk about being more suspicious of old friends who come out of the woodwork.

"I think it's great that you do whatever it takes to get it done." Tinsley smiles and squeezes my leg as a suggestion to drop it.

"How about you, Tinsley? Before you sold, how did you make money?"

Tomas knows. I *knew* he knew she sold her company. I don't trust this bastard.

"I worked coding jobs for various people during the day and developed on my own at night. When I got close, I had an angel investor who covered me while I worked on the software. I was the only one working full time. I hired a small team, but they had other jobs, some part-time and some full-time. We had enough to be able to do this a little while longer, but not forever."

"It also helps that you have wealthy parents," Tomas reminds her, and my dislike for him continues to grow.

Tinsley smiles, but it doesn't reach her eyes. She shrugs. "My father has not been in the picture since I was young, and my mother has worked her ass off for everything she's earned. I don't expect anything from her—ever."

I'm impressed. I knew her mother was her angel investor, but Tomas has the nerve to think Tinsley wasn't smart enough to have a good idea? His idea is shit. That's why he doesn't have any investors interested in what he's doing.

"I'm getting hungry, and I can't have anything else without food." Tinsley looks around the table. "Anyone interested in dinner?"

"I could use something to eat," I say.

"Claire and Tomas, are you guys hungry? We can probably get a table for four in the restaurant."

Tomas looks down at her, and if he goes in for a kiss, I won't be able to restrain myself. I'll kick his ass and not even feel an ounce of remorse.

"I can't stay. I've got a few hours of coding to do tonight. While I was at the Y swimming this morning, I think I had a breakthrough."

"I totally understand. You need to harness it when it comes." Tinsley gives him a hug goodbye.

I glare at him with a tight smile. He knows I didn't fall for his bullshit.

Claire seems disappointed he's leaving. "We hope to see you again."

How is it that I'm the only one who sees through his crap?

We work our way over to the hostess. She looks me up and down, but I couldn't care less. When she places the menus in front of us, she leans down and gives me a strategic view of her breasts. I'm not interested.

As we look over the menu, Claire blossoms. "I think Tomas is great."

"I was hoping you'd like him." Tinsley beams. She takes a sip of water and eyes the breadbasket on the table.

"You two make such a great couple." Claire has a giant grin.

I almost choke, and Tinsley sprays water out of her nose and mouth. She coughs, and I pat her on her back.

Finally, she shakes her head. "No way. Tomas and I dated for a half minute in college. We figured out quickly we weren't suited for each other."

Claire has a puzzled look.

"I ran into him this morning. It was a total accident. I told him I was seeing someone. I wanted to hear what he was up to, but I thought he might be a good fit for you."

"Me? But I'm dating Nick."

Tinsley shrugs. "I understand. But you didn't seem in love with Nick, so I thought I'd offer you another option."

Claire bites her lip and looks away. "He *is* kind of cute, but I'm not giving up on Nick, yet."

I'm relieved to hear that.

Tinsley nods agreeably. "No worries. I've worked out at the Y for years and never run into him. I may never again. And anyway, he knows nothing has changed for us since college."

Claire eyes me skeptically. "Why are you so grumpy?"

"I'm not grumpy," I reply.

She looks at Tinsley. "He's grumpy."

Tinsley gives me the side-eye. "I agree."

Claire turns her attention to Tinsley, as if I'm not even sitting at the same table. "Tell us more about this guy you've started seeing. You told me less than a week ago you were footloose and fancy-free."

Tinsley gives a nervous laugh.

"Yes, I want to hear about this guy," I prod.

"We've spent some time together, but it's still new. We've decided to give it a try." She shrugs. "We'll see. I don't have a great track record with keeping men around. My dad was not a good example."

"Hopefully he figures out what we know, and that's that you're a prize."

Claire declares this with such authority that I know she believes it. If I do anything to hurt Tinsley, Claire will kick me to the curb. No family loyalty.

Tinsley cracks a grin. "You've officially become the co-president of my fan club. Chrissy is probably ready to share the title, but you can ask her."

We spend the rest of our dinner laughing over silly things, and the girls make plans for a weekend in Napa — without me.

I hate this.

Tinsley looks down at her Apple watch. "It's after eleven. I need to go. I have an early morning, and then it's working the afternoon away at Landon's."

She tries to put some money on the table, but I wave her off. "Don't worry about it. I have it."

"It's not worth the fight," Claire says. "His stupid caveman pride requires him to buy."

I frown at my sister. "It's a business expense. I'm putting it on my company card."

After Tinsley departs, Claire turns to me. "If you fucking sleep with her, I will cut your balls off. Don't even think of going there."

Leave it to my sister to play along all night, knowing full well what's going on. "We're friends," I tell her. "Nothing more. In fact, we're meeting in the morning to visit the Ferry Plaza Farmer's Market before she comes over and codes. And to be clear, I don't have girlfriends in my apartment—you know that. And I will add that she works at the kitchen table, and I work in my office. No comingling."

She crosses her arms and studies me. "Peter Landon Walsh, Tinsley and her team are a good addition. Please leave her alone."

I nod. "I'll tell you, I didn't like Tomas at all. I think it's no secret Tinsley sold her idea, and he wants her to invest in his stupid water purifier."

She sips her decaf coffee. "I agree. He won't be the first who comes sniffing for her money. We'll need to broach that subject carefully. But she doesn't like Nick? She's never met him."

While Claire can read the way I'm feeling better than I can, it's like she's in a blacked-out cave when it comes to herself. "Baby sister, you're not excited about this guy. And Tinsley pointed out something today when she told me she was inviting Tomas along."

Claire sits forward.

"He hasn't Googled you."

She sighs. "I find it incredibly refreshing. I want a guy to like me for me, not our balance sheet."

"I agree, but if he were interested, he would look you up."

"I deserve a nice guy," Claire cries.

"I know. Of everyone I know, you do. But I don't think Nick is it."

A little while later, I'm back home and watching the ceiling, hoping the sandman will come for a visit. Too many things are running through my brain. It's like a never-ending stream of consciousness, a loop on repeat. My conversation with Claire keeps bouncing around in my head, and I can't get Tinsley out of my mind. I want to talk to her. I know I'll see her in only a few hours, but I want to talk to her now. Because it's so late, I text her.

I type out a message. *Claire lectured me about you tonight.* I erase it. That will only upset her.

Claire saw right through me tonight. I think she picks you over me.

No, that's not right. She might think Claire will never buy into us getting together.

Claire and I think Tomas is after your money.

That's a bad text to send. That's a conversation for Claire and me to have with her together.

I think about what I want to say. I realize I just want to talk to her.

Me: Hey.

I wait.

Tinsley: Hey back. Did you get a lecture from Claire

after I left?

Me: How did you know?

Tinsley: She's not stupid. I saw the looks. What did she say?

Me: That she'd cut my balls off if I had my way with you.

Tinsley: So, I take it you didn't tell her we fucked in the coatroom at the bar the night before the sale.

Me: No. And I didn't tell her I want to do it again and again.

Tinsley: You're very bad.

Me: I have a feeling you like it when I'm bad.

CHAPTER 8

Tinsley

My fingers hover over the keys. We're supposed to be friends for the next six months. I'm standing atop a slippery slope, but maybe we could just walk down it.

Me: What do you think is bad? Sex with a woman you just met in a coatroom?

Landon: That's not bad, maybe a little naughty, but I like naughty.

Me: Okay then, what makes you a bad boy?

I hit send on that too quickly. I groan. No dots are rotating. Did I go too far? I can't help myself.

Me: Stop trying to talk yourself out of telling me and spill.

Landon: I like being in charge.

I think all the blood in my body just went straight between my legs.

Me: What else do you like?

No response. I pushed too hard. I type *Goodnight,* and my finger hovers over the send button. Then I see the dots.

Landon: You.

I quickly erase the Goodnight and respond.

Me: Tell me what you'd like from me.

Landon: You kneeling before me with my cock in your mouth and your hands behind your back.

Landon: You with your arms tied down and your legs open—my tongue buried in your pussy, making you come multiple times.

Landon: You on all fours with me pounding you from behind and Bob massaging your clit and my balls.

Landon: I can keep going...

My heart is racing, and I'm very wet.

Me: I think Bob and I are going to be busy tonight.

Landon: Is watching a violation of our six-month rule?

I read and reread his question. If he offers to come over,

I'm not sure I can say no. I need to think with my brain and not my vagina.

Me: It's probably not a good idea.

Landon: You're not saying no. Your turn. What do you like?

I bite my lower lip.

Me: The list is shorter if I tell you what I don't like.

Landon: Don't hold back now.

Me: I don't like to be gagged. I want my mouth free to kiss, lick, and suck.

Me: I'm not crazy about whips or canes, but I do like to be spanked and pulling hair is okay.

Me: I don't share with others. No minors. No animals.

I can't think of any other hard nos at this point.

Landon: That's a pretty broad spectrum. The rest is on the table?

Me: I reserve the right to add to my list, but for the most part those are my hard nos.

Landon: You're killing me. I need to go tug on the slug. I look forward to seeing you in the morning.

Me: I'm off to find Bob and visit the bat cave. We'll forget this conversation by morning, right?

Landon: I definitely won't forget, but we won't talk

about it. 171 days. Goodnight.

Me: 171 days. Goodnight.

The coffee shop is off the Ferry Building, and as usual, it's crowded and crazy with people getting their early-morning fix before fighting the crowds at the farmer's market. I spot Landon and Claire at a table against the wall and wave as I walk over.

Claire stands and greets me with a hug. "I hope you don't mind me crashing this morning. Landon mentioned you were meeting."

"I'm just going to torture him and make him visit all the stalls before we head over to see Jim." I wink at Claire, and she grins.

Landon pushes a white paper cup toward me. "Claire says at the lawyer's office you always had Earl Grey with two sugars."

I'm stunned, but I shouldn't be. Nothing gets past Claire, and her being here isn't a coincidence.

"Thank you. It's perfect."

I sink into my seat, between them, and wait for what Claire needs to say.

"What are you looking for at the farmers market this morning?" she asks.

"Salad fixings and some fruit. Not much since it's only me, and I hate to see things go to waste."

Claire nods. "I love the bread stall."

It's my turn to nod. "My favorite is the dried apricot and walnut bread they had a few weeks ago."

Claire reaches for my arm. "It's better than any orgasm I've ever had."

I can't go there. I turn to Landon. "What are you

looking for?"

"I thought since we're spending the day together, I would make dinner for us tonight. The fishmonger has great mahi-mahi steaks, maybe with a broccoli rabe—"

"The one with the caramelized onions?" Claire asks.

"Yes," Landon continues. "Depending on the dry-goods stall, we might get a high-carb side like cheesy rice."

"You had me at cooking dinner," I tell him. "Bob will understand."

"Landon's a great cook. He took a bunch of cooking classes at San Francisco Culinary Arts," Claire says.

"You went to a professional cooking school on top of everything else you do?"

He turns away and blushes a bit. "They offer a few classes for novices like me."

"She doesn't offer those classes to anyone else," Claire explains. "She was smitten, and this Bozo was into food play."

I take too big of a drink of my hot tea, and it burns my throat and tongue. I try hard to disguise that my mouth is blistering. "I'm sorry." I wave my hands in front of my mouth. "That was too hot."

"My sister, as you know, is direct." Landon glares at Claire, and she gives him a tight smile.

"I'll make a salad," I offer. "Maybe I can get some wine from the wine stall."

"Salad is great, but I have tons of wine," Landon responds.

"He went out with a sommelier for a while," Claire adds. "I liked her, and she helped me find my place in Napa."

I'm howling with laughter. "At least you benefit from all his girlfriends."

"Yes! I have an amazing personal shopper at Nordstrom, my hairdresser, I have someone to call at Tiffany—and you saw what a great eye she has." Claire looks across the table. "I love my brother, but he does get around."

I'm pretty sure that's a comment directed more to me

than to him.

"Not like you're married with three kids," Landon counters.

"You're right. And I've been thinking about what you said last night. I didn't call Nick to find out our plans for tonight, and he didn't call me. You're right, he's not that into me. His loss."

"Amen!" I raise my cup, and we toast. "This town sucks when it comes to decent men. They're all about getting shagged and heading off to look for the next best thing."

Claire gives a noncommittal shrug. "You'll meet some of my friends. Some of them have met great guys. But there are a lot of stinkers out there."

I agree. I gave up on dating a while ago.

"At least I know I'm not on any revenge-porn sites." Claire looks across the table at Landon through squinted eyes.

He holds his hands up. "I've never posted on a revenge site."

"No, but Jim's team had to pull a photo of you *off* a site where one of your *friends* had posted it." Claire uses air quotes.

"It wasn't me," Landon says. "She *said* it was me. My dick is much bigger than that putz's was, and it was obvious my head had been edited into the picture."

I roll my eyes. "You're a mess."

"You can tell me about that all day." Landon stands. "I want to get good fish before all we're left with is fatty tuna."

We meander through the stalls. It's tough to keep my buying to a minimum. I find every size and shape of tomato, carrot, and potato — plus every other vegetable I've heard of, and some I haven't. On another row there are all sorts of artisans, and my favorite is the flower seller.

There are buckets and buckets of flowers. They're so fragrant, and it's a cacophony of color. Landon hands his sister a brightly colored bouquet. I can't decide if their relationship is like an old married couple that constantly bickers or if they have that twin communication thing going on — even though they're not actually twins.

Then Landon heads my way. "These are for you," he says. "May they be the first of many." He hands me a bouquet of pink cabbage roses with white bouvardia. "Thanks for putting up with my sister and me."

"Oh my goodness. Thank you. You both are great." I take a deep sniff. I'm convinced this is what heaven must smell like. "I love it."

Landon steps away to pay for the flowers, and Claire stands by me. "My brother likes you. If you didn't have Bob in your life, I'd be more concerned. Landon's a great guy, but he had his heart broken when he was in college, and since then, he's been on a tear with women. Each time I think, *this is the one*, I realize she's only the one for right now." She sighs. "One day."

We've come to the end of the market.

"I'll catch up with you later," Claire tells us. "I'm off to get a mani-pedi and have my girl parts waxed." She waves goodbye as we head over to Greg. "See you tonight."

"Did she scare you off?" Landon asks.

"I think she confirmed the need for six months."

Greg opens the door, and Landon and I climb into the back of the Suburban. Our little fingers are close as we settle into the seat. I reach out and put my finger on his, and it's electric.

"We can do this." My platitude could be about anything, but I know what his sister said earlier about his manwhore ways bothers him.

We don't drive far before we arrive at a giant, warehouse-type building in an industrial area. A man comes walking out as we exit the car.

Landon shakes his hand and turns to me. "Tinsley, this is Jim Adelson."

Jim is huge. He's at least 6'4" and looks like he could bench press me without breaking a sweat. But his blue eyes are kind, and that lessens the threat of him breaking someone in half.

We follow him into a generic-looking reception area, and he leads us to an elevator.

"Have you been out to the Magnolia Homestead ranch in Montana yet?" Jim asks Landon.

He shakes his head. "Nope. Mia sent me the paperwork this week. I'll probably get over there in a few."

"It's a beautiful place." Jim turns to me. "Did he tell you about the poker tournament in Maui a few weeks ago?"

I nod. "He said he won the whole thing."

"This guy ran the weekend. There was no stopping him, and in the end, he won a five-thousand-acre ranch in Montana just outside Yellowstone."

My eyes widen. "I bet that's impressive."

"I was there last fall while Mia still owned it," Jim says. "It's beautiful."

When we exit the elevator, I stop to look around. The reception area may be generic, but up here there are at least twenty people busy around high-end computers and an entire wall of large monitors. It's as if I'm on the bridge of a futuristic spaceship.

Jim leads us to a conference room, and right behind him is another man equally as tall and muscular. With all these shoulders, I'm almost claustrophobic.

"Tinsley and Landon, this is Gage Easton. He's our computer expert. Most of the team out there look to him when they run up against something tough."

Gage takes a portable hard drive from under his arm and places it on the table. "Nice to meet you both."

Jim motions to the chairs. "Please have a seat."

"Tell me what's going on," Gage says to me.

"Can I start my computer?" I ask because if I have a virus, I could infect their network, and people don't typically like it when you do that.

"Go right ahead." Gage hands me a card. "This is the

server and password we use. It's a private network for just this kind of thing."

While my computer goes through the startup sequence, I walk him through what's going on.

He nods. "That must be frustrating, and it only happens on the network in your offices?"

"Yes," Landon confirms. "We can see her on the network, but it's like there's a line of code that's shutting her computer down."

"I've gone through the code, but I don't see it," I say, trying not to sound defensive.

Gage nods as he studies the code. He types a few lines and sets the code, and the program takes them just fine. "Hmmm… The computer takes it fine here…" He studies the computer while it downloads my hard drive to his portable drive.

I nod.

"What does your IT guy say?" Gage asks.

"He doesn't like me very much. But I think he believes I'm making it up."

Landon crosses and uncrosses his legs. "I tried it on her computer, and it did the same to me on the office network."

I watch Gage bring up my code on the portable drive. He looks through it carefully. It makes me nervous. Jim and Landon talk about Landon's plans for the Magnolia Homestead ranch. I listen to their conversation while keeping an eagle eye on what Gage is doing.

He looks up, and the room stops and turns to him. "Landon, I want to load this on another computer and tunnel into your network. I want to see if it's a glitch in her connection to the network or something else."

"What else do you think it could be?" Jim asks.

"I've read about a failsafe some programs have put in if someone is spying on a computer."

Landon and I sit up straight. "Corporate espionage?"

Gage holds his hands up. "Let's not get ahead of

ourselves." He motions to a woman out in the office, and she walks in with a laptop and leaves.

Gage hooks up the portable hard drive. "We connected to your network this morning. Let's see what happens."

Gage connects and asks me to write a basic line of code. I do, and when I try to set it, the computer seems to stutter a minute. Then it goes to a black screen and begins to reboot.

Whew. Nothing is worse than taking something in for repair, and once it's in front of the repair person, it works fine and they think you're a little left of nuts.

I watch as Gage transfers the connection to a different Wi-Fi network. He turns my computer to me. "You're a much more elegant developer than I am. Please, type any line of code."

I type.

Elif answers==1:
    Print "It is certain."

Landon smirks. "Magic 8 Ball?"

"I'm impressed. Yes. It's all I could think of. Do you want any more?"

Gage shakes his head. "Set it."

I push enter, and the computer code sets.

It isn't the software. It's something else.

Gage studies the computer. "I think this is going to take some work." He looks at me. "This may take some time, but I don't suggest you connect your computer to the network at the office."

Landon sits up straight. "Do we need to pull all the developers off the network?"

"They're not having problems right now?"

Landon shakes his head. "No."

"I don't want anyone to panic. We need to do some sniffing around. We'll work on it today and tomorrow. We can meet here Monday morning. Would that work?"

I nod. "I'll need the address, but yes."

"I'll pick you up. Don't worry," Landon assures me.

As we walk out, Gage leans over. "Would you like a tour?"

I nod. This is my type of porn.

When we go back out to the car, I can feel the anger and frustration rolling off of Landon. *I'm* the one they seem to be stealing from, so that makes me nervous. I know Landon and Claire vetted my code when they bought me.

"Should we call Claire?" I ask.

Landon looks up. "I'm so blinded by rage right now, I hadn't thought about it." He gets on the phone, and I hear Claire's voice mail.

"Claire, we met with Jim and Gage. They don't want Tinsley on the network until we get this figured out. There's a possibility of corporate espionage. We need to let Mason know. I'll wait for your call."

We stop in front of The Adams, and Greg parks and comes around to open the door. We gather our purchases from the farmer's market, and Landon turns to Greg. "Can you take Tinsley up with the bags? I'll be back shortly."

I don't feel comfortable hanging out in his apartment when he's not home. "I can come back later. Don't worry about me."

He hands me a fob. "This is for you to keep. Please, stay. I need to think a minute. I'll be up shortly. Promise." He puts his arm around me and kisses my temple. "We're going to get this figured out."

It's strange to walk into the building without Landon. Tiffany shimmies into the elevator with Greg and me. "He doesn't do monogamy, you know."

I look at her. "Who him?" I hook my finger at Greg, who looks at me like a deer in the headlights.

"No, Landon." She puts her hands on her hips, and I wait for her to point at me.

"That's fine. He's an adult." I look away from her, bored with the conversation.

"He likes the way I suck his cock."

Wow, that was not necessary. "If you're good with it, that's fine with me."

"He's totally into ass fucking."

The elevator doors open.

I have no idea how to respond. "I think this is your floor."

"You should have more respect for yourself," she admonishes.

I hold the door open as she exits. "Me? You just said you got on your knees for him, and he fucks your ass. I'm his business partner. I have plenty of self-respect. Maybe you should look in the mirror."

I step away, and the elevator doors begin to close. Tiffany's mouth is open, and she's turning bright scarlet. After the elevator begins to move again, I look over at Greg. "Sorry about that."

He smiles. "I think you handled that well. She wants him bad."

"I know. Crazy isn't it?" I sigh as the elevator arrives at Landon's floor. "She'd wet her pants if she knew where he lived."

"I'll park the car and be back."

"I don't think I'm going to stay. It wouldn't be right. I'll unpack the groceries and put what needs to be kept cool in the fridge. Then I can grab a rideshare home."

"The direction I was given from Jim was to stay with you. So, if you want to go back to your place on Nob Hill, I can do that."

"Oh. Let me think while I unpack the groceries."

"No problem." Greg walks away.

I quickly put away the fish and vegetables, and I find a pitcher and put the flowers into some water.

There's no sign of Landon or Greg.

Me: Hey, I'm thinking of heading home to work. What time do you want me back?

Landon: Please don't go. I'm on my way there. Plus, you can't work on your network.

Me: Be careful. Your crazy, redheaded girlfriend informed me that you like her BJs and are into anal, and I should have more self-respect.

Landon: She did what?

Me: I wasn't very nice, so be aware. I told her to look in the mirror because I'm your business partner.

Landon: That seems pretty nice given what she said.

Me: I'll care if she's this worked up in 170 days.

Landon: I'm walking in the building now. Stay put.

CHAPTER 9

Landon

Fuck Tiffany. I knew she was a mistake. She's like a cat in heat, looking to claw the eyes of anyone who gets close. I need to figure out how she got an apartment in the building. I know she's not an owner…someone's propping her up. She needs to be evicted and quick. I should ask Mike about that. Maybe he knows.

And Claire is right. I need to stop fucking every pussy I meet.

Jesus.

I'm way into Tinsley. She's all nerdy and sexy at the same time, but once you get beyond the veneer, she's a hellcat.

Six months is an eternity. *It'll be worth it.*

The elevator doors open, and Tinsley's standing by the table in my apartment with her backpack open, her computer tucked away.

"Sorry about that," I tell her. "I'm even more sorry about Tiffany. She shouldn't have talked to you that way."

Tinsley reaches for my arm. "It's okay."

My eyes widen.

"Claire and Tiffany seem to be on a shared mission to make sure we don't get together."

"I'm going to show you I can go the six months. It won't be easy, but I'm hoping for a few saucy text sessions to tide me over with visuals."

"You're too much." She grins, and I notice how well she fills out her T-shirt…and the shape of her ass.

My dick is at half-mast. "If you only knew."

"I think I do. Everyone is filling in the details."

My hands go to my chest like I've been shot. "Ohhh."

She giggles and begins to unpack her computer.

"I'll start prepping dinner. Please sit down and do what you wanted to do this afternoon." I go into the kitchen, but there isn't much to keep me busy. I have a marinade for the broccoli rabe and the mahi-mahi filets. I'll get everything set up in my outdoor kitchen, but beyond that, I'll have to resort to working in my home office.

A little while later, I'm trying to distract myself by going through the coding my team has done for the satellite we're building when Claire calls.

"Hey."

"What happened over at Clear?" she asks.

"Jim and Gage took a copy of Tinsley's hard drive. They can't pinpoint the issue right now, but they don't want her on the network."

"Should we pull the rest of the team off too?"

"I asked the same question, but they don't think it's necessary since they're not having a problem. Have you heard from Mattis?"

"I haven't. He knows I was pissed at him for treating Tinsley so poorly," Claire says. "What about you?"

"I got a text from him yesterday saying he'd be out. Jim is doing a trace on him. Tinsley asked me a good question. She wanted to know if he was a failed developer."

"Is he?"

"I didn't remember that he was, but Jim is going to do another round of background. And, Jim and Gage will be in the office on Monday to meet with him."

"Okay, good. I'm about twenty minutes out. I need to stop and pick up a dessert. I'm sorry about everything I said this morning to Tinsley. I like her, and I can tell you two have great chemistry. I need at least one of you to be strong, and I got a little desperate. At the smell of female pheromones, you're lost."

"Tiffany went after Tinsley in the elevator this afternoon."

"That's the redheaded skank in your building?"

"Yes. She told her things we'd done together and said Tinsley should have some self-respect."

"Are you fucking with me? Tinsley needs self-respect?"

I snort. "Right? Tinsley told her to look in the mirror."

Claire laughs. "I like her."

"I know. So do I. See you in a few." I disconnect the call and think about the first time I met Tinsley. She was fun—and not just the naked-tango part.

I shut down my computer and ask the Alexa on my desk to turn on a Coldplay mix. When I hear it flowing through the speakers throughout the apartment, I join Tinsley in the kitchen.

"Claire's on her way," I announce. "Dinner will be in a little over an hour."

Tinsley smiles. "Perfect timing. I'm at a good place to stop." Her head bobs as the music fills my apartment. "You're a Coldplay fan?"

"Yep. Claire and I saw them here and again up in Vancouver. What a great show."

"Definitely. I saw them in Denver last year at Mile High."

We both begin to dance. She has such a grace about her, and her laugh is music to my soul. I'm completely at ease being goofy and shaking off the seriousness of our day.

Claire comes in and joins us. "I love Coldplay!"

"Me, too!" Tinsley sings.

We all dance to a few songs and talk about the music we like. I didn't realize I had a mental checklist for my ideal woman, until I discovered that so far, Tinsley's hitting all the big boxes. It sends a jolt through me — good or bad, I'm not quite sure.

Eventually, I get the mahi-mahi filets on the barbeque, and we sit outside with the space heaters going. We laugh our way through dinner, and it's an easygoing, fun night.

"It's easy to forget we're living in the middle of the city here." Tinsley rests her head on the back of her chair, her eyes closed.

"Absolutely," Claire replies.

As we finish our second bottle of wine, Tinsley turns to Claire. "Did you know your brother won a five-thousand-acre ranch in Montana when he was in Hawaii?"

She looks at him. "No, I didn't. Who did you win it from?"

"Mia Couture." I know Claire and Mia are both in a small club of successful women.

"How did you manage that?" she asks.

"Mia had three aces, and I had a full house, jacks high."

Claire shakes her head. "What are you going to do with it?"

"I'm supposed to host a poker tournament out there over Labor Day weekend, which I'm hoping you'll help me plan..."

Claire sits up straight and looks at him. "Oh, no. That's not my thing. I'm not your assistant."

I know she isn't my assistant, and I can ask Wendy — who *is* my assistant — to do it, but Claire will enjoy this group. They're our friends.

"Listen a minute. Gillian Reece, the guest-relations manager at the Shangri-la, will do all the organizing, and your friends will be there. Caroline always comes with Mason. Jonathan Best will bring dealers out from the Shangri-la, and his wife, Maggie Reinhardt, will be there. Jim comes with Kate."

Her face lights up. "I'll go, but I'm bringing Tinsley as my date," Claire announces.

Tinsley sits up. "Me?"

"Sure, why not? If they're all going to be wrapped up in the game, at least we can enjoy the ranch and hang out together."

"Great," I tell them. "It's called the Magnolia Homestead. I also think it might be a good place for Mom and Dad to go — get out of Vancouver and the craziness there and truly retire."

Claire nods. "We can check it out and decide. Their friends are there with them in Van City. I don't think they're in any hurry to leave."

"It's at least something for them to consider."

"Okay," Claire relents.

"When are they coming again?" I ask.

"I think they'll be here on Wednesday. Aren't you reading your email?" Claire looks at me, confused.

"You know I don't go into the family email account that often."

Claire rolls her eyes. I hate it when she does this. She's stubborn as shit. It's great in the workplace. She's tenacious and doesn't take no — that's how she landed Tinsley and her team — but on personal issues, she's determined it's her way or no way, and that's hard.

Tinsley stands and picks up her plate.

"I'll get that," I tell her. Now I want to throttle Claire. Her arguing made Tinsley uncomfortable. I give Claire *the look,* and she closes her eyes.

"He has a housekeeper who can do that," Claire offers.

"That's okay. Landon cooked, and you brought appetizers and dessert," Tinsley says. "I made a salad. I can do some dishes."

"Not necessary," I insist.

"Well, I'll at least put these in the kitchen. I should get going. I'll probably work from my place tomorrow," she says.

The idea of not seeing her tomorrow bothers me, but also, for business reasons, if she's going to work, she needs to do it here.

"I need you to work here. We're worried about the network, remember? I gave you a fob today, and you can come and go as you like."

Her brow creases. "I'll think about it."

"I'll call Greg."

"I can take a rideshare," she insists.

"Tinsley, you need to use Greg. Right now, Claire and I both use Greg and Stan to cover us seven days a week. I spoke with Jim this week, and he's looking for a third, female agent to do more with us. I'm not trying to control you, but we don't know what this threat is. Please?"

"Fine. But I'm only a partner because you paid me some money. Honestly, this isn't that big a deal."

"If someone is going after you or trying to steal your work, that's a threat to us too," I assure her. "We're one company now. We're in this together."

Claire gives her a big hug, and the look on Tinsley's face tells me she finally understands. My sister may piss me off a thousand times a day, but I love her.

"Okay," Tinsley acquiesces. "I guess I didn't see my computer issues as anything outside of the norm in Silicon Valley. Everyone is hyper-paranoid about it."

I text Greg that she's on her way down.

"I think we can all agree we're beyond the paranoid stage. Greg is in the garage. He'll be waiting for you."

She nods. "I guess I'll see you tomorrow."

"Come over whenever you're ready. I'll try not to walk around in my boxers."

Claire shakes her head. "That would be disgusting.

Please don't do that. Tinsley will run away for sure."

The last glance I have of Tinsley is a grin from ear to ear as the elevator doors close. Then she's gone.

"Thanks for getting her to understand," Claire says.

"We should have talked about Tomas tonight." I shake my head. A missed opportunity. "We can't put that off."

"I agree. I just didn't think of it."

"She's naïve, and it's refreshing, but I also want to be sure we protect her."

Claire nods. "I think she has a good best friend and a few others. We'll help her navigate this like Tom Sutterland did for us." Her phone pings. "Stan is downstairs to take me home. Get dressed before she gets here tomorrow."

I kiss Claire on the cheek. "Promise. Are you going to come over and make sure I haven't charmed the pants off of her?"

"You better not. I will absolutely castrate you if you cross the line with her."

"I was only teasing. Don't make Stan wait."

"I *will* be by to check on you tomorrow," she says as the elevator doors close.

Me: I'm sorry we ran you off.

Tinsley: You didn't! You both are great at not making me seem like a third wheel.

Me: You certainly aren't. We're a good threesome.

Tinsley: ???

Me: Ewww. She's my sister. You're the only one I want to bend over the furniture and fuck.

Tinsley: That's better.

Tinsley: Are you sure you want me to come by tomorrow?

Me: I'd much prefer to come in your pussy.

Tinsley: Not my mouth or ass?

Me: I'm going to find out who Tiffany's landlord is and make sure she's evicted.

Tinsley: Don't do that for me. It'll be fun to keep showing up and making her crazy.

Me: Okay. For you, anything.

Tinsley: Will you wear one of my thongs while you play poker?

Me: What?

Tinsley: Just checking your boundaries.

Me: Come early and have breakfast with me?

Tinsley: Will you be in your boxers?

Me: If you want me to.

Tinsley: What did Claire say when she left?

Me: I have a feeling she texted you first.

Tinsley: What did Claire say when she left?

Me: She'll be stopping by unannounced at some point, and I better not be balls deep into you. What did she say to you?

Tinsley: The first part. No threats of you being in balls deep, though. Has she walked in on you before?

Me: More than once, when we lived together. The second she could move out, she did. But I walked in on her once.

Tinsley: You would have had sex with me at the bar in front of everyone if I let you.

Me: No, I respect you too much for that. I don't want to share you with anyone.

Tinsley: It's after midnight. 169 days.

Me: Breakfast is at 9. See you then. I'll be dressed.

Tinsley: Goodnight.

Me: Counting the days.

CHAPTER 10

Tinsley

Landon was in my dreams again last night. I release a deep sigh.

As promised, he didn't walk around in his boxers yesterday, and I was able to get about five hours uninterrupted coding done at his place before meeting up with Chrissy last night. She had so many questions about Landon, and I had no answers other than saying we're going to be friends only for the next six months. Chrissy seemed skeptical, to say the least.

I stretch, debating on getting out of bed. It's Monday, so I know I have to eventually… For the last year, I've been working from home, which can be lonely, but working out has been my saving grace. I don't want to go to the gym, and I know if I don't do it as soon as I get up each morning, I won't go—despite all my best intentions.

I throw the covers back. As summer creeps in, it becomes colder in San Francisco. The fog pulls over the city and wraps her in a cold gray blanket.

I can do this.

I throw my gym bag over my shoulder, along with my computer bag, and head downstairs. Yolanda Martinez is waiting for me in front of the Suburban.

"Hello! Nice to meet you," she says as I approach. She extends her hand and gives me a firm handshake.

Yolanda is my height, with short, glossy black hair, and carries herself as if she might have been in the military. She's dressed like someone from the tech world—jeans and an American Rejects T-shirt. She'll blend in well as a friend I'm hanging out with rather than sticking out like Greg would following me around. I need to thank Jim for finding her.

I smile. "Hello! Thanks for getting up so early to join me at the Y."

"No problem," she says. "I love it when clients want to hit the gym, because I usually get a workout, too."

"Off to the Y then," I tell her.

"I understand you're a swimmer?"

I nod. "Is it okay if I swim?"

"Absolutely. I'll do my best to keep up."

I shake my head. "Slow and steady wins the race."

She chuckles as we navigate the streets of San Francisco.

She moves the large Suburban around as if it's a sports car. Yolanda is not talkative, but that's fine. My head is full of thoughts. I'm still trying to figure out what's going on with my computer, and I can't get rid of that ache of desire for Landon.

Just a few minutes later, we walk into the pool area, and I push off to start my forty-five minutes of swimming. Yolanda seems to have no problem keeping up with me.

When the end finally comes, we pull ourselves from the pool.

Toweling off, Yolanda turns to me. "You do this every day?"

I shake my head. "I wish I could, but I try to do it at least three times a week."

"You're not slow and steady; you're fast and determined."

I smile. "Thanks, but I swam with Olympic swimmers. *They're* fast."

Yolanda laughs. "Lead the way."

After a quick shower and a little bit of prep, we head out of the locker room. As we exit, I spot Tomas. If I had to bet, I'd say he was waiting for me.

"Hey! Great to see you." He goes in for a hug as we approach.

I watch Yolanda out of the corner of my eye. She's ready to take him out if I give her the signal.

I put my hands on his shoulders, so he gets nothing but arms. "Good to see you. I'm glad you got to meet Claire and Landon the other night."

"Yeah, me too." He looks me over. "Do you have time for coffee?"

"Sorry, I don't. We have a staff meeting this morning, and I can't be late."

Tomas touches my shoulder, which seems like an invasion of my personal space. *Huh.* When Landon does it, he lights my body on fire.

"Maybe you can make it up to me later?"

It's time to let him down a little more clearly. "I already told you, I'm seeing someone, so I don't think that's a good idea."

He seems surprised. "Why did you invite me for drinks?"

"We're old friends from college. I thought you might like to meet Claire."

"Oh." He looks crestfallen. "I didn't get that."

"Maybe we can try drinks another time."

"I was hoping you might be able to help with an introduction to Jackson Graham over at Soleil Energy."

I shake my head. "I don't know him. He could walk by me on the street, and I wouldn't recognize him."

"Can you ask the Walshes if they would do it?"

I'm not comfortable with this conversation. "I'm sure you'll find your angel funder," I tell him, taking a step back. "You're certainly resourceful."

I give Yolanda a nod, and she begins to walk me out. "I'll see you later," I call to Tomas.

"That's it?" he says. "That's all you're willing to do?"

He grabs my arm, and in two seconds Yolanda has him flat on his back.

"You don't touch her again. Understand?"

A crowd forms to watch the spectacle. Lying on the floor, he holds his hands up in surrender. "Okay, no problem."

Yolanda points me to the elevators, and we get in.

"Thank you," I murmur.

"Just doing my job. No one is supposed to touch you unless you want them to. I could tell when he touched you the first time it was unwelcome. I was going to discuss it with you once we got to the car, but then when he grabbed you, I had to put him down."

I giggle. "I think he definitely got the message."

She smiles. "Couldn't help myself."

She walks me up to the office. "I'll need to go to Clear Security to file an action report. If you need anything, Greg and Stan should be here. I'll be back before lunch to escort you."

"I'm not sure of my plans quite yet."

"No worries."

Once Yolanda is satisfied that I'm securely in the office, I don't know what to do. It's stunning to think I have nothing to do without a computer.

On my way to grab a coffee from the kitchen, I notice Mattis isn't in yet. I wonder where his spineless self is hiding. But I forget about him as soon as I enter the kitchen. I debate a donut or the egg-and-meat thing warming on the food bar. It smells like heaven, but the calories would negate all the swimming I did this morning. I grab a banana instead.

As I walk back to my office. I see Claire has arrived.

"Hey." I peel the banana and take a bite.

"How was your night?" she asks.

"Good. I didn't work much, but I'm okay with that. I'll get more done over at Landon's this afternoon."

"Did I see Yolanda leaving?" Claire asks.

"She said she had to file an action report with Clear Security."

Claire stops what she's doing. "What happened this morning?"

I'm not clear what she's asking for a moment, but then it hits me. "We went to the Y and swam, and when we were walking out, I ran into Tomas. He hit on me, and I rebuffed him, as I was leaving, he grabbed my arm and Yolanda took him down."

"Are you okay?"

"I'm fine."

She motions through the glass wall to Landon. He comes in, and she shuts the door. We sit at the round conference table Claire has in her office.

"Tell us what happened," she says.

I walk them through my morning's adventures, which concluded with Tomas lying on the floor of the Y.

"That asshat," Landon exclaims.

Claire looks at Landon, and I see a subtle nod. "We wanted to talk to you about Tomas and the new world you've entered."

What is she talking about?

"It's no secret that we bought your company, or that you were paid ten million dollars," Claire explains. "We know you gave some of that to your team, but the public doesn't. *You* are the face of Translations. People are going to crawl out of the woodwork with ideas they want you to finance or introductions they want you to make. And many will be interested in your money."

"You need to be cautious," Landon interjects.

Claire holds up her hand. "Yes, you need to be cautious. People who've been around, like Chrissy or Bob, are fine. More concerning are the people you've lost touch with that suddenly reach out—like a man you dated in school." She gives me a look. "You can work with Yolanda to figure out when she needs to step in, though it sounds like you're figuring that out already. She's an expert at reading people's intentions and your reactions. She's there to protect you."

I nod. "That's a lot to take in."

"Not everyone has bad intentions. We're only suggesting—as two people who are a little farther ahead on this same road— that you be careful who you meet, and pay attention to what's going on around you." Claire reaches over to me. "Yolanda will hang out with you for a while. It's the hardest thing to adjust to. Landon and I have kept a pretty low profile with Disruptive, so at least we're not recognizable like Nate Lancaster."

"He can't go anywhere without a team around him," Landon says. "And the list of suspects in his wife's murder is huge. I think he wonders if he's next."

Nate and Cecelia Lancaster founded a high-tech prosthetics company and became famous overnight. One of their daughters was kidnapped at one point, and Cecelia slipped her protection detail last fall and went missing in Las Vegas. They found her body six weeks later. Since then Nate's grief has been on the front page of every tabloid. I can't imagine the pain of living like that.

I know Claire and Landon are right, but this part of my new reality is depressing.

"Jim will be here in a little over an hour," Claire says. "He'll probably want to talk to you about this, too. I promise there aren't many action reports."

"It'll get easier," Landon adds. "My team will drop me

places, so I can blend in at a bar." He adds that a member of the team goes with him if he's out at night, and most people don't even realize it. I'm sure he's hinting at the night we met. "And Claire and I carry panic buttons in easy reach at all times," he concludes.

Claire nods. "Right now, your success is being discussed by people who knew you before. You're not paparazzi fodder — that's good news. Once any of us becomes that, we'll need more help. But we'll do this together."

Claire and Landon smile at me, and I give them a firm nod.

"Thank you." I stand. "I should meet with my team."

I've spent my morning in meetings while my team has been immersed in their projects.

I walk up and have to tap them on the shoulder to get their attention. The trend in the office is to wear high-end, over-the-ear headphones and ignore everything around you.

"Join me in my office in five, and we can go over a few highlights from my meeting," I tell them.

Once we get settled, with drinks and plenty of snacks, I share what we discussed. "Ginger, the Disruption team is trying to work on the uplink with the integration, but they're having problems. Can you reach out to Sean and see what they need from our side?"

She nods and types into her tablet.

"Thank you." I turn to Vanessa. "Everyone loves the design you've created. They're looking at this adjustment," I point to some changes on my computer screen.

She taps her fingers on the desk. "That will increase the size of the earpiece by at least twenty percent. I think if they did this..." She points to a piece of hardware on my screen. "And flipped these two chips, we might be able to go smaller.

Maybe another five percent?"

I'm stunned by what such a simple adjustment could do. "Get with Glen and see if that can happen. I love it."

I turn to the next lady. "Danica, I'm getting closer with the algorithm that should pick up the slang. How are you doing with the dialects?"

She walks us through eight Spanish dialects we haven't touched. She's charted the similarities and differences, pointing out some patterns that give me an idea.

"This is so helpful," I tell her. "If I adjust the code here and here, we may fix a major problem."

The room erupts in excitement, and I look at this team in awe. Damn, these women are smart. How did I get so lucky to have them take a chance on my idea? I have goosebumps.

Landon knocks on the glass door to my office. "Are you ready?"

I nod. "Be right there."

"I have a meeting with a tech security team to figure out why I'm not able to work on our server," I explain as I gather my things. "If they can't get it fixed, I'm heading back to Landon's this afternoon, so I can code."

"If you weren't pushing out several thousand lines of code a day, I'd be convinced you and Landon were screwing like rabbits," Vanessa says, a glint in her dark eyes.

The heat rushes to my face. "We're not! He's a giant flirt, but a good guy. We're becoming friends."

Ginger's eyes grow big. "Are you friends with benefits?"

I mostly ignore the comment and search for a pen that isn't pink. "I've told you before — he works in his home office on the other side of the apartment. I work at the kitchen table"

"Too bad," Ginger remarks. "He looks good enough to eat."

I stand. "Cross your fingers that we get some answers."

The ladies all nod.

"You got it, boss," Danica says.

I join the group — which I see still does not include Mattis — in the large conference room. It looks like they've started, so I take the first available seat. "Sorry," I mumble, trying to be inconspicuous.

Claire and I are the only women in a room full of male models — or at least that's what they look like. Not an ounce of fat on any of them. Chrissy would go nuts in this room. I smile, thinking of all the things she'd be saying right now.

"No problem." Jim says. "Claire and Landon haven't heard from Mattis. Have you?"

"No. I wouldn't expect that I would…" I shrug. Mattis wouldn't contact me if I were the last person on Earth.

"That's somewhat puzzling," Jim replies, turning to Landon and Claire. "Has he ever not shown up for work and not called?"

"He's only worked for us about eight months," Landon says. "He keeps to himself, but that's not abnormal around here. I think he goes out and plays darts after work with a few of the guys on the team. But he's pretty much been here every day." Landon looks to Claire to see if she has anything to add.

She shrugs. "Yes, Mattis has been a decent employee. He doesn't work any overtime — just comes in, does his job, talks to a few of the guys, and goes home."

Jim's head does a slight bob. "Hmm…We may want the police to do a wellness check on him."

"What does that entail?" Claire asks.

"We'll explain that he left work on Thursday and texted he wasn't coming in on Friday, but we've been unable to reach him since, and he hasn't come in to work."

"We don't have to tell them he got in some trouble before he left?" Claire asks.

"If you're concerned, we can have my team go over first. If Mattis opens the door, we'll know he quit his job without telling anyone. If he doesn't, we can tell the police that."

Claire bounces her fist against her mouth. "I like that

idea."

Jim makes a call, reciting Mattis's address. When he disconnects, he looks at Claire. "Bash is going over now. He'll call us as soon as he knows something."

She nods.

"While we wait…" Gage takes the mirror of my laptop he created and places it on the table. "Let's see how this is behaving today."

As he opens the computer, he motions through the glass wall to one of the women from his team, who walks over to the server room.

"Colleen is going to run some additional diagnostics," he explains. "As soon as she gives me the thumbs up, we're ready to go."

Colleen gives her signal to Gage.

He pushes the start button, and my computer boots up. He bypasses the password and opens my Python coding screen. Pushing a few buttons, he puts in a basic command. Colleen watches from across the room. When he gives a thumbs up and sets the command, the room is silent. We're all holding our breath as we wait to see if it works.

The screen goes black, and the reboot starts.

I sigh audibly.

"We did anticipate that," Gage says. "We haven't made any changes to the code, but Colleen's able to watch you on the network now and capture the error code that comes up when it happens."

Her brow creased, Colleen walks back into the conference room, shaking her head. "You're on the network, and then it's as if you log off."

Gage clears his throat. "We've gone through your code — which looks pretty impressive — and we're not able to see what's triggering the reboot. We'll continue to run a few tests. Are you okay working from The Adams for a few more days?"

I look over at Landon, since it doesn't matter if I'm

okay with it; it's more a matter of whether he's okay with it.

He nods.

"I suppose so," I say. "I just don't want to encroach on Landon's prolific love life."

"The girls can make us both breakfast," he quips.

I look over at Claire to see her dropping her head into her hands, and everyone in the room snickers. We spend the next forty minutes discussing logistics before the meeting finally breaks up.

Gage and his tech team move to another conference room across from the server room. Jim asks Landon, Claire, and me to remain.

"I spoke with Yolanda about what happened this morning," he begins.

"It was my fault," I respond immediately. "Tomas had the wrong idea and wanted something from me. I think Yolanda made things pretty clear for the future, though."

Jim clicks a few buttons on his tablet and turns it around. It's a TubeIt page, and the video shows me talking to Tomas in the lobby of the Y. The entire interaction is recorded, along with my walking away. You can hear what Tomas says, and he looks at the camera before following me and grabbing my arm. Yolanda comes into the shot, grabs him, and puts him down.

My hand goes to my mouth. "Who recorded this?"

Jim clicks a few things, and a security feed from the Y comes up. There's no sound, but it shows a black-and-white view of most of the lobby, which I'm guessing comes from a camera stationed to the wall. "Do you know who this woman is?" he asks.

I look at the image of a dark-haired woman with pale skin. "She looks familiar, but I can't place her. What does she have to do with this?"

"The video was uploaded to TubeIt less than an hour ago from this woman's account. The name on the account is Bridget Shepherd. Does that sound familiar?"

I shake my head and look over at Claire and Landon. "I ran into Tomas last Friday and invited him out for drinks with the three of us." I turn to Jim. "Was any of that recorded and posted, too?"

"We'll check. The link to this footage was sent to a private group. We're looking into who the members are."

"What should I do?"

"For now, don't go anywhere without Yolanda."

I nod.

"And, let's continue to have you work at Landon's apartment in The Adams."

"Of course."

"You can't go back to the Y," Landon insists.

"We'd prefer you not go back for the time being," Jim agrees.

"I have a pool. It's certainly not Olympic size, but you can always swim there. It's heated," Landon adds.

"Okay," I murmur.

My head is bouncing around. The conversation with Tomas was pretty innocuous. He was a bit too friendly, and I kindly reminded him I was seeing someone. Then he got all aggressive. That didn't make much sense.

What the hell is going on?

After Jim and Landon leave, Claire comes and sits next to me. "Are you okay?"

"I don't know. Today has not turned out like I expected when I got out of bed this morning."

"Do you want to take the day? We can head up to my place in St. Helena? Maybe spend the day at Meritage?"

I shake my head. "No, I should get some work done."

"How about lunch then, at the Waterfront Café? I'll invite some friends, and afterward, you and Yolanda can walk the last bit to The Adams."

"Sure, why not?"

I stop in the kitchen to look for something to lighten my mood. But as I stare at the fridge, full of every kind of soda you could ever want, and the bar full of snacks, I can't make up my mind.

I don't hear or see Landon come in, until he says, "Are you okay?"

I jump, startled, and turn to find him smirking. "I'll get there. It's a bit disconcerting to see that someone has posted a polite interaction that went sideways on TubeIt."

"You were a complete lady. He was the ass."

"Thanks." I look around to make sure no one else has snuck up on us. "You're only saying that to get into my pants."

"You're like a sister to me. That would be disgusting." He smiles broadly and wiggles his eyebrows.

"Okay, big brother. Claire and I are meeting her friends for lunch at the Waterfront Café, and then I'll walk down afterward and work the remainder of the afternoon at your place."

"That may not happen," he says. "Claire is determined to get your mind off all this. There's no way I'll see you this afternoon at the apartment. Enjoy it. I need to visit my lawyer anyway."

"Everything okay?"

"Yeah, uh… It's just some procedural stuff related to what happened with Cecelia."

I whip around and stare at him. "What do you mean? Cecelia Lancaster?"

He nods. "Everyone who was in Vegas for poker when it happened is a suspect. Even Nate."

"No way. The way he's had to mourn in public is terrible."

"It wasn't any of us, but your video incident has just introduced you to the ugly side of having money. People go out of their way to embarrass you and try to take advantage."

"I'm sorry." I hate that all I have is an empty platitude.

He shakes his head and smiles. "It's going to be fine. Enjoy your afternoon. Tell Caroline I said cowboy boots are a requirement at the Magnolia Homestead ranch."

"Okay. Who's Caroline?"

"You'll see. She's one of Claire's good friends. You'll have fun at lunch today."

"Why do I think you're setting me up?"

Landon smiles again and walks away.

CHAPTER 11

Landon

"Mr. Walsh, please follow me." The law firm's receptionist sashays down the hall.

Usually, I might flirt and gauge her interest—get her number and meet her later for drinks and maybe a quick romp. But not today. Not interested.

"Would you care for coffee? Tea?" She smiles, probably waiting for me to offer "Or me?"

Yeah, she's flirting. I see bottled waters on the table. "Water's fine."

Her face drops for a half-second. "Ms. McPhee will be with you momentarily."

"Thank you." I sit down and stare out the window. The view is striking, but what I see from my apartment is the *most* spectacular. I watch cars cross the Bay Bridge and start to count red ones. I get bored once I reach twenty-five.

My mind wanders. I wonder if Tinsley is free for dinner? Maybe we can hit Quince. They have three Michelin stars. Or there's a great place up in North Beach for pizza or something more relaxed. I hated lying to Tinsley about why I was meeting with my lawyer. I don't know what's worse, saying you're a murder suspect or that you're being accused of having fathered a child. I *will* tell her, but once I know more about what's going on.

The pressure in the room changes as the glass door opens. "Landon, great to see you. Thank you for waiting."

I turn away from the window. Fiona McPhee, a fine Irish lass, has been my attorney and our personal fixer for years. She helped Claire and me with our immigration papers when our permanent resident cards were expiring and there was a rumor they weren't going to be renewed. She's never met a challenge she wasn't up for. I'm sure today will be no exception.

Fiona puts a folder down in front of her and clasps her hands together. "I sat down with Heather McCoy. She's taken a blood test that shows some of the father's DNA and would like you to complete a prenatal paternity test."

It's just like Fiona to come right to the point. No greetings, no formalities. Get down to why we're here. "How is it possible that I got this woman pregnant? Do you have a picture of her?"

Fiona opens the file and shows me a picture of a woman with platinum blond hair and over-tanned skin.

I don't recognize her. "I've never seen her before."

"She claims she met you at Tate's last October, and you talked for a short time before going across the street to the SOMA Hotel, room six twenty-four. There you had vigorous sex twice and wore a condom, but she insists it must have broken because she became pregnant."

"Fiona, look…" I'm trying to not scream that *this didn't happen*, because it didn't. I've been reckless in my personal life, but I know who I've slept with. Okay, I know the names they *gave* me, but Jesus, she isn't one of them. "I didn't sleep with Heather McCoy."

"This test will prove it." I can tell Fiona believes me. She's gotten plenty of people out of jams similar to this.

She motions, and a woman comes in with gloved hands and a swab. She stands before me. "Please open your mouth. I'm going to rub this on the inside of your cheek."

She practically chokes me as she shoves the thing in my mouth.

"We'll have an answer tomorrow," Fiona assures me.

That's great, because I want this crazy woman to go away.

The nurse covers the swab with a fancy plastic cap and places it in an evidence bag. She nods at Fiona before she leaves.

I fucking hate this. I'm positive I haven't even met this woman. "Can I countersue her for harassment? What's to stop anyone else from doing this?"

Fiona eyes me carefully. "There will be others. But next time you're accused, we'll be able to use this DNA swab. The other option is to become celibate." She gives me a plastic smile.

I don't like Fiona today.

"I've met someone," I tell her.

"Really? Do I need to do a background check on her?"

"No. Jim did that when we bought her company."

Fiona introduced me to Jim Adelson and Clear Security back when Claire and I first started having problems.

"Oh, so you're going to pee in your own sandbox." Fiona cocks her head to the side. "Landon, we've been down this road before. You should know better."

I take a big breath. If I wanted to be lectured, I'd have come clean with Claire. "There's something here. We've talked about it, and we've decided we'll be friends for six months. After that, once we get Claire's buy-in, we'll figure out how to go from there."

"How adult of you."

I put my hands on the table in front of me and push

myself up to stand. "Let me know when you get the test back and have let that woman know she's mistaken."

Fiona stands. "That's fine."

"And please don't tell Claire about my six-month plans. I don't need another lecture."

Fiona puts her hand on my arm. "Landon, I'm sorry. I don't mean to lecture. You're a self-made billionaire, very handsome, and extremely successful in your work and hobbies. People who read about you feel like they know you and feel entitled to your good fortune. You have a target on your back."

"Tell me about it. Our new partner had something happen this morning along the same lines. It's exhausting."

"Let me know if you need me to get involved." Her face softens. "I hope it works out for both of you."

"I'll see you later." I head for the door.

I can't get out of Fiona's office fast enough. I zip down to Greg and the waiting car.

As he drives me home, I stare out the window of the Suburban. People in San Francisco are young and active. They're outside running, walking dogs, relaxing, and enjoying life. I love this city. Claire and I have made it our home. I miss Vancouver in the summer, but this is where I want to be.

My phone rings, and Jim's on the caller ID. "Hey, Jim. What's up?"

"My team went by Mattis' apartment, and I'm afraid I don't have good news."

I sit up straight.

"He seems to have moved out in the middle of the night last Thursday. They found his crushed cell phone on the floor with the battery taken out."

My stomach drops. "What does that mean?"

"We're doing some investigating. His employment background check was routine. I want to stop by later today and show you the file and his picture. As you know, we recently encountered someone impersonating someone with another client, so I want to be sure that isn't the case here."

"Sure. I'm heading back to The Adams. I'll let the building manager know you're coming."

"I'll see you in a bit."

This day keeps getting worse and worse.

CHAPTER 12

Tinsley

Claire winds her way through the restaurant to a back room with a large, round table. It looks like we're the last to arrive.

"Caroline, please let me introduce you to Tinsley Pratt. We acquired her company, and I adore her."

My mind spins. Caroline Arnault is *famous*. She and her twin brother, Trey, were billionaires before they were ten years old. They've grown up under the watchful eye of the paparazzi. Caroline now runs a highly successful cosmetics company, and when someone tried to ruin her a while back, I heard she personally stepped in and paid her employees' salaries. She's amazing. I've seen her around town—she's a true local celebrity—but I never expected to *meet* her.

Caroline brings me into a friendly embrace. "So wonderful to meet you."

"I'm…Oh…Thanks me." I turn eight shades of red before I can pull myself together. "It's great to meet you."

Caroline turns. "This is my best friend, Emerson Healy, my sister-in-law, Sara Arnault, and three other wonderful friends, Mia Couture, Alyssa March, and Viviana Prentis."

This room is a who's who of San Francisco. I'm star-struck and overwhelmed.

We take our seats, and the waiter makes his way around the table.

"I heard you may have figured out a way to translate every language, including slang, as it's being spoken," Viviana tells me.

"How very Star Trek," Emerson remarks.

I blush. "It's not done yet, but we're close."

"This is going to change how we do business," Viviana says. "Can you imagine putting a hearing-aid-size device in your ear and being able to understand everyone you speak to?"

"Will it work with mumblers?" Mia asks. "I speak Mandarin, but I still can't understand my grandfather sometimes. I think he mumbles his opinions so I *can't* understand. I suspect he doesn't think much of my clothes or the current non-Asian boyfriend."

The table erupts in laughter.

"No guarantee on mumblers," I tell her with a laugh. "Right now, I'm trying to manage basic slang like *cool* or *awesome*."

"Old-school slang. I love it!" Caroline exclaims.

"Where are you from originally?" Viviana asks.

"I grew up in Denver."

"Me, too," Emerson cries. "Where about?"

"Wash Park. And you?"

"Boulder. My dad was a professor at CU."

"Nice."

Emerson and I talk for a while about what we love and miss about Colorado.

By the end of lunch, I have plans with everyone at the table. We've set a date for a weekend up in St. Helena and talked about a weekend in Victoria, Canada. My world has just grown exponentially.

"We're a small group, and a few couldn't make it, but each of these women has at least a billion in the bank," Claire says as we head for the car. "They're wonderful people, and it's great to know they're your friends because of you, not your money."

I shake my head. "I'm not a billionaire, and despite you paying me ten million dollars, after paying bills and giving the employees their share, I have about half left."

Claire smiles. "That's still a lot of money, and one day you'll be a billionaire. I've no doubt about that. For now, though, we have a party to plan in St. Helena."

Yolanda meets me at Claire's car, and after we say our goodbyes, she walks with me toward The Adams. I'm excited about the new friends I've made and what's ahead. I just need to get this network connection thing figured out so I can work a regular day in the actual office.

Yolanda and I step into the lobby and wave to Dee. I catch a flash of red hair in my periphery.

As we approach the elevator, Tiffany appears. "You don't live in this building."

"No, I don't."

"Guests are not allowed beyond reception without a resident escort."

Yolanda has stepped ahead of me to call the elevator. When it arrives, I step in, and Tiffany tries to follow. Taking the fob from my pocket, I wave it over the pad.

As the elevator doors close, Yolanda extends her hand. "This is an express elevator."

Tiffany turns red. "You can't—" The doors close, and we don't hear the rest of her sentence.

"Thank you."

Yolanda shrugs.

"Will you have to write an action report on that one?"

"I don't have to, but I will. She's a feisty one, and we'll

want each interaction with her documented. She's probably going to be a problem for Mr. Walsh. Greg told me she confronted you previously."

"I addressed it, but it looks like I only made it worse."

"We'll see."

"I'll mention today's encounter to Landon when I see him. Do you know if he's in the apartment this afternoon?"

Yolanda taps her ear. "Is Rabbit in the hole?"

Rabbit in the hole? What does that mean?

She nods. "He's home."

"Why Rabbit?"

She just smiles.

"What do you call me?"

"Cottontail."

Then it hits me. Peter Landon Walsh is Peter Rabbit, and he has three sisters—Flopsy, Mopsy, and Cottontail. "Does that mean Claire is Flopsy or Mopsy?"

"Josephine."

"The mother? I bet she loves that." I grin from ear to ear.

When we arrive, I look around but don't see Landon. I pull my laptop out and start it booting up as I wander around. He isn't in his office either.

I sit at the kitchen table, pop in some Mozart brain music, and begin working from my notes to accomplish what I can.

Suddenly, Landon is in my face, waving. I pull my earbuds out and look at him.

"Have you heard anything I said?"

"Sorry. I've been working on this. The lag is driving me crazy."

"There shouldn't be any lag."

I don't know how to tell him I wouldn't lie about a lag. Instead, I change the subject. "What time is it?"

"Almost six. I was asking if you wanted to grab some dinner."

"What were you thinking?"

"Do you want to stay in or go out?"

I'm feeling behind, I don't have time to eat, and nothing sounds good. "You know, don't worry about me. I'll get out of your hair and grab something on the way home. I'm still behind and need to work."

"Wait, you have to eat. We can grab something, and plus, we'd rather you work from here on the secure network."

I stand, trying to decide what to do. I would much prefer to put on yoga pants and a sweatshirt and code in my fuzzy slippers. But security is an issue.

"How about we order a pizza?" I ask.

Landon relaxes. "I'm open to any toppings. What sounds good?"

"Pepperoni and mushroom?"

"Sure. I'll order right now. There's a place in North Beach that will deliver."

I nod and sit back down.

Landon orders our dinner and returns. "How are things going? You're working on a lag?"

"I can show you. Can you pull up Univision on your television?"

"I think so. I'm not sure what channel it is."

"Well, if you can find a Mandarin station, that would work, too."

"I found it."

He clicks to Univision, which is playing a telenovela—lots of expression, and they don't always talk superfast. I set a microphone next to a speaker, and we sit down to listen. It takes a few minutes for the software to get going, and then a voice starts speaking through my computer. The lag is still about five seconds, but we've shortened it considerably. The translation software still struggles with what I'm guessing is abnormal sentence structure or unknown idioms. But I also wonder if it isn't something else—something separate from the software and more about the network. Or maybe I'm just paranoid about all networks now.

After a few minutes of listening, I ask, "What do you think?"

He nods. "There's still a delay, and it misses sections, so the translation doesn't always make sense."

I nod. He's right—the delay is getting longer and not shorter—but he's not seeing the big picture. "That's what we're working on. But there's nothing on the market today with this short of a delay. We're also working on idioms and slang. It's more important to get the translation correct in closer to real-time."

He sighs. "We need it soon, and with a much shorter delay. Otherwise it will be a bad *Saturday Night Live* skit where everyone is awkwardly waiting around."

There's no pleasing him. "I understand. I'm working on it. It would be great to be able to work from the office or even my home."

"That's not possible."

I take a deep breath. This can't be about me. What is his deal tonight? "What's going on?"

"Nothing. I'm frustrated. I thought this would be going smoother."

"It seems like there's something else going on. Did Jim's team locate Mattis?"

"He moved out and destroyed his phone before he left."

I sit down hard. "I need to run anti-spyware software on my computer."

"You think he was some sort of spy? Mattis' background check came back clean, and Jim's team has run checks on everything."

I stop and look at Landon, wondering why he isn't considering this link. "Yes, absolutely, and without a doubt I think he was spying. And I'm not running spyware on your network. I want to be on *my* home network that I know is safe."

"My network is safe."

Our pizza arrives, so we table the discussion for a moment to make up our plates.

I take a big bite of pizza, and Landon watches me, his eyes hooded with desire. He was pissed at me two minutes ago and now he's ready to pounce? Men and their libido…

I sigh. "I need to go. And by the way, your little friend Tiffany was waiting for me in the lobby today. She tried to get in my face about visitors not being allowed in the building without an escort. Yolanda had to stop her from joining us in the elevator, and we shut the doors in her face."

His jaw clenches, and his fists become tight, white balls. Looking to the sky, he says, "I'm having her evicted. That's it. This needs to stop."

I gather my computer and stuff it into my bag. I hit the button on my phone that tells Yolanda I'm ready to go.

"You're not going to stay?"

"No, I should go. I'm tired, and we're both crabby."

"Fine." He crosses his arms. "You should run the anti-spyware here."

"I'll take it up with Gage and Jim."

Yolanda appears, and I run the fob over the elevator. I'm mad at Landon right now. I get that he's upset about something, but he knew my software was still a work-in-progress when they bought us.

I'm angry with him for not celebrating how close we are. He knows this is *huge* to only be five seconds off of real-time. There will always be a few-second lag, mostly because direct translations don't make sense because sentence structures vary from language to language. *Whatever*. This has to be about something else.

When I finally make it home, I sit in my dark

apartment. I've been all over the place today, but right now I'm scared this isn't going well. Joining Disruptive Technologies was supposed to help me, but I'm still working on my own.

What if I can't get this to work?

What if they give my software to someone else to finish because they aren't happy with me?

What if they terminate me? I'll owe them their money — and I don't have all of it anymore. I won't be able to work in this area of software again. And I won't see any stock options. My eyes pool with tears, and I let them fall.

After a few minutes, though, my fear turns to anger. I fire up my laptop, download two spyware catchers, and begin to run them on my hard drive.

My heart stops when they show three red flags.

There are two sniffers, transmitting both keystrokes and sound.

Shit.

I examine them more closely, and they're ugly. Someone loaded these on my computer. I suddenly feel incredibly violated. I'm not sure what's safe and what's not.

It occurs to me that I probably have something similar on my phone. I leave my computer in the living room and use my cell phone to turn on some music close by.

For once, I'm grateful for the landline phone bill I get each month. It's something my mother always insists on.

I pull my home phone into the bathroom, turn the water on, and make a call.

I ring Yolanda. "Sorry to bother you," I explain when she answers.

"I can be back in twenty minutes."

I nod even though she can't see me. "That's not necessary, but I need to see Jim and Gage. Can you let them know I'm coming in the morning? And Landon should be there, but I'm not sure me calling him is safe."

"Do you want to meet tonight?"

"No, I need to be fresh."

She agrees, I assure her I'm physically safe, and we hang up until tomorrow.

I take screenshots and close down my computer. I turn the television on and sleep with it that way all night. The noise helps me relax, and maybe it will drive the person listening a little insane, if I'm lucky.

CHAPTER 13

Tinsley

In the morning, Yolanda arrives at our agreed-upon time: 6:45. I would prefer to be going to the Y to swim, but I don't want to run into Tomas. He wouldn't like what I have to say. I didn't sleep so well with the television on, but at least I know whoever is listening didn't hear me even murmur anything.

The drive over to Clear Security is farther than I thought. They're south of Market Street, close to the baseball park. There's a big technology pocket here, and I interviewed with a few companies in this part of town.

We pull into the garage, and I get out. Jim comes to meet me.

I hand him a note I've written.

I found spyware on my computer last night and possibly on my phone. It includes voice and keystroke capture. Do you have a room with a jammer where we can meet?

Jim reads it and looks up at me, surprised. Landon pulls in behind us, and Jim hands him my note. After a moment he shakes his head, confused.

We silently follow Jim. He puts us in a room where the walls are padded, and Gage joins us. They look at me expectantly.

"I'm sorry for all the cloak and dagger. Yesterday I was having lag issues at Landon's apartment in The Adams. Landon thought it was an excuse, because we've not made as much progress as he'd like. Part of me wondered if it was caused by something besides the software. From my home network, I ran the McMillan Spyware Detector and the Julian Spyware Sniffer. Both identified different spyware on my computer, and I have to believe it could be on my phone. There may be others." I show them the photos from my cell phone of the spyware, just in case the alerts don't show up here.

A woman appears with a carafe of coffee and cups.

I boot up my computer and hope for the best. Thankfully, the alerts are still there.

"What the fuck?" Landon demands.

"This wasn't on my computer three weeks ago, before I joined Disruptive," I tell him.

"We ran the Thompson Spyware check, which I suppose Mattis would have known about and been able to work around." Gage clenches his hands in frustration. "Did you call Yolanda from your cell phone last night?"

I shake my head. "I have a landline, so I called from the bathroom with water running."

Gage stands. "I need all your cell phones."

We hand them over, and he steps out of the room.

"I believe Mattis did this," I announce. I want it out there. He's gone off the rails, and now I discover this.

"What made you decide to look?" Jim asks.

Suddenly, I'm not sure Jim and Clear aren't behind the

intrusion. What if they put it on? "My program was lagging, and I didn't realize until last night that each day it got subtly worse. Landon had indicated he was frustrated by my output, and when he mentioned Mattis, it finally clicked—"

"I didn't think the lag was your fault," Landon counters.

"Everyone was so insistent that I work on the networks in the office or Landon's home, but not on my home network." I look at Jim. "Did you put these on my computer?"

He shakes his head. "We put a tracker on to see where your computer is at any time. You also have one on your cell phone. It's a security protocol. It's just a GPS tracker, which tells us if your computer is stolen or if someone says you're one place and we know better—that happens."

I turn to Landon. "Did you put this on my computer?"

He shakes his head. "I swear I didn't."

Claire appears at the door. "What the hell is going on?"

Jim explains the situation.

"Who put spyware on her computer?" she demands.

"Right now, we believe it may have been Mattis Yung," Jim confirms.

"Gage took my phone from me when I arrived. Are they bugging us, too?" Claire asks.

"He's checking, and if there is anything, he'll clean it away."

"The issue of my computer rebooting while on the network wouldn't be caused by the spyware, though," I muse.

Jim nods. "You're probably right, and we still haven't figured that out. Gage is pulling in Cameron Newhouse from SHN. He's a brilliant coder and might have some ideas."

My head hurts. Claire and Landon talk in hushed tones, and I try to think when my computer was unattended so someone could load spyware on it. Other than at my desk in the office, I can't recall anything. I don't open mysterious attachments.

Gage returns with our phones and puts them in the

center of the table.

"Each of your phones had spyware. It was recording all passwords, email, texts, and voice mail messages."

I look at Landon. His eyes are closed.

We'll need to come clean with Claire sooner than we'd planned. That'll be World War III for sure.

"I'd like to hold on to your computer for the day," Gage tells me. "I want to trace and see where the connection trying to retrieve your information is located. We'll give your computer a different signal than our offices, so they'll think it's in a coffee shop or something. I'll also have a team run a spyware sniffer on your office and home routers and networks."

Everyone looks shocked. I nod, not knowing what else to do. Claire and Landon agree.

Jim stands. "I'll give you guys a few minutes. I need to make some calls."

Landon nods at Jim as he leaves, then turns to his sister. "Claire-bear?"

She looks at him, alarmed. "What did you do? Did you load this on her machine?"

"No. I have something to tell you."

"What did you do? Why did you need to meet Fiona yesterday?"

My ears perk up. *Who's Fiona? The lawyer?*

"We can talk about that later," he says. "But I thought you should know that Tinsley and I met the night before the closing with her business. We both used a fake name. I was Peter, and she was Amanda."

Claire looks confused.

Landon can't look her in the eye. "We hooked up."

Claire moves from confused to angry. "What do you mean, *hooked up*?"

"Claire, I was out with Chrissy celebrating the sale of Translations to Disruptive. I don't usually pick up strange men in bars."

Claire slams her hand down on the table. "Why are you just telling me this now?"

"Because we've exchanged some messages, and if someone's been spying on our phones, they have them. We wanted to tell you the truth. I'm embarrassed by my behavior," I add. "I don't want you to think that reckless girl is my typical self."

"If those messages are going to come out, you need to have already heard the news from us," Landon adds.

"What about your boyfriend, Bob?" she asks me.

I try not to laugh. "Bob is my vibe—battery-operated boyfriend."

Claire doesn't seem to find this funny or clever. "Is that why you wanted to set me up with Tomas? So you two can fuck like bunnies?"

Landon puts his hand up. "Hold on. We've not been together since that night. Tinsley suggested we be friends for six months before we explore anything, and even then, we agreed you needed to be on board with anything that happened."

Claire closes her eyes, and I can tell she's doing Ujjayi Pranayama breathing—a calming yoga technique. "I'm upset with both of you for not telling me."

"I'm sorry, Claire." What a mess this is.

Jim and Gage return and join us at the table.

"It looks like when you were on the office network, you were transmitting information—though fortunately not your code—to someone not far from here."

Landon looks over at Claire. "Morgan Bennett. How much do you want to bet he's the bastard behind this? He was probably using Mattis."

Claire rolls her eyes. "Transitive wouldn't dare."

"Bullshit. Just because *you* had feelings for Morgan doesn't mean he isn't trying to beat us to market."

Claire's eyes fill with tears. "Stop it!" she yells.

I reach for her and hug her while she cries.

"I'm sorry," Landon says after a moment. "But I hate the asshole. He hurt you, and you didn't deserve it. And he is a competitor."

I didn't realize Jim had gotten up until he placed a box of tissues beside us. It takes a few moments before Claire notices it's there.

She blows her nose and wipes her eyes. "Please investigate Transitive. We're in a race to release direct translation."

Jim nods.

"We've removed the spyware," Gage explains. "And your computer and phones are clean. As far as your computer, Tinsley, we've learned that currently, with the reboot issue, they're not getting the coding information, from what we can tell. The lag caused the information being captured by the spyware to spin in the router, so it was unable to send it to the thief."

Gage is watching me carefully. I'm not going to cry. Not yet.

"We'll check the office router and Landon's home router for spyware. We focused just on Tinsley's computer before, because she was the only one having issues. But I believe there may be spyware on the office router, which would transmit to whoever is behind this breach."

"I'm curious. Would it have transmitted the code after I worked at Landon's if I'd reconnected to the office network?" I ask.

"We need to figure that out," Gage replies.

I'm almost shaking with rage. This is my hard work. If someone else takes it to market before I do, everything I did was for nothing. Zilch. I'm so grateful for the incredibly annoying black screen of death. It seems to be the only thing saving me right now.

Landon turns to Gage. "I'll take you into the office and The Adams. I doubt they've bugged us, but I think we should check for that too."

"What should Tinsley and I do?" Claire asks.

"The sun is shining for a change," Jim says. "There's a great garden on the roof. Why don't the two of you get some vitamin D, and we'll get lunch ordered before too long."

He leads us to the elevator and up to the top floor, which is obviously his apartment.

I stop and stare. "This is beautiful."

"My fiancée, Kate, did most of the decorating."

"You'll love Kate," Claire says, but without much enthusiasm. "She runs a national nonprofit affiliated with Bullseye's foundation. We'll participate in some of their projects as a company so you'll get the chance to work with her."

I nod. Jim having a life outside of his work is a little surprising. He seems like a guy who splits his time between work and the gym.

Jim shows us where to go before he disappears back downstairs. We walk to a set of stairs, which takes us up to the roof. There's a well-manicured yard with a picnic area, swing set, trees, a small pond, and when you look closely, a solid glass fence around the edge to prevent anyone from stepping over, but without obstructing the view.

We walk along a path to the pond and a bench without saying a word. Claire periodically sniffs and sniffles.

She sits down, and I sit next to her. "Do you want to talk about Morgan Bennett?"

She snorts. "The man ripped my heart out, slammed it against the wall, and then stomped all over it."

I wince. We've all had someone do that to us at one point, and it changes you. I watch a mama duck come out and look at us before she gets into the pond with three ducklings behind her.

"I met him after Landon and I sold our video-conferencing company to Tom Sutterland at PeopleMover. It allowed them to do video chats on social media. It was huge. Morgan worked as the head of technology at PeopleMover and did well when they went public. He's beautiful. Everyone stops talking and stares when he walks into a room. I couldn't believe he talked to me."

She wipes a tear away. "We got serious quickly. We talked about everything—our future, kids, where we'd live and vacation. We met each other's families, and we spent as much time together as we could. Then one day, he just ghosted me."

"Ghosted you?"

"Yep. He wouldn't return my calls, texts, or emails. I'd sold my apartment and had movers coming to move me into his place."

"He never told you not to move in?"

She shakes her head. "Landon took the key I had to his place and went to talk to him, but the locks had been changed."

"Jeez. That's harsh."

Claire starts crying all over again, and I'm a moron. *Nice going. Rub a little more salt in her wound.*

"Landon was great and made sure my belongings went into storage. I lived in his guest room, and I had to explain to everyone, even people I didn't know, what happened. It was awful."

"He's the ass, not you."

"A while after that, I was out with Caroline and a few other friends, and we saw him. I confronted him about ghosting me, and he was with a date. He told me he'd never loved me."

"That's horrible. I hate him for you."

"I didn't get out of bed for a week. Landon was ready to punch his lights out."

I giggle. "I can totally see him doing that."

"I know." She smiles, and I know she's going to be okay. "Eventually I found the house on Lombard, and renovating has been a great distraction outside of work. And I knew we wanted the next evolution of our communication technology to come with translation, so I found you."

"So, Morgan's working on his own now? Not at PeopleMover?"

"Yeah, Landon had lunch with Tom Sutterland a few weeks ago, and he mentioned that there was a race between us to get translation software done."

I suppose that makes sense. There are a lot of people trying to do what we're doing. The basics aren't hard, and you can find translation software all over the internet, but doing it well, in a way that's truly useful, is what's challenging — and what will set the ultimate winner apart.

The woman who brought us coffee earlier appears. "Hi, ladies. I'm Stella Dupont. I've ordered some lunch downstairs, and I'm serving it buffet style in Jim's apartment. Would you like to join us?"

I squeeze Claire's hand. "We can do this."

Claire stands and looks around. "This is beautiful up here."

Stella nods. "My girls love it. Jim had it built to keep them occupied and busy while their dad and I work. Their favorites are the ducks and rabbits Jim put up here. But the gardener hates the rabbits because they're getting into his vegetable garden."

I laugh. "Is that why our code names are from Peter Rabbit?"

She smiles. "Probably. It's been a topic of conversation recently."

Claire turns to me. "How do you know our code names?"

"I heard Yolanda refer to Landon as Rabbit, and his apartment as the rabbit hole."

"I love it!" Claire laughs. "That was one of his favorite books as a child."

We walk downstairs to Jim's apartment, and a crowd has gathered around the counter in the kitchen, which is packed with a feast of fajitas and all the fixings.

"Here they are," Landon announces. "How are you doing?" he asks Claire.

She nods.

"You were fast," I say. "Did you figure anything out?"

Landon gets behind me in the line for food. "Gage and I left a team there. I think he'll have an update in a few minutes."

We fill our plates and move over to a large table. When we introduce ourselves, and I learn that Cameron Newhouse with SHN, our investor, is among those here for lunch.

Claire and I take seats on either side of Landon. Once everyone is settled, our unplanned meeting begins.

"We did find spyware on both the company's and The Adams' routers. They were buried, and it seems logical to assume they were put there by former Head of IT Mattis Yung," Gage shares.

"Do you know how long they've been there?" Claire asks.

"Not exactly, but we're finding that packets of information were sent each evening." Gage wipes his mouth with his napkin. "The reboot that kept Tinsley's computer from working also kept her code from being transferred. When she worked from The Adams, the router was collecting packets of her work. But The Adams' router couldn't transmit the data, so it kept storing it, which in turn caused the lag."

"But I only began to notice a lag yesterday when I was on The Adams' network."

"Well, we can't find any record of the information being moved, so perhaps it finally reached the tipping point and built up into a noticeable delay."

Claire and I breathe easier. Landon doesn't, though, and I quickly see there's another shoe to drop.

"I understand from Landon that there's a rush to market with what you're working on," Cameron says.

I nod. "No pressure there."

"I've looked at what you've done." Cameron puts a

napkin in his lap. "I can see why you're having some challenges with the slang and some dialects. I have some ideas — that is, if you're open to hearing them. I don't want to step on your toes."

Cameron Newhouse is a genius developer. He's helped several of SHN's investments be successful. If he has ideas, I'm in. "I'm definitely open to hearing what you think — unless you tell me to scrap it all."

"Not exactly, but it could mean a lot of work ahead of us."

My palms start sweating, and I itch everywhere. *Not exactly* means I'm scrapping everything I've done.

"We can meet at The Adams tomorrow morning, if that works?" he says.

I look at Landon. "Are you okay with that?"

"If he's not, I'll whip his ass into shape," Claire interjects.

I look at Landon, and we both smile. Our Claire is back. *Fuck you, Morgan Bennett.*

We spend the next two hours planning our next steps. Gage's team is replacing the routers with newer and better models that have heavier encryption.

Before we break, Jim pulls me, Landon, and Claire aside. "We ran bug detectors through Landon and Claire's homes," he says. "Landon's had one that came in with a piece of mail, and Claire, you had several in the wiring at your house that's being renovated."

Claire gasps, suddenly white as a sheet.

"We caught them," Jim assures her. "You're fine, and we're changing some things around. We'll be more vigilant about checking your homes."

Jim looks at me. "We'd like to go through your place. Are you okay with that?"

"Of course."

"May I have a key to your apartment?"

I stand and dig my keys out of my backpack, handing

them to Jim.

"I'm sending Yolanda," he says. "She's also going to pack up a few outfits for you for the next few days."

"Where will I stay?"

"Landon and I were talking, and he has his parents coming, but there's still a guest room where you can stay."

"I don't want to be underfoot with his parents visiting."

"You won't." Landon looks at Claire, waiting for her to object. When she doesn't, he continues. "I have five different guest rooms, plus you can work out in the pool each morning."

"How long do you think I'll need to do this?" I start calculating what needs to be done.

"I'm not sure right now," Jim says.

My mind is going a thousand miles a minute. "What if I stay with my best friend, Christine Matthews? Or at a hotel?"

"If you don't mind, I'd prefer you stay with Landon," Jim says. "We'll have a team inside the apartment in the house manager's quarters, and it's a little less intrusive that way than having a team sitting on someone's couch, or accommodating them at a hotel."

"Where are the house manager's quarters?"

"The door next to the fridge leads to a two-bedroom apartment," Landon explains.

I had no idea.

I look at Claire. "Are you sure you're okay, given what we disclosed earlier?"

Jim excuses himself.

Claire clasps her hands in front of her. "You're both adults. I expect you to behave professionally at work, and when this all goes sideways, I don't want the office dragged into your drama."

"There won't be any drama," Landon assures her.

Claire cocks her head. "What about Tiffany?"

Landon sighs. "I'm looking into who Tiffany's landlord might be and trying to evict her. And Erin was a special case.

That won't happen again."

"Just remember Erin and what happened and promise me you'll both be friends at the end of this." Claire gives us a pointed look.

Okay, I need to know what happened with Erin. "Claire, right now, our focus is on the software. Your folks are arriving tomorrow, and they'll be here how long? Two weeks? A month?"

"Probably."

Okay… I guess when your children are billionaires, and you have access to a private plane, you don't exactly have a return ticket. "So for now, Landon and I will continue to press on as friends and only friends."

Claire smiles. "And we're still going to St. Helena in two weeks."

"Oh, yeah!" I give her a high-five.

CHAPTER 14

Landon

My parents' visit is another layer of stress I don't need right now. Tinsley and I need all the time we can get to figure out this mess with her software and how the integration will work, though Cameron will be a huge help. This is one of the many advantages of having SHN fund us. They do a lot of our operations work for us, so we can focus on what we do well, and sometimes when you can't get the software to do what you want, they have a top-notch development team that pitches in at no extra charge.

Before leaving the lunch meeting at Jim's, Cameron, Tinsley and I agree that he will be at the apartment by ten tomorrow morning. Then Greg drives Tinsley and me back to The Adams.

I look across the backseat at her. "Are you okay with this?"

"I will be. I'm a little lost without my computer. At least I have my phone." We're stopped at a light, and there's a man next to us in a metallic purple Mercedes convertible with the top down. We can hear Cher's "Believe" as clearly as if it were being played in this car.

I shake my head. "I think he's recently broken up with his boyfriend."

Tinsley giggles as she bounces in her seat. She pulls out her phone and forwards the song to my sister. "I think this should be Claire's anthem for a while."

"I'm good with that." I smile and feel warm as I remember how she looked out for Claire today.

Her cell phone pings. She chuckles. "Claire sent me 'It's Raining Men'."

When we arrive at The Adams, we're still grinning.

"I know another one I can send her." She clicks on her phone and Diana Ross begins to belt out "Ain't No Mountain High Enough."

Once we get upstairs, Tinsley dances around my living room. Her cell phone rings, and she puts it on the table as she answers.

"I love you both," Claire bellows through the speaker.

"I love you, too," Tinsley yells.

"Claire-bear, you're my favorite sister." I wink at Tinsley.

"That's because I'm your only sister."

"Do you want to come over here?" Tinsley asks.

"I do, but I've drawn a bath, and I'm going to relax. Thank you both for understanding how tough today was for me."

"Call me if you want to talk," Tinsley says. "We'll be here tomorrow." She hangs up, clicks on her phone, and shows me she sent Claire the classic Motown tune "I'll be Around."

Motown continues to rule the playlist, and I join Tinsley as she sashays around my living room. I grind my cock into her backside as we dirty dance. I can smell her perfume, and I want her.

She grinds back into me. I lean down and kiss her softly. She needs to drive this since we're only three weeks into our six months.

The song ends, and she backs away. I pour a glass of bourbon and offer her one. She nods. She takes a drink and continues dancing alone. I sit on the couch and watch her, mesmerized.

"What are you thinking?" I ask when her song ends.

She doesn't immediately look at me. "Who is Erin?"

I should have been prepared for that question, but I'm not. Claire mentioned a colossal mistake on my part earlier today, and I would have told Tinsley about it eventually… No time like the present.

"When we founded Disruptive Technologies, Erin was one of our first developers. She was right out of Berkeley, and she was brilliant. We got involved. It was a mistake. She was young and impressionable, and I was stupid. She wanted more than I did, and it caused a lot of problems for us. Eventually I had to write her a sizable check. I'm not proud of what happened, but with you, everything is different."

"No strings attached?" Tinsley offers.

"Oh, there are always strings attached."

She laughs. "Not always. If we hadn't run into each other, we never would have connected again. Sometimes two adults can screw without head games or emotions."

I frown. "I can't believe I'm even having this conversation with you. I wasn't kidding when I told you I'd planned to find you again. I have the resources, and I would have searched until I found you. Instead, you came right back to me. How do you not see that as some sort of sign?"

Tinsley looks as if I've grown a second head.

"Claire gave us the green light."

"I'm not sure about that. We told her six months."

Dammit. I nod, disappointed.

She crooks her finger at me, and I stand, prepared to do whatever she asks. "Thank you for staying with me," I tell her, "even if it's only for work purposes."

She looks at me with her big brown eyes and nods. I can't stop myself from brushing my lips against hers. She doesn't kiss me back at first, but then her arms stretch around my neck, and our tongues explore — heating up quickly.

I break the kiss and murmur, "This is probably a bad idea."

She nods. "Probably, but don't you at least owe me a goodnight kiss?"

I chuckle. "I suppose it is the least I can do." I grasp her shoulders, and she looks up into my eyes and sighs.

I lower my head, closing the distance between us again.

"Thank you," she whispers against my lips.

As my mouth moves softly over hers, she takes a step forward, pressing her body against mine. She moans softly as the hard ridge in my jeans brushes against her thigh. I groan. She's the most intoxicating thing I've ever felt. Our tongues dance for several long moments until I reluctantly draw back.

"I should go to my room," I whisper.

"But you won't." She smiles as she leads me down the hall and turns the knob on her bedroom door. Without looking back, she steps inside. She doesn't bother to turn on the light; enough light filters through the open curtains to illuminate the way to the bed.

She lies back on the bed and pulls me down on top of her. Our lips lock and once again find the perfect rhythm to keep the doubts at bay. She moans her pleasure when I cup her breast through her T-shirt.

My cock is not happy being constrained by my pants, but I want to take this at her pace. I slide my hand beneath the cotton of her shirt and find a nipple pushing hard against the lace of her bra. I play with it.

"Please," she begs in a throaty whisper.

What a sexy siren. She makes the most delicious, soft, needy noises, and I didn't realize how much I'd missed them until now.

I trail hot, wet kisses down the side of her throat as my other hand brushes up the inside of her thighs to cup her heated core. Her hips arch into my caresses as I rub her seam through the rough material.

My mouth finds her hard nipple, and I bite at it through her shirt and bra. She cries out in ecstasy.

I find the button of her jeans, and the sound of the zipper is loud in the quiet of our little world. I pull them off and admire her in a sexy T-shirt and lacy panties.

Her panties are wet, and I move them aside, my fingers sliding easily between her folds. I push deep inside of her, pivoting in and out. Her internal muscles tighten.

"Oh God," she cries as she grips my shoulders.

I want better access. She lifts her hips, and I slip her panties over her legs and drop them to the floor. I lean in and draw a deep breath. She smells like I remember — musk and honey.

I paw at her shirt. She lifts her head to allow me to pull it off, taking her bra with it. She's naked. Naked in her bed, and she wants me naked with her. She's tearing at my T-shirt as impatiently as I was. I'm already working on my belt buckle and jeans. She manages to tug my shirt off seconds before I push my jeans to the floor next to hers.

My hands are all over her — skimming her stomach and heating a trail to her firm breasts as I capture her nipple and suckle. She whimpers and moans, rubbing against my hand, and her bliss returns once more.

I spread her legs. This time instead of pushing inside her, my thumb finds the hard nub, and I circle, coming closer and closer, but not actually touching it — until she cries out, "Please…"

I stroke it hard and fast as three of my fingers plunge inside her wetness. She arches up as I bite her nipple. She pushes herself into my hand, her body off the bed and head and feet holding her steady as pleasure overtakes her. Her sounds and heavy breathing only make me harder. Her wetness covers my fingers, and I can't stop. I'm going to explode at any moment, but I want to see her come again.

She reaches for me. "It's your turn," she whispers.

I scramble to my jeans and pull a condom from my wallet. She licks her lips as I roll it on. "Are you okay?" I ask.

She nods and sucks in a deep breath. I line myself up. Pushing in is like putting on a warm glove. She's so tight. I rock in and out of her as she adjusts to my size. Her nails sink into my back. She's the perfect lover, an aberration. She holds on, drawing me deeper as she arches her hips up to meet my thrusts.

"So fucking tight," I groan.

I'm inside of her, pushing deep—hard and fast, pounding mindlessly. It's what we want, what our bodies desire. She explodes yet again, and this time it's more intense because of the frantic way I'm moving inside of her. I follow her, and our climax together is complete.

She's gasping for breath, her body limp and exhausted. I roll to the side, taking the bulk of my weight off of her, but our legs and lower bodies remain intimately locked.

"We do that well," she breathes.

"I agree."

My breathing slows, and she caresses my shoulders.

"Thank you," she murmurs as her eyes close.

Her body is too satiated—after a long day of work and the release of her orgasms, it's impossible to fight slumber.

We'll have several weeks of living together, and I plan on making the most of them. We wake twice more in the night and find each other. Each time seems better than the last.

As she falls asleep in my arms, my heart is racing. I know if I'm not careful, I could get used to this.

CHAPTER 15

Tinsley

Waking up next to Landon is surprisingly comfortable, though I'm shocked I slept at all. The man is like the Energizer Bunny—he keeps going and going.

"How are you feeling this morning?" he murmurs as he kisses the top of my head.

I run my fingers through the sparse hair on his chest. "I think I'm going to be feeling this for a few days."

"We'll have to continue to work those muscles."

"Let's see where we are after your parents leave," I suggest.

"That's right. My parents arrive today. Maybe I can put them up at The Fairmont?"

"Why? We held off for three weeks. We can hold off again."

"We said we'd wait six months, and we only made it three weeks. What if they're here a month?"

I giggle. "We can manage that. Just think of it like I'm

on my period for a month."

"There are other things we can do, if you're on your period."

Her eyes become hooded for a moment. "I think we can be friends for a few weeks. You'll need to spend time with your parents. They're coming here to see you."

"Not necessarily," I protest. "My mom's coming to help Claire with decorating her new house, and my dad is looking at a sailboat. Sailing is his retirement hobby."

"You didn't grow up sailing?"

"Not at all. We did a lot together as a family, though. We went out to Vancouver Island every summer for the month of July and stayed at a beach rental on the northwestern coast. We spent a lot of weekends in the winter going up to Whistler. It's under two hours each way, so we'd go downhill or cross-country skiing one day during the weekend."

"Do you still ski?"

"Not as much as I'd like. I miss the day hikes you can take in Vancouver. Even if you didn't want to leave the city, Stanley Park has some great trails."

Landon is caressing my back, and he may lull me to sleep again.

"What did you do growing up?" he asks.

"My mom worked most every Saturday —"

"I thought she was a lawyer?"

"She is, and she was the first female partner in her firm because she worked hard. She was quite the role model. But on Sundays, we'd find someplace to go do something outside. That was always her thing."

"Maybe we can take my sister up to Mount Tamaulipas and do a fun hike this weekend?"

"That sounds good." I stretch. "I need to get up and get ready. Cameron's going to be here in an hour."

"Do you need the whole hour?" His hands start to wander.

"I suppose another twenty minutes or so won't hurt."

I've dried my hair, and I'm running my hairbrush through one more time when Landon walks into my bathroom.

"Cameron's here and on his way up."

"Thanks." Just looking at Landon makes my insides melt, and I'd much prefer to spend the day in bed with him. *Focus.*

I walk out of my guest room and dig my computer out of its bag as the elevator pings its arrival. When I spot Cameron, I do my best Vanna White impression. "Welcome to my office away from my office."

"Good morning." He looks around. "This is a great place."

I nod. "It is. Landon's parents arrive later today, though, so I'm not sure how long we have it."

"No problem. Let's see how far we get. Our offices aren't that far, and we can always move there if need be. The network is secure, and I guarantee you'll be fine working there."

We settle down to work. Landon joins us and watches. Cameron is super easy to work with. His mind is amazing. He thinks about eight steps ahead. I'm so engrossed that I don't notice when Landon steps away.

Cameron and I go through numerous lines of code. In no time we're making huge progress.

A little while later, I see Landon out of the corner of my eye. "It's after one," he says. "Do you guys want any lunch?"

My stomach growls, but I look to Cameron. We've been going for four hours nonstop, and I think we're getting somewhere. If he wants to keep going, I'll grab a granola bar from my bag.

Cameron stretches. "Sure. Who delivers to this fancy address?"

Landon chuckles. "Everyone. What sounds good?"

"A burger from Waldo's in the Marina."

"That does sound good." Turning to me, Landon asks, "Burger okay? I can pull a menu and see what else they have, or we can order from more than one place."

"Burger sounds great."

We give Landon our order, and I escape to the restroom.

When I return, Landon is giving Cameron a tour of his apartment. "Yeah, they want to do a *San Francisco Living* spread on the place, but honestly, I love that people don't know I'm the mysterious guy living here. My neighbors don't even know."

When I join them, we talk for a short time about what we've accomplished this morning. The food arrives, and after we've eaten, Landon has some suggestions for integration with the technology the other team is building, which we decide to work on in the afternoon.

Sometime later, the elevator pings and I hear Claire. Cameron and I look up, and I realize it's dark outside.

"Mom, Dad? This is Tinsley Pratt," Claire announces. "She's our new business partner."

The couple exiting the elevator smile wide and embrace me. "Call us Peter and Edna," the woman says.

"Nice to meet you both." I'm going to need to change Landon's name in my cell phone. I can't confuse the two.

"We're so excited you've joined the kids," Edna tells me.

"I'm excited, too." I turn to Cameron. "This is Cameron Newhouse. He's the technology partner with our investor. He's helping me get some things with my software figured out."

Cameron has been packing up his computer and stops to shake their hands. "So nice to meet you both. We're excited about what Disruptive is doing."

"I can't wait to buy in myself." Peter rubs his hands together.

Cameron has zipped up his bag. "Great day today," he tells me. "I'll see you at our offices tomorrow at nine?"

"Sure. Should I bring coffee or anything?"

"Only if you like something in particular. Otherwise, we have almost everything in our kitchen."

"All right. See you in the morning. Thanks so much."

I step toward the elevator and watch Cameron leave as Peter and Edna turn their attention to their son.

Landon's mother gives him a hug so tight and long that you can see the love.

"Welcome to San Francisco," Landon tells her. "How was your flight?"

"Just beautiful. We're so spoiled on that private plane you sent."

"Glad it works for you."

Peter and Edna wander off with Claire and Landon. I clean up my computer and all the trash from our lunches before I head back to my room.

I need to give them some family time *and* clear my mind, so I pick up my Kindle and begin to read a fun, steamy, romantic suspense novel. We had a late lunch, and I can grab something later if I get hungry.

I'm so completely engrossed that I jump at the knock at my door.

"Are you joining us for dinner?" Landon asks as he ducks his head inside.

"No, I thought you'd like to visit with your parents. I don't want to intrude."

Landon steps into the room and closes the door behind him. "Are you okay?"

I nod, feeling shy all of a sudden. I want to reach for him, but I put my book aside and stand up.

He leans down and kisses me softly on the lips. "Please

join us for dinner. My dad loves a Greek place nearby, and we've ordered a ton of food."

"You don't think they want to visit with just the two of you?"

Landon's face scrunches up. "Definitely not."

"Okay. Greek food sounds good."

Landon takes my hand and pulls me out.

As we enter the room, everyone sees he's holding my hand, and Edna and Claire exchange a look.

"She didn't want to intrude and was going to hide in her room," Landon explains, releasing me. "I had to drag her out."

A look of relief crosses Edna's face, and an uneasiness settles in my stomach. She isn't comfortable with a personal relationship between her son and me.

"You're not intruding. Come on, sit down and join us," Peter exclaims.

Dinner is fun. We laugh our way through multiple conversations, and I learn all about Claire and Landon as children. My sides hurt from laughing so hard.

It's gotten a little late, and Claire leaves for home since it's a work night. Edna and I finish cleaning up the kitchen.

She's wiping counters down. "Landon likes you," she says.

"He's a good guy. And I know Claire is nervous about it, and I understand."

"She is, but she adores you."

"As I adore her. I wouldn't be here without her."

"You all will figure this out."

When I finally retire to my room, I change into pajamas and return to my book. My cell phone pings softly.

A picture from Landon arrives: a flaccid, sad penis.

Landon: Missing you.

Landon: Wish you were here in my bed right now.

Me: So close, yet so far away.

Landon: You could always sneak over here.

Me: We can hold out for a few days. Plus, I need some sleep tonight. With you in my bed, I don't sleep well.

I snap a picture of my right breast and send it to him.

Landon: God, woman. Are you trying to kill me?

Me: I thought that might help your friend reach his full glory.

A short video arrives of him stroking his hard rod.

Landon: I wish I were there, biting, sucking, and twisting that nipple.

I pull the covers back and take a picture of my obviously wet panties with Bob in the shot.

Me: And what would you do with this?

Landon: I'm on my way.

My heart beats quickly. I'm positive his mother is listening and waiting for that. She may be a guest in Landon's house, but she's his mother and has both his and Claire's best interests at heart.

Me: Don't. It's a bad idea.

Landon: We're adults. This is my house.

Me: Your mother doesn't like the idea of us together.

Landon: That officially killed my erection.

Landon: What did she say?

Me: Nothing, but I think she's worried about Claire. And you guys haven't even told her what we're dealing with at work, or that you think Morgan Bennett may be behind it, have you?

Landon: No. They would find Morgan and hunt him down. They really liked him until he did what he did.

Me: Let's stick to our plan. We need to keep our distance—for now.

Landon: You know how to put a damper on great sex.

Me: It is great sex, isn't it?

Landon: The best.

Me: Goodnight.

Landon: Sweet dreams.

CHAPTER 16

The alarm on my phone wakes me from what I'm sure was a delicious dream, but I have no idea what it was. I slept soundly last night. I was exhausted. I'm still sore, but that's to be expected.

I put my swimsuit on and make my way to the pool. The house is quiet. I open the door to the outside and *holy shit,* it's cold. My goosebumps have goosebumps. Vapors rise from the water, so I know it's warmer than the air outside, but that may not be by much. I stretch my nylon swim cap over my head as I dip my toe in. It's warm enough.

Landon's infinity pool gives you the impression that you could swim off the top of the building, but it's only an illusion. It's about a quarter of an Olympic-sized pool, but it'll work. It's more about the routine. I set the alarm on my phone to alert me at the forty-five minute mark and dive in. I swim freestyle back and forth, thinking about the software, my mom, living here at The Adams, that I need to call Chrissy...

My mind has just wandered to Landon as the alarm signals that I'm done. I know with the shorter distance and all the pushing off the sides of the pool, I didn't get as good a workout as usual, but it's something. I'll have to adjust for that tomorrow.

As I towel off, I look inside the house and can see everyone in the kitchen preparing breakfast. Wrapping myself in a beach towel, I join them. Edna walks over with a cup of Earl Grey tea.

"Good morning," she singsongs as she offers it to me.

"Good morning." I take a sip, and it's perfect.

"You're an inspiration to be swimming laps so early. I'm impressed."

"Thanks. It gives me a chance to think about what I need to do each day. Plus, I sleep better at night when I've worked out."

"Would you like breakfast?" She opens her arms to the kitchen. "I'm making eggs to order this morning. So far, I have requests for poached, an omelet, and over easy."

"Thank you, but I should take a shower. Probably the tea and a piece of fruit are enough for me. Now that I'm working in an office with a bunch of guys, I've noticed they seem to eat big lunches and dinners. I have to watch that. It's making my jeans too snug."

"You look fine," Landon shouts from the kitchen.

Peter holds his hands up. "I could get myself in trouble if I comment, but as a retired physician, I will say men can consume more calories than women."

"And you seem to rub our noses in it," Edna mutters.

I chuckle. "I'll be right back. I have to meet Cameron at nine at his office. That way we're not in your way today."

I sneak off and quickly shower, dry my hair, and put on a little bit of makeup. When I step out, I have twenty minutes before Yolanda is going to meet me downstairs.

Everyone is sitting around the table now.

"Here's a fresh tea for you," Edna says. "I'm a tea

drinker myself. My parents were from England, and we had afternoon tea most days. I prefer the taste to coffee."

"You're spoiling me. Thank you." I take a hesitant sip. The temperature is perfect, and she's steeped it just as I like. "Pure nectar of the gods. Thank you."

She crosses her arms and grins.

"What are your plans today?" I ask the group.

"I have a meeting with a man about a sailboat," Peter says with a big smile.

"I'm meeting Claire and her decorator," Edna chimes in. "We're working on the tile for the bathrooms and kitchen. I suspect we'll do some furniture shopping at some point, too."

"I'm going into the office," Landon says. "I'll be working with the SHN team to figure out if the router is working like it's supposed to. It wasn't working yesterday, and the spyware keeps coming back, so we're going to work on that. What about you?"

"As I mentioned, Cameron and I made plans to meet over at SHN. We'll be working on irregular sentence structure today." I turn to Edna and Peter. "My team is developing an in-ear translator that's designed so anyone can talk to anyone in real-time in any language."

"That's so exciting!" Edna says. "I won't deny, I'd love to go to my local Asian market and understand what people are saying. I'm sure it's about whether or not the dragon fruit or something is fresh, but when you aren't sure, you wonder. They could be laughing at me for having my skirt tucked in my pantyhose."

We all laugh. I can see where Landon and Claire get their sense of humor.

"When was the last time you wore pantyhose and a skirt?" Peter looks at her, puzzled.

"That's exactly why I don't. It only needs to happen once, and never again." Edna crosses her legs with a look of triumph.

I'm still giggling. "Our software has a lot of

applications," I tell her. "Of course, it would be the company's goal to have everyone wear an earpiece for all communication. It's very Star Trek. And now that I've partnered with Claire and Landon, we can make sure there is always a satellite connection, regardless of climate or location."

I look at my watch, and I have five minutes to get downstairs.

"I should go before Yolanda comes looking for me. Thank you for the tea," I say.

"We have dinner reservations at our favorite fish house. I hope you'll be coming," Edna offers.

"I don't want to intrude on your family time."

Peter shrugs. "The kids consider you family, so please come."

I get the impression this isn't something I'll be able to get out of, so it isn't worth trying. "What time?" I ask.

"Seven. Landon can text you the address," Edna confirms.

"See you then." I stand to leave, and Landon stands with me.

"I'll go down with you." He looks at his parents. "I'll be right back."

They study their newspapers, and we get in the elevator.

Landon pushes me up against the wall as soon as the doors close. "You look beautiful today." He leans down and kisses me. I can feel his hardness through our clothes. It's difficult to break away, but when the doors open, I spot Tiffany stalking him, and I continue toward the car at the curb as he follows.

"I should be at SHN all day and on my cell."

I look back and see Tiffany still at the door. "Someone is waiting for you," I tell him.

"She'll love this." Landon bends down and our lips meet. His tongue sweeps deep in my mouth, staking its claim. He grabs my ass and squeezes.

My toes curl, and I'm light-headed when we break. "Wow. You know how to kiss." Tiffany is now visibly angry. "Good luck getting by that without a scratch."

"It would only make evicting her from the building that much easier."

"I'll see you later." I get into the car with Yolanda.

As we drive away, I see Tiffany sashay up to Landon, ready to pounce. I do not envy him in this moment.

CHAPTER 17

Landon

As the Suburban drives off, Tiffany shimmies up to my side and pushes her ample breasts against my arm.

"Hey, handsome," she coos.

I turn to walk back into the building. She's practically running to keep up with me. "I understand you've been rude to my house guest."

"She's lying. I've been nothing but polite."

I stop and turn to look at her. "Her bodyguard reported it to me, along with the security footage. Those are all lies?"

Tiffany steps back. "I'm just keeping with the rules of the building."

"She's registered with the HOA as a long-term guest, which is what she became two days ago. She's also my business partner and has every right to work with me in my apartment. Leave her alone."

I'm getting upset, and it's obvious. I continue moving back toward the elevator, willing myself to calm down.

Tiffany catches up with me as I wait for the elevator to arrive. "When can I see you?" Her voice softens, and she runs her fingers up my arm.

"Tiffany, please don't touch me. Don't you have a job? Why are you always in the lobby waiting for me?"

She stands up tall. "I have a job, and I pay my rent. I'm not always in the lobby waiting for you."

"Good. Keep your distance from my friend." I enter the elevator angrier than I've been in a long time and leave her watching me as the elevator doors close in her face. She's lucky she didn't try to get in. I would have been brutally honest, and she'd probably sell the story to some tabloid. *Ugh.*

As the elevator rises to my floor, I text Mike Spencer again to follow up on Tiffany.

Me: Have you figured out who Tiffany Reynolds' landlord is?

Mike: Yeah, I was messing with you, man. She's my tenant.

How did I miss that?

Me: She needs to be evicted.

Mike: That's not easy in San Francisco, particularly because she pays her rent.

Me: She's stalking my business partner.

Mike: She can suck a golf ball through a garden hose. Tell him to give it a try.

Me: My business partner is a woman.

Mike: Nice! Some girl on girl action. Can we watch?

Me: Jesus, man. She's a psycho. We need to get her out of the building. She's always in the lobby. Where does she work? How does she make rent each month?

Mike: I don't remember.

My mom comes around the corner just as I exit the elevator. "Oh good, you're back."

I tuck my phone in my pocket. I have more questions for Mike, but they'll have to wait. "Where are you off to?"

"Claire should be here shortly. Your father is meeting with the sailboat dealer at one, and I'll meet him and go with him to the marina. If I don't, he'll buy the boat without asking any questions."

I nod, knowing exactly what she means. If he's excited about something, my dad will ignore neon flashing signs that say it's a bad idea.

"I'm going into the office. You both have fobs to come and go as you please."

I grab my gear and let Greg know I'll be ready in five.

I've been sitting across from Gage for three hours. We're still struggling. Against my better judgment, I've asked everyone to work from home because we keep rebooting the system, and the router keeps reinstalling the spyware. Nothing we've tried seems to be working.

"I need a break," I announce.

"Understand. We'll be here until we get this figured out," Gage says.

I have Stan pick me up and take me to SHN's offices. I want to see how the coding is going for Tinsley and Cameron.

When I arrive and ask for Cameron, the receptionist is flustered.

Mason walks out. "Hey, man, what brings you by?"

"I'm looking for Cameron and Tinsley. They're working on our software."

"Come on back." He motions for me to follow.

I trail Mason into his company's workspace. SHN covers the entire floor, and everything is modern and bright. Easily over a hundred people work in this space, and almost all the walls are glass.

Mason takes me to his office, and we sit down.

"Do you want anything to drink?" he asks.

"Bourbon is my preference, but it's far too early in the day for that. Coffee is fine."

He alerts someone and looks at me. "Caffeine doesn't have the same punch. A friend of mine talks about a jazz bar here in the city that has a bourbon tasting room. We should check it out sometime."

I like that idea. "Sure."

"How are you doing with the spyware?"

"I'm working with Jim's team, and they're struggling. But it did bring to light a challenge Tinsley's been wrestling with in our new software. Her skills are well beyond mine, so I'm no help. Cameron has been a godsend."

"He's brilliant. Glad he can help. He also has a team with all kinds of coding skills, so we can utilize them if he thinks it's necessary."

"Speaking of which, he and Tinsley were supposed to be here working today. Where are they?"

"Good question. I was late this morning. One of our companies was bought by Cloud Source, so this place is crazy."

I look out over the offices, and everyone is standing and social. I haven't been here a lot, but it hits me that this most likely isn't the norm. "I suspect they've gone someplace quiet to work—which would not be here today."

I pull my phone out and text Tinsley.

Me: Hey, I'm at SHN. Where are you?

I don't see a response. I'm still glancing at my phone over and over again when Dillon, the finance partner, comes into Mason's office. We shoot the shit for roughly an hour, but still no text from Tinsley.

What could she be doing? Could something be wrong?

Cameron's married—and I believe happily—but why isn't she responding to me?

Tinsley's beautiful and smart. He'd better be keeping his hands to himself.

Where the fuck is she?

I can't stall any longer, so I stand. "Well, my break is over. I need to see if Gage and his team are making any progress."

We shake hands, and I head downstairs.

Maybe they're at my place, and we just passed one another?

I ask Greg to drop me at home. I wave to Dee as I enter the building and take the elevator upstairs. I'm pleasantly surprised not to see Tiffany. *Good.* Maybe she's gotten the hint.

I find my dad sitting on a chair in my living room with his feet up and a newspaper in hand. "Hey, did Tinsley come back?"

"Nope, I've been here alone all morning. Your mom is due back in..." My dad looks at his watch. "Fifteen minutes ago, which means she'll be here in fifteen. We're meeting that guy down at the marina at one."

I nod and walk back to Tinsley's room. She isn't there. *Where is she?*

Me: Where are you?

Maybe Claire knows where she is.
Me: Have you talked to Tinsley this morning?

Claire: No. How are things with the router going?

Me: Not as well as I'd hoped. I sent everyone home to work since they keep stopping and restarting the Wi-Fi.

Claire: Mom has left to meet Dad. I was going to head over to the office and check in.

Me: I'm heading back myself.

My dad begins to tell me about the boat he's going to look at. "It's ideal for racing with a crew of four. It can accommodate six on a coastal cruise and eight on day trips."

"How will you get it home? Sail or transport?"

"It has a double berth and single berths on either side of the keel box, so your mom can easily have her own space. There's a small galley with a hob and icebox, chemical toilets, and an electric pack combined with solar panels. Those make the yacht fully autonomous. We could easily make it in about six weeks of casual sailing. It would be great."

I blanch internally. My mother is not a huge fan of sailing. She's okay with the occasional day trip around the islands, but she hated when my dad talked her into a trip around Vancouver Island a few years back. That was five days on the water. Six weeks would probably land them divorced. I'm not going to get involved.

The entire time my father is talking, I keep wondering where Tinsley is. When my mother arrives, I kiss her on her forehead and leave to return to the office. I text Jim.

Me: Do you know where Tinsley and Yolanda are?

The few moments it takes Jim to respond seem like forever.

Jim: They're at Cameron Newhouse's place in Pacific

Heights.

They're at his house?

I breathe in a few times to get my bearings. Why didn't they go back to my apartment or somewhere public? And why isn't she getting my texts? I swear, I'm going to kill Cameron. He may be bigger than me, but I have no problem playing dirty when it comes to my woman.

My woman?

What. The. Fuck. Where is this coming from?

I thank Jim and ping Tinsley one more time. I get nothing. *That's it.* I'm going over there. Nothing's going to stop me.

I call Stan as I head downstairs, and when I arrive, he's at the curb and ready to go. We drive across town. I hardly notice the people on the streets, the other cars, taxis, or buses. I hope Tinsley's okay. I don't know what I'll do if she's in the hospital. Why wouldn't Cameron have called to tell me if something happened? Is the battery on her cell phone dead? I rub my hands over my face. Can't we get there any faster?

The Suburban is hardly at a stop when I'm out of the car. Cameron's house is part of some group of modern row houses—elegant, light taupe stucco and all the accents. The garage door, gates, shutters, and trim are black. I'm ready to pound on the door when Stan comes running up.

"You're at the wrong home, sir."

I look at him, my hand inches from banging on the door.

"Thanks." I back away and walk around to the correct driveway. I'm too worked up. I take the time to collect myself. *What am I doing?*

Once my heartbeat is at a reasonable level, I knock on Cameron's door. One of Jim's guys answers and lets us in.

I see Cameron first. He comes over and shakes my hand, all smiles. "I think we had a breakthrough in how to improve the lag in translation. We'll need to redo some work, but it will make a huge difference with the timing, and I think it will give us the chance to fix the slang and obscure sentence structure we've been struggling with."

I nod. I'm so relieved Stan stopped me from making a fool of myself.

I walk into the kitchen to find Tinsley sitting at the table. She's so focused you could probably throw a party in here, and she wouldn't even notice. That explains so much. She likely has no idea where her phone even is.

What an idiot I am.

I reach out and touch her arm, and she jumps. "Where did you come from?"

"I've been texting all afternoon, and you didn't respond. I was worried when I went over to SHN's office and you weren't there."

"Oh! There was some sort of celebration going on at SHN, and it made it hard to talk," she tells me. "So, Cameron suggested here. We couldn't go back to your place with your parents there." Her eyes sparkle with excitement. "I think Cameron figured out our issue."

"You figured it out on your own," Cameron remarks with a grin. "I only helped you formulate a plan."

"I'm going to have to rewrite most of the code, but this is going to work. Plus, Vanessa can design a smaller device."

Cameron hands us both a beer. "Let's talk about what we did today and what we need to do to move forward."

Tinsley starts talking so fast I struggle to understand what she's saying.

Then I catch enough to make sense. She's designed her software in Python, which is considered cutting edge for these kinds of uses, but it isn't fast enough to deal with the translations. She'll rewrite everything in Java, which is older, but nimbler.

Her enthusiasm is infectious. *Shit!* This is big. "How long is this going to take?" I ask. "You've been working on this for months. Is this going to take months?"

She shakes her head. "Cameron and one of his team members are going to help. And you're a decent Java developer. We might be delayed a few weeks, but with four or five of us pushing through, we should be able to get caught up and move ahead."

I nod, and my blood pressure calms.

Cameron's phone rings, and he steps out of the room to take it.

"Why are you here, Landon?" Tinsley studies me.

"You weren't responding to my texts."

"I was working. But you went looking for me at SHN. Why?"

"I already told you why. I was frustrated about how things were going at Disruptive. I couldn't get ahold of you, and I got worried. They still can't figure out the routers and—"

"Landon, were you worried about me and Cameron alone together?"

"No! But—"

"Because Cameron's happily married to a beautiful redhead."

"Yes, I know Hadlee. You don't understand—"

"So, explain it to me," she demands.

"You're mine, and—"

"The hell I am." Tinsley stands up and begins shoving her belongings into her bag. "I belong to no one but me. If you can't approach this like an adult and treat me with any kind of respect, I don't want anything to do with you outside of work."

"Too bad. You live in my guest room. We need to have better communication."

I can see Tinsley getting angrier as each moment passes. "Don't exchange your lack of trust in yourself for a lack of trust in me."

I take a deep breath. *Why won't she understand?*

"I have too much work to do tonight to join you for

dinner," she says. "Please apologize to your parents for me."

With that, she picks up her bag and walks out the door.

I start to follow her, but see Cameron standing behind me.

"I might let her cool down a bit," he says as I turn.

"How much of that did you overhear?"

"More than you'd probably like."

I sit down hard in his living room chair. "I've never been like this. I know you're a complete professional, but when Tinsley wasn't responding, my head went to the wrong place. I was worried something might have happened, and you were too busy to call, or that her phone died... But I don't know why. I don't usually move directly into freak-out mode, especially for no reason."

Cameron laughs a deep belly laugh. "You're in for it now. Ask Jackson Graham, Mason, or Dillon Healy from my office. We've all hit that cliff. We all jumped and have settled down. Good luck. I'd be lost without Hadlee."

I'm late to the Fish House, and my parents, sister, and—oddly enough—Tinsley are waiting when I arrive. I sit between my sister and my dad.

"Can you believe Tinsley planned on working through dinner tonight?" my mom asks.

I look over at Tinsley, and if her eyes could shoot lasers, I'd be dead.

"It's my fault," I tell them. "I interrupted her mojo while she was working this afternoon."

"She tells me she and Cameron had a breakthrough. You'd better stay away from them so they can get it figured out," Claire warns.

"He's going to help, too," Tinsley says. "I should have it divided up between Cameron and his team and the two of goes dry, and my eyes bulge. Holy crap, he looks good.

Edna explains her phobia, and I quickly pour the tea she made into a travel cup and gather my belongings.

"Are you taking your computer?" Landon asks.

"I was planning on it."

"You're supposed to be taking the day off. Twenty-four hours with your computer here will be fine."

I shrug. "Alright, I'll leave it here. I have my phone if you need me for something, and I can be back in an hour."

He takes my bag off my shoulder. "I'm walking you downstairs."

"Only if you put a shirt on. Tiffany will be lurking. I have no doubt."

He rolls his eyes and pulls on the shirt he has in his hands. "Happy?"

"I am," his mother chides.

We get in the elevator, and once the doors close, Landon's mouth is on mine. His lips are salty with sweat, and his tongue is aggressive. It takes all my willpower not to call Claire and cancel.

The elevator arrives at the lobby, and as we walk out to Claire's waiting car, I spot Tiffany perched in the library on the second floor.

"Twenty-four hours is going to kill me, but at least I know you'll come back if I have your computer," Landon says.

"I promise to be good." I wink at him and reach for his cock.

He nuzzles my neck. "I'm glad, because I have plans for you when you get back."

He bends and gives me a toe-curling kiss.

"Are you trying to piss your sister off?"

"Nope." He opens the door, and I can tell she's not happy. "If you look in the lobby, you'll see Tiffany waiting for me. I did that for her benefit. Don't be upset."

Claire's eyes narrow, and her lips purse. "I know you

us later tonight. Tomorrow we'll need to be at Cameron's about nine, if that works for you." She looks at me coldly.

"Of course."

As dinner progresses, the angrier I get. So, I overreacted to her disappearing today and not answering her phone—but I was worried about her. That's not a crime.

After we're done with dinner, Claire pulls me aside. "You'd better check yourself there, mister."

"What are you referring to?"

"You know damn well you're all upset because Tinsley didn't respond to you today. Sure, she should have, but you're getting wound up, and that's not going to go over well with her. Take my word for it."

"I—"

"I don't care what flimsy excuse you have. Step back. You're wrong."

I watch my sister hug and kiss our parents and Tinsley goodbye, like she hasn't just chastised me.

When we pile into the Suburban, Mom and Tinsley crawl into the last row, and I sit in the middle next to my dad. He's excited about the sailboat he saw today.

"Are you going to buy it?" I ask.

"Your mother thinks we may have a problem getting it over the border."

"Why?"

My mother starts in on a long list of problems related to the boat. She begins with how Dad's planning on getting it up to Vancouver. "It's been sitting in the water for years and probably needs its hull cleaned because of the barnacles border inspectors for Canada get particular about, and then there are the mechanical issues." She rolls her eyes and continues her laundry list.

I chuckle. My dad probably won't win this one. "Do you have a slip in mind at the marina?" I ask.

"No!" Mom practically yells. "And that's another reason. Not only is he looking at dropping almost a half-million dollars on a sailboat he will take out a dozen times a year at most, he also doesn't have a place to store it. There are no available slips in Vancouver for a boat of that size, and I doubt he can head north or down into Washington."

My parents bicker as we drive back to my place and walk into my building. I let them lead the way and hold back so I can grab Tinsley's hand.

"I'm sorry about today," I tell her. "I didn't mean to be stalking you. I *was* curious about how the coding was going, and the office Wi-Fi is a mess, so I was looking for a break. Then when I couldn't get a hold of you... I don't know why I freaked out."

Tinsley squeezes my hand. "I've worked the last three years on my own. I know I need to be better at letting people know where I am. I'm sorry you were worried."

"I'm sorry for getting all worked up. My head went to a thousand places, including you in a hospital. I can't even explain why."

"Things like this may happen again. Let's try to remember we're both new to this relationship thing."

She gives me a smoldering look, and I raise my eyes to the skies, wishing to God my parents were staying with my sister.

CHAPTER 18

Tinsley

As we walk into the building, I notice Peter and Edna have stopped and are talking to none other than my *best friend,* Tiffany. Does this woman have any sort of life? What. The. Fuck.

Landon must notice at the same time. "What the hell…" he murmurs.

Peter is laughing, and Tiffany is hanging all over them. Landon swings the door open, and her eyes turn to him, traveling to his hand on my lower back. He steps in protectively. Her eyes narrow. If she were a cartoon, she'd be a twelve-foot green monster spewing fire.

"I thought you were business partners." She sounds like a petulant sixteen-year-old.

I try to step away from Landon, but he stops me. "I see you're still hanging out in the lobby."

Landon pulls me past her and shoos his parents into the elevator.

When the doors close, his mother turns to him. "What was that?"

"Mother, stay away from that woman. She's nothing but trouble, and I don't want her to know where I live."

Edna looks at Peter, and I know immediately they've already said something.

"How could you?" Landon sighs. "You know how much I value my privacy."

"What's the big deal?" Peter asks.

"The owner of my apartment — me — is considered one of the biggest secrets in all of San Francisco. I want it to remain that way."

"I didn't know," Peter murmurs.

"He's told almost everyone he's met," Edna says sadly. "We're proud of you. We didn't understand it was a secret."

When we get upstairs, I leave them to discuss and walk back to my room.

I can still hear them talking after I've changed and crawled into bed. I pull my computer out and continue working through what I'm hoping Cameron and his team will do. There are code converters, but Cameron and I both agreed we were best served by recreating the code. That way, if it breaks down, the error will be easier to spot. I'll take on the oldest code, and Cameron and his team can take the newest. We'll start with Spanish first and then make the changes to other languages.

It's after midnight when my cell phone pings. I shut my computer down and turn the light off.

Landon: I'm sorry.

Me: What do you have to be sorry for?

Landon: For today. For my parents. For Tiffany. For the continued problems with the routers... Should I go on?

Me: You're fine. Nothing to worry about.

Landon: I came clean to my parents about us.

Me: They already knew and didn't approve.

Landon: Trust me, it's not you they don't approve of. It's me.

Me: We can wait until they're gone.

I send him a pic of my breasts.
Me: These will still want to play with you when they leave.

Landon: You're killing me, woman.

Me: I'm doing my best.

Landon: I like it when you do your best.

Me: What else do you like?

Landon: Toys.

I take a picture of a small vibe I brought with me.
Me: Like this?

Landon: That could be fun, but I'm thinking bigger.

I search the internet and take a screenshot of a huge dildo.
Me: I don't think I can do this.

A picture arrives of a high-end vibrator that twists and turns while it pulsates inside.
Landon: I was thinking about this while I eat you.

I look around the website and find a vibrating cock ring.

Me: Add this to your cart for when I eat you.

Landon: I've added both and a surprise.

Me: I'm going to Napa with Claire and the girls this weekend.

Landon: Maybe I'll join you in your room. No one will know.

Me: I can be loud. That may not be a good idea.

Landon: I love it when you scream my name when you come.

Me: What else do you love?

Landon: Your big brown eyes staring up at me with my cock down your throat.

Me: Has anyone ever told you you're a naughty boy?

Landon: I do the punishing.

Me: How do you plan on punishing me for making you worry today?

Landon: It's in the surprise.

Landon: I wish you were here with me now.

Me: Your mom has better hearing than an owl. Guarantee she'd know you were creeping down to my bedroom. I'm sure she got up early this morning when I got

in the pool.

Landon: When you talk about my mother, you destroy my erection. The same can be said for Claire.

Me: We'll have lots of erections in our future.

Landon: How can you be so patient? You turn me on with your mind, body, and soul. I think of the look on your face when you come all the time.

Me: Tomorrow, we're working all day together.

Landon: I can't wait.

Me: Goodnight.

Landon: Goodnight.

I put my phone down, but I'm so amped I can hardly sleep. I think about our texting and the last time we were together. I run my hands down my ribcage and across my hips. I'm wet and needy.

I move my fingertips to my nipples, concentrating the sensation into one spot. Butterfly touches send flickers of pleasure along my skin and nerves. My whole body responds to this touch in two places.

My fingers find my clit, and I slowly circle it, imaging it's Landon and his tongue.

My fingers slip inside. My hand rocks and strokes, inside and out. I can no longer stop my hips from jerking or my thighs from twitching as I ride my hand. My breasts sway, and my toes curl and point over and over. Wet sounds mingle with soft, hungry moans, breaking the quiet of the night and releasing all my pent-up energy.

The word *please* forms in my mind, but I can't tell if I've said it or thought it. The frantic energy of the moment is so good, so right, so perfect — and then pleasure rushes through me as I come undone.

It would be better if Landon were here, but he is in my dreams.

CHAPTER 19

Landon

I had to take care of myself after my text session with Tinsley last night, and my sleep was filled with thoughts of her. I love my parents, but I need some alone time with Tinsley. *Quality* alone time.

Rolling over, I see it's after seven. I'm sure everyone is awake. My morning wood is strong. It wants Tinsley, not my hand.

I hop in the shower and set it a little cold to simmer myself down. I may need that erection later today, if I'm lucky.

When I join my parents in the kitchen, I'm just in time to see Tinsley exit the pool outside. *God, she's beautiful.*

"What would you like for breakfast, sweetheart?" my mom asks.

Tinsley. I turn to my mom. "Toast is fine."

After a moment, Tinsley joins us with a towel on her head and coverup over her suit. "Good morning."

"Same as yesterday, or would you prefer some eggs this morning?" Mom asks her.

"Tea and fruit are perfect."

Mom hands her a cup of tea, and I go back to reading my email. Fiona McFee wants to meet again early this morning. I'm hoping we can countersue the bitch who filed this paternity suit against me.

I wander back to Tinsley's room. "Tinsley?"

"Come on in," she yells.

I walk in, and she's standing in a thong and a demicup bra. My cock is immediately hard and ready. I shut the door behind me. "You're killing me."

She smiles and touches a nipple, which is straining behind her bra.

"I have to go see my lawyer this morning. Are you going to SHN or is Cameron meeting you at our offices?"

She pulls a T-shirt over her head, which fits snugly across her tits. "SHN. I'm meeting with him and his team."

I watch her pull on a pair of jeans, and they fit like a second skin. I love the way she looks, but a guy would have to be dead not to notice how hot she is. I'm about to object to her outfit when she grabs a big sweater and pulls it on, hiding all of her assets.

"Thank you."

She kisses me. "Only you get to see it all."

"I'm getting a hotel room this afternoon, and I'm going to fuck you until you can't walk."

She cocks her head to the side. "You can do that after we've finished this coding and get caught up."

Always focused, this one. I sigh.

We walk out together, and I tell her where I'll catch up with her later today as I sprint out the door. I need to get a good answer out of Fiona.

Greg is waiting for me downstairs, and we head over to the financial district where Fiona's offices are. I call Claire.

"Hey," she answers, out of breath.

"Am I interrupting?"

She laughs. "I ran to the phone in the bedroom from the kitchen."

"Sure." I know she's telling the truth, but it's fun to yank her chain. "What are you doing with Mom and Dad today?"

"They're on their own." She sighs. "I have to get some work done. Why?"

"Tinsley and I need to work, and the office is out. At home, they'll keep interrupting us."

"Okay, I can have them come to the office and take me to lunch. I'll send them shopping after. Would that work?"

"Yes, but don't bring up the sailboat. Dad's still dying to buy it, and Mom's holding firm since there isn't a boat slip available anywhere near them."

"No problem there." Claire is grunting and breathing heavily. "I got you covered."

"Are you sure you're alone?"

"Yes." She's not happy I've asked. "My boot was stuck in the back of my closet. Grow up. I'd tell you to go get laid, but I don't want to unleash you on Tinsley, yet."

Oops. Too late.

"Alright. I'm off to see Fiona this morning and will catch up with Tinsley and Cameron. I'll leave Mom and Dad to you."

"Thanks. You owe me."

"Me? You're the one who invited them."

"Whatever. Bye."

My sister is something else sometimes. "Bye."

When we arrive at Fiona's building, Greg parks in a no-parking zone and walks me upstairs to her office.

The receptionist greets me, her cleavage once again on display. She's a sexual harassment suit waiting to happen.

She invites me to follow her to a conference room. "Can I get you anything?" she mewls.

"I'm good." *Does she act like this all the time or just with me?*

I wait patiently for Fiona, which is saying something since it takes her close to twenty minutes to join me.

She embraces me and gives me an air kiss on the cheek. "Sorry about the delay."

"I want to countersue her for harassment," I begin.

Fiona sighs and pushes a piece of paper at me. I look down, and it says I'm a ninety-two percent match to be the father to Heather McCoy's child.

"This is impossible!" I murmur.

"We can ask for a blood test after the baby is born, but for now, she's asking you to pay all medical bills and her rent."

I study the paper and its aligned genetic markings. "This must be a scam. How is this possible?"

Fiona shakes her head.

"So, what happens if I pay what will probably be close to fifty thousand dollars and it's not mine, making this whole thing a scam?"

"You can sue her for that."

"She probably doesn't have a pot to pee in. This is bullshit. No. If a test after the baby's birth confirms I'm the father, I will take responsibility. But that isn't my baby. I was never with that woman."

"How can you be sure?" Fiona asks.

I'm stunned. That was a complete kick in the chops. "Perhaps I've been a bit reckless with my personal life, but I know where I was that weekend. And the day she's talking about, I wasn't with her."

Fiona nods. "That's good news. I want to see your calendar. Did you have sex that weekend?"

"Yes, but in Las Vegas. And with a woman I see on occasion when we aren't dating others. It can't get out." I click two buttons on my phone and email the contact to her. "This Heather McCoy says I was with her on October fifteenth. I was playing poker in Vegas at a hush-hush game with Nate

Lancaster. That was the weekend his wife went missing. I would think that's more than enough to at least delay until the baby is born."

"How did you get to Vegas?"

"I flew in with Walker Clifton and Jackson Graham on Jackson's plane."

"Will Jackson verify this?"

"He'd better." I scroll through my contacts and dial his office.

"Hello, Jackson Graham's office," a woman states efficiently.

"This is Landon Walsh. Can you see if Jackson has two minutes for me?"

"One moment, please."

"Hey, loser," Jackson's voice bellows through the phone.

"Hey. I'm here with my attorney. Can you tell her when I flew with you to Vegas last fall?"

"Sure. Is everything okay?"

"It will be as soon as you verify."

"Okay, give me just a second... Here it is. We went to Vegas in October from the twelfth to the eighteenth. That was the weekend Cecelia went missing."

"Thanks. That's what I needed to hear. I have a psycho saying I was somewhere else."

"Let me know if you need more info from me. I can pull the flight manifests and give a sworn statement — Clifton too. I'm sure having a United States Attorney swear on your behalf would help, too."

"Thanks. I appreciate it."

We disconnect, and I look at Fiona. "So, I have Jackson Graham and probably Walker Clifton swearing I was in Vegas."

"But you could have flown back," Fiona reasons.

"Why? For some nameless piece of ass? If I'd wanted that, I could have gotten it in Vegas. Why fly back? Honestly, I was in a tournament with these guys. It ran all afternoon and into the evening. Twelve big-name people will verify that I was there, plus the Las Vegas Police were all in our shit over that weekend. I was there, and the woman I sent you will verify that I spent the nights with her. So no, I'm not paying for some other guy's baby."

Fiona taps her pen on the glass table. "Let me pull all this together. We can fight this. The problem is that the paternity test is conclusive."

"Could it have been faked? I wasn't there. I've never been with that woman." I debate a moment, and then I pull a file from my phone and forward it to her.

"What is this?"

"It's a list of every woman I've been with in the last three years. Of course, these are the names they gave me."

"You think some of the names are wrong?"

I nod. "The last entry for *Amanda* is actually Tinsley Pratt, the new partner at Disruptive Technologies."

"Why did you put her down as Amanda?"

I walk her through how Tinsley and I met and what happened the next day at the closing.

"Sounds like you may have met your match."

"Fiona, I think I'm off the market for good."

Her eyes bulge. "That's…that's good news."

I'm not sure *what* she thinks with that response, but I don't care.

"Call this woman's lawyer and let them know if we have a blood match after the baby is born, I'll pay her a million dollars plus an additional hundred thousand a month. But I promise you, that is not my kid, so I'm not giving her a penny until we test again."

I leave Fiona's office with a black cloud over me. I don't mean to be an ass, but I have not slept with that woman. Yes, she seems to know how I operate, but that only means we know someone in common—not that I slept with her.

When the car arrives at the office, I don't even notice.

"Sir, is this where you want to be?" Greg asks.

I look up at the building and realize where I am. "Yes, sorry. Thank you."

I hop out and walk into the office, trying to put aside what happened this morning. Upstairs, I go in search of Gage and his team. I find them with deep, dark circles under their eyes and wearing the same clothes from yesterday.

"How's it going?" I ask.

I get the rundown on their many unsuccessful attempts at fixing the router and the network issues.

My blood pressure rises. "Do you think this is a sabotage attempt to slow us down? Or is it someone stealing the software?"

Gage sighs. "I think it's both. We've figured out what might have been stolen from the original Disruptive software, but we're struggling with why the reboot keeps happening. We have a mirror image of Tinsley's computer, and we're running it in a controlled environment, but something is still causing the reboot. The only advantage is that none of the information has been shared. It's like the reboot is a fail-safe."

"Could that be embedded in the software she's using for her coding?"

"I don't think so. I usually call in the big guns at SHN, but Cameron hasn't called me back."

I know why. He's with the five-foot-six-inch dynamo that gets my dick hard. "I'll see what I can do. You all look miserable. I'm glad I didn't pick up any coffee. You need to go home and get some sleep."

I walk back out to the car and have Greg drive me over to SHN. When I arrive, I'm shown to the conference room where four people are already working.

"Hey, welcome. Everything go okay this morning?" Tinsley asks.

I nod. I'm surprised at how in tune she is to me. "Nothing to worry about. How are things here?"

She studies me carefully. "I've divided up the code.

Cameron and his team are working through the dictionary part. I'm taking the oldest code. You can help me if you have the ability, but if you need to do other things, don't worry. I can do it."

"Happy to help." I turn to Cameron. "Gage is in our office having an issue and is looking for you."

Cameron nods and excuses himself.

I turn back to Tinsley. "Point me to a place to start, and I'll get to work."

"Your wish is my command." She winks at me, and I feel a little more like my old self. If only what she said were true.

CHAPTER 20

Tinsley

I can tell something is weighing on Landon, but I guess when he's ready to share it with me, he will.

Our team of developers sits at SHN for the remainder of the day, each of us recoding the software. We know there are going to be issues with the code, so we're testing strings as we go. And there are more than a hundred thousand words in the Spanish dictionary.

While all Spanish dialects adhere to approximately the same written standard, spoken varieties differ to varying degrees. Getting all those sounds right makes this challenging, and I'm loving having a team to discuss things with as we work through.

In the afternoon, an alarm sounds from the phone of someone on Cameron's team. He blushes. "Sorry. I have to go or my son doesn't get picked up from daycare today."

"I understand," I tell him. "No worries. This will take a few weeks. No use in all of us burning out today." Everyone stands and begins to stretch. "We can start again on Monday."

Cameron smiles at Landon. "Do you miss the days of coding?"

He shakes his head. "Hardly. It reminds me how bad my typing skills are. My brain works so much faster."

Cameron laughs. "It's a skill, that's for sure."

Landon and I climb into the back of the Suburban, and he still seems off. He's slouched, and his eyes seem unfocused. "What's going on?" I ask.

He squints at me. "I have a few things on my mind."

"I'm here if you want to talk about it."

He nods. "I'd rather go back to my empty apartment and enjoy you for a few days."

"We'll get there," I promise.

When we arrive at The Adams, there's Tiffany in the lobby. I hold my breath, waiting for her to say or do something. She's even more immature today. She pretends to cough as we pass and shouts, "Asshole."

I roll my eyes.

Landon smiles.

When we step into his apartment, we're engulfed in the smell of simmering tomatoes and spices.

"What's for dinner?" Landon asks.

Claire peeks around the corner. "Maria, Landon's housekeeper, made us her eggplant parm, and Mom's made her garlic bread."

Landon rubs his hands together. "Tonight, we're eating good."

He isn't wrong. After a few glasses of a nice red wine from Claire's vineyard and lots of eggplant parm and garlic bread, I'm stuffed.

"Roll me to my room," I sigh. "Oh, I think I ate too much."

We all laugh and giggle.

After helping Edna with the dishes, I go back to my room, tired after a long week. I don't have time to go to Napa with Claire and her friends tomorrow, but it will be a great diversion.

I crawl in bed, trying to decide if I want to text Landon when a text from him shows up.

Landon: You're beautiful when you smile and laugh.

Me: You're hot when you're naked.

Landon: I was going to ease in, but you took us right there.

Me: I figured you had a rough day and needed the help.

Landon: I'm going to miss you this weekend.

Me: I'm only gone one day and night. I'll be back on Sunday afternoon. I will need to get some work done, so my plan is to leave first thing.

Landon: What if I were to come up and spend the night with you tomorrow night?

Me: I'm at Claire's house. She'll know.

Landon: It was wishful thinking.

Me: Once we get beyond this, I think we should find a place to go away for a week, and be naked for most of it.

Landon: I like that idea.

Me: Me, too. Goodnight. Sleep well.

Landon: Goodnight.

Still seems like something is bothering him. Maybe I should have let him lead the conversation. I may have messed that up. *Crap.*

"Are you ready?" Claire's voice echoes through the speakerphone. It's barely six a.m. on Saturday morning.

"I'm up," I tell her. "I don't have any caffeine yet."

"I'll stop and pick you up something."

"That's probably not necessary. Your mom takes good care of me, and I would bet the kettle is on and ready."

"I forgot you were a tea drinker. You're better off with her. We should be there in about fifteen minutes."

"I'll meet you outside. I have to watch for the redhead from hell. That woman has it bad for Landon. I'll tell you all about it on the drive up."

"Great. See you in a few."

Claire disconnects, and I grab a cute dress for dinner tonight and head into the kitchen to find Edna and Peter.

"Has Landon already left?" I ask.

"He's on his bike." Peter points to Landon's exercise room. "I don't know how he can do that where it is. His pool would kill me too. All the illusions of falling off a fifty-story building leave me shaking in my boots."

I chuckle. "Honestly, it makes me nervous, too, but I think it increases my speed. I'm constantly working hard to make sure I'm swimming away from the water going over. And, I make sure not to look at the traffic and the Bay when I'm underwater. I just focus on the wall in front of me."

"Oh, my God. The wall is see-through? I'm never going in that pool. Ever," Edna proclaims.

"Where aren't you going?" Landon questions from behind me.

I turn to look, and he's shirtless and sweaty. My mouth

better than you know yourself, Landon. You know how I feel."

I climb in the car and wave goodbye to Landon. As Yolanda drives us north, I tell her and Claire all about what Tiffany is doing.

Claire is furious. "He shouldn't have gotten involved with her."

"Probably not, but I don't understand why she keeps putting herself out there and not taking the hint," I say.

"I agree. Both Yolanda and Greg have reported incidents with her. She's not the sharpest tool in the shed, that's for sure." Claire changes the subject. "We're going to have so much fun with the girls. I have the vintner coming to talk to us over lunch, we'll go to Meritage for spa treatments this afternoon, and tonight Caroline has gotten us a private room at French Laundry for dinner."

I kick my shoes off and put my head back, closing my eyes. "I need this getaway. Thank you for including me."

"Of course," Claire says, squeezing my hand. "Everyone adored you when they met you. There will be fifteen of us tonight, so we'll be a rowdy bunch."

"That's the best kind."

CHAPTER 21

Landon

The twenty-four hours with my parents wasn't too bad. They took me out for dinner, and my mom dragged me along as she went shopping for fabric for one of my guest rooms. "All-white rooms have no personality," she told me.

Still, I was grateful when Claire and Tinsley returned. I missed them both. Claire was great and took my parents out for dinner that night, while I enjoyed a date with Tinsley that ended with me ravishing her. Being with her centers me. I wish I knew how to explain that to Claire — and most importantly, to Tinsley.

It was hard to get up this morning. I wanted more time with Tinsley, but it's Monday, and we need to get back to work. As we leave for the office, Tiffany is yet again in the lobby. She doesn't hide her disdain.

"Pig!" she shouts.

I shake my head. Tinsley reaches for my hand and gives me a tight smile. I know I brought this on myself by sleeping with Tiffany, and I wish I could turn back time and never go near her.

As Stan drives us over to SHN, Fiona, my attorney, calls.

"What's up?" I ask in greeting.

"Have you seen today's *Gossip Gorilla*?" she asks.

"Nope. I've heard of it, but can't say I've ever read anything in it."

"I sent you a link."

"To what?" Why would I care about a *Gossip Gorilla* article?

"I'll hold."

She needs her coffee this morning. She's rather testy.

I open the link on my phone while Fiona remains on the line. It's an article about me. This is going to fucking blow up. Great. They have all the information about me impregnating a woman — who, of course, is not named for her privacy — and that I deny paternity, despite the test coming back with overwhelming odds that the baby is mine.

"Fuck! How did they get this?" I screech into the phone.

"I'm only speculating, but my guess is your baby mama wasn't happy with your offer."

I see red. "You know this only proves I'm not the father."

Tinsley looks up from her phone at me. *Shit*, now I have to drag her into this.

"I agree," Fiona says. "Something was up with the test or the facility where it was done. If she knew a payday was coming, she wouldn't be scorching earth."

"This is a smear campaign. So, what are you going to do?" This is what I pay Fiona for, and I expect her to shine right now.

"I have a few ideas. But I also thought you should warn your business partners and your family. This may get ugly."

"I understand what you're saying." I look over at

Tinsley, who's back to studying her email. "Call me back with a detailed plan to make this woman pay."

Tinsley turns to me again and furrows her brow.

"I'll have a plan for you within the hour," Fiona confirms.

We disconnect the call.

I turn to Tinsley. "That was my attorney, Fiona McPhee. What's been weighing on me is that a woman has claimed I'm the father of her child. But I'm not. I assure you." I pause to hold her eyes a moment. "She knew a few things about me and how I might have hooked up with people in the past, but there are problems with her story. We weren't even in the same city when she says this happened. She requested a paternity test, and I obliged because I knew I hadn't slept with her. However, on Friday morning, the test came back with a ninety-two-percent probability that I was the father of the child."

A look of disappointment crosses Tinsley's face, but it clears quickly. "What does that mean?"

"Despite what the test says, I can't be the father. For starters, the day she said we were together, I was in Las Vegas. I was at a poker tournament, so there are multiple witnesses that can attest I was there." Now for the hard part. "Second, given what I have to lose, I keep a list of all the women I've slept with and where I slept with them."

Tinsley's eyes bulge.

"This was advice given to me when we sold our video conference software to Tom Sutterland and PeopleMover. Tom warned Claire and me that we should keep meticulous records of who we meet and what we do, because there are a lot of people out there looking for a quick buck."

"You keep a list of *everyone*?"

"I only include the date, the name they gave me, and the location of our time together — no ratings or comments." I reach for her hand. "I promise I did not sleep with this woman. Fiona thinks the test or the testing facility may have been compromised. She showed me a picture of the woman, and I'd never seen her before. I'm positive I've never been with her."

Tinsley rubs her temple. "What are you going to do?"

"I'm going to drop you at SHN, and then I'm heading back to my place to talk to my parents and Claire. I need to let them know what's happening. We're going to get a plan from Fiona. She's not only my attorney, she's a fixer."

"What's a fixer?"

"She fixes problems."

"What other problems has she fixed for you?"

"We had a problem with our immigration paperwork when our permanent residency looked like it wouldn't be renewed. She also helped on a matter with Morgan Bennett and a few other difficult subjects, including a past employee."

"How is she different than what Jim does for you?"

"Jim tends to deal with issues like you had with Tomas. Fiona becomes involved if there's a legal matter."

After a moment, she nods. "Okay, let me know how it goes. Or would you like me to join you with Claire and your parents?"

"They probably wouldn't yell at me if you were there, but I need to let them yell." I reach over and squeeze her hand. "But thank you."

"Okay, you know where I'll be."

"I'm sorry about this," I tell her.

"What do you have to be sorry for? She sees dollar signs and is looking for easy money. You said it before — you're a target."

I appreciate that she sees it so black and white. I only hope my parents and sister feel the same.

As we pull up in front of SHN's building, I help Tinsley out of the car. "I truly am sorry."

She stands on her tiptoes and kisses me on the cheek. "Keep me posted."

I watch her walk into SHN. She doesn't look back or

wave. I hope that isn't a bad sign.

So now, at least for readers of *Gossip Gorilla*, I'm the asshole who isn't holding up his end of the responsibilities. I always swore that if I had a child, I'd do everything I could to be a part of his or her life and support both them and their mom. But I won't be blackmailed into supporting someone else's child.

As Stan drives me back toward home, I phone Claire.

"Where are you?" I ask before she can even greet me.

"I'm leaving my house for the office. Where are you?"

"Heading back to my apartment. Meet me there. Fiona called, and I have an issue we should discuss with Mom and Dad."

"Is everything okay?"

"Probably not, but I want to tell all of you at the same time."

"I'm on my way."

I then call Mason Sullivan at SHN. I could have gone inside when I was there, but I'd rather have this conversation over the phone.

"Mason?"

"Hey, you want to grab lunch today?" he asks, recognizing my voice.

"No, I don't think I can. Say, is your PR person pulling media hits on Disruptive?"

"Yes, her name is Greer Ford. I haven't gotten that far in my email. What am I going to see?"

"A woman is suing me for paternity."

Mason whistles.

"Where is it reported?"

"*Gossip Gorilla*."

"A second-rate tabloid," he scoffs. "What do you know?"

"She reached out to Fiona McPhee, claiming I impregnated her last October. She took a blood test and asked for a cheek swab. I gave that, and supposedly, there's a ninety-two-percent chance that I'm the father."

"I'm sorry, man."

"Well, the date she said we were together, I was with you and everyone in Las Vegas. That was the weekend of Cecelia Lancaster's disappearance."

"No fucking way. This baby can't be yours. Could she have gotten the dates wrong?"

"No, gestation is firm within the dates I was in Vegas."

"That's good news."

"Yeah, that's what's passing for it right now. I asked Fiona to draw up a contract saying I'd pay a million dollars to the mom upon birth after conclusive blood tests prove the baby is mine. I also offered an additional one hundred thou a month for maintenance until the baby is eighteen. But the story in the gossip rag is what I got in response. She apparently knows her payday's not coming, so she's doing a smear campaign instead."

"Let Fiona know all of us would sign affidavits verifying you were in Las Vegas," Mason says. "And probably the police would chime in since we're all people of interest in Cecelia's case."

"Thanks. I appreciate that." The car has arrived at my building. "I'll keep you posted. Fiona suggested I keep you informed."

"Good thinking on her part. I'll have Greer reach out to her, and they can work some PR magic."

"Thanks, man."

I hang up and get out. I want my family to hear this from me and not a gossip rag. As I walk to the elevator, Dee, who usually greets me, barely smiles as she turns away.

I'm going to kill this Heather McCoy woman.

Upstairs, my parents are waiting for me.

"Claire called ahead?"

My mom nods. "We googled your name and saw the story. We're going to be grandparents?"

I shake my head. "Wait until Claire arrives, and I'll

walk you through what I know."

Seconds later, the elevator announces her entrance.

We all sit at the kitchen table, and I explain everything that's happened and what Fiona and I suspect.

"That's a load of crap," my father announces.

"She's a gold-digger," my mother exclaims.

I explain that we have to wait to hear what Mason's PR person and Fiona have as a plan.

Claire opens and closes her fist. "If you hadn't been so fucking careless with these women, you wouldn't be a target. We're trying to beat Morgan to market, and now we're focusing on this shit? Regardless of whether or not this is true, you created this mess. Where the hell is Tinsley?"

I take a deep breath. "You're right. I've been careless with my personal life, but I didn't do this on purpose. I was most likely targeted to take our attention off of what we're trying to accomplish. But we can't take our eyes off of our goal. We need to get our translator to market. Tinsley is working with the development team at SHN's offices to convert the code, and I *should* be there helping. If you want me to hire a developer to cover me, I'll do that and pay for it myself."

Claire slams her hand on the table. "No! You're a distraction. Right now, I don't want you anywhere near the company *or* us."

I look at her, taken aback. Claire and I have always been close. She's always been supportive. She knows all about gold-diggers.

"What do you mean?"

She takes a deep breath and clenches her jaw. "I mean you need to leave. Tinsley's apartment has been cleared, so she can move back there and work with me. You can do something else — anything else. But you can't be part of Disruptive Technologies."

I stand, hands going to my hips. "Are you joking? I own as much of the company as you do. You can't make the decision unilaterally."

"Until this is done and taken care of, you are on leave."

"You're playing into just what Morgan Bennett wants."

My parents visibly cringe.

Claire shakes her head. "I don't think so. Your decision to sleep with Tinsley and a whole list of others, including the crazy woman here in your own building, has put the company at risk. You need a break."

I turn to my parents, and they won't look at me. I want to kick them all out of my apartment, banish them from my life. But I know there's an element of truth in what Claire is saying.

Without looking back, I leave. I'm not sure where I'm going, but I need some fresh air.

CHAPTER 22

Tinsley

The last time I spoke to Landon, he told me about the paternity suit, said he needed to discuss it with his family, and said he would meet me later at SHN. That afternoon, I received a text that said he was going away and would be back in touch after he'd sorted some things out. But he hasn't texted, called, or *anything* since. I've reached out more than a dozen times with no response.

When he didn't show up as promised, I texted him and got no response. I didn't push it, because I didn't want to interfere with whatever he was dealing with. When I returned to his apartment that night, no one was there, so I ate and retired to my room early. I heard Edna and Peter return after eleven. I sent Landon a text, telling him I missed him and goodnight.

The next morning, I didn't see his parents. When I checked his room, it was clear he hadn't slept there, and I saw his suitcase was gone. My anxiety began to rise. I texted him, and again he didn't respond. I waited in the kitchen for Edna and Peter, but when they finally appeared, they didn't seem to have any answers. Edna's eyes were red from crying.

I checked the hospitals, just in case, but I knew he'd gone somewhere. I just couldn't figure out where.

Claire asked me to meet her at the Disruptive offices. When I did, she dropped the bomb that she didn't know where Landon was, but given that my apartment was free of bugs and spyware, she thought I should move home where I'd be more comfortable. It was certainly going to be more awkward at Landon's with his parents now that he was gone, so I did.

I tried to give Landon the space he'd told me he wanted, but as the days went on, his absence became harder for me to understand. He'd left me in the lurch at work, and I just plain missed him.

In the weeks that followed, the paternity story moved from the gossip pages to the mainstream news. The paparazzi have been staked out at his apartment, and Tiffany has been interviewed a dozen times, always throwing him under the bus. Through it all, he's been mysteriously silent. So, everyone else filled in the gaps: He's a billionaire who owns the most prestigious piece of real estate in San Francisco and an entitled jerk who's not paying for his mistake with this mysterious woman.

Could they be right? Did she have the date wrong and he's actually the father? It's not like pregnancy is a precise science. Due dates are wrong every day.

But that's not who he is, and it hurts my heart to think anyone believes that.

After a while, I sent him a few less-than-cordial messages, trying to convey the urgency of the situation. But when he still refused to respond, I stopped trying. I had to preserve a little of my dignity.

Claire continued to tell me she had no idea where he was, nor did she have any interest in discussing it. She wanted our interactions to be strictly business, but unfortunately, she didn't have much of a plan for how we were going to integrate the Disruptive and Translations software, which left both teams twisting in the wind. I've had to step up as best I can.

So, each day I go into the SHN offices, but I'm an outsider at SHN. I don't feel part of their team, and I don't feel part of Disruptive. Without Cameron's help, I'd have been working eighteen-hour days to try to hold it all together and keep things moving forward. I'm still working long hours and seven days a week, and I'm still behind, but at least I'm not doing it alone. Cameron and his team are getting close to the end of their side of the project. Nevertheless, I'm exhausted and in need of a break.

I believe in my bones that Claire knows more than she's saying, but I can't seem to get her to tell me anything. Why isn't she more upset? And why has she shut me out? She acts like Landon's dead to her, and that hurts me, too. It's like neither Walsh wants anything to do with me anymore. Which is unfortunate.

At night I lie in bed and ask myself if I made the wrong decision. And sometimes I cry because I miss Landon. I feel like a fool for allowing my personal and professional lives to get this tangled.

Has he blocked me?
What the hell is going on with the paternity suit?
Why won't anyone get the paparazzi to back off?
How could he have left Disruptive at such a crucial time?
Why isn't he helping me with this software?
Where the fuck has he gone?

It's now been almost seven weeks.

Despite the strangeness between us, Claire has invited me to return to St. Helena for the weekend to relax and get away from the craziness of San Francisco. Leaving is a luxury, now more than ever, but it should be worth it. We're supposed to leave at lunchtime today and start our weekend a little early on a Friday afternoon, so I'm making the most of every moment this morning.

When noon hits, my cell phone pings, alerting me that Claire is downstairs. I pack up my belongings, wave goodbye to the team, and go downstairs. Claire is in the backseat of the Suburban, studying her cell phone.

"What's wrong now?" I ask.

"Fiona says two more women are stepping forward, saying Landon's the father of their children."

"That's a way to keep it in the news, I suppose. What does Fiona think?"

"Don't know. Landon's not talking to anyone," Claire says.

I can't quite decipher the emotion in her eyes — anger? "Why did he disappear?" I ask. "It doesn't make sense that he'd abandon our project and his commitment to helping me fix the coding." My mind flashes to his last text, which essentially said, *don't call me, I'll call you.*

"How is the code conversion going?" Claire asks.

Okay, she doesn't want to talk about this. *Fine.* I take a big breath. "Cameron and his team are done with the Spanish and English dictionaries. I've gotten through the various pronunciations on my own, but I still need to tackle grammar, regional dialects, and slang."

"Why do you think converting the code is taking so long?"

Wow. She knows how hard I've been working. I haven't felt this defeated while talking to a manager since I worked in what's considered a sweatshop kind of development place, where nothing was ever enough.

I take a minute to compose myself. "Maybe this weekend is a mistake. Without Landon's help, I'm behind. I should remain in the city this weekend and work."

Claire looks at me, and I see tears in her eyes. "I'm sorry. I miss him, too. He's so fucking careless — always thinking with his dick. I'm angry with him. He's not doing a thing, and it's getting worse."

"Where is he?"

"I have no idea." She shakes her head. "I told him he was a distraction. I asked him to step down from the company, and he walked out of his apartment and never came back. My parents waited almost two months for him to return, but they gave up and left for Vancouver this morning. They're mad at me for banishing him."

What? Why is she just admitting this now? "Claire, I've asked you about this for weeks. I know you're used to managing the company on your own, but I'm a partner, and this should have been discussed with me."

"He was destroying the company."

"His being gone is destroying the company." I take a deep breath. "I need his help, and he needs to fix this mess with the crazy woman. Maybe he was too cavalier, but he's kept records—"

"Which you're in."

"I know that. But I was a willing participant. I wasn't there for his money or the company. As I understand it, when Morgan Bennett sabotaged you, Landon was right there to support you. Why aren't you doing the same?"

"Maybe getting out of town *is* a mistake."

I can't believe it. Claire refuses to take any ownership of this.

"I'll have Greg drop you at your house," she says.

"No, that's okay. I'll get out here." I look at Greg in the rearview mirror. "Greg, can you pull over here, please?"

"Yes, ma'am." He maneuvers the car to the curb.

"Claire, we need to find Landon before this gets worse. I'm going back to SHN."

She's crying. I know she's stubborn, but her demanding he take a leave during this pivotal time was the wrong move. I need his help with the development, and he needs to push back against this smear campaign.

I get out of the car, expecting Claire to at least try to

stop me, but she doesn't.

I can tell Greg's not wild about it, but I walk the ten blocks back to SHN. When I get upstairs, I see Mason Sullivan working away, so I knock on his door.

"Hey, do you have a minute?"

He nods and points me to a chair.

I shut the door and sit down. "Were you aware that Claire asked Landon to step down from Disruptive?"

He straightens his posture. "I wasn't. When did you learn this?"

"She told me just a few minutes ago. She's understandably angry at him, but I'm not in support of her pushing him out. I know I'm a minority holder, but I need his help with coding, and he needs to respond to the allegations against him. Cameron and his team have been amazing, but I need help from Landon."

Mason nods. "Greer Ford, our PR guru, told me she and his attorney have put together a plan and are waiting for him to approve it."

"You don't know where he is?"

Mason shakes his head.

"He left his apartment after Claire made the demand — which was almost two months ago now — and he hasn't been back. Where could he have gone?"

"I have an idea." Mason puts his phone on speaker and dials. After a moment I hear, "Hey, Mason."

"Jim, I'm sitting with Tinsley Pratt. Do you know where Landon Walsh is?"

"I do."

We wait, but Jim doesn't say anything.

"Jim, can you call him and ask if I can go to him? I need his help." I'm begging, but I don't care. I need him back.

"I'm not sure he's going to listen," Jim warns.

My heart breaks. "Can you tell him Mason and I disagree with Claire? We want him back. If he doesn't want to return right away, I'll go to him."

"I'll call you back." Jim disconnects from the call.

Mason hangs up, and I close my eyes, willing away threatening tears.

"Do you want something to drink while you wait?"

I shake my head.

We wait. And we wait.

No return call from Jim.

We both have work to do, so I move back to my conference room and return to coding.

I've been working by myself for a few hours when Mason sticks his head in. "It's after six, and I haven't heard back from Jim or Landon. Caroline and I are having a night in. Why don't you join us? At least we'll be together if Landon or Jim calls."

I lean back in my chair and think for a minute. I feel anxious about everything at this point. Maybe a distraction will help. "Okay. I guess so. It's better than hanging out at my place."

I follow him to the car, and I text Yolanda to let her know I'm with Mason Sullivan and his girlfriend, Caroline — not out of town overnight as planned.

She sends me back a thumbs-up emoji.

We drive across town, into Pacific Heights.

"I thought you lived on Nob Hill," I tell him.

"I do, but Caroline's home is on Jackson Street off Alta Plaza Park. Is that okay?"

"Of course. I live on Nob Hill, and I've seen you out with a golden retriever."

Mason breaks into a grin. "That's Misty. She's a real love. Don't let Caroline know this, but I'm pretty sure Misty prefers Caroline's house to mine."

I laugh. "I can keep a secret."

"We're getting married next spring, and we'll convert my place to a rental or maybe sell it. I live in an apartment off the garden on the ground floor of a high rise. It's pretty decent in size, and the garden is beautiful, but it still isn't a house like

Caroline's."

I look at him. "I'd love to see it before you sell it. I recently came into a little bit of money, and I'm looking to get out of my tiny apartment."

"There are a lot of those in San Francisco."

"I love the neighborhood, though."

"It doesn't have much of a view, but it has a huge courtyard between four buildings, lots of grass, and a great tree to climb." He pauses a moment. "I've been to Landon's place — now that's a nice apartment."

I nod. "I love the pool. When I was staying there, I swam most mornings, and it was nice to walk the fifty feet to the pool and do my laps. Granted, it's not Olympic size like the Y, but I swam a bit longer to make up for the extra wall pushes."

"You belong to the Y?"

"I do. It's a nice mix of people, though security has asked me not to go there for now."

"My best friend — I think you've met Dillon — belongs to the Y. He plays basketball there all the time."

I nod. "It's a great deal for being on a budget or looking to shake up a workout."

When we arrive at Caroline's, we walk in through the garage off the alley. Her chef's kitchen is bright, cheery, and spectacular.

Caroline gives me a big hug and presents each of us with a drink in a martini glass. Her hair is mussed from cooking. "Welcome to our home."

"Thank you for having me, last minute."

"Of course! Now we need to find Landy." She raises her glass. "To good friends."

We clink glasses, and the drink goes down smooth. I've never heard anyone call Landon Landy, but I'm not sure anyone corrects Caroline.

"Let's sit in the living room."

I follow her, and I almost stop short. The room has floor

to ceiling windows, and it's a little foggy today, but I can make out the Golden Gate Bridge, Sausalito, Alcatraz, and the East Bay. On a clear day, I'd bet she can see north of Berkeley.

"Believe it or not, I had a hard time deciding which view was better," she says. "The front looks out on Alta Plaza Park. The gardens are spectacular, particularly in the spring. The only problem is how busy Jackson Street can be out front."

"I'll work on feeling sorry for you," I tease.

Caroline rolls her eyes. "I know, first-world problem."

"I'd call it a one-percenter problem, but who am I to say?" I like that Caroline doesn't take offense at my ribbing.

"My housekeeper made a Mexican fiesta for tonight. I hope that works for you?"

"Sounds fantastic."

We talk for a short time about what I'm doing and all the help I'm getting from Cameron.

"You know, he's married to my oldest and dearest friend, Hadlee," Caroline says. "She's a pediatrician. I knew when I saw the two of them that they belonged together."

"He's a great guy. I'd be in a real jam without him." I take a sip of my drink. Whatever it is, it's outstanding.

"He's so smart," Caroline agrees. "So, what's the plan for Landy?" she asks after a moment.

"Greer and Fiona McPhee have worked out a PR plan, but he's gone silent," Mason explains. "Claire told him off several weeks ago, and he's disappeared. Jim knows where he is, so we at least know he's fine, but—"

"Did he go to his place in Montana?" Caroline asks.

Mason looks at her, and his eyes go wide. "I've checked everywhere, but not there. I forgot about the Magnolia Homestead. That has to be where he is."

My jaw drops. Of course he's gone to Montana. "I'll send him a note and tell him I'm flying in tomorrow."

"I think that's perfect. Get him back to work and figuring out how to fix this," Mason says. "We're all due there in a few weeks for the poker tournament. He needs to put this behind him."

I text Landon.

Me: I'm flying to Montana. I miss you, and I need your help.

Landon: Okay.

I pump my fist in the air. "I found him. Thank God!" I jump into Caroline's arms and hug her tight. My heart is beating fast, and I can't wait to get some answers.

"I think we need to celebrate," Caroline says.

"I need to book a flight and a rental car." I start working my way through a mental checklist of everything I'll have to do to get to the middle of nowhere.

"You can land a private plane on the property," Mason says. "It has a runway. That's probably easiest."

"I don't have a private plane or any clue how to charter one for this kind of thing," I tell him. I'm a simple girl from Colorado.

"Let me make a few phone calls. When do you want to be there? Before lunch?"

I nod. "That sounds great." I turn to Caroline. "Can you ask Greer if she'd send me the PR plan she worked up with Fiona?"

"Of course." Caroline taps away on her phone. "What's your email address?"

"Send it to my personal address," I tell her, rattling it off.

And with that, I feel a weight lifting.

After dinner, Mason informs me that a chartered jet will meet me in the morning at the private terminal at San Francisco International.

I alert Yolanda and Jim via text.

Jim: I'm so glad you found him. Now bring him home.

Me: My thoughts exactly.

CHAPTER 23

Tinsley

I slept like crap last night. I miss Landon, and I'm both excited and nervous to see him. Why did he leave? What has he been doing all this time? What will I do if he won't come back? What will I do if he's changed his mind about us? What will I do if he won't help me?

When I left Mason and Caroline last night, they offered to come with me. I declined because I wanted to spend some time with Landon alone, but maybe that was a mistake. Maybe I need people who've known him longer than I have.

Simply put, it's time to get Landon home and move forward. I can't imagine what's been going on with him, and I don't know where all this leaves us. But even if he's only going to be my business partner, we need him back.

I arrive at San Francisco International Airport's private plane terminal shortly before eight, and the pilot introduces himself. "The flight will be a little over two and a half hours. We'll be landing on a dirt field, so don't blame me if it's a little bumpy." He smiles and winks.

"I understand." I take my seat and buckle myself in. I'm too anxious to care about any food or anything.

The flight seems more like five hours than the two and a half I was promised, but we finally arrive. When the plane comes to a stop, I'm expecting Landon to be here to meet me, but he's not. No one is here, and I'm not even sure how far away the house is or which direction I'm supposed to go.

I look back over my shoulder at the pilot. "Which way is the residence?"

He points in the direction the plane is facing, and I pick up my bag and begin the walk. My suitcase, plus my bag with my computer, seem like I'm pulling two hundred pounds. The ground is uneven, and I stumble as I walk. I could easily turn my ankle. I hear the plane take off behind me, and my heart races. Did Landon forget I was coming? Am I in the right place?

A pickup truck approaches. "Hey there, little lady. I wasn't expecting anyone. Who are you here to see?"

"I told Landon Walsh I was coming. Is this his ranch?"

"Get in."

I don't see what choice I have, so I follow his instructions. The man is in his early fifties and doesn't seem to have much to say. We drive in silence for a few minutes before we arrive at a beautiful estate tucked up against the mountains in a green valley. The house is enormous, with a giant wraparound porch.

As I get out, an older woman approaches, drying her hands on an apron tied at her waist. "Welcome. What brings you here?"

"I'm one of Landon Walsh's business partners, and I've come to see him. Am I in the right place?"

She nods and eyes me speculatively. "You are. Did he know you were coming?"

"I texted him last night, and he said he'd be here. Has he gone?"

"Yes, and I'm not sure when he'll be back. He left early this morning, going toward town."

"I see."

"It looks like you were planning on staying a bit." She eyes my suitcase and computer bag.

"Well, as long as it takes for him to come back with me." I extend my hand. "I'm Tinsley Pratt."

"Come on in. We'll put your suitcase here."

I notice they don't introduce themselves.

"Can I get you some lunch?" the woman asks. "I was going to serve leftover fried chicken. But I can heat you some chili or beef stew, if you prefer."

"Leftover fried chicken sounds wonderful, if you have enough for one more. Otherwise a can of soup or anything will do."

"There are no cans of soup here, but I have plenty of chicken."

Great. I'm trying to be low-maintenance, and I've insulted her. "Thank you."

She shows me to a living room, and the view over the ranch land is different than I expect. Being from Colorado, which is high desert with rolling mountains and looks more brown than green, I'm shocked at the jagged mountains and green land as far as I can see.

I text Landon.

Me: I'm here at Magnolia Homestead.

I want to ask when he'll be back or if he's even coming back, but instead I leave it at that.

After a moment, my hostess calls me for lunch, and I find the table set in the dining room. Table for one. I enjoy my lunch—the chicken and potato salad are outstanding—but I jump whenever I see a trail of dust approaching the house or hear anyone. After I finish, I bring my plate into the kitchen and see the man and woman sitting at a table. Their conversation stops as soon as I walk in.

"You didn't need to clear your place," the woman remarks.

"I don't mind. You didn't need to serve me. I've texted Landon to let him know I'm here."

They look at me, and I can't help but worry they just *said* this was his place and actually they're going to kill me and leave me for the wild animals.

I haven't had any response from Landon, so I return to the living room, open my computer, and begin to work. Surely, he'll be back any minute.

I hardly notice that it's getting dark until the woman turns a light on. "You're going to ruin your eyes, sitting here in the dark."

I smile at her. "Thank you." I sigh. "I reserved a room a little while ago at the Holiday Inn in Lewiston. Do you think your husband would mind driving me there tonight?"

She nods.

"Thank you."

I hear them talking in the kitchen, but I can't make out what they're saying. The man appears, lifts my suitcase like it weighs nothing, and takes it out to the back of his truck.

The drive is nearly an hour into Lewiston.

"I'm sorry," I tell him. "The location service on my phone said Lewiston was the closest town. I didn't mean to make you go out of your way."

"It is the closest town," he replies.

I look out the window, and my tears fall. How did this go so colossally wrong?

When my driver pulls into the hotel, I thank him and go inside to check in. My room isn't fancy, but it's clean, and the people at the front desk have told me where I can eat. However, there isn't any car rental place in town. If I need a car, I'll need to take a shuttle into Butte on the other side of the Rockies. I guess they don't get many visitors here. I still haven't heard anything from Landon.

Me: I've left Magnolia Homestead. You can go back now.

I cry, feeling ridiculous and angry all at once. Why tell me to come and then hide? Why didn't he at least talk to me? I email Jim and Mason, letting them know where I am in case I'm robbed or murdered in this crazy town, and I cry myself to sleep.

I toss and turn all night, but that's not much of a surprise. I miss swimming. The hotel has a cute little pool, but it's not made for swimming laps. I keep waiting for my cell phone to ring or at least alert me I have a text.

Nothing.

When I finally give up and get out of bed, I wipe the crusted tears from my eyes. My head is pounding from lack of food. I didn't have any dinner last night.

I walk next door to McDonald's, order an Egg McMuffin meal, and return to my room to eat. I still have a lot of work to get done, so I use the desk in my room to make some coding progress. Thankfully, I don't need the internet to code. I occasionally look at my phone and check the time, hoping maybe Landon called and it didn't ring, or I missed a notification.

When it begins to get dark out, I realize I'm hungry again. I look at the takeout menus and decide to try the diner across the street.

I navigate the somewhat busy street, and all I see are giant trucks and a bunch of cowboys. *What am I doing here?*

I sit in a booth that faces the hotel in case Landon drives in. I know it's silly, but I don't want to miss him.

"Welcome," a waitress greets me. "You're not from around here."

Her nametag says Darlene.

"No, is it that obvious?"

"Pretty much. What brings you to Lewiston?"

"I was going to meet a friend, but it looks like he's stood me up."

"I'd say it's time for a new friend." She smiles and seems friendly. Right now, I need a friend.

"I think you're probably right."

I order a cheeseburger and fries. When it arrives, I devour it. I knew I was hungry, but I would swear this is the best cheeseburger and fresh-cut fries I've ever had.

Darlene gives me my check and, on top, places a paper bag. "This is a piece of apple pie for later."

"Thank you. I may need the sugar to keep working."

I wave as I open the door. It was nice to talk to a human being.

I walk back to my hotel room and cry myself to sleep again. Everything two months ago was incredibly right, and now I don't know the bottom from the top. What did I do?

Morning comes early, and still, I'm waiting. I reach out to Claire, but she doesn't take my call, so I leave her a message.

"Claire, I found Landon out at his ranch in Montana. I told him I was coming, but then he stood me up. I'll be working from here for a few days, hoping to connect with him, and then I'll fly back to San Francisco. Call if you need me."

I spend the day much like I did yesterday, except I order the fried chicken dinner on Monday evening. It's not as good as what I had out at the Magnolia Homestead, but it's still tasty.

It's clear Landon doesn't want to see me. I look at commercial flights back to San Francisco, and there's one that connects through Salt Lake, but it's full until Friday afternoon. I guess that's as good as I can do. I book myself a ticket home and cry again.

I'm broken and don't know what to do. But finally, as my tears dry, my anger begins to boil. This entire situation is ridiculous, and none of it is my fault.

I email my attorney.

TO: Charles Arnold
FROM: Tinsley Pratt
SUBJECT: Translations sale to Disruptive

Charles,
Disruptive is imploding right now. How do I
take my company back? Is it even possible?

Tinsley

He responds the following day.

TO: Tinsley Pratt
FROM: Charles Arnold
SUBJECT: RE: Translations sale to Disruptive

Tinsley,
I'm sorry to hear that. It hasn't been very long.
You can ask if they'll let you repurchase it. We
can find someone else who might buy you out.
Or, if they declare bankruptcy, you can pull the
company back. But for now, if they're not
interested in any of those options, you can only
wait.

I spend the next couple days mulling that over, trying
to decide if *I'm* interested in any of those options. Finally, I
realize I need to lay it all on the line, so I text Landon. If he
isn't coming out of hiding, I'm not sure what else to do. I've
been here for almost a week now, and I can't stay indefinitely.

Me: I'm going home. I've talked to my lawyer about
taking Translations back. Please speak with Claire and
Mason and let me know what it will cost to buy it from you.

I can't work like this.

I'm all cried out. But I'm going to continue to work because I have every intention of making sure my software sees the light of day. My fingers fly across the keyboard — almost nonstop for the next two days.

By the end of my visit, I know I'm going to miss Darlene at the diner. Talking to her each evening is the highlight of my day. I give her a hug on my final night, and she sends me off with more apple pie. I'm not sure I'll ever return to Lewiston, but it's been nice to work here, unencumbered by San Francisco.

My flight isn't until two, but I take the lone cab in town and arrive at the Lewiston airport early. There isn't a huge waiting area, but I find a corner and quickly become engrossed in my work.

"You're leaving already?"

I look up, and Landon is sitting across the table from me. The rush of emotions barreling through me renders me nearly speechless.

I settle on cold anger. "I've waited five days for you. You didn't even acknowledge me when I came." If we weren't in public, I'd be yelling. Instead, I stand and stuff my computer into my bag. "I want out. I won't be in the middle of you and Claire. I don't know what she said that made you run away, but you've shut me out, and you've turned your back on all your responsibilities for two months. That's unbelievable, Landon. What on Earth have you been doing? I needed your help."

"I'm sorry."

I shake my head. "Fuck you and grow the hell up. You told me that woman was full of shit, yet now you've let it get so bad that two other women are saying you've done the same to them. I told you I was coming here, and you agreed. Then I sat in a hotel for almost a full week, and you've ignored me. No more. I want out."

He nods. "Then you're out."

"I want my software."

He shakes his head. "Sorry, you sold it to us."

"At the rate you're going, Disruptive will join the thousands of companies that have gone before you and die. I'll sit back and wait."

He shrugs, his eyes unreadable. "I accepted your resignation. The software belongs to us."

"You don't seem too interested in working on it. Good luck getting it to work."

The gate has security, and I walk through, knowing he can't follow me. My flight is boarding anyway. I get on the plane and ugly cry the entire hour and a half into Salt Lake.

I'm not going to go back to San Francisco. *Fuck them.*

Upon arrival in Salt Lake, I find the customer service desk and ask about changing my flight from San Francisco to Denver.

I want to go home, and I want my mom.

"I'm sorry," the woman behind the desk says. "That's a busy flight for us, and I don't have any open seats. We run four flights a day, though, and you're welcome to try to fly standby tomorrow. You might also check with other airlines to see what they can do for you."

At this point, I'm just overwhelmed. I manage to thank her without falling apart, walk over to the gate for my flight to San Francisco, and watch the flight board. They call my name over the loudspeakers, warning me I'm going to miss my plane. Still, I sit and allow the cacophony of travelers rushing to their desired destinations to engulf me.

Once the doors close and my plane pushes away from the gate, I stand and walk out to the rental car counter. I rent myself a car to drive the eight hours home to my mother and the comfort of my childhood bedroom — far away from the mess my professional and personal life have become.

CHAPTER 24

Landon

"What do you mean you accepted her resignation?" Claire bellows at me.

I thought after all the messages she'd sent me, Claire would be thrilled when I walked into the office this morning. I came right here and didn't even stop at my apartment. I also thought Tinsley would be here. Turns out I was wrong on both counts.

"She said she couldn't be in the middle of us. She asked to buy us out and take her company back."

"So how does that translate to her quitting? Besides the fact that she's a fantastic addition to our team and we want and need her, you must realize we don't have anything beyond the work she did in Python before we bought her company?"

I look at her. "Why the fuck didn't we get an update? What did you do while I was gone?"

"She still can't use the fucking internet, Landon. Plus,

why did it matter? She was a partner. You had zero right to treat her the way you did. This is exactly why I told you not to sleep with her. *Fuck*, she flew in to see you — to get your help — and you left her there and ignored her until the last day. This is all your fault."

"My fault? You told me to get lost."

"I wanted you to take a break from the company and fix your personal life, not neglect all your responsibilities."

I know she's right, but I'd rather blame her than sort through any of this mess. "She was flying back. Where is she?" I rant.

"How the fuck do I know? She wasn't on the flight from Salt Lake into SFO. You need to *fix this* before Mason gets involved and we lose Tinsley forever."

I cover my face with my hands. How did I manage to fuck up so many different things? I was hurt when Tinsley told me she wanted out at the airport. It felt like she was rejecting *me*, and I need her. But I suppose she's heard nothing from me for two months. How could she possibly know that?

I put my pride away, tuck myself in my office, and make my first call.

"Landon, what have you been up to?" Jim asks.

"Getting the ranch ready for the poker tournament over Labor Day."

"Uh, okay. We'll go with that. I'm looking forward to it. I see Tinsley got you back."

"Well, not exactly. I fucked up. Do you know where she is?"

Jim snickers. "This seems to be a reoccurring theme with you two."

"I said something I shouldn't have. I watched her get on a flight to Salt Lake, but it seems she didn't board her connection to SFO. Do you happen to know where she is?"

I hear Jim click away on the computer. "Hmmm." More clicks. "Her GPS is not locating her."

I sit up straight. "What does that mean?"

"The history has her leaving Salt Lake two days ago down I-15. My guess is she's in a car, and chances are her phone has died."

"Where does fifteen go?"

"San Diego, but there are multiple interstates that connect, including I-70. Isn't she from Colorado?"

"Yes. She grew up in Denver."

"I'd start there."

I thank him and make the next call.

"You rat bastard. Where have you been?"

"At my ranch in Montana."

"Why didn't you return any of my calls or texts?"

Fiona is definitely upset with me.

I hardly know where to begin. "I'd like to blame it on everyone else, but it's all my fault. I just… I got overwhelmed."

"You bet your ass this is your fault. You helped it get a lot worse, though I suppose lately you being all low-profile has killed the paparazzi on this since they can't find you. But if you'd cooperated, we could have done this with a lot less damage to your rep."

"I'm back in San Francisco now, and I'm at your disposal, but I've managed to scorch some earth with the woman I love."

"Sounds to me like *you* need to fix that — and that isn't the kind of fixing I do," Fiona counters.

"I know. I just wanted you to know I was around if you needed me."

"Well, I'd say continue to lay low. Just answer when I call. Heather is due to have her baby in the second half of August. Then we can do all the shows about how being young, single, and rich makes you a target."

"I can manage that. Thanks, Fiona."

I hang up with her, find Claire, and share what I know.

"While I desperately want to see Tinsley alone, maybe we should both go," I tell her. "It's what would be most professional."

"I agree. And so you know…" Claire sighs. "I wasn't exactly kind to her while you were gone, so you don't deserve all the blame for how she felt."

"What did you do to her?" I demand.

Claire shrugs. "I suggested she move out of your place and worry about the software she's developing, not you."

"Did it ever occur to you that without me here, she was doing the work we'd been splitting by herself?" I'm trying to contain my anger. Claire's supposed to be the rational one.

She shrugs. "Cameron's group could have stepped in."

"How do you not know what's going on? If you kick me out of the company, you have to be prepared to take over." I begin to pace, trying to figure out why my sister is so clueless. "She gave Cameron and his team half the work, and she and I had the other half. Cameron and his team have other commitments."

"I said I wasn't nice…"

No wonder Tinsley wanted out. "Do we have her mother's address?"

"I'll get it," Claire says. "Let's call and see if we can get a jet out to Denver."

Within two hours, Claire has packed a bag that looks like she's moving to Denver. I still have my carry-on from my stay in Montana, and we're on the way to the airport. We'll hit Denver before rush hour. We'll be on our own, without anyone from Jim's team, but hopefully we'll be in and out without anyone noticing.

The flight goes smoothly, but private planes the size we're arriving in don't land at Denver International. We land in south central Denver, and a Land Rover sits at the base of the stairs waiting for us. We program her mother's address into the GPS, and we're off. Well, sort of.

We didn't expect the traffic to be so tight at four o'clock in the afternoon.

"Shit! The time to her mother's just doubled," Claire

laments. "We have less than ten miles, and the GPS says it's going to take fifty-five minutes. What the hell?"

"Don't people work here?" I respond.

We white-knuckle it down the interstate and finally navigate off into a beautiful neighborhood. As we follow the directions from the GPS, and the little flag appears showing the destination is getting close, my stomach tightens.

What do we do if she pulls what I did and refuses to meet with us?

I will throw myself at her mercy and hope she is kinder to me than I was to her.

Her mom's house is across the street from a huge park. The giant oak trees edging the grass are beautiful, and it's great to see so many people enjoying the sunny afternoon.

"I don't think people here work," Claire says. The park is filled with joggers, dog-walkers, and people flying kites.

"Of course, they do. They just apparently have a better work-life balance than we do in San Francisco." Despite my distress, I discovered the power of that in Montana.

"Look at all the dogs. It must be a requirement to live here — you have to have a dog," she responds.

"We've stalled long enough," I sigh after a moment. "Let's at least see if Tinsley's here."

There's a gate at the sidewalk to cross into the fenced yard. I look at Claire as we approach, and she nods, encouraging me to open it. The gate creaks loudly as I do.

We walk up the path to the shiny, black door with a large, brass door knocker. I push the bell and a voice from the camera attached to the doorbell responds, "How can I help you?"

I lean down. "I'm Landon Walsh, and this is my sister, Claire. We're looking for Tinsley. We're hoping she's here."

There is no response.

Then the front door opens, and Tinsley stands with her hands on her hips. She's wearing khaki capri pants and a loose-fitting green blouse. It's odd to see her in something other than jeans and T-shirt, but I like it.

"Why are you here?" she demands.

Claire, thankfully, is much better at this than I am. "We've come to talk to you," she responds. "May we come in?"

Tinsley looks us over. "My mother is upstairs and ready to call the police if you are jerks in any way. She's a big-deal lawyer around here, and you'll find yourselves in jail."

I hold my hands up. "We're here to apologize."

Tinsley scoffs. "You want your software. Don't lie to me."

I press my hands together in front of me, as if I'm praying. "Please, Tinsley. Can we talk? I need to tell you how sorry I am—for everything."

"We both owe you more than an apology," Claire adds.

Tinsley steps back and points us toward the living room.

"Is this the house you grew up in?" Claire asks.

"Yes."

Not seeming discouraged by the clipped answer, Claire continues. "What's the name of the park across the street?"

"Washington Park."

"It's popular for a late afternoon."

"You should see it on the weekends. There isn't a parking space on the street."

"I believe that." I look at her and smile. "I'm sorry."

If looks could kill, Tinsley would turn me to ashes on the ground.

"Look, I'm sorry for many things," I continue. "I'm sorry I've rushed our relationship instead of sticking with our agreement. I'm sorry I sucked you into the mess with this woman who's accusing me of fathering her child. I'm sorry I disappeared. And when you tracked me down, I'm sorry I hid from you."

She looks at me, her breathing staccato bursts.

"Originally, I thought you were coming on a

commercial flight from Salt Lake, so I drove into town to get you. When Molly called and said you were at the Magnolia Homestead, I panicked. I realized I didn't know what to say, so I hid. I hadn't talked to anyone in weeks. I'm an idiot."

Her eyebrows raise, and she crosses her arms at her chest. "You left me high and dry, both professionally and personally, when you disappeared. Claire tells you to get your act together and you run away and don't return *anyone's* call? That's ridiculous. It's self-sabotage. I don't need that shit."

Of course, she's nailed it. "You're right. I spent seven weeks depressed and beating myself up for the way I've lived. That opened the door for Heather McCoy to lie to me, and then when she couldn't extort me, she went to the press. I've behaved badly for so long that of course everyone believed her."

I scrub my hands over my face. "It came to me as I was driving back from the Lewiston airport to see you at the ranch. Here I am, absolutely crazy about you, and I've given you no reason to believe me. Shit, look at how we first met! And, as for professionally, that was another huge failing. Claire and I both handled that aspect of this poorly. I should have pushed back when Claire asked me to step aside, instead of acting like a child. I should have shown her how I could fix this with the media and still be around to help you."

Tinsley's mouth is pursed and her hands are fisted at her sides. Claire doesn't look thrilled either, but what I said was true.

"I was an utter ass, but because I was paralyzed by the realization that I'd let everything important slip through my fingers. When I finally got the nerve to talk to you at the airport, you were understandably angry, but for some reason I wasn't prepared for that, and I responded poorly. In spite of everything, somehow, I wanted you to be excited to see me. I see how ludicrous that was. There's a lot I can't explain about how I've behaved. But I promise I have my head on straight now. Claire and I are back on the same page, and we are determined to make it up to you. We want and need you as a business partner and as a friend."

She sighs. "I'm not committing to anything."

"Landon and I both made huge mistakes," Claire adds. She looks like she's going to cry. "We need to earn back your trust, but we want you standing with us."

"Who was that couple I met at your ranch?" Tinsley asks.

I smile. "They manage the day to day operations. They're the managers and caretakers."

"They didn't even introduce themselves to me. You hadn't told them I was coming, and they treated me like I was a process server."

I cringe. "I know. That was terrible. But they're very protective."

"You hurt me, Landon. You cut me deeper than anyone ever has."

"I don't know if this matters, but I came into town each day to catch a glimpse of you at the diner. Darlene knew and kept texting me to man up and come inside to see you. I behaved badly. I know that. But please tell me it's not too late. I don't want to lose you—not as a friend and not as a partner."

Claire is crying. "I was wrong, too. I was mad at him, and I took it out on you. I'll admit I was jealous of your relationship. You had everything I wanted—a great guy, even if he is my brother, you're awesome at your job, and everyone likes you."

Tinsley eyes grow wide. "That is not true. A lot of people *don't* like me. I fall into the category of you either like me or you hate me."

I turn, hearing someone approach. It's an older version of Tinsley. They could be twins. When she stops, I fan my hand in a half-wave. "I'm the prime, number-one asshole, Landon Walsh."

Her face softens. "Nice to see some honesty."

Claire stands and offers her hand. "I'm the number-two

asshole, Claire Walsh."

"I'm Tinsley's mother, Layne Stapleton. I'm ordering in Indian. Do you want to stay for dinner?"

"We'd love to," Claire gushes.

Tinsley stares at her mother. She clearly doesn't forgive us yet.

"Can I talk you into a walk around the park so we can chat?" I ask Tinsley.

She hesitates but agrees. Claire settles in with her phone as we exit.

We walk side by side across the street.

"This is so different than San Francisco," I say.

"It is. It's cool when it snows. It's a white blanket out in our front yard."

We skirt around a man with three labs — one brown, one black, and one yellow. "Claire was wondering if a dog was a requirement for living here?"

Tinsley chuckles. "It almost seems like it, doesn't it?"

"I am sorry."

"I'm going to fight you for my software. My mom and I have looked into it, and given the short time we've been connected, we can nullify the contract, and I will return your money."

I nod. "What if we put more rules in place and work together?"

"I've also informed Mason of my desire to separate. He'll back my new project."

"I bet he would. He sees a winner. But so do we. We believe in you, Tinsley." I can't let her give up on us. "I want to help you. I'm here to beg forgiveness and do whatever it takes to earn back your trust."

"I don't know if that's possible," she says.

We watch the Canadian geese around the lake for a while. "You know, they don't require visas or any paperwork for these Canadians," she finally teases.

I have to believe that's a good sign. "They have no idea

how easy they have it."

Next I fill her in on what I learned from Fiona.

"So, where are you going to hang out until August?"

"I originally thought we could go back to Montana for the summer. But if you'd prefer to stay here, I'll rent something close by and can meet you for work wherever you'd like."

She turns and looks at me. "You'd live here in Denver for me?"

I nod. "I screwed up. I'll do whatever it takes to fix it." I dig my hands in my pocket. If I don't, I'll reach out and touch her, and we're not there yet.

After a few more minutes of walking, we've circled a decent-sized lake, and we're back to the house. When we walk in, I can smell the Indian spices. My stomach growls. I realize I haven't eaten all day.

"Ms. Stapleton, I've told Tinsley I'd rent an apartment or something close by through August to help her get this coding done. Do you know of anything available?"

She looks at Tinsley before she answers. "I might have a partner in my law firm who has something."

I nod.

Claire claps her hands. "I've always wanted to spend time in Denver."

I shake my head. "You're going to need to go back to San Francisco to manage the company and get the team on track for the sale to Tom Sutterland."

"Okay. Can I at least stay a few days?"

"You both can stay as long as you want." Tinsley stands up, and her chair scrapes across the wood floor. "I'm leaving."

I shut my eyes as I hear Tinsley stomp up the stairs. I look over at her mother. "What do I do?"

Layne seems to debate whether to be Tinsley's attorney or her mom.

I shut my eyes again. This isn't how it's supposed to

work. She needs to forgive me and come back. How do I make her understand?

"I'm sorry for disrupting your evening." I stand to leave.

Her mother sighs. "Stay the weekend. Let me see if I can talk to her."

"Thank you," Claire and I say in unison.

CHAPTER 25

Tinsley

"They've gone," my mother informs me from the doorway. "I thought you were making progress…"

I'm lying on my childhood twin bed with my head buried in the pillow to muffle my sobs.

The bed dips as my mom sits down next to me. I immediately feel better. It's always been us against the world.

She rubs my back. "Are you sure this is what you want? This is a mess, but I know you. I know you can shape this company into what you want it to be. They seem genuinely sorry."

"Oh, don't worry, they are. Or they will be, once they realize I won't just forget everything they've done to me. Satellites in the sky are worthless without my software. My software, however, doesn't need them."

She sighs loudly. "It may not need you, either. It's theirs whether you stay or go, according to the contract you signed. You've always been like this. So stubborn. You'd cut your nose off to spite your face."

I hate it when she says that. It's not true. "Honestly, when did I ever not stand my ground and come out ahead? I said no to Berkeley because I wanted Stanford, and I got it. I told Michael Foster that since he kissed Mona Linsky, he could go to prom with her instead of me. Now they're married with a dozen kids, and I didn't go to college pining for a guy who wanted someone else. You tell me when I've stood my ground and come out behind."

She cocks her head to the side. "When you kicked Landon and Claire out of our house."

"I didn't kick them out. They left."

"Stomping up the stairs like you were three again and telling them you were leaving isn't exactly kicking them out, but it pretty much signifies you're done with the conversation."

I hate disagreeing with my mother. Her lawyer's mind is always four steps ahead of me and always without emotion. "I was. I don't need them, their money, or their help. Turns out it's not much help at all."

"Are you sure about that?"

"Yes, absolutely."

"Okay. But as your attorney, I'd tell you you're in breach of the purchase agreement, and anything you create with Translations belongs to them."

"You told me that wasn't the case."

"I did, presuming they were closing their doors. Now they're pushing to remain open, and they've extended a genuine olive branch, so it will belong to them."

I turn away from her. I don't want to give up my company.

"I'd suggest you meet with them and determine how you'd like to move forward."

My mother is rarely wrong. If I wasn't so angry, I'd probably tell her that, but right now, I want to wallow in self-pity.

The bed shifts as she stands. "Fixing this could be a great thing for Translations. But you know I'll love you regardless, Tin. Just remember that."

She leaves, and I continue to lie in bed, eventually getting up to plug my cell phone in to see if I have any messages. I haven't charged it since it ran out of battery on the way here. I haven't wanted to face what was on it. But now my week-long technology break is over. I have to figure this out.

It must take twenty minutes for my phone to muster enough battery to turn on, but once it does, it dings nonstop.

Claire: I haven't heard from you? Are you both buried in code? I miss you.

Claire: I'm sure Landon blocked me. Did you block me, too? I'm sorry for being a bitch. Truly. Please talk to me. I'll grovel.

Vanessa: Hey, what's going on? Claire's acting weird. We miss you. Drinks after work at Whitley's?

Chrissy: Hey, chica. Missing you!

Ginger: We wish you were here.

Ginger also sent me a picture of the three ladies on my team. Seeing them makes me smile. They're amazing. As I study the picture, I realize Tomas Vigil is in the background, looking in the direction of the camera. He's talking to someone. Why the fuck is he hanging out at Whitley's?

There are a dozen more messages, mostly from Claire and Landon.

Landon: I'm sorry we surprised you today. We deserve what you said. Please be assured, we're sorry. Most

**importantly, I'm sorry. For everything. We can do better, and
we will do better, if you'll give us a chance.**

I glance at the clock, and it's after eleven. I must have
dozed off for a bit at some point. If I want my software to see
the light of day, I have to work with Claire and Landon. That's
the choice I made when I sold my company to them. So, I can
forgive them and we move on, or I can walk away, have no
software, and owe them a lot of money.

As I stare at this picture, another reality comes into
focus: Disruptive didn't have issues until Translations joined
them. And whomever is trying to steal my software isn't
interested in Disruptive's technology. They're going after
mine. I don't have the resources or the knowledge to fight
them on my own. So, there's yet another reason I need to find
my way forward, rather than trying to undo what's done.

I refuse to be like Landon and hide from the world and
all my problems because things are difficult.

I copy the photo of my team, take a deep breath, and
forward it to Landon and Claire.

**Me: Look in the background. Why is Tomas at
Whitley's, the bar my team frequents?**

Landon immediately responds.

**Landon: Holy crap! I'm sending it to Jim to
investigate.**

Claire: Can you tell who he's talking to?

Me: Not sure. Can't tell from behind.

Landon: Does Whitley's have security cameras?

Me: ???

Landon: Jim and team will look into it. I've told him we want details on who he's with. Jim says there's a bank ATM machine across the street with a camera. His team will pull that and check to see who she might be.

Me: Thanks.

If I'm doing this, I guess I should get on with it.

Me: Should we meet for breakfast?

Claire: We'd love that. We're at the JW in Cherry Creek.

Me: I'll meet you at the Cherry Cricket on 2nd Street at 8.

Landon: We'll see you then.

I sleep restlessly. I'm getting back on board with doing business with the Walshes, but I'm not at all sure my heart wants any more of Landon Walsh. I wish we could go back to before that bitch came into his life and wreaked havoc with her fake paternity suit. I still can't fully process that he disappeared for nearly two months and refused to communicate.

But anyway, I need to focus on the present. *What the hell is Tomas doing?* I sit up in bed and send a text.

Me: What do you remember about Tomas Vigil?

Chrissy: You're alive.

Me: Sorry. Hiding at my mom's. Long story, but I'm curious what you remember about Tomas from Stanford?

Chrissy: You dated him for a minute. He was scrawny and pretty granola even by Bay Area standards.

Chrissy: He was friends with a group of nerdy guys who were always angry that no one wanted to go out with them.

Chrissy: He had a lame idea about water filtration and nothing beyond that.

Me: Do you recall who his friends were?

Chrissy: Dan Tanenbaum was one. He had a tiny one. Oh, and that Jimmy guy.

I skip over her penis joke. *Who was Jimmy again?*

Me: Fallon?

Chrissy: No! Jimmy Fallon is on TV.

Me: Duh! I'm going back to bed.

Chrissy: Come home soon.

Me: Miss you too.

I lie awake and try to remember Jimmy's last name. There was another guy named Michael Goldie they hung out with…

By five, I have my computer open, and I'm on PeopleMover. I have to be careful because I'm not friends with these guys, and if I search too close, I'll show up in their friends suggestions. I'm trying to stay below the radar.

On Tomas' page, I find a Stanford group he belongs to—the Stanford Octagon. It's a closed group, so I can't see who the members are, but I search a few friends from school and find one who is also a member.

Me: Dana, I have a question for you. You open for a quick chat?

Dana: Sure. Wow, it's early where you are. I'm on the East Coast.

She gives me her land line number, and I call.

"Hey, sorry to call so early," I tell her.

"Don't worry about me. I have a new baby, and we're in Boston, so I never sleep."

"Congratulations. Boy? Girl?"

"She's a girl. We named her Kennedy."

"Boston's the place to be a Kennedy, I suppose."

She chuckles. "We need to come up with a funny Boston story about why we named her that, but actually, it's a family name."

"Tinsley is a family name. I like that."

"What's going on?" she asks.

"It's a bit of a long story, but I saw you were a member of a closed PeopleMover group from Stanford—the Stanford Octagon?"

"Yes, but I haven't been on the page for a long time. I hid the comments because they're all bitter guys who can't face the reality that they have shitty ideas."

"Any chance I can talk you into going into the group and grabbing some screenshots of the members and any interesting conversations?"

"Sure. I'm not sure when I'll be able to, but I'll try when I have a chance."

"You're awesome. Are you guys planning any trips out to the Bay Area?"

"I'm not sure. Kennedy is only three months old. And I'm only telling you this because I need to tell someone, but I'm pretty sure I'm pregnant again."

"No way! Is that bad?"

"We pulled the goalie to have Kennedy, and between the forever-long period you have post-birth and nursing, I didn't think I could get pregnant. I've been waiting for my period to come back again, and it dawned on me this morning that I could be pregnant. My palms are all sweaty."

I laugh. "Well, think of it this way, if you are having another one, your kids will be close in age and super tight."

"You're right. I need to look at the positives. But after this baby is born, Phillip is getting a vasectomy. He looked at me, and I got pregnant."

"Somehow, I think the mechanics were a little more than that."

I hear her giggle. "Thanks for listening."

"No problem, and send those screenshots over when you can."

I disconnect the call as my mother walks in. "You're up early," she says.

"I couldn't sleep. I made the mistake of turning my phone on for the first time in over a week."

"Anything interesting?"

I tell her about everything that's happened with Tomas, and then him showing up at the bar where my team was hanging out—and where I'd been invited.

She takes a leisurely sip of her coffee. "What are you thinking?"

"I decided to meet Landon and Claire this morning for breakfast."

"I like that, but what are you doing about this Tomas guy?"

"I don't know yet. I reached out to Dana from Stanford. Do you remember her?"

"Dirty blonde with glasses?"

My mom has an impeccable memory. "Yes, she recently had a baby and is with her husband in Boston." I recount our conversation, minus the part about her possibly being pregnant again.

"Smart thinking. Your private investigator should be made aware of anyone you can figure out is a member of this group. Sounds like they'd be worth exploring."

"I thought so, too." I take a deep breath. "I think I'm going to keep working with Landon and Claire."

My mom doesn't react. She knew last night what buttons to push to get me thinking straight. I was being overly dramatic and a spoiled brat.

"I think that's a great idea. What time are you meeting them?"

"We're meeting at the Cherry Cricket at eight."

She nods toward the clock. "You'd better hurry."

I've got fifteen minutes. Even on a Saturday morning, traffic can be severe. It'll be tight, but not impossible.

I throw on clothes, and I'm out the door to my waiting rideshare.

When I arrive, Claire and Landon are already sitting at a table, and it looks like they've been here a while.

"I'm sorry. Am I late?" I ask.

"No, we were early and in need of coffee," Landon says.

"We walked over, giving us time to get lost," Claire adds.

I shake my head. "It's hard to get lost here. The city is on a grid."

"The concierge told us to head east and then north, and I was lost."

I chuckle. "Well, if you're going north, the mountains are to your left. South they're on your right. West, you're driving toward them, and east away."

Claire looks at Landon. "That would have been useful information from the concierge."

"At least you found it," I offer.

The waitress arrives, and without looking at the menu, I order the huevos rancheros.

"I'll have the same." Landon winks at me.

"I'd like an egg-white omelet, with spinach…" Claire orders like Sally from *When Harry Met Sally*.

Landon shakes his head, and I chuckle. I have missed their company.

Once the waitress leaves, Claire looks at us. "What?"

"Could you make it more difficult to get a silly egg-white omelet?" Landon asks.

"I like it a certain way," she says with a shrug.

"And we like that about you," I jump in, before they start to argue. I change the subject. "I couldn't sleep last night. I'm bothered by Tomas being at that bar. I know it could be a chance meeting, but honestly, I don't think so."

"We don't either," Claire agrees.

"I found out he's part of a closed group on PeopleMover called the Stanford Octagon. I think it's a group of my classmates who used to get together regularly to talk about how they were going to take on Silicon Valley. I wasn't invited, probably because Tomas was one of the founders and we only went out for a minute. But a friend of mine, Dana Schwartz, was. I reached out to her this morning, looking for information on the group."

"We need to let Jim know, but when we're in a private place."

"I agree. I'm still not convinced they don't have something on our phones. I texted Dana from my cell phone and called her from the home landline. I hate that all of a sudden, I'm worried about big brother, but I started thinking—how did Tomas know I might show up at Whitley's? The girls from my team had texted to invite me."

Landon shakes his head. "He went to school with you and probably knows you grew up here. We need to get ahead of them, so you should move."

I nod. "I don't want to agree, but you're probably right."

"You can't go back to San Francisco. Where should you go?" Claire asks.

"We can fly back to my ranch in Montana," Landon offers. "At least if they're coming there, we'll see them. I can lock the cell phone booster down to only us."

"Is it safe for Claire to be in San Francisco alone?"

"I think so, but if I can get Jim to sign off on this, I want Gage working out of our offices, and…" He turns to Claire. "You should have a team of two bodyguards with you at all times."

"I'll agree to that if you take someone with you to Montana."

Landon nods. We finish our breakfast, return to my mom's, and call Jim from the kitchen phone, filling him in on what we've learned about Tomas and the Stanford Octagon. Jim promises to investigate and makes plans to send a plane for us. He says he'll meet us with supplies when we land. We're to disconnect our cell phones and leave them here in Denver.

Jim also arranges for Claire to come back to San Francisco. He's sending a team to meet her. Since she's been living in a rental during her renovations, she'll move into Landon's place at The Adams, along with her security. Landon and I are heading to "Vancouver" with a quick stop in Montana that will put us at the Magnolia Homestead undetected.

I have just a little time to pack up my things, and then we're off.

"I love you, sweetheart." My mom holds me tight.

While I gathered my stuff, Claire and Landon educated her about keeping an eye on her surroundings, and she's going to spend some time at her boyfriend's. If she sees anything out of the ordinary, she's going to call Jim and will have her own security team.

"You have the landline number for the ranch?" I ask her.

"I do, and I have Jim's number, plus the burner phone he's sending." She looks at Landon. "I encouraged this reconciliation. If you make me sorry, I have no problem making sure you sit for a long time in a dark cell."

He gives a curt nod. "I understand."

We're standing in the terminal as two Gulfstream jets touch down, one right after another.

The pilots disembark and file new flight plans for Vancouver and San Francisco while we walk out to our planes.

I give Claire a hug. "You be careful. Tiffany is super possessive of your brother. She wants him all to herself."

Claire laughs. "I think Tiffany is the least of my worries."

"I know, but I thought if you focused on that, rather than the mess we're in, it would be a little easier to manage."

"I'll miss you," she tells me.

"Hey, stop hogging my baby sister." Landon jostles me.

Claire grins and seems to relax as they banter.

Greg comes out and greets Claire, taking her bag. She waves to us.

"We'll talk soon. I promise," Landon yells after her.

We walk up to our chartered Gulfstream, and Yolanda sticks her head out and waves. I'm excited she's joining us in Montana.

"Great to see you," I gush.

"This should be fun," she agrees.

The pilot returns and gives us the details of our flight, reminding us that when we stop in Montana, we'll need to immediately get off the plane so he can continue on to

Vancouver without anyone figuring out we've landed.

Once the plane comes to altitude in the air, Landon adjusts his seatbelt. "Molly and Frank were pretty upset with me when I didn't show up at the ranch after you arrived."

So those are their names. "They're good people."

"Be ready for a heroine's welcome, and I'll still probably be in the shit house."

"I'm good with that." I look away from him. "We have a lot to keep us busy. You'll be fine."

"How far have you gotten on the software?"

I give him the highlights.

He nods. "That's amazing. We can get this done." I'm not sure if he's assuring himself or me, but I believe it.

"I agree." I pull out my Kindle and begin to read.

Before I know it, we're doing our quick landing. The plane is on the ground less than five minutes before it continues on as if we never stopped.

Unlike last time, when I was left in this field alone, there are two trucks waiting for us. Yolanda and other members of Jim's team move the gear and our bags to the back of the two vehicles.

"Frank, this is Tinsley Pratt." Landon says.

Frank nods. "We've met. I didn't think we'd see her again after you pulled that stunt and stood her up."

I smile.

"I wasn't sure I would either," I tell him.

When we arrive at the house, Frank's wife meets us, and she's all smiles — so different from the last time. "I'm so glad you're back. I'm Molly Pierce. Landon was so scared to see you when you came a few weeks ago."

"He knew he was in trouble." I look at Landon, and he's taking the teasing, mostly because he knows he deserves it.

I walk in with Molly and Landon.

"One day, I'll tell you what happened with Frank when we were courting," she says. "Men have a foolish gene in them sometimes."

Landon sighs. "I already told her I was in the doghouse, and if the house burns down, you're savin' her and leaving me to figure it out on my own."

"You bet your ass," she replies with a wink.

I can feel the smile on my face.

"How about the Yellowstone room for Tinsley?" Molly suggests. "And you can have the Rockies room."

Landon's eyebrows arch, but he nods. Landon may own the ranch, but Molly is in charge around here.

I follow her to my room with my suitcase after she sends Landon off to his room on his own.

All the teasing does make me feel a little better. I wasn't crazy to feel the way I did.

"Dinner will be at six thirty, but feel free to come down whenever you're ready," Molly says. "We have a full bar, and we can make you a drink before dinner, if you'd like."

"Thank you." I hesitate a moment. "Don't be too hard on Landon. He has some real crazies chasing after him."

She nods and leaves me to my room.

When I turn to look at it, I know why Landon was surprised. This is usually his room. I'm sure of it. The king-sized bed faces windows that look out over the land, which is a stunning patchwork of greens, blues, and golds. Montana is God's country. There's also a massive fireplace, and the bathroom is bigger than my apartment in San Francisco.

The entire team gathers for dinner, and Molly has gone all out. Molly and Frank definitely continue to jab at Landon, but I see it as admiration, not anger.

"Dinner was outstanding." Landon pushes his chair back from the table and pats his belly.

Frank makes us after-dinner drinks, and Landon and I sit in the living room, alone for the first time since we arrived.

"This place is pretty spectacular," I tell him.

"It is. Mia Couture owned it for a few years, and I think Jim has used it a few times. Molly and Frank know Jim and his team — they even seem to have an office here."

"Wow, I can believe it. So handy if they want to keep a client off the radar. The pilots had the landing and disembarking down pat."

"It's my turn to host the next poker game, which will be over Labor Day weekend. I don't know if we'll still be working from the ranch, but Mia assures me that will be a great time to be here."

"Will you try to lose it back to Mia?" I ask as I take in all the details around me, like a collection of Royal Doulton figurines and a bookshelf of what looks like first editions of classic books, including Jane Austin's *Emma*, and Ian Fleming's *Casino Royale*. A collection of Fabergé EGGS SITS ON A TABLE. THE HOUSE HAS SO MANY BEAUTIFUL PIECES. I'M SURE MIA MISSES IT.

"I don't know," Landon says. "I like it. I have a ski chalet in Whistler I may try to lose instead. I've been looking at another place that's a little more secluded and would accommodate my parents better."

"Does it have a boat slip for your dad?" I tease.

Landon laughs. "No. There's an inlet not far away, but it's probably only deep enough for a canoe, and not close enough for the size sailboat he was looking at. That boat's a pipe dream of his."

We watch the last bit of sun dip below the mountains as the fireplace snaps and crackles.

"I am sorry about everything," Landon says after a moment.

"I know. It's just going to take me a while to trust you again. I know you were honest about the paternity, but it hurt when you disappeared on me."

"I can't even truly explain why I did it." He reaches for my hand. "You can take as long as you need. I'll wait. You are worth waiting for."

My stomach does a somersault, and my heart leaps, despite my lingering fear.

CHAPTER 26

Landon

It's fun being at the Magnolia Homestead with company. When I was here before, I needed the time to come to grips with my behavior and anger. The staff was here, but I felt alone, which is what I needed. But now it's definitely better with the additional people.

I did accomplish at least one thing in my solitude, though, as I did coordinate with Gillian Reece at the Shangri-la to prepare for the upcoming poker tournament. She'll bring in dealers and is working with Molly to organize food and whatever other help is needed for the weekend. The ranch has plenty of room, and we'll have day trips into Yellowstone, horseback riding, whitewater rafting on the Snake River, golf, spa activities, and then a traditional chuckwagon jamboree with a stage show performed by a local group—Molly and her brothers.

It should be a fun weekend.

It has taken Tinsley and me a few days to find our footing, but we've developed a nice routine. We meet in the kitchen each morning for breakfast and work in the dining room—her on one end and me on the other. We work through early afternoon before we have lunch, and then we try to get out each afternoon for some kind of exercise. We then typically come back and work until dinner. Sometimes we even work after dinner, and other times we watch a movie. Either way, we say goodnight at the end of the evening, and she heads off in one direction while I go in another with a serious case of blue balls.

It was a delicious lunch today, but it's made me sleepy as I return to my computer. I'm trying to work out something complicated, and my mind wanders as I look away from my screen. Tinsley must also be restless, because she stands and moves to the open floor. I watch her stretch and bend in her yoga pants. She puts her hands flat on the ground, moving to all fours, and pushes up. Her ass looks heavenly, and I want to reach for it, smooth my hand over her perfect globes. I have the urge to spank her.

She moves her feet wide apart, her knees pointing in opposite directions, and bends into her pose. Her pussy is wide open... What I wouldn't give to taste it again.

When she lies on her back and stretches her feet over her head, my dick becomes extremely uncomfortable behind my jeans. I haven't been with anyone since her, and she's making it exceedingly difficult to concentrate. Not that I was doing great there to begin with...

Her brow furrows. "What's wrong?"

My cock is weeping in my pants for you. I debate whether I should blow off the answer or address the situation. "I've missed you."

She looks at me but doesn't reply.

I hurt her, and I need to make it up to her. I know this. I stand. "Let's go for a hike. We need the break, and it'll be good to get some fresh air and stretch our legs."

"I should put on different shoes."

I notice the pink fuzzy slippers she's slipped on. "Yeah,

those might be difficult to manage the rocks with."

Tinsley goes to her room and returns in a pair of runners. "I'm ready."

I pick up our coats and the satellite phone, and we start the trek. "I did this hike several times when I was here before. I think you'll like it."

We walk behind the house and barn, and she follows me to a trailhead that leads into the foothills. It has a subtle climb to it, but we won't get too high.

We set off, but after a few minutes, I hear Tinsley behind me. "I haven't been swimming for over a month. I'm out of shape."

I turn, but she's barely breathing hard. "You're doing great. If you want to stop, say so. This isn't a race."

We walk another five minutes, and we're at the steepest part of the hike. Tinsley looks back over the ranch below. "Wow, that's positively gorgeous."

I stand next to her. We're about three hundred feet above the house. You can see the runway and the green fields where I have five hundred head of cattle and what I thought were commercial crops. But I was informed that they grow alfalfa for the cows and horses on the ranch there. Plus, there are groves of fruit trees and rows of vegetables sourced for the ranch.

"I can see why you'd want to hang on to this," Tinsley adds. "Where does your property line end and the next ranch begin?"

I point over my shoulder. "I go to the Lewiston city limits."

She shakes her head. "That's nearly an hour away."

Landon smiles. "Frank took you the long way into town, hoping I'd call you back. It's closer to thirty minutes."

I see a flash of hurt in her eyes.

"That's still a lot of land," she says.

"It is. There are four houses outside the valley and closer to Lewiston, where some of the ranch hands live."

"That makes sense." Tinsley puts her arm around my waist. "Thank you for bringing me here."

I nod. I know if I look at her, I'll pounce, and I want her to make the first move. I'm not sure putting her arm around my waist as we stand together counts as anything more than a side hug. "We can head back now, but there's a great spot a little farther up the hill, about fifteen more minutes."

Tinsley claps her hands. "Let's do it."

We continue hiking until we get to a flat spot where there's a large rock, and we sit down. I offer her water as we take in the vastness of the homestead and the land. "I love it here, but I do miss the city. Maybe by the time we go back, after this mess is over, I won't miss it. But Fog City Diner, Saipan Gardens, Soulva Greek..." I sigh. "Molly is an outstanding chef, but I miss the options."

"Makes sense."

I put my arm around Tinsley's shoulder, and she leans in. She smells so good. I kiss the top of her head.

We stay like that for a good twenty minutes. I don't want this to end, but I know if we don't start back soon, the sun will set, and we'll have to navigate in the dark. My backpack has a flashlight, but I'd rather not look like an idiot trying to figure out how to use it.

The hike back to the house is almost harder than the walk up, but we make it. When we enter the house, Molly's in the kitchen. "People were starting to worry," she says. "Getting ready to send a search party out for you."

"We didn't go far." I smirk. "Just up to Bitterroot Midpoint."

Molly shakes her head. I know she doesn't like that I've hiked it, but she has to know I would never take Tinsley up that far. The trail becomes too steep if we'd gone much farther without rock climbing gear, and my goal was just to spend some time with Tinsley. What we did was perfect.

After an amazing dinner, Tinsley excuses herself and disappears into her room. I pour three fingers of bourbon over a large cube of ice and go to my room. The satellite television doesn't have much to offer tonight, so I stop at ESPN, where they're going through baseball scores and updates. This will be the first year since I left Vancouver that I may not make a Giants game.

I pick up my phone and text Tinsley.

Me: Thanks for today.

I wait, but she doesn't text me back right away.

Tinsley: I'm happy to be here and happy you're here with me.

Me: Well, I'm not with you. Molly put me on the other side of the house.

Tinsley: Are your parents or Claire here?

I sit up straight. Is she saying what I think she's saying?

Me: No.

I hold my breath, type my next comment, and push send before I change my mind or she says something that moves us in another direction.

Me: Would you like some company?

She doesn't immediately respond.

Tinsley: Maybe. What are you promising?

My dick is instantly hard. I throw caution to the wind and take a picture of myself, sending it with a caption.

Me: To go at any speed you'd like.

Tinsley: Fast or slow?

Me: Yes.

Tinsley: Have you been with anyone since we were together last?

Me: No, have you?

Tinsley: No. Do you have condoms?

Me: Yes, many.

Tinsley: Then you better come quick, or I'll be getting Bob out to do that task tonight.

I jump out of bed so quickly I almost trip. I run a toothbrush through my mouth and grab several condoms. My heart is pounding, and I'm ready to be with my woman.

I knock on the door, and Tinsley opens it wearing a tiny robe. I can see her nipples through the fabric. I pull her to me, and this time I kiss her, closing the door with my foot. I kiss her with all of the feeling I can muster. I want her to know I missed her. She returns my kisses with vigor.

After a few precious minutes of making out, she says, "Please, I've missed you."

I lift her up, lay her on the king-size bed, and return to kissing her. As our tongues dance, she sucks on my lower lip, and my hands move to her firm breasts. I've missed these magnificently perfect mounds. Taking a handful, I squeeze softly while stroking her diamond-hard nipple with my thumb. She moans into my mouth. Her hands wander to my rock-hard shaft, and I press against her.

I pull away and open her silky robe to slide it down her body. I'm hungry for her and ready to feast.

I spread her dripping wet lips with my thumb and attack her clit ravenously. Her aroma is intoxicating. Her taste is addicting. Licking down to her opening, I tongue as deeply as I can. Licking and sucking and slurping her juices, I find her sweet spot and drive her orgasm home. My fingers probe, rubbing the place I know will set her off. She tenses, and I know she's close. As I stroke and press, her body shakes as an orgasm erupts. She cries out in pleasure, pulling my head into her as deeply as I can stand it. With a final shiver, she lets me go, reveling in the aftershocks.

When she sits up and slides toward the headboard, I follow — not by choice, but because she doesn't let go of my cock.

She finally catches her breath and growls, "I want to suck you and return the favor."

I smile and kiss her. "Tinsley, you don't have to reciprocate anything. I'm not keeping count."

She shakes her head. "I've missed you and need to taste you."

"Who am I to complain about that?"

She slides down and strokes my shaft while licking my balls. Taking each into her mouth, she tests my pain threshold by sucking deeply, one at a time. I moan my appreciation. She licks my shaft, slowly working her way to the top. She licks every drop of precum, and then, taking a deep breath, she wraps her lips around the head.

She makes it a third of the way down before I hit the back of her throat. Tinsley strokes me and twists her hand, moving up and down. She pauses. "I know with practice, I can take it all."

"I promise you, I'm not complaining," I manage.

Tinsley grins, and one of her hands disappears. I'm sure she's playing with herself. The thought of her mastering her satisfaction while bouncing up and down on my cock with her mouth completely turns me on. I warn her. "Baby, I'm close."

She moans and strokes faster. Pulling her head back, she licks her lips. "Give it to me, lover. I want every drop."

It only takes a moment once she wraps her lips back around the head before I unload stream after stream into her hot, willing mouth.

She slurps it down and licks her lips. "That was so worth the wait."

I pull her up and kiss her deeply. This woman does something to me that I can't explain. She strokes and caresses my member, and it doesn't take long before I begin to get hard again. Her long, languid strokes bring me to full hardness, and she looks at me, her eyes hooded with desire.

Reaching for one of the condoms, she rips the foil package, but before she rolls it down my aching shaft, she takes me into her mouth and down her throat.

"I want to feel the inside of you," I groan.

She releases my cock with a pop and rolls the condom on. Straddling my hips, she guides me to her and gasps as I enter. Taking a deep breath, she moves her hips from side to side as she adjusts to my size.

I reach for her breasts and tweak her nipples. No words are spoken as Tinsley moves up and down, going deeper and deeper until I'm fully seated, deep in her tunnel.

Her hair covers part of her face, and she looks at me with a half-smile.

"God, you're beautiful."

Tinsley sets her own pace, and my thumb circles her hard nub as I begin to move my hips faster.

"Yes, baby, yes!" she moans. "Like that, don't stop!"

As she shakes from her orgasm, her vaginal walls pull and squeeze me, milking. Her wetness leaks down to my balls. But she doesn't break her rhythm and continues to ride me until her breathing returns to normal. "I'm going to turn around."

I nod. I don't care what she does as long as she doesn't stop. My own pinnacle is slowly building. Now I'm looking at her beautiful heart-shaped ass, and she rolls my balls in her hands. She lifts a little bit, and I drive in and out beneath her.

"Oh, yes," Tinsley cries as I make love to her slowly.

"Come for me, baby. Fill me up," she demands as I pick up speed.

"So close, ugh, yes, I'm coming," I manage.

After I erupt inside her, she collapses back on top of me, and I kiss her feverishly. Rolling to my side, I pull her into me and drift toward sleep.

We're finally together, where we need to be.

CHAPTER 27

Landon

I'm working through my final pieces of the code when my phone vibrates on the table. The caller ID tells me it's Jim.

"Hey, man, what's up?"

"Heather McCoy is in the news today."

I'm surprised because I would expect Fiona to call, or maybe Greer from SHN, but not Jim. "Did she have her baby?" It is the second half of August now...

Tinsley looks up, so I put the phone on speaker.

"That would be good news," Jim agrees.

He doesn't add anything, which makes me nervous. "What did she do?"

"She's disappeared," he informs us.

I lean back in my chair. I feel a bit grateful this mess is close to being over, and then I realize there's a reason Jim is the one calling me.

"She knew the baby wasn't mine," I say slowly. "Could she have snuck away to have the baby somewhere else, without the embarrassment that she lied?"

"The police are investigating that theory," Jim hedges.

"Okay, so why all the cloak and dagger?"

"They found her blood in the apartment. I spoke with a detective I've worked with a lot, and he let me know you were SFPD's number-one suspect."

Tinsley shakes her head. I've been by her side nonstop since we returned to the ranch three and a half weeks ago.

"Did you tell him I'm here in Montana at my ranch and have been for almost a month, with Tinsley and a house full of staff?"

"I did, and I shared that we have statements from all the players at the poker tournament last October, including Walker Clifton, which verify that you were with them when she claimed you were getting her pregnant. We also have video of you from the Shangri-la on those dates and video of her at Tate's bar in San Francisco, where she claims she met you, that same day. She leaves with a guy."

I feel a little better knowing that. "If they have her blood, they can also test that to determine I'm not the father. Something was shady about that first round of testing."

"They did test it again. It looks like she wasn't pregnant."

I pump my fists in the air. "Then I'm done?"

"I wish it was that easy," Jim whispers into the phone.

My stomach drops.

"My detective friend let me know that the detective handling the case is ambitious," he continues. "He's convinced a lot of people that you had her taken out because you were nervous about her."

Taken out? This has gotten way out of control. "But I always knew the child wasn't mine. I offered to give her a lot of money once we had proof. She's the one who went to the media saying I refused my responsibility."

"I understand that. Fiona is on her way to you and should be landing in a little over an hour, and the police are flying into Lewiston commercially on the two thirty flight from Salt Lake. They will either be at the ranch tonight or first thing tomorrow."

"Do they have an arrest warrant?"

"Not when they left, but they may have one by the time they land."

I sigh. "Okay. Thanks, Jim, for the heads up."

Our call disconnects. I close my eyes for a moment before I look over at Tinsley. "You know Claire is going ape shit over this, right?"

Tinsley nods. "Why don't you call her?"

The thought sours my stomach. "She's going to scream at me."

"Better now than later, I suppose." Tinsley gives me a tight smile, but her eyes are soft.

I take a deep breath and hold it. "You're only saying that because she won't be yelling at you."

Our last week here at the ranch has been perfect. We usually make love when we wake up. Who needs caffeine when I can hear Tinsley scream my name before breakfast? That's my adrenaline. Then we're at the dining room table by eight. We break for lunch at twelve-thirty and work until at least two before we quit for the day and usually do something to explore the property. We are back for dinner by seven. We watch a movie snuggled up in bed and make love at least one more time before we go to sleep. We're living in a carefully crafted bubble and loving every second of it.

I talked to my sister last week. Her house should be done after Labor Day, and the interest in our communications product continues to be high from PeopleMover. We've also been approached by others outside of social media. Now I have to alert her to the impending nightmare of more PR cleanup.

I look at Tinsley, and she kisses me softly for encouragement. I finally make the call.

"Hey. What's up? It's not our day to chat."

Claire is bubbly, and I'm going to pop that bubble and incur her wrath.

"Jim called," I tell her.

"What's going on?"

"Heather McCoy is missing."

"I saw that on the news this morning. We dodged a bullet on that one."

"We'll talk about why you didn't call me as soon as you saw the news another time, but Jim's heard otherwise."

"What do you mean?"

"Despite my confidence and the proof of my non-paternity, the detective on the case supposedly thinks I hired someone to take her out."

"What? Do they know you at all?"

There goes the bubble. *Pop.*

"Well, no. They don't know me, but they're on their way here. They arrive this afternoon."

"Oh shit," Claire breathes.

She's taking this much better than I expected. I thought she'd go crazy on me like she did before she banished me from the company.

"Jim put Fiona on a plane, and she arrives within the hour."

Tinsley stands and leaves the room. I hope she's not pissed off.

Claire and I talk through some things she's going to do to protect the company, including the thing I dread the most — my possible removal. It's *my* company.

"If we have to go there, it will be temporary," Claire assures me. "And we'll make that legally binding."

Tinsley returns with a bottle of bourbon and a glass of water. She scribbles a note: *I told Molly Fiona was on the way. Frank will be there to meet her. We'll manage this together.*

I look at her and mouth, "Thank you."

She winks at me, and my shoulders relax. My heartbeat slows.

"I should go. Fiona will be here, and I need to prepare."

"I love you. This is all going to be fine," Claire says.

"I love you, too," I tell her. "I'll call you, or if I get arrested, I'll have Tinsley call you."

"You'll be fine."

I wish I were as confident as Claire and Tinsley that this is all going to be okay. I don't know what it was in Jim's voice, but something has me scared, despite the truth on my side.

We hang up, and Tinsley crawls into my lap. She stares at me with her big brown eyes. "I know we haven't said this, but I want you to know that I love you."

I feel like I could leap tall buildings.

Tinsley leans down and kisses me, her tongue swiping languidly in my mouth. My hand goes to her breast, and I can feel my erection growing. Rather than meet with Fiona, I'd much prefer to make love to my girlfriend.

"I love you, too," I murmur between kisses.

"We're going to get through this. If Fiona can't or doesn't want to help, my mom went to law school in Los Angeles, and she has many friends who are still there. Her network can help us."

I pull her in and hold her tight. The buzz of the plane can be heard long before we see it enter the valley.

My pulse quickens as we walk out to the porch.

Molly joins us. "Do you think she'll be staying?" she asks.

I turn to her. "I'm sorry. Yes, I imagine she's going to want to stay on the property. I should also warn you that the San Francisco police are coming to meet with me."

"That's fine. I don't mind doing up a room for your lawyer, but I'm not doing up a room for the police." Molly disappears with a sniff.

Tinsley squeezes my hand. "We should call Darlene since chances are they're staying at the Holiday Inn and will eat at the diner across the street. She can give us the scoop."

"You read my mind. We should also call Jason at the Holiday Inn. I'll make sure they have the room next to the elevator and the ice machine."

"You're pure evil." Tinsley grins at me.

"That's why I'm so easy to love." I lean down and kiss the top of her hair, savoring the floral scent of her shampoo.

Frank's truck drives up, and Fiona jumps out in jeans and a sweater. I'm shocked that in place of her usual stilettos, she's wearing cowboy boots.

"Surprised to see me?" she asks.

Her enthusiasm is infectious, but I'm going to play it cool and yank her chain a bit. "Naw. Jim warned me you were coming."

"That bastard," she shouts with a wide grin. "You must be Tinsley Pratt." She rushes over while Frank unpacks five suitcases.

"Are you moving in?" I tease.

"I brought my computer and a printer and some files and an outfit or two." She blushes, and it's rather funny. She's going to be sorely disappointed when she learns there isn't anyone here to dress for.

"Come on in. Jim said you were on your way and gave me the rundown." I show her where she can set up in the living room, so she has her own space.

"What do you think is going on?" Tinsley asks.

"The detective on this is Nick Robards. He's young, kind of cute, and looking at jobs in Sacramento," Fiona says.

"What does that mean for me?" I ask.

"The downside is he's looking for headlines, so a billionaire playboy who denies paternity, and then the mother of his baby goes missing, is perfect for him."

I groan. "Except that isn't what he has," I protest. "It wasn't my baby, and it actually wasn't a baby at all." I've never been so grateful to have Tinsley in my life. My dick is permanently wrapped up and put away. "Did you know the blood they tested indicated she wasn't pregnant?"

Fiona nods. "We also found out the boyfriend has a conviction for assault and battery."

"Jim was told the police are trying to get a warrant for my arrest. Will they ship me home in handcuffs?"

"Probably not. If they do, I'll make sure the media are there to talk about Robards overlooking so many issues with her story." She smiles. "Is he coming today or tomorrow?"

"Jim thought he'd be here tomorrow, though possibly in town tonight. He doesn't know he's lost the element of surprise, so do you think he's expecting to show up and haul me off?"

She shrugs. "Good question. We'll see. I suspect he has a lot of questions he needs answers to in order to get his arrest warrant."

Frank shows Fiona where she'll be staying, and Molly insists on making her a cobb salad for lunch.

When Fiona gushes about it, Molly is gracious. "Thank you. The only thing that didn't come from the ranch was the avocado and the blue cheese crumbles. The chicken and egg are from our hen house. We cure our own bacon twice a year, and the greens and tomatoes are grown right here on the land."

"I'd love to see your garden," Fiona says.

"I'm sure we can make that happen."

Molly is so proud of the garden, and she should be. It feeds the ranch and all its visitors almost year-round.

After lunch, we move to the dining room to talk. Fiona sits down with a big file in front of her, along with a yellow legal pad and a fancy pen.

Tinsley sits next to me, and while they're still doing small talk, I send a text to Darlene at the diner and Jason at the hotel about Robards coming in, letting them know he's not to be trusted.

Jason: Perfect. I've got a family with eight kids in three rooms. I'll make sure he's next to them.

Darlene: We'll conveniently be out of whatever he orders, and he'll have to eat the leftover trout from yesterday.

My leg bounces, and Tinsley reaches over to still it, calming me with her touch. Fiona opens her file and brings out a packet of paper. "Mason Sullivan obtained these affidavits from each person you were with at the Shangri-la in October. Having Walker Clifton is good sway, given if anyone's going to Sacramento, it's him."

"Wouldn't Robards have checked that out first?" Tinsley asks.

"I'm not sure he's that bright," Fiona snarks.

I hope she's right. I know ambition can get in the way of success.

Fiona holds up a CD with a fob attached. "This is the jump drive Jonathan Best compiled for you. It's all your comings and goings around Las Vegas the weekend she insists you got her pregnant. They have each night you entered and when you left your room."

My stomach turns. "Each time?"

"They say you're always on a camera in Vegas." Tinsley smiles, clearly thinking this is a good thing.

It's not—at least not for my standing with her. I wasn't alone.

Fiona nods. She knows I'm nervous because I spent a lot of time that weekend with Viviana Prentis.

"The compact disc is a video of Heather McCoy coming and going from the bar on the date in question, taken from the bank ATM across the street." Fiona holds up the paper square with a CD inside. "She does leave, but we're unable to validate who she's with. It's blown up and grainy, but we recognize her from the photos Jim has shown me."

"That shows I didn't get her pregnant, so I wouldn't be worried about her doing anything to me," I muse. "So, I'm guessing they're going after what's happened since she went to the press, and as you know, I left. I did go to Denver and back to San Francisco, but for the last month or so, I've been here. I'm sure they must have pulled all my phone activity since I've been gone. What else could be motivating them?"

"We'll find out," Fiona says.

Molly comes into the dining room. "Please don't be upset with me, but I overheard why Ms. McPhee was here, and I called my brother and told him someone from the San Francisco police was coming, and they'd be reaching out."

I forgot law enforcement needs to check in with the local law.

"Who's your brother?" Fiona asks.

"He's Sheriff Scott Lambert." Molly gives almost an evil smile. "Nothing goes on here that he isn't aware of, and Landon did donate five thousand dollars to his campaign after he bought the ranch."

Fiona smiles. "Sounds like Robards might find it difficult to get a lot of support. Where's the local FBI office?"

Molly purses her lips and shrugs. "There's an office of two in Butte, and the Crow and the Northern Cheyenne reservations each have a team, but they usually don't act on anything outside of reservation land unless someone from their tribe is involved."

Fiona grins. "Sounds like some things are working in our favor."

Tinsley leaves to do some work while I continue to go through what we know about the McCoy situation, and Fiona drills me with questions.

Eventually, she relaxes into her chair. "I think we're in good shape. Now we need to learn what they have."

"They won't be able to sneak up on us here." I say that with more confidence than I'm feeling. "We'll spot the dirt plume behind them as they approach. But hopefully, we'll know even before then because Jason or Darlene will have called."

My cell phone pings. It's shortly after four thirty.

Jason: Your friend has arrived. He has a stick up his ass big time. He's heading over to see Darlene for dinner. She's not going to take to him at all. I'll let you know when he drives off.

Me: Thanks, man. You're a true friend.

Jason: We always look out for locals.

I relay what I've learned to Fiona, and she nods. "Keep me posted."

Over dinner, Frank tells us he's locked the outside gate. "They won't be trying to come in tonight."

"They'll have bolt cutters," Fiona warns him.

"Nothing's chained. The gate's electric. If they cut the power, it'll remain locked, and even a battering ram on the front of an F350 truck wouldn't be able to open it. The gate's in twenty-five feet of concrete underground."

Frank's proud of the security features he set up with Jim a few years ago.

"Scotty hasn't sent me a message saying this guy's checked in with them," Molly reports. "He's supposed to let them know. If he doesn't, Scotty will be following him out."

"Scotty is your brother, the sheriff?" Fiona asks.

Molly nods. "Yes, ma'am."

Fiona is busy eating her pot roast, but chuckles. "Don't piss off the locals."

"You have no idea," Tinsley exclaims.

Molly pats her on the leg. "You didn't piss anyone off." Molly jacks her thumb to me. "He, on the other hand, did, and he paid for it the entire week you were staying at the Holiday Inn."

"Don't remind me." I shake my head.

CHAPTER 28

Landon

After dinner, Tinsley reaches for my hand and guides me upstairs to my room. Pushing me back onto the bed, she pulls her T-shirt over her head and her shorts down her hips. She stands before me in a lacy, navy blue bra and thong.

I begin to sit up, and she shakes her head. "I think you need some therapy."

"Really? What kind of therapy?"

"Blow-job therapy."

My cock is at rigid attention.

"Tonight is all about getting your mind off what's going on."

She licks her lips, and I can see her nipples straining behind her bra. My cock is ready to slide between her slick folds.

She leans down and kisses me softly, reaching for my shirt. My hands go to her breasts, but she stops and shakes her head. "No touching."

I think I'm going to explode.

Her hand grazes the length of my hardness. "I want to taste you first."

"Your wish is my command," I growl.

She kisses me again and pulls my shirt up over my head. Standing back, she palms her breasts, and it's pure torture.

She pops the button on my shorts and watches me as she unzips them. I stand up enough for her to slide them down.

Her hands roam over my chest and legs as my cock bobs at her.

"You have the most incredible body." She runs her fingers over my tight stomach.

Reaching for a pillow, she places it on the ground between my legs. She grasps my cock tightly and begins to stroke. Precum seeps, and she leans in to lick it up. "Mmmm, you taste so good."

In one long, slow, smooth motion, she places her lips around the tip of my cock and works me into her mouth until she's engulfed my entire length, gagging a bit as I reach the back of her throat. Maintaining a slow tempo, she draws her cheeks hollow, and the suction careens me close to my pinnacle. She bobs up and down, finding a rhythm with her motions.

Increasing her speed, she takes less of my length into her mouth, but uses her hands on the base of my shaft. Her brown eyes stare up at me, and I cup her face. She pulls off and flicks her tongue over the head. I twine my fingers in her hair and guide her deep onto me again. She doesn't even falter as she takes my entire length into her throat.

"Oh yeah, Tinsley, you like that, huh? You like it when I push myself deep into your throat?"

She looks up, unable to speak, and squeezes my balls.

"I suppose you'd like a little attention as well?"

She pulls away long enough to answer. "Oh no, this is

all about you. We can't evaluate the effectiveness of the blow-job therapy unless we follow through to the conclusion."

"Very well then, continue." I interlace my fingers behind my head and enjoy Tinsley's ministrations.

She cups my balls in one hand and begins jacking me off with her other as she sucks the last few inches of my cock. I clearly love this combination of motions, so she sticks with it, gradually increasing her tempo as she responds to my growing excitement. After a few minutes, I reach down and unhook her bra so I can fondle her tits, gently at first, but then more firmly. And finally, I squeeze her nipples, like I know turns her on.

I'm getting close, and I want to enjoy her, too. "You don't have to finish me," I say through clenched teeth.

She doesn't stop. She bobs up and down with added enthusiasm, groaning as she moves me closer to my climax. I push my hips forward as she struggles to keep my throbbing length in her mouth.

"I want to come in your pussy," I hiss breathlessly.

Tinsley gives my cock one last long suck before letting me out of her mouth and jumping to her feet. Leaning over the back of the stuffed side chair, she spreads her legs and looks back at me over her shoulder, a clear invitation to take her from behind.

I grab a condom and begin to roll it on. "We need to have a conversation about birth control. I want to feel you."

"I'm on the pill."

I stop what I'm doing. "Do you prefer I use a condom?"

She looks at my swollen member in my hand. "I've never had sex without a condom."

I finish rolling it on. "I can't wait, but we can figure it out later."

I move behind her, pulling her wet thong away and slowly pressing my hard cock into her. She groans loudly as I fill her, and she reaches down to finger her clit as I begin pounding in and out. She knows I won't last long — but neither will she, as turned on as she is. I catch a glance of her tits rocking back and forth in the reflection of the glass, and I reach around to pull and twist her nipples.

Her pussy clenches around my cock, and I whisper in her ear, "Yes, Tinsley, yes, yes," as my cum shoots deep inside her. My legs become jelly, and I collapse against her, panting over the armchair.

When we finally stand and reach for our clothes on the floor, I smile. "Well, it seems the treatment worked wonders."

Tinsley stands on her tiptoes. "I'm glad I could be of service. Let me know when you're ready for another round."

After such excellent therapy, I slept well last night. I'm not nervous about this defective detective. He may have me in his sights, but I'm in good legal shape.

I get out of bed before Tinsley and head to the gym. I don't want to leave the main house until this conversation with the police is behind me.

When I'm done exercising, I smell bacon. Molly's looking out for me again. I walk into the kitchen covered in sweat, only to find it full of all the ranch hands, plus Fiona and Tinsley. "What's going on?"

"The guys here want to make Detective Robards' life miserable, but I won't let them," Fiona says.

I pull my shirt on. "Guys, you're the best. I can't tell you how much it means to have your support. This asshole is going out of his way to try to surprise us. He hasn't, but we should pretend at least a little bit."

"He hasn't checked in with my brother yet either," Molly huffs.

"Look, I have a top-notch team here." I motion to everyone in the kitchen. "If this guy arrests me, this team is going to expand greatly. He can't link me to this woman in any way. As bad as it sounds, I don't care about her, nor have I been worried about her threat. The things I've done have more to do with protecting my company and the work we're doing there. Unfortunately, people want to take advantage of me."

"What can we do to help?" Jimmy, the horse wrangler, asks.

"We prevented him from coming in the middle of the night…" I look at Fiona. "Should we open the gates? We'll know he's coming."

"How would that work if we didn't?" Fiona bites her lip and squints.

"When he arrives, just off to the driver's side of the gate is a house phone, which rings here." Frank points to a black phone I never noticed before. "He'll have to ring and announce himself. I have the option of buzzing the gate open from the phone, or I could get in the truck and drive down to open it with a nine-digit code."

Fiona thinks about it. "Let me know when he arrives. We can determine how nice he's playing and decide whether we're going to make him wait or buzz him in."

"There's still a few-minute drive, even if Frank doesn't go to the gate to let him in," Molly says.

I can tell everyone is nervous. Turning to Molly, I ask, "What smells so good?"

"I've got scrambled eggs, bacon, biscuits, and a small bar of toppings people can add to their eggs. I can make you something else if you prefer."

"This is perfect. Anyone want to join me for breakfast?"

The team lines up for food. Molly stands next to me, and I put my arm around her. "Thank you for taking such good care of all of us. I know you sent out the rallying cry to get everyone here."

"Actually, it was Frank. He was fuming mad about this fellow coming."

I eye her. "I would bet someone knew which buttons to

push to get him to do that."

Molly looks away. "I have no idea what you're talking about."

I kiss her head, and she blushes. I look over and raise my coffee to Frank. "Thank you for all of this."

Frank nods. "We don't take kindly to people harassing our residents."

After breakfast is eaten and cleared, people go about their daily jobs, and I sit with Tinsley. She's in the zone and coding away.

She looks up at me. "Do we need to go upstairs for another therapy session?"

God, I love this woman. "Yes," I say immediately. But it's not a good idea. "No. I want to, but I don't want anyone to interrupt us."

"Is there anything else I can do?" Tinsley comes over and sits in my lap, putting her arms around me.

"This is perfect," I whisper.

My cell phone pings.

Jason: He's left the hotel.

We stand and let Fiona and Molly know.

"My brother has a cruiser watching him," Molly assures me.

The landline phone rings a few minutes later. Molly answers it and has a short conversation.

"Robards blew past a speed trap, and they've pulled him over on a county road," she reports. "Scotty's guys are not letting it slide."

Fiona chuckles. "He's going to be pissed by the time he gets here."

Molly makes us a nice lunch, and not too long after that, she's started prepping a dinner that smells fantastic.

At one point she comes in to report the update from her brother. "Robards admitted he was coming to the ranch, and my brother won't allow it until he talks to his boss in San Francisco, who isn't in today."

Frank snickers. "I learned the hard way not to piss Scotty off." He looks at Molly lovingly. "So, he won't be here today."

"Is he going to be so pissed when he finally gets here that I take the brunt of it?" I ask.

Fiona shrugs. "Hard to say, really. Right now, the sheriff and his office are trying to irritate him, and I imagine it's working. That may be to our advantage. He'll be mad at them, not at you."

"It'll be hard to dismiss Scotty as a backwater, small-town cop since before he was sheriff, he was a captain in the Dallas Police Department," Molly says.

"Why didn't I know that?" I look at Molly. "I thought you were from here."

"We are. Scotty went to Texas to play football and then joined the police force and worked himself up the ladder. When he retired, he moved back here and was talked into running for sheriff. He grouses about it, but he loves it. Even the FBI likes him."

"Wow. I'm impressed," Fiona says.

With the pressure off for today, I want to stretch my legs. "You up for a mountain-bike ride up the river trail?" I ask Tinsley.

"Sure."

It takes three days before Detective Robards finally gets it worked out to be on his way here, and he's also had to assure Sheriff Lambert that this upstanding citizen (me) will not be arrested and extradited out of this jurisdiction without his knowledge.

"That's excellent news," Fiona assures us.

When Robards finally gets to the front gate, Frank allows him entry, and when he arrives at the house, Fiona greets him at the door.

"Detective Robards. What brings you to Montana?" she asks.

"I'd like to speak with Peter Landon Walsh, please."

"I'm his lawyer. What can I help you with?"

"That's why the sheriff slowed me down. He wanted to wait for you to arrive," he snipes.

She shakes her head. "I've been here for four days — ever since you announced on the San Francisco news that you were making Mr. Walsh the prime suspect in your missing-person case."

"Getting all the lies lined up, I see."

Fiona shows him into her living room office, and we can hear everything, but we can't see or be seen. "May I get you something to drink?" she asks. "Coffee? Tea? Water?"

"I'm fine."

"What can I help you with?"

"I'd like to speak to your client."

"I tell you what, you tell me what you want to know, and I'll answer your questions."

"If he doesn't want to talk to me himself, I'll arrest him, and he'll be forced to talk to me."

There's a pause, and I know that Fiona is letting him think he has her.

"Really?" she says. "You'll arrest him?"

Another break and I hear her boots scuff across the carpet over the wooden floor. "I don't see the sheriff with you. Do you have permission from your captain for that?"

"Look, I flew all the way here to speak to him. It's either here, or I can do so at the precinct in San Francisco."

"Well, before you decide to go there, I have a few ideas for you to consider. I'll release everything I'm giving you to the press, so you may want to see what it is before you make demands that will make you look like a fool."

Tinsley looks at me with a giant, goofy smile, and I have the strongest urge to kiss it off her right now.

"On the weekend Heather McCoy claimed she was with my client, he was actually in Las Vegas. Here's a list of twelve prominent Bay Area residents who were with him. You might want to note the top affidavit from the United States Attorney for the Northern District of California. Walker Clifton would not lie for his own mother."

"These could all be falsified."

"You can check them. That's fine. This is the time-stamped footage of my client's comings and goings while he stayed in Las Vegas at the Shangri-la."

"This can be faked," Robards counters.

"You can subpoena the footage from the Shangri-la directly, if you'd like. The numbers for Jonathan Best and his head of security, Travis Deck, are noted on the cover."

"I'd like to speak to your client."

"We'll see. And this CD is footage from an ATM where Ms. McCoy was filmed entering Tate's bar in San Francisco and leaving with someone who is not my client, because he was in Las Vegas."

"He was embarrassed by the publicity she brought down on him, and he ran here to his ranch."

"Embarrassed? Quite the opposite. He was prepared to support her and the child, once the baby was born and a blood test determined he was the father. He offered her a lot of money. If she went to the press to embarrass him, all it did was make him move from his downtown condominium to his ranch so he could work in peace. You do know that Disruptive Technologies is close to doing what their name says and upsetting the way we communicate. Turning everything on its ear—literally."

"Why was he harassing her?"

"He has had zero communication with Ms. McCoy except through me, and I assure you, I didn't speak to her."

Robards sighs. "Since you've shared all your client's

cards, I'll show you some of mine. Your client emailed Ms. McCoy on six separate occasions with threats."

"I'd like to have those sent to me electronically so I can verify their geo-tag."

"I've already done that, and they were sent from right here in Lewiston."

"The geo-tag for the ranch isn't Lewiston. It's Crow Nation," Molly whispers to me.

I didn't even realize she was standing next to me. I give her a thumbs up.

"I also have some of his DNA found at the scene in her apartment. Your client has a private airstrip I drove by, doesn't he?"

"He does."

"Has your client been here the entire time?"

"For the most part, but he's not under house arrest. He traveled to Denver, Colorado, a little over a month ago. I can provide you with flight manifests and signed affidavits by the staff here—"

"They're on his payroll. Those are worth nothing."

"They may be on his payroll, but they're kind and honest people who would happily verify that my client was here when he says he was."

"He still threatened her," Robards insists.

"That remains to be seen. My client is a man of great wealth who may have been a little cavalier with his personal life. Ms. McCoy is not the first to place a bullseye on his back, looking for a big payday. She also won't be the last. But let me assure you, he isn't worried. And before you go, here's the contract I sent to her, and this is the receipt she signed upon delivery."

"I'd like to speak to your client now."

I hear Fiona walk toward the door we're standing behind. We step back as she opens it.

Fiona steps close to me and whispers, "He doesn't have anything, and I'm pretty sure the documents he has are fake."

I tell her what Molly said about the geo-tag for the ranch.

She nods. "That's great. Let's keep that to ourselves for now. We're going to walk back out there, and you can answer his questions, but don't expand. If he asks if you've been here the whole time, you answer no. You don't offer where you've been."

I nod. "Got it."

I follow her into the living room and lay eyes on Detective Robards for the first time. He's probably in his late thirties, if I had to guess. Blond hair and blue eyes. He's almost unmemorable—he'd be great for undercover work, as he seems to blend in with his surroundings.

He doesn't shake my hand, just hands me his business card. "You're not only hiding in Montana, but you're hiding behind your lawyer."

I don't respond.

"Cat got your tongue?" he jabs.

"I'm sorry, was that a question?" Fiona asks.

"Why are you in Montana, Mr. Walsh?"

"To work," I say.

"You can't work in your offices in San Francisco?"

"No."

"Why is that, Mr. Walsh?" Detective Robards asks.

"My business partners and I thought this would have fewer distractions."

"Who are your business partners?"

"My sister, Claire Walsh, Tinsley Pratt, and Sullivan Healy Newhouse is our investor."

"I understand Ms. Pratt is here with you?" Detective Robards says.

"Yes."

"You're a man of many words, Mr. Walsh."

I look at him.

"He's answering your questions, Detective," Fiona not so subtly reminds him.

His questions continue for over an hour. I get the feeling he isn't used to people who claim to be innocent and don't overshare. For the most part, he gets yes or no answers from me.

When he circles back and begins to ask the same questions a second time, Fiona steps in. "I think we've answered all your questions. Thank you for coming out. If you'd like to speak with my client again, please call me at the number on the card."

"I'm not done with my questions," Detective Robards, says looking a little panicked.

"What else do you want to know?" Fiona asks.

"Is Ms. Pratt your lover?" he blurts.

"You're done. Goodbye, Detective," Fiona says as she stands.

"Ms. Pratt could be behind this."

Fiona smiles. "If you can link her to this, you let me know, because I'm her lawyer, too."

Frank appears and opens the front door for Detective Robards, who reluctantly goes.

As he steps outside, Fiona stands in the doorway. "Thank you for coming, Detective. Please be sure to contact United States Attorney Walker Clifton about my client's alibi. I'll make sure he's expecting your call."

Molly stands at the side window. "That man is pissed, as he well should be—at himself." She shakes her head in disgust.

"I know you couldn't see him, but he was surprised at the information I gave him," Fiona says, closing the door. "Walker Clifton's affidavit was on top, but Robards isn't done with this yet."

CHAPTER 29

Tinsley

Jason sent Landon a text letting him know Detective Robards had checked out of the Holiday Inn and left town almost five days ago, but Landon is still on edge. We set a goal to finish the development of this layer of the translations, but he gets distracted easily. He's told me he's waiting for the other shoe to drop. I can't blame him.

Fiona is going to stick around. She says she's staying because people will be arriving for the poker tournament in less than a week, but I believe it's because she knows Landon feels better having her close in case something goes sideways. I'm sure he's paying her a fortune as well, but I don't want him to disappear back into the anger and despair that engulfed him for two months not long ago.

Today I'm going to drag him on a fat-tire bike ride. One of the ranch hands told me about a great trail that skirts the river and ends at a waterfall. Hopefully this will get his mind off of what's going on. His friends are arriving in five days for the poker tournament, and I'm ready for fresh faces.

The alarm on my phone sounds, indicating it's two o'clock. I shut my computer and look up at Landon. "Are you ready?"

"Sure. I'll follow wherever you go, as long as I can stare at your ass."

I roll my eyes. "You're incorrigible. Is there ever a time when you're not thinking about sex?"

"Of course. When we're in the middle of it. Then I'm thinking about satisfying you."

I roll my eyes like the comment bothers me, but secretly, I love it. I've never before felt the power he lets me have—like I have a magic pussy or something. It's heady.

"Come on," I tell him. "We need to go now, or we'll not make it back before dark."

I pick up the backpack with all our essentials, and Frank sets the bikes out for us at the bottom of the porch steps. I swing my helmet on and clasp it beneath my chin.

"Are you sure that bike's not too big for you?" Landon asks as he fumbles with his helmet.

Frank has a funny sense of humor; Landon's helmet has a wide strip of rubber spikes, which look like a mohawk. I pull my phone from my back pocket and take a picture.

"I'll be fine. Try to keep up." I push off, and we head down a path that skirts the river in the valley. We're heading uphill as we ride, and it doesn't take long for it to get difficult. I'm out of shape since I'm not getting to swim, and our afternoon hikes aren't as rigorous.

I spot a large rock and slow to a stop. "I need a break."

"I needed one about a mile ago."

I grin. "You should have said something."

"What? And look like a wimp? No, thank you. You'd tell Claire, and then she'd tell everyone here this weekend, and they'd use it to break my concentration. These guys play some serious poker. No one has ever won two games in a row, and I'm going to break that streak. I want to win again."

"But you're not going to lose Magnolia Homestead, right?"

"No, I'm going to put up my house in Whistler for my final collateral, if I need it. When I won this place, I didn't need any additional collateral. I had the majority of the chips."

"Is your place in Whistler grand like this?"

"Not at all, but it's nice. We should go. Maybe if I win, we can host next time up there, and I can show you where I used to seduce the women I met on the ski slopes."

"Why? So you can seduce me there, too?"

"Of course, along with all the other places I plan on seducing you."

"You're too much." I chuckle, shaking my head. "Mikey told me at this point, we have another two miles or so to the waterfall. It gets rocky, and he suggested we walk the last few yards."

"Mikey the ranch hand?"

I drink from my water bottle and nod.

"I'll follow your lead." Landon mounts his bike and looks back over his shoulder. "Maybe you should stare at my ass for a while."

"That works for me."

We push off, and as Mikey predicted, the incline gets pretty steep. I'm about to suggest we walk when I see Landon's bike pitch. He puts his leg out to stop the fall, but momentum torques it the wrong way, and he crumples to the ground.

I fling myself off my bike and rush to his side. "Are you okay?"

His ankle is swelling up like a balloon. He groans. "I'm okay."

He's not okay. When he tries to stand, his face contorts into real pain.

I pull the satellite phone out of the backpack and call the house.

Molly answers after the first ring. "What's wrong?"

"I think Landon broke his ankle. It's swelling, and he can't put any weight on it." I explain to her where we are, and she puts Frank on the phone.

"How far back is the meadow?" he asks.

"A few miles." I do some mental calculating, trying to figure out how long ago we rode through there. "I'm not sure I can get him there."

"I'll call a helicopter in. Mikey, since he got you into this mess, and I will be right there. Hold tight."

"Thanks."

I disconnect the call and look at Landon. He's trying to be tough, but I can tell by the crease in his brow that he's hurting. "Mikey and Frank are on their way. They'll have the helicopter in the meadow, which I believe is going to take you right to the hospital."

"I'm never going to live this down. You know that, right?"

"Hey, I'm on your side here. You weren't showing off or anything. You were trying to keep the mama bear from charging me. You got into the middle of it and scared her away, but in doing so, you lost your footing. Nothing but heroism here."

"You'd tell that lie?" Landon cocks his head, seeming surprised.

"Of course. How romantic is it to say you were showing off and pushing beyond your abilities when you lost your balance on your bike?"

"Yeah, I like the mama bear much better. You're awesome, you know that?"

"I am." I grin widely and kiss him.

"Hey! Aren't you going to tell me I'm awesome, too?"

Before I can answer, I hear dirt bikes. "Here comes the cavalry."

"And?"

"And what? I'm telling everyone you were a hero, not a show-off. I should get extra credit for that."

Frank and Mikey come barreling up on their bikes. Mikey takes his helmet off. "You rode this far up?"

I nod. "He took the lead at the meadow."

"I told you to be prepared to *walk* after the meadow."

I'm positive he told me we could ride beyond the meadow, but it's not worth the argument.

"Well, there was this bear…" Landon says.

Frank looks at him dubiously. He won't be fooled by our story.

"He doesn't want anyone to know he was showing off and turned his ankle," I explain. "We're telling his friends he got between a mama bear and me and scared her off."

Frank shakes his head. "We have grizzly bears here, but not in this area. Not enough food. Plus, if you had seen a mama grizzly, she would have charged you at thirty-five miles an hour, taken you both out, and left you half-alive for the coyotes and wolves to enjoy."

"My friends are all city folk," Landon grunts. "They won't know the difference."

"Whatever." Frank looks at his watch. "The medivac will be here in twenty minutes. How's your other leg?"

"Fine, I think."

"We're going to walk you to the meadow."

I watch them stand Landon up. He puts an arm around each of them, and they slowly walk him down the trail. Two more ranch hands arrive as we're halfway down, and Mikey tells them where our bikes are.

"What will you do about the dirt bikes?"

"We'll go back for them after we get him on the medivac."

The helicopter blades chopping through the air can be heard before it appears. Its blades are still spinning when we arrive, and a nurse comes running over.

"How's he doing?"

"He's fine," Frank says. "Turned his ankle, and it's most likely broken."

"Let's hope he doesn't need surgery," the nurse says.

Landon looks up, eyes wide. "Surgery?"

"I'll let the orthopedist from Butte make that determination."

"We're flying to Butte?" I ask.

"Yep. The best ortho is there. Hopefully she's sober." The nurse winks at Landon so I know she's teasing — at least I hope she is.

"We have room for you," she tells me. "Would you care to join us?"

"Yes." I turn to Frank. "Should I rent a car to get him home?"

"No, I'll leave after dinner and head into Butte in the Range Rover. If they determine he needs surgery, call and let me know when they'll be discharging him."

I nod. I wasn't nervous before, but now I'm scared. Do I call his parents? Claire? Do I cancel his friends coming? *Shit.* I don't know what to do.

I take a deep breath and figure I'll take this one step at a time.

The nurse checks Landon's vitals and gives him a choice between lying down on the gurney on the outside of the helicopter or sitting in the back. He immediately signals that he'll sit upright.

"I warn you, this is going to throb because it isn't elevated," she says.

"That's okay."

I sit next to him and lift his leg onto my lap. "This might help," I yell into the mic of the headphones, but I'm not sure he can hear me.

In under an hour, we land at the hospital in Butte. As the helicopter touches down, people come running at us from all sides. They move Landon to a wheelchair and elevate his leg.

"How are you doing?" a nurse asks me.

"I'm fine. We were out on fat tires, and he took a rock

wrong. To keep from falling, he put his leg out, and it got twisted."

"That happens a lot around here. Don't worry."

I lean in. "He's kind of famous. Can we register him under a different name for privacy?"

"Let's talk to admitting. We do that every now and again."

My cell phone pings, and I look down to see I have an email from Dana. I'd completely forgotten I asked her almost three weeks ago to snoop on the Stanford Octagon page.

I'm so sorry about the delay. I AM pregnant, and my energy is gone, but I didn't forget. Attached is the list of members of the Stanford Octagon group, and I included several screenshots of conversations about you. I'm sorry I didn't get to this earlier. I hope it's still useful.

Miss you,
Dana

There are eight attachments. This is great, but I'll have to look at everything later. I now have all Landon's admitting paperwork in front of me, and I have no idea what to write.

I call Claire and explain what happened — using the bear story.

"I know my brother well. You do know he wouldn't jump in front of a bear for our mother. My guess is he was being a show-off."

"I don't know what to tell you... She was a big grizzly bear." I shuffle through the mountain of forms. "Can you help me with some of the information for these forms?"

I run through the questions, and she's great about answering them.

"Is he going to be okay?" she asks as we finish up.

"He's angry at himself more than anything. He's in xray right now, and I got stuck with this. I did at least make sure they registered him in the hospital under a different name. He's Peter Pratt."

"That's hysterical." Claire chuckles. "I may have to call him that. Mr. Pratt. I love it."

Landon rolls up in a wheelchair pushed by a medical assistant, and we're moved into a small room off the ER. His chart has VIP stamped horizontally across it in red.

"No hiding that." I point Landon to it.

"Did they recognize me?"

"No, but given Detective Robards' recent interest and other things going on, I thought it was smart to have them admit you under an assumed name."

Landon's shoulders drop. "Good thinking."

A tall woman walks in wearing green scrubs. "Hello. Is it Mr. Walsh or Mr. Pratt?"

"To admitting, I'm Mr. Pratt."

All of a sudden, recognition crosses her face. "I completely understand." She pulls up a seat between us. "I'm Dr. Whitefeather. Let's get a look at your ankle."

She begins to manipulate it, and Landon flinches. "You've definitely broken it. But I don't see any tendon damage, which means you may escape surgery—at least for now."

She makes some notes in his chart. "We're going to put you in an air cast because of the swelling. I want you to wear it even to bed, and wrap it in plastic to take a shower." She reaches behind me for a pamphlet. "Here's how you manage it. I'd like to see you back in a few days."

I nod.

"I have fifty people coming out to my ranch this weekend, and it's been planned for several months," Landon says.

She thinks for a moment. "It can wait until after Labor Day, and I'll make you a deal. I do house calls. I can come to you on Tuesday, after Labor Day."

"Sounds great."

"Stay off the fat-tire bike for a while," Dr. Whitefeather warns.

"I promise."

I step out and call Frank. "No surgery," I tell him. "We should be out in an hour or so. They're putting him in an air cast."

"Molly and I are in the waiting room."

"Here in the hospital?"

"Yes, and Molly has dinner for the two of you when you're ready."

My heart melts. "I'm so glad. I'm starving, and she was teasing us all day with her pot roast smells."

"Let us know, and we'll pull the Range Rover up when you're ready."

"Thanks."

I return to the room, and the doctor is working with a casting technician to fit the air cast.

She turns to me. "He needs to keep it elevated for the next three days and ice it down to help with swelling. Don't let him take the cast off for any reason. The bone will not heal correctly and will require surgery if he's not diligent."

She turns to Landon. "You understand?"

"I don't want surgery. The cast is to remain on always."

She signs some paperwork and heads out the door. "I'll be in touch about seeing you after Labor Day."

"Molly and Frank are in the waiting room, and Molly brought dinner."

Landon looks up to the fluorescent lights. "Thank the maker. I'm starving."

I kiss his forehead. "Me, too."

I call Frank to let him know we're on the way as I wheel Landon down the hall.

When we arrive in the waiting area, Frank is gone, but Molly is standing with a picnic basket.

"Thank goodness you're alright." She gives Landon a

hug. "I heard about the grizzly."

She winks at him, and I know it's going to be okay.

CHAPTER 30

Landon

I'm stuck in a chair with an ottoman and my foot up. The first time I tried to get up to go to the bathroom, both Tinsley and Molly were all over me. Now, I'm much better on my crutches after two solid days of practice.

Claire is our first arrival for Labor Day weekend later today. Tinsley is excited to have her here, and I am too—but also apprehensive. I know Tinsley had to tell Claire about the accident to get my medical information, but Claire told everyone, and then the text messages started. *Giant eye roll.*

Jackson: A grizzly bear? Your woman had better know how lucky she is.

Trust me, I know I'm the lucky one.

Mason: Nature is not your thing. Time to lose the ranch to me.

No way, I'm beginning to like it here. I'm staying put.

Mia: You do know the grizzlies aren't in that part of the ranch because there's no food source, right?

Hopefully, Mia will keep that little tidbit to herself.

Walker: Shall I bring a nurse to push your lazy ass around so you can keep up with us?

Me: Don't you worry, I'm fast on my crutches, and I can still beat you at poker with my broken ankle. You wait.

Like it's going to be difficult to beat him? Ha!

Viviana: Make sure you can get it up to play.

Viviana brought a guest to Maui. We've gotten together at these events in the past. I hope it's not too awkward this time around. A lot has changed for me.

Jonathan: None of my team can explore. I don't have enough workers comp to cover bear maulings.

Maybe we should order more satellite phones, now that I think about it.

Christopher: Your face is too ugly for a bear to chase.

Me: The bear wasn't looking at my face. She saw my big dick and ran away, asshole.

Take that, pretty boy.

Tinsley has spent the last couple days working hard, and she's planning on showing Mason an update to the software once he arrives. She's cleared her workspace and moved it to the bedroom we've been sharing for the last few weeks.

Molly has spit-shined the entire house. There isn't a hair out of place, and she's ready for the arrivals.

When we hear the rumble of the plane coming in, Frank drives down to the runway. He returns a little while later with Claire, Jim, and his security team. Frank and the ranch hands are unloading the equipment they've brought with them, and I hobble over to greet everyone.

Claire rushes into my arms. "Landon!"

"Claire-bear!"

When she lets me go, she eyes my cast and crutches. "No one can sign that thing," she says, disappointed.

"I'm okay with that," I tell her with a chuckle.

"I brought all sorts of pens so people could sign it, and then when it came off, I thought we might auction it off to someone with far too much money for charity."

"It tends to stink when he takes it off," Tinsley warns as she arrives.

"Tinsley!" cries Claire, rushing to her.

The girls wander off, leaving me with Jim and his team. "You guys know where to set up?"

"Definitely. We've been here before, as Mia allowed us to use this spot when I needed to hide someone. We'd love to continue that agreement, if you're up for it."

"I don't know why that would be a problem," I tell him. "Let's talk about it after this is all over, and you can explain to me what you need."

"Great. And by the way, I heard you were protecting Tinsley from a bear?"

I nod, waiting to hear him tell me there are no bears in the area, but he just shakes his head. I shrug.

He grins, and his smile is wide. It'll be one of our many secrets.

I hear the next plane approaching already. Arrivals will

continue throughout the day and into tomorrow. Several people are coming together, which will save Frank a few trips down to the runway, not to mention saving the environment.

A few hours later, a party is starting to take shape as a few more guests have trickled in.

"Do you guys have some time before everyone arrives?" Jim inquires.

Claire, Tinsley, and I join him in the living room, previously Fiona's "office." He walks us through the updates from his team.

"Gage tells me they've wiped the new routers at your office, and they believe they've finally got it figured out. We can't exactly determine what's setting it off, but they think the spyware's a trojan horse that could have been attached to anything."

"Do you know who's behind it?" I wish he'd say Mattis Yung was working for Morgan Bennett, so I could go kick his ass.

"Not yet," Jim says. "We know generally where the information was supposed to be going, but we're not sure who would have collected Tinsley's code, because she couldn't get on the network. And bottom line, we still believe your information is safe and didn't get transmitted."

"How do we know they won't be right back at it another way once we finally get this cleared?" Claire asks.

Jim nods. "That's a great question. Gage and his team have replaced all the routers, and one file at a time, they've moved everything to a different cloud account, making sure to clear it of any cookies that could be carrying the trojan horse. We've installed a sniffer that hopefully won't slow everything down but will be an invisible wall to your internal staff."

"Does that mean no working on a network outside the office?"

"I think, for now, that's a good idea. It's your call, but your work is almost complete, and none of the staff should work in a coffee shop or their home because we can't be sure they won't get the trojan horse by accepting the terms of service for a public Wi-Fi system or opening an email."

"Do you have any updates on Tomas Vigil?" I ask. "Is he stalking the team?"

Tinsley suddenly stands. "Oh my God. I'll be right back."

We all stop, a bit stunned by her reaction.

In a few short moments, she returns with her laptop. "I totally forgot."

She offers no further information, but clicks through her email and plugs her laptop into Fiona's screen.

"I got these pictures from my friend from college, Dana, right when you were heading into the hospital. With all the commotion, I forgot and never looked at them."

We watch as she opens the attachments. They're screenshots of a PeopleMover private group page. The first is the list of the group's twenty members.

"I think most of these guys are working around the Valley," she notes.

Tinsley moves to a screenshot of the announcement about her selling to us. The comments are full of haters. Wow.

They only bought her company because she's a woman.

She's getting on her knees for Landon Walsh. I've had that pussy. It was cold fish.

The cunt doesn't have an original idea in that empty head of hers.

I bet her family is behind the purchase, so she looks good to their friends.

Tinsley is frozen. Claire moves to the computer and navigates to the next screengrab. It's a picture of us at the bar with Tomas, posted by Tomas. *She thinks she's a Stacy when she's actually a Becky*, he wrote.

"What are Stacy and Becky?" Claire asks.

Tinsley shakes her head, looking a little pale. "Stacys are attractive women who reject men for sex or are involved with someone else. Beckys are women too ugly to have sex with. It's incel language."

"You're definitely a Stacy. Fuck them." I reach for her hand.

Tinsley's hand goes to her mouth as she reads the vitriol in the posts. Tears glisten in her eyes, and I stand, wincing at my ankle, and pull her in. "These guys are assholes. Don't pay them any attention."

"They have images of every interaction I've had with Tomas, and they're saying horrible things. What did I ever do to any of them?"

Claire joins our hug. "You were successful. They can't take anything away from that."

This is supposed to be a fun weekend, and it's starting with tears. I want to rip Tomas Vigil's dick off. He's an involuntary celibate because he has a shitty idea, and he's disrespectful to women.

"This behavior isn't because you did anything other than work hard," Jim says. "But it does raise some questions about your vulnerability for a while. You can see here…" Jim points to a post titled *Where's Tinsley Pratt the Spoiled Brat?* "They don't know where you are. Hopefully, they've used the time while you've been away to focus on someone else. Regardless, when you return to San Francisco, for all public events, and possibly even other activities, you'll need to go with a team — more than only Yolanda — at least until we have a better feel for the risk."

Tinsley's weight shifts, and I'm afraid she's going to fall to the floor.

"It's nothing you need to worry about this weekend," I assure her. "And we'll figure out a plan for when we return."

"Tinsley, may I forward this email to myself and a few people on my team?" Jim asks. "I'd like to investigate a few things, and now that we've identified the group members, we might be able to get in through a backdoor with some help from people we know at the FBI and PeopleMover."

Tinsley nods.

"I think we need a glass of wine. How does that sound?" Claire suggests.

"I know I need a drink, but I want something stronger," I add. "Would you like a glass of bourbon, or should we get out the tequila and some shot glasses?"

Tinsley smiles, and I know we're going to find our way out of this mess. I just wish I was a little more mobile.

"Since everyone is arriving, we should take it slow," Tinsley says. Always practical. "Can you guys do me a favor?"

Jim, Claire, and I all look at her.

"Can we not tell anyone about this?" she implores.

Jim smiles. "I will promise not to tell, but I know everyone coming today, and I promise you'd find an enormous amount of support if you decided to share. Unfortunately, several of them have experienced some similar situations."

"But you won't say anything and let me say it if I feel it's right?" she confirms.

Jim crosses his heart and holds up a three-finger Boy Scout salute.

Claire and I do the same. I lean down and kiss Tinsley's head.

CHAPTER 31

Tinsley

The next day, I'm still feeling twinges of embarrassment and pain. It was hard to see those pictures and postings from men I respected and liked. I know I was red as a stop sign and radiated heat like a hot pan. No one could miss how I was feeling.

The memory will be seared into my brain forever, ready to pop up and torment me when I'm in a quiet moment.

I'm not aware of anything I've done to merit this level of hatred and contempt. I've just worked hard. I'm also kicking myself for forgetting about the email and not looking at those attachments before I opened them in front of everyone.

"Hello?" rings out from the other room, breaking me out of my thoughts. It's Caroline.

I jump up from my spot in the living room and head for the door. "Hi! Welcome to Montana and the Magnolia Homestead ranch."

We embrace.

"I need a stiff drink after that ride in," she says. "It was a bit bumpy there at the end, and you know these private planes are the most dangerous of all."

Molly appears to meet our needs, and a few minutes later, with drinks in hand, the ladies and I are sitting on the back porch in rocking chairs. Our view is the lush green mountain base.

"Ahhh. This is exactly what I needed," Caroline sighs.

"Agreed," Claire exclaims.

Caroline eyes me over her glass. "What has you so stressed? Is your software going left when you want it to go right?"

I bite back the tears. I don't want to go into any of this right now. With Chrissy, I'm safe, but she's not here. But I can't ignore her question. "No, I recently found out some of my friends are not my friends."

Caroline rocks in her chair. "The first year you have money is always the hardest. People you thought were your friends want to see you do well, only not better than they're doing. It's jealousy at its core. I know it sounds flippant for me to say you'll learn to ignore them, but you will."

I figure if anyone has dealt with this, Caroline Arnault has. She's been in the gossip rags since I was in elementary school.

I decide I can trust her. "There's a PeopleMover group that many of the people I went to grad school with are —"

"They're a bunch of incels, so they don't want to see any female be successful," Claire interjects.

Caroline nods. "You do have the disadvantage of technology being so dominated by emotionally stunted men. But it's jealousy. They aren't going to be happy for you, because they aren't happy for themselves."

I roll that over in my brain. *They're a bunch of unhappy people.* "Thank you. That helps me put their crap in perspective."

"I dealt with the same thing while I was in school. Mean girls ran amok. But I had two friends, who are still among my closest friends today. I'd be lost without them. Look for those of us who are happy for your success, and after a while, you'll find a great support system. No one can manage everything alone. It's that village thing."

I smile. "Thank you." And now we need to move on. I don't want to dwell on a bunch of idiots who, no matter what I do, won't like me. That's their problem, not mine. "What do you do while Mason plays poker?" I ask her.

"I saw all the activities, and some I'll want to do with Mason after he loses, but until that happens, I tend to stick close — with one eye on the game, the other on relaxing."

"You don't expect him to win?"

"Honestly, I don't think *he* ever expects to win. He's competitive, but not when it comes to this. This is about hanging out with his friends outside of Silicon Valley and letting his hair down. It's good for him."

"You both travel in different circles than I do," I tell them. "I'm worried about people who know me. You have people who *think* they know you to worry about."

Caroline shrugs. "I pushed Mason away for a long time, worried the baggage that came with my family name was too much. But he was persistent."

"I don't even want to think about men right now." Claire fills us in on Nick, her latest relationship failure.

"I know someone perfect for you," Caroline assures her. "I'm working on it. Please be a little patient with me. And you…" She turns to me. "How are things going with Landy? That boy has it bad for you."

I blush and shrug noncommittally. "We're stuck together here, trying to finish up this software."

"How did he actually break his ankle?" she asks, an eyebrow raised. "Was it some fancy sex move?"

"Oh my God, don't answer that!" Claire covers her eyes and ears. "I don't want to know what my brother does."

We all giggle.

"What's so funny?" Landon crutches in with Mason behind him, holding his drink.

"I want the real story about how you broke your ankle," Caroline says. "I think it was some fancy sex move with Tinsley."

"How did you know?" Landon teases.

"I have stories—"

"Not with me," Mason quickly interjects.

Caroline shuts her mouth and grins while Mason blushes. It's rather cute and definitely funny.

I hear the roar of a plane coming in. "Who's due to arrive next?"

"Walker Clifton is flying in with a guest, along with Mia and her latest," Landon says.

"Who's she seeing?" Caroline's interest is piqued.

"His name is Quinton O'Hara, and he's out of Austin. They went to CalTech together. He's substituting in to play for Christopher Reinhardt, who can't make it this weekend."

It isn't long before the house is overflowing with people. Everyone's in jeans, new western shirts, and cowboy boots that haven't been broken in. I chuckle. It's out of respect that these people want to blend in rather than stick out.

Of course, Viviana's red and black boots with sparkles don't exactly scream *Montana*.

CHAPTER 32

Tinsley

When Fiona decided to stay until the poker weekend, I was sure she'd come to Montana for Landon, and I mean romantically for him. But now that I've seen them interact, I know she has no interest in him beyond his legal needs. We asked her to stay here to work through the weekend in case something happened with the investigation.

"It's slow in San Francisco anyway," she declared.

While we're waiting for our massages on Saturday morning, I turn to her. "Do you think Landon is going to get out of this mess with Heather McCoy unscathed?"

"I guess it depends on how you define *unscathed*. He's already taken quite a bit of heat for it. And Landon's crazy about you. If you walk away, despite him being exonerated, he's not unscathed."

What does she know that I don't?

"But I think it's going to be difficult for them to pin this on him," she continues. "If Robards is persistent, my next step is to go to the media and put pressure on his bosses, and I'm sure they know that."

I nod. That's what I'm looking to hear.

"How do you feel about all of this?" she asks.

I shrug. "There's been so much going on, but I've tried to be supportive of Landon."

"What's been going on?" she asks.

"You don't want to know."

"Actually, I do. The more information I have, the better. What if something troubling you factors in to what's going on with Landon?"

I chuckle. "Then they knew we were going to join forces long before we did." I walk her through everything with Tomas and the Stanford crew, and eventually we're called into the massage room.

Fiona continues to ask questions intermittently. She's not relaxing, and her masseuse tells her as much.

She finally stops talking, and as the room falls silent, I begin to let these problems go and focus on the fun of this weekend. We have the western dinner and a show tonight, and I may also try to offer Landon some therapy, so he's relaxed for his game tomorrow.

Claire and Corrine rotate into the massage room as we finish up and move over to the pedicure chairs.

I'm about to drift off to sleep when Fiona asks, "Do you know if Jim and his team have had any luck breaking into the closed group on PeopleMover yet?"

I shrug. "I don't know. I think he's been working on it, and I got him some additional information yesterday."

We walk back in our sandals, and Fiona grabs me by the hand as we enter the house. She leads us back to the security room.

I'm a bit stunned when we walk in. The room has become a network operation center. I look at the wall of monitors and see feeds from all over the property and throughout the hallways in the house.

"Do you have cameras in the rooms?" I ask, feeling mildly panicked.

Gage laughs. "No, you're safe. Although rumor has it, you guys had a serious sex swing going, which is what broke Landon's ankle."

Jim looks at him, and he shrivels.

"Nope, I pushed him off a rock."

Jim smiles.

"Have you had any luck getting into the private group that's targeting Tinsley?" Fiona asks.

"We're trying, but currently struggling with that," Jim says.

Fiona pulls her cell phone from her back pocket. She scrolls through her list of contacts and pushes a button. I can hear the phone ringing.

"Hey, Steve," she says after a moment in a low, seductive voice. "Yes, it's me. I have a client being harassed by a group of men in a private group."

She listens for a few minutes.

"No, I don't think we want to close them down yet. I was wondering what I'd need to do to get you to let us poke around the group and their chats?"

She's quiet a moment.

"I think that's doable. I'm in Montana for the weekend. I should be home Tuesday night. Would that work?"

She listens.

Fiona looks at me. "The name of the group is the Stanford Octagon."

She makes a motion to Jim for a pen and something to write on.

"Okay, see you Tuesday. Make sure you bring the toys."

She disconnects the call and looks at me. "My friend is head of security for PeopleMover, and we're both into a bit of kink. It works well both ways for us."

I seem to be the only one surprised by this, so

obviously I'm the only one who didn't know.

She hands Gage the passwords. "We need to get in before they realize the group's been breached. Steve thinks they have a tertiary group that's even smaller and darker."

Gage opens the group and begins to scroll.

"Are you able to capture all of this?" Jim asks.

"Yes, I'm copying as we go," Gage responds.

"Great. We'll need copies of all the linked video if we can get them before they shut those down."

"They won't know you're here," Fiona says.

"But they will, and they'll shut down."

"The pass I gave you should be invisible unless you announce yourself. But before you get too excited, the password only works for this group."

"This is all we're looking for?" Gage asks as he works his way through the pages.

I pull my phone out and begin searching the members of the group on the Stanford alumni page, writing down what they're doing and where they're working. I stop short when I come to Tomas Vigil's name. "That can't be," I mutter.

"What?" Jim looks at me, alarmed.

I show him what's on my phone, and he looks at me with his brow raised.

"This says Tomas is working in internet security," I report. "Though I've never heard of this company... He could be the person behind at least some of our problems."

That evening, everyone is dressed in their finest western wear, and we have a fantastic time enjoying Molly's feast. I'm sure I've gained fifty pounds from all the fabulous food I've consumed. I'm stuffed.

Then Molly and her brothers pull out their fiddles for a good, old fashioned hoedown.

What a blast.

Molly's helpers teach us to line dance, and it's the first time all day that I'm able to put the mess with the Stanford Octagon out of my head.

As the evening winds down, Landon gets up on his crutches to dance with me — mostly just swaying back and forth.

"Thank you." I kiss him softly on the lips.

"It's you I should be thanking."

The crowd begins to dissipate. The poker games start tomorrow, and they're throwing relentless shade at each other, but it's all in fun. I like Landon's friends.

"Shall we go upstairs? I think you might need some therapy."

"I thought you'd never ask."

CHAPTER 33

Landon

Waking up with Tinsley in my arms feels right. I know the last few days have been trying for her. Finding out people you know and might have considered friends have gone out of their way to belittle you and your accomplishments is a tough nut to swallow.

Tinsley. She's everything I never thought I'd find. Perfect in every way. But what I find most attractive is how her brain works. She's more than smart. She's brilliant, and seeing her move intuitively through the Java development to build our new software has been jaw-dropping.

The fact that she shares my bed makes me the luckiest man alive.

I hurt her, and I know she doesn't fully trust me yet, but when we return to San Francisco, I want her to move in with me — and not because of the security she needs, but because I sleep better with her cuddled up beside me. We love each other, and I know together we can get through anything.

She's so peaceful as she sleeps. She nuzzles in close, and that always seems to calm me — even when my life is spinning out of control. I think I do the same for her. Or at least I want to. I'll never disappear on her like I did again. It's as if we're different sides of a coin that took a while to find each other and stick together.

I watch as the sun comes up and washes over her. I pick up a pillow, trying to shade her face from the direct sunlight. We need to be better about closing the curtains so we can sleep in.

"Why are you moving so much?" she mumbles with her eyes closed.

"Sorry, babe." I kiss her forehead.

She rolls on to her back and throws her arm over her eyes. "We forgot to shut the blackout blinds again last night."

"I'm sorry." I reach for her breast. "I was distracted by your beauty."

She lifts her arm and gives me a side-eye. She has to feel my morning wood pressing against her hip. I palm her nipples to hardness before rolling them between my finger and thumb. Her body goes stiff as she gasps. I pull and twist.

"Do you need more therapy this morning?" she moans.

"I do," I whisper as I bite her shoulder.

We spend the early morning having slow, leisurely sex as we prepare for the game this afternoon. I'm centered and calm. I have the confidence I need to win.

With Tinsley satiated and splayed across me, I figure it's time to talk about the future. "We'll probably go back to San Francisco this week," I tell her. "Time to get back to reality."

"I know. Everything is going to change." I hear sadness in her voice.

"What do you think will change?"

"No more of this." She caresses my soft cock.

My heart begins to race. "Why not? I was hoping you'd move back into my apartment — and my bedroom."

Tinsley sits up and gathers the sheets around her. Her eyes narrow.

I hold up my hand. "I don't want a fight. We love each other. You made it clear you don't want to get married, but are you okay with living together?"

Her brows crease, and her anger seems to dissipate. "I *don't* want to marry. It's a stupid piece of paper. We can sign a medical power of attorney and —"

"Alright, but I thought we could take this in baby steps. You move in, or we can find somewhere else to live, we live together for a while, and when we both believe it's right, we'll make a commitment to one another."

Tinsley jumps out of bed. "How can you say that?"

I take a deep breath, because I'm not sure where I've gone wrong. "Look, we don't have to discuss this right now. But given the requirement that you have twenty-four/seven security coverage, at least for the time being, why don't you stay with me? I'd love it if we were together in the master bedroom, but I understand if you'd prefer to stay in the guest room and leave me with the worst case of blue balls ever seen. I mean, they'd be massive." I kiss her softly on her lips. "But only you will have access to them."

Tinsley's shoulders drop. "I don't know what I want." She sighs.

"We don't have to decide right now. I swear, I don't have the medical power of attorney in my back pocket."

"You're not wearing pants," she points out.

I look down, and my erection is back. "No, I most certainly am not."

I roll her on her back and cuddle in close. "What I'm trying to say is I love waking up to you, and I've been hoping I might continue to do that when we return to San Francisco."

"We'll talk about it after you win the tournament. If you lose, it's a nonstarter." Tinsley wiggles her eyebrows and runs to the bathroom.

I jump out of bed and hobble behind her. "After the

therapy you gave me last night, I'm going to win this thing."

"Good, because I want to go up to Whistler this winter."

"We always close the company between Christmas and New Year's," I tell her. "We can invite your mom and her boyfriend, plus Claire and my parents."

As Tinsley steps into the shower, she looks over her shoulder. "I guess you'd better win."

Even after our leisurely morning, we're among the first to the breakfast buffet.

"This smells fantastic." Tinsley opens the various chafing dishes and peeks at the contents. "Molly, did you sleep at all after that huge dinner you made last night?"

"Of course I did." She blushes. "I didn't even get up as early as you think. Jeannine, Jimmy's wife, Dolores, and my friend Margie all were here at six. We had the ovens going here and in two different guesthouses. It's what we do, and the ladies love the extra cash, so they're great with getting everything ready."

"I agree. This is incredible." I see scrambled eggs, bacon, sausage, ham, biscuits, sausage gravy, pancakes, and a frittata.

"What can I get you both to drink?" Molly asks. "There's juice at the end of the table—including fresh pineapple juice from Jackson Graham's estate in Maui—and I have drip coffee and hot water for tea, but I'm happy to make any espresso drink."

"Tea is perfect for me," Tinsley responds.

"I'm good with pineapple juice, and the drip coffee is fine. Have you and Frank eaten?" I ask.

"We're fine."

I hear the shuffle of slippers behind me.

"Good morning." Claire rubs the sleep from her eyes. She's dressed, and her dark hair is pulled into a bun.

"Good morning. How did you sleep last night?" Tinsley asks.

"Fine. It's a little quiet here."

"It does take some adjustment," I agree.

"What can I get you to drink?" Molly asks while I hand her a warm plate.

"Can I have a nonfat latte?"

While Molly gets Claire her drink, I grab a pitcher and begin filling it with pineapple juice.

"What are you doing?" Tinsley asks in a low whisper.

"Saving this for later. I don't want to share it."

Tinsley shakes her head.

I store the pitcher behind a plant in the dining room. Soon most of the guests have wandered in, and we're all making plans. We have a good part of the day before we meet in the barn for the tournament at one.

I relax and enjoy watching people wander around. After a while, I've stored five pitchers of pineapple juice around the downstairs.

"Who drank all the pineapple juice?" Jackson asks. "I didn't even get any."

"It was fantastic, but I was one of the first this morning," I say with a shrug.

"Lelani sent over five gallons. I thought that would be enough for the weekend."

I'm trying so hard to hide my smile. "It was pretty damn good. Guess I wasn't the only one who thought so."

Jackson walks off, clearly puzzled, and I'm holding back the giggles.

"You're bad." Molly gives me a look. I don't get much past her.

"We give each other a hard time. It's all about the mental game that comes with our tournament," I tell her. "I have to throw him off. When he was getting serious with

Corrine, I asked him if I could ask her out while we were on a phone call. If I'd asked him in person, I'm sure he would have punched me."

"What's he done to you?" Molly asks.

"When we were getting ready for the final round in Las Vegas, he asked me to throw in my interest in the apartment building I own in San Francisco because he thought it could use some changes in design. I was in the zone, and that comment distracted me long enough to knock me out. He beat Viviana for her estate in Hawaii, and I wanted it."

Tinsley shakes her head. "You guys need to find other people to play with."

"Nah, this is fun."

At one o'clock, when we're finally ready to start, Gillian gathers us together and reminds us of the rules. "I will pull the names from the hat to determine where you will sit," she says. "Today, the cost per hand is five hundred thousand. We'll play until we have six players for tomorrow night. And the winner takes all."

My table includes Walker and Mason, who I see as my biggest competitors, though I know both Mia and Viviana, who fill the other seats, are tough as well.

The play plods along. Everyone is conservative. Everyone wants to win.

Dinner and snacks are served, and we've still not lost any players. The sun sets, and spectators come and go. After we've been playing for ten hours, Nate goes all in and busts. Finally, we've lost the first player.

We continue to hold steady for another couple hours, and then during a bio-break, Gillian pulls me aside.

"Do you want to keep going?" she asks.

I shrug. "What do you think? Everyone is playing it

safe."

"We can pick it up tomorrow earlier than we planned and play through, but my dealers are dead on their feet. I suggest we go another hour at most."

I nod. We've played for twelve hours, and we're only down to eleven players. "Let's call it now."

When she makes the announcement, everyone seems grateful. We agree to reconvene tomorrow.

Since we were a bigger group than usual for day two, we started before lunch. It's been a long and grueling day, as we've now played through dinner, and the sky is black outside. It's finally down to Walker Clifton and me. Walker is a shrewd player. Rumor has it, he's going to run for governor in the next election, with eyes on 1600 Pennsylvania Avenue. He's from an old San Francisco mining family whose money started with gold and moved into property. They own most of the Nob Hill and Pacific Heights neighborhoods' retail property and multiple apartment units.

He's a nice-enough guy. He brought a date this weekend, but she's more interested in him than he seems to be in her. There's pressure here to bring someone along, so I get it. You don't want to be the only one at the dinner table without a date.

We've been playing now for twelve hours after playing twelve yesterday. The flop shows several face cards, but it also completes a full house for me — a pair of aces and three sevens. Seven is my lucky number. Two hands can beat me at this point: a straight flush and a four of a kind. I calculate in my head the probability of him having either one. Walker isn't a mathematician, so I believe I have him beat that way. But he's a big-time lawyer who's gone up against some serious criminals, so he's the master at disguising his emotions.

I shuffle my chips as a way to fight sleep.

I don't think he can beat me. He has a higher chip count, so I throw in the chalet in Whistler. "I'm all in."

Everyone is in the barn, and they're practically breathing as one. They know this is the hand that will crown winner and all the bragging rights.

He calls.

I'm feeling pretty good.

I turn my full house over and watch him carefully. Walker smirks, and immediately I know he has me beat.

He turns over four twos. A four of a kind beats my full house.

"No fucking way!" I laugh and shake my head. He didn't have it until the flop when the dealer put down the king of diamonds and the two of spades.

The barn erupts.

I can't believe I just lost with the best hand I had the entire tournament.

Walker stands and shakes my hand. "That was fantastic. You should have beaten me."

"I know!" But surprisingly, I'm not disappointed. This was a great weekend. Tinsley is standing next to me, and she gives me a giant hug and kiss. I couldn't be happier.

We all celebrate and pass the torch to Walker for our next gathering in Whistler.

"It's not big enough for everyone to stay," I warn, "but it can host a party, and the Four Seasons is close by. Whistler will open for ski season at the end of November, so I suggest early December for our next tournament—if that works for Walker, of course."

He nods, and everyone is quick to agree.

The planes begin arriving shortly after eleven on Labor

Day to shuttle our guests to their next destination. We're all a bit tired since last night's marathon game ended so late. A few have made plans for stops on their way home. Mason and Caroline have helicoptered into Yellowstone and are spending a few days at the Lake Yellowstone Hotel and exploring.

Claire catches a ride back with Mia. They're taking some sort of detour to go shopping. She told me what she was doing, but I wasn't paying attention.

Jim and his team are beginning to wrap up. He's going to fly out with our personal team, Tinsley, and me, after I see Dr. Whitefeather tomorrow to get my release to my doctor in San Francisco. I'm going to miss it here, and I'm already trying to figure out when I can come back. But it's time to be home in San Francisco.

CHAPTER 34

Landon

We're mid-air on the way home when Jim's phone rings.

"Okay, I understand," he says. He listens a moment. "Yes. Fiona is with me, and we're an hour out. Find out where they're taking him. What does the media look like?"

Everyone stops and tries to hear the conversation.

Jim ignores us and stares at the carpeting on the floor. I can't follow what he's saying. Fiona has moved to the seat next to him, my guess is to hear his part of the conversation over the jet engines.

Jim looks at his watch. "We land in about an hour. Keep me posted." He hangs up.

Fiona looks at him, waiting.

"Nate was arrested when he landed."

"What? Why?" Tinsley asks.

"He was arrested for the murder of his wife last October." Jim looks at Fiona.

They seem to know something we don't.

I sit back hard in my chair. We had a great time with Nate in Montana. Whenever his foundation or Cecelia was mentioned, a dark cloud covered his face. I know he still hurts when it comes to his wife. They were an incredible team together. The Las Vegas PD is in a cluster, and I guess they just decided they needed to make an arrest.

Nate mentioned over Memorial Day weekend that he was a suspect. But we were all suspects—everyone who was together when she disappeared. No way he was involved in her death. They had a special kind of love that blooms from shared experiences, trust, and understanding. I was also with him when he learned Cecelia was missing, and I would have bet my last dollar he was devastated and surprised.

I play poker with that man. I know his tells. It broke him when they couldn't find her, and *devastated* doesn't even come close to describing him after he learned she'd been murdered.

Why would they think he had anything to do with it? "Holy crap," I breathe.

Jim bounces from phone call to phone call for the remainder of the flight, and Fiona does the same. I learn that the police surrounded the plane when they landed. Jackson Graham and his girlfriend, Corrine, as well as Viviana and her date were there.

"Damn it. All they needed to do was ask to speak with him, and we would have made him available," Fiona screams into her phone. "This is a publicity stunt for the stupid cunt mayor. God damn it. Totally unnecessary. I'm going to make it my job to see that she suffers. Nate and I and everyone we know will be donating to her opponent in the next election, and I will run a PR campaign that shows her to be the self-serving idiot she is for trying this stunt to hang this on Nate Lancaster."

I've seen Fiona mad. Most of the time, that anger is focused on me. Though I also saw her upset dealing with a less-than-scrupulous immigration officer. She went to town on him, and he lost his job, but this is as angry as I've ever seen her. A part of me almost feels sorry for the Las Vegas mayor and police department.

Tinsley gets up and brings her some golden liquid in a glass.

Fiona looks at her gratefully. "I shouldn't…" She reaches for the glass. "…given what I'm walking into, but thank you. I'm absolutely helpless here on the plane."

Fiona downs the drink.

"Would you like another one?" Tinsley asks.

"Yes."

Tinsley stands, but Fiona reaches for her arm.

"But I won't. When this happened, I planned for this scenario and several others. We knew he'd be the number-one suspect after it happened. Honestly, we expected this in February. Not almost a year later."

"Why would they suspect him? He adored Cecelia," I implore.

Fiona knows whatever she tells me is violating confidentiality, but she must figure it's going to come out with the arrest, because after a moment she sighs. "The Mayor has set up a press conference once they secure his transfer from San Francisco to Las Vegas. Cecelia moved a large amount of money out of their account, and they've asserted that she was preparing to divorce him."

"Where did she move it?" Tinsley asks.

Jim shakes his head. "We're not sure. We can't figure out where the money went. It bounced offshore and through several banks without any ability for us to follow it."

My phone pings.

Jackson: Let Fiona know I'm sending over my criminal attorney, Damien Lewis. He's good and helped me when LVPD came knocking. He'll irritate the crap out of them until she can get there.

I pass the message on to Fiona.

She nods. "I've heard of Damien. He's over at Colfax Day, and he's good. He was on our shortlist. Knowing he's already dealt with the Las Vegas Police on this matter makes it even better. Tell him we need to know where they're taking him. Nate's arraignment is going to be a circus. I'll make plans for the getaway."

I relay the information to Jackson.

Fiona has her phone to her ear. "Damien and I may need to get to Vegas. After you guys drop me, can we hitch a ride? If their plan is to extradite him to Vegas tonight, I need to be there. "

I nod. "That's not an issue. Do what you need to do."

Fiona's fingers fly over the keyboard on her phone. As we come into our final approach at the airport, I see easily twenty police cars below, with lights flashing.

"Are they still dealing with Nate at the airport? I would've thought he'd be long gone by now."

Fiona reaches over me to look out the window. "God damn it. When it fucking rains…"

The pilot comes on the speaker. "We've been notified that we're to proceed to the private plane terminal, where they'll be arresting Mr. Walsh."

My mind shoots in a thousand directions. I had nothing to do with Cecelia's death. I know they said I left a fingerprint in her room, but I was never in their suite. "I didn't do anything." Then another thought piles on. "Is this Detective Robards again?"

"We're going to manage this." Tinsley reaches for my hand and gives it a reassuring squeeze.

Fiona gets on a call, and I hear her speaking Gaelic to someone. It sounds nothing like any language I know. When she hangs up, she writes something down and walks up to the pilots.

When she returns, she takes a deep breath. "I've asked

the pilots to land and then take us to a hangar that belongs to a friend of mine. The police will have to run after us, but that's fine. We're not trying to outrun them, but we're not letting the media make a spectacle of two of my clients today. I'll exit the plane, and you'll sit here until I call Jim. He will escort you down. Take as long as you need to come down the stairs and make them wait. You broke your ankle, after all."

"What about the press? Won't they follow the police?" Tinsley asks.

"They can't. They won't be able to access the tarmac and won't know where we're stopping the plane. They'll figure it out, but hopefully not until after you're long gone. This is how you get arrested at an airport — without the press and with dignity. And this is how we're going to knock Detective Robards' legs out from under him."

Dammit. It is Robards. "Did they find Heather McCoy?"

"Not that my contact in the DA's office was aware of this morning," Fiona says. "This is also a publicity stunt."

"If they arrest me, I won't say anything until you arrive," I assure her.

"When I spoke with the district attorney this morning, we both agreed that this was a fishing exhibition for Detective Robards. I don't think the DA knows this is going down, and I'm going to call in a good and expensive favor."

I'm not sure what that means.

Tinsley pulls her hand away from mine and stretches her fingers. I think I was squeezing too hard.

We hit the tarmac, and the police are parked where we would normally go when we land. The plane makes an early turn and drives past several access points before turning into a large hangar far away from the main private terminal.

The pilot comes to a stop, and the flight attendant opens the door and extends the stairs. I hear Fiona tell her to shut the door behind her.

The flight attendant nods and does as she asks.

Through the window, I watch Fiona descend and speak

to a large gentleman. I wonder if he's the guy she was speaking to in Gaelic. After a moment the police come blazing up with their lights and sirens. Detective Robards runs over to her. He's yelling and screaming and pointing at the plane.

Fiona puts her hands on her hips and points to the plane as well. I wish I could hear what they're saying.

Detective Robards gets right in her face, and the hair on the back of my neck stands up. Jim grips the seat in front of him, no doubt ready to jettison himself from the plane and right to her side.

The large gentleman steps between the two of them, but Robards doesn't back down. The large man points to several places in the ceiling of the hangar. I'm not clear what he's pointing to, but I hear Jim chuckle.

"He's pointing to the cameras, reminding Robards that his anger is being recorded and will most likely be shared."

Robards keeps pointing at the plane, and I'm sure he's insisting I come out and be arrested. Someone in a police uniform rushes up with a telephone. Robards snatches it and paces back and forth, his arms moving so frantically, I'm sure he's going to take flight.

Suddenly he throws the phone to the ground, and it crashes into a thousand pieces. But he's not finished. He struts over to a paint can sitting off to the side, and it's almost in slow motion as I watch him rear back and, in a perfect kick, send the can into the air. The lid spins toward Fiona, and yellow paint sprays as the can sails toward the plane and out of my sight.

Tinsley gasps. I'm not sure where it landed, but I hear something crash against the front of the plane.

"That asshole!" one of the pilots yells.

"I have a feeling someone is not going to be happy," Jim says.

The pilots swing open the cockpit door, and I can see the front window spiderwebbed and yellow paint running down the outside.

Detective Robards is now pacing back and forth, his arms flapping as he yells, his face so red it looks almost purple.

The pilots grab towels and drape them over the plane's electronics as the bright yellow paint seeps through the broken safety glass.

Jim's phone rings. I see Fiona's name on the screen. He listens a few moments. "Okay, we'll call up the car, and they'll meet you at his place."

Jim disconnects the call and looks over at us. "You both are going to Landon's with your team."

Tinsley pulls her belongings together and is ready to exit the plane with her head held high, not as if twenty people are watching.

Jim's phone pings, and a Range Rover comes up to the base of the plane. He looks at me. "We're going to exit. Some media has found us, but they're outside. We're going to walk down the stairs, and we'll get right into the Range Rover. My team will take care of your belongings. Only take your purse and wallets and anything you can't wait an hour for, but leave your computers. If they're going to try something, we don't want to give them the excuse to go through your hard drive."

Tinsley and I nod. My heart is racing, and she's taking short breaths. We line up behind the flight attendant, ready to exit.

I turn to Tinsley and paint on the best smile I have. "Ladies first."

She kisses me and mouths, "I love you."

When she's about halfway down, I hobble behind her. I spot zoom lenses, so I'm sure that they can see every pore on my face. Tinsley stands at the open door of the Range Rover and watches me awkwardly descend the stairs. I focus on her and ignore all the commotion around me. *I can do this.*

As I step off the final stair, I see a large Suburban arrive with flashing lights in its grill. Before it comes to a complete stop, a large man exits the car.

Fiona steps in and greets him. He embraces her. She points to the dent and paint all over the nose of the plane. For the first time, I turn and look at the damage. I knew the window was cracked, but there's also a dent above the nose cone and paint not only all over the plane but also the hangar. That's going to be a costly fix, and it may have totaled the plane.

Robards is done.

Detective Robards rushes over to the large man and seems to bicker with him. We're seated in the Range Rover, and one of Jim's drivers settles behind the wheel. Detective Robards isn't as aggressive with this man as he was with Fiona. He seems to be pleading his case.

Jim chuckles. "I'm delighted not to be Detective Robards right now."

"Who is that man?" Tinsley asks as we drive away.

"That is Eddy Martinez, the chief of police," Jim says. "Detective Robards has probably ended his career."

"But that doesn't mean the hunt for Heather McCoy has ended or that I'm not still the number-one suspect," I muse aloud, mostly to remind myself.

"We have some leads we're working on." Jim looks out the window as we pull onto the freeway, heading into the city.

I glance behind and see one of the police cars tailing us. "Are they going to arrest me when we get to my building?"

Jim shakes his head. "I don't think so. No one knows where Heather McCoy is. It's not even a bona fide missing person case, so hanging it around your neck seems to be more about publicity than anything else."

"I can't help but wonder why both the Las Vegas and San Francisco police were making arrests at the airport today," I note.

"I was thinking the same thing." Jim looks down at his phone.

When we arrive at my building, Jim's team takes us in through the garage, and we go directly up to my apartment. It smells a little closed up, so we open the windows to get some fresh air. Jim and his team move toward the security room. I'm not sure what they're going to do.

Before Jim goes inside, he says just above a whisper, "I need to see what's going on with Nate. I'll be back in a bit. Your belongings will arrive shortly, but try not to go anywhere. If you do feel the need to get out, take two members of your team with you. They'll be in the security room and have access."

I extend my hand to shake Jim's.

"After I get these guys settled, I'll check on my team at the office and be back shortly," he says.

He disappears behind the door to the security room, and Tinsley collapses into me. She's so strong and beautiful. I look in her big brown eyes, grateful she's here with me. "Thank you."

"For what?"

"For being here. For putting up with the chaos that is my life."

Tinsley holds me tight. "There's no place I'd rather be."

After much wrangling, Tinsley has agreed to stay here in my apartment, but I'm still nervous about my next question. "Have you decided where you want to stay? I won't lie; I want you in my bed. I've grown rather fond of taking you before I go to sleep and again in the morning." When she doesn't respond, I add, "Or I can always sneak into a guest room, if that's where you'd be most comfortable."

She grins. "Your room is closer to the pool."

Yes! I sit down on the couch and pick up the remote control. ESPN comes on, and I mute it.

"It's weird to be without my computer," Tinsley frets.

"It'll be here before too long." I smile. "I know a way to keep ourselves entertained until they arrive."

She smiles. "Really? Maybe a little therapy?"

"How did you know?" I pat my lap. "How about you take your pants off and sit on my lap."

"Leave the panties on?"

I nod. "For now," I whisper.

She looks over at the door to the security room and then to the elevator.

I pick up my phone and call Dee downstairs. "Dee, I'm home. I'm expecting someone to bring our luggage. When they arrive, can you let me know? Thanks."

Tinsley looks again at the security room door.

"Jim already told me they were going to be busy and to let him know when we need them," I tell her. "And no going out without two people." I give her a look. "Take your jeans off."

"You're so bossy."

She unbuttons her jeans and kicks off her shoes. She's wearing plain white cotton panties, which totally works for me.

"You like it when I'm bossy."

"And you like it when I'm naughty." She reaches for the hem of her Atari T-shirt and lifts her brows. I love that she's sexy, even in her software-designer uniform.

I shake my head. "You have no idea. Stop stalling and come here." I pat my lap again.

Tinsley climbs on top of me, and my fingers go to her center. Her panties are already wet. "You're so turned on."

She moves her hips over the bulge in my pants. "What are we going to do about that?"

My hands reach up into her shirt and slip inside her cotton bra. I tease and pinch her nipples. "I think I'm going to make you come twice before I fuck you in front of all the windows in my workout room where anyone can see." My pants are becoming incredibly uncomfortable as she rubs against me. There's too much fabric between us.

"I like that idea." She breathes into a kiss and moves her hips, never breaking their rhythm.

My fingers slide inside her panties and find her hard nub.

I apply a bit of pressure, and Tinsley moans. "Right there, don't stop."

I lift her shirt off and have the bra unhooked in no time. Her tits are free and bouncing in my face, the beautiful pink nipples begging to be sucked. I take one deep in my mouth while I strum her clit. Her breathing hitches, so I know she's close. I plunge one finger inside her and then two.

Tinsley grinds her pussy on my hand and throws her head back. Three fingers stroke her deep inside, while I apply firm pressure to her clit. The contractions create an explosion of wetness on my hand.

I roll her off my lap and onto her back beside me on the couch. I tear her panties off and dive in — licking, nibbling, and sucking in all of her juices until she comes again.

As she eases down from her blissful state, my cock is hard and ready. Tinsley reaches for it. "What's easiest for you?"

I lead her by the hand out to my workout room. Moving a sturdy chair to the center window, I push the seat up against the glass. She holds on to the back of the chair, and I bend her over at the waist. My pants are half off, and my dick is in my hand. She's so wet that in one hard thrust, I'm balls deep into her.

Tinsley groans and pushes back. "I want it hard and fast," she pants.

I won't last long, but I don't care. I pound her from behind, overlooking the Bay Bridge, Treasure Island, and the traffic leaving the city below. Tinsley clamps tight on my cock, and I can't move. She screams out my name, and the vice of her channel milks my cock of all its seed.

Breathing hard, she pushes herself to stand. My cock moves to a semi-hard state as I watch our bliss ooze down her leg. I have no doubt in the world that I love this woman.

The house phone rings, and I know it's Dee letting me know Jim's team has arrived with our gear.

"How about you go take a shower? I'll get our luggage

taken care of. Are you okay staying in my room, or do you want your things in the guest room?"

"I'll stay with you, but if you start to snore too loud, I'm moving back into the guest room."

I kiss her forehead. "That's fine. I don't snore."

"I'll record you."

I pat her on the derriere and walk out to the foyer, looking for Greg with my luggage.

I stop short when I see Jim and Fiona standing in my living room.

Nate's the one I thought they'd be helping right now, not me.

CHAPTER 35

Tinsley

I don't know how Landon does it, but he knows how to make my body sing. I like it when he's slow and deliberate, but I also like it when he's fast and hard. I know we have a lot of stuff to work out, but I think we can do it. And that's a huge relief. Because I need to focus and get this software over the finish line.

I don't have a lot of clothes here, and I don't want to prance around naked with Jim's team delivering our stuff, so I pull a pair of his sweatpants from his drawer. They're giant on me, so I roll them at the waist and have a giant roll around my middle. I pull on one courtnayof his button-down shirts, and it hits me well below the ass. I'm drowning in his clothes, but I smell him on me, and I love it.

On my way to find out where my clothes and belongings are, I see the pool. I need to get in there to work out the kinks in my back and neck. I've missed that pool.

Through the glass, I spot Fiona and Jim in the living

room. I can't hear them, but I see that they're talking. Fiona spots me and nods since I'm to Landon's back.

He turns around as I approach. "Hey."

"What's going on?"

He takes a deep breath. "The FBI has gotten involved. That's good news because they're less likely to want to make this about press conferences, but it's bad news because they want me to come in with an attorney. Jim has a referral for a federal litigator, and we're negotiating my surrender."

All of the blood drains from my face. "Surrender? Why?"

"They believe they have enough evidence to hold me."

"He was with me," I exclaim.

Jim steps forward. "We know. This is not fun or pretty, but we have some contacts within the FBI — and this is also under Walker Clifton's purview — so we believe we'll get a fair shake."

Landon's shoulders are rounded, and as he reaches for a glass of water, his hand has a slight tremor.

I search my brain for anything I can do to help him. I circle my arms around him and hug him tight. I know he's scared, but we're going to weather this storm. I turn to Fiona. "When does he need to go in?"

"Tomorrow morning," she remarks softly.

"Will they keep him, or will they question him and send him home?" I ask.

"We don't know," she replies.

Landon moves to the living room, sits back on the couch, and stares up at the ceiling. I sit next to him and grip his hand. Suddenly, he stands up and crosses the room to the kitchen. He opens a drawer and pulls out a blue booklet. He hands it to Fiona. "Thank you."

I cock my head, puzzled.

"In order to wait until morning, the judge required him to forfeit his passport," Fiona says.

I want to run. He has a plane. I'd get on the plane with

him and fly wherever he wants to go. I don't care that we'd be running from the law. I know in my heart of hearts, he didn't have anything to do with Heather McCoy's disappearance. What if they never leave him alone?

But in the next breath, I know facing this is the only option.

I look at Jim where he's seated on a chair. "Your best friend has been arrested for his wife's murder and now this. Where is your focus?"

Jim's face softens. "I won't deny, I'm split between the two, but I have a team standing behind me." He leans forward, his hands clasped together. "Bash Pontius and Levi Holden are working hard on this case exclusively. Right now, they're in Illinois talking to Heather's parents."

"From what I've seen, no one has searched her boyfriend's place since she went missing," Fiona adds. "SFPD has focused purely on Landon. Our hope is that giving up his passport and being on time tomorrow for questions will make him a cooperating witness."

The house phone rings, and I answer. After listening a moment, I report, "There's a Marci Peterson here to see Mr. Walsh."

Jim nods, and Fiona mouths, "That's our attorney."

"Send her up, please," I tell Dee at the desk below.

"I also have a large amount of mail here for Mr. Walsh," Dee says. "Would it be okay to send it up with Diego?"

"That would be fine. Dee, I know I'm a guest, but Mr. Walsh is distracted. Can you help me order dinner?"

"I'd be happy to."

"Do you have the last order of Chinese we made when Mr. Walsh's parents were here in May?"

I hear her flip pages. "I do." She recites the list.

"Would you reorder that? I can give you my credit card, if you prefer."

"No, Ms. Pratt. Mr. Walsh mentioned you were his

guest. We're fine."

"Thank you, Dee."

I step out of the room to call Claire and give her the update. She agrees to come right over.

When I return, I'm introduced to Marci. She's a 1950s pin-up model with short, curly, blond hair and porcelain skin.

"Hello," she says. "I'm sorry we're meeting under these circumstances."

"Nice to meet you. I've ordered Chinese for dinner. I hope that will work for everyone. Claire is also on her way."

Marci's brow furrows.

"Claire is our business partner and Landon's sister."

Relief crosses her face. "Perfect. Let's sit at the table, and we can go through everything."

Claire arrives shortly, as does our food. Marci asks questions and collects information, and then Fiona gives her everything she's shared with the San Francisco PD.

After she's organized everything, Marci nods. "So, if everything stands, we should be home by the end of the day tomorrow."

I didn't realize I was holding my breath until she said that.

"I'll meet you tomorrow morning at my office at eight," she tells Landon. "We'll make our way over to arrive at the Federal Building by eight thirty. Bring your driver's license. I'm assuming it's current with this address?"

Landon nods. "I've given Fiona my passport, but I'm still carrying my permanent resident card."

"We don't need to advertise that you're not a citizen. They already know."

Landon nods.

"Do you think there will be any press there?" Claire asks.

Marci smiles. "If there is, it's not because *they've* told anyone you're coming in."

"We're close to finishing some pretty significant

software," Claire laments. "Tinsley has a stalker. My ex-boyfriend seems to be trying to steal our work. And Jim and Fiona are busy with another client. Now we have this to deal with." She begins to cry.

I pat her on the back.

"That is a lot at one time. I'm so sorry." Marci looks down at the leather notebook in front of her. "Tinsley, tell me about your stalker."

I tell her about Tomas Vigil and the Stanford Octagon.

"Jim, what have you found out about this guy?"

Jim goes into the security room and returns with a folder over an inch thick. "Tomas went to school at Stanford. He graduated at the top of his class, but he's emotionally stunted, which is obvious from what he's said about Tinsley in the group, but I'm not sure he's an incel. Tinsley has found out that he works for an internet security company, which is a subsidiary of a subsidiary. We can't be sure exactly who he works for yet, but Gage and his team are working on it, and I'm considering having Cora Perry, head of cybercrimes at FBI Cyber, look into it."

"Okay." Marci turns to Claire. "Tell me about your ex-boyfriend."

"His name is Morgan Bennett." Claire tells her how they met, and she cries as she tells her about the plans they made and his disappearance.

When Claire's hurt and anger overtake her, I fill the gap to close the last piece of the puzzle. "She was out with friends, and they saw him on a date and confronted him. It wasn't pretty, and he said some awful things."

Marci makes a few notes in her book. "What can you tell me about Morgan Bennett?"

Jim quirks the side of his mouth. "I wish there was something to say. He's a devout bachelor. He never spends the night with anyone in his home. His company is competing with Disruptive to come up with communications software. We've been unsuccessful in linking anything directly to him."

"Why do you think he's behind it?" Marci asks.

"Tom Sutterland said both of our companies were competing for the contract with PeopleMover, and when we pinged where the spyware was coming from, it was within Bennett's building."

"His office building?"

I nod.

"Does he have the whole building?"

"No, which is what saves him right now," Jim notes. "There are thirteen tenants in the building, including a coffee shop, eight technology startups, two retail stores, a technology recruiting firm, and the final is a broker of high-end Egyptian antiquities."

"Egyptian antiquities?"

Jim nods.

"Can you give me the overview of what's going on with Nate?" Marci asks.

Jim begins, and Fiona finishes. They don't say too much more than what's been in the press.

"And you can't tell where the money Cecelia transferred went?" Marci asks.

"We can't, and I don't think the FBI can either," Jim says. "The funds went to Cypress, and we lost them when they bounced from there."

"This seems like an awful lot at one time." Marci chews on her pen. "Could this be planned?"

"I've wondered that myself," Jim agrees.

"We need to find the thread that strings everything together. Just about everyone who was there the weekend Cecelia went missing has had something troubling going on since then—the missing money for Nate, Jackson had issues with theft by a Chinese company, and now you guys have this strange set of events. It's possible the company Tomas Vigil seems to be working for and Morgan Bennett are also related somehow." Marci puts her pen in her mouth and stares at her paper. "I have to think about this." She stands and turns to me. "I'll see you in the morning at my office."

"I'll be there," I say with more enthusiasm than I actually feel.

"Is it okay if I come?" Tinsley asks.

Marci smiles. "It is, but they'll stick you in a waiting room—no internet and no computers allowed."

Tinsley nods, and I know she'd sit in a room and wait. I love her for that, but it's not necessary.

"You have work to do," I tell her. "I'll call you as soon as I'm done." I look over at Claire. "The same goes for you."

"You're going to do great tomorrow," Marci assures me.

Tinsley and Claire begin clearing the trash and plates from the table as I wrap everything up with my team.

"Try to get some sleep tonight. You've got this," Marci calls as she slips out.

"Tomorrow the mayor of Las Vegas is having a press conference about Nate's arrest and his being transferred to Vegas," Fiona reports. "I have some reporters planning to ask her some hard questions, but I'll need to be on the ground there in Vegas. I'd take your plane, but..." She shrugs.

I smirk. "You pissed off Detective Robards today."

Fiona crinkles her nose. "I did. I ruined his plan, and he got himself fired in the process. Not even the union is backing him after he probably totaled your airplane."

"Are you releasing the video?"

"Not yet, but let's see how the FBI does tomorrow. I've released some of the affidavits from the friends you were with in Vegas."

I take a deep breath. "Do you think all of this could stem back to Cecelia's disappearance?"

"I hadn't thought about it until we laid it all out together with Marci," she says. "She's good, and she may be on to something."

I nod. "You'll be in Vegas. What about Jim?"

"He's here. He's got his team working overtime on

Heather McCoy, Cecelia's money, and this mess."

"I should send Kate flowers."

"Jim's fiancée?"

I nod.

"She might like that," Fiona agrees.

I kiss her on both cheeks, and she heads out.

Claire rounds the corner and gives me a tight hug. "I want updates as you get them. Text messages are fine. And do whatever you need to do to get a decent night's sleep."

"What are you saying, baby sister?"

"I like Tinsley a lot, and I know you do, too. But just, you know... Make sure you get some rest."

I roll my eyes as I nod, and she gets into the elevator. "Let's get this wrapped up tomorrow."

The door closes, and fear washes over me. I'm surrounded by material things, and I'd miss them, but I'd be lost without Tinsley every day.

CHAPTER 36

Landon

I'm up before my alarm sounds, and I dress in workout clothes. Despite Marci's assurances, I worry I may not be home for a few days, weeks — or God forbid, months. Tinsley gave me lots of therapy last night, but despite the exhaustion, I didn't sleep.

I enter my workout room, closing off the house and opening all the windows. It's fucking freezing outside.

I set my Peloton bike for a moderate workout, and I carefully ride with my cast. After forty minutes of pounding on the bike, my legs are like jelly, my lungs are going to burst, and every pore on my body is sweating.

I smell coffee as I exit, and look out at the pool to find Tinsley doing her laps. She's so graceful as she swims. I know she'd like a bigger pool, but she doesn't complain. After I get my coffee, I stand and watch her for easily ten minutes. It's after six when Tinsley pulls herself out of the pool and sees me. She smiles and grabs a towel to dry herself. She must be freezing.

Turning the kettle on, I pull down a mug and a teabag.

She comes over and pats me on the backside. "Good morning."

"You looked good out there."

She smiles. "I missed the water while we were gone."

"We can always add one of those pools that creates drag, so you can swim at the ranch."

"Maybe. I've never tried one of those."

She pours hot water and steeps her tea. "Are you ready for this morning?" she asks.

"I guess as ready as I'll ever be."

"I thought I'd walk over with you to the lawyer's and maybe to the federal building. I'll meet up with Claire. We can work close by, and when you're done, we'll meet you again."

"You don't have to do that."

Tinsley steps in. "I know." She kisses me softly. "I want to."

My heart soars.

"I've told you this several times, we're going to manage this together."

"I'm scared," I whisper.

She pulls me in. "I know. I am, too."

We're quiet a few moments. "We should shower."

I smile, hoping for a shower together, but she sees right through me.

She shakes her head. "You go wrap up your cast and shower in our room, and I'll shower in the guest room."

"But that's not nearly as fun. Plus, you might need some help getting those hard-to-reach places."

"I'll never be ready on time if we take one together, and I want to look good today."

"You always look good," I assure her.

"I'll be ready in an hour. See you right here."

"If you're late, can I spank you?"

She smiles. "Your wish will be my command."

"Damn, woman. See what you do to me?" I reveal my erect penis beneath my shorts.

"I have big plans for that later," Tinsley calls over her shoulder as she walks toward her room.

An hour later, I'm dressed in an altered suit that allows my cast. The collar is too tight, and I can't get the cufflinks to work.

Tinsley walks in, and she's beautiful in a dark green silk brocade Chinese jacket, with black pants and beautiful black strappy sandals.

I stop fiddling with my cufflink and admire her. "You look stunning."

She blushes. "Thank you. Can I help you with those?"

"Please."

In mere moments, she has my cufflinks done. She then stands behind me and fixes the collar, which loosens it up.

"That's so much better. I was worried my neck was getting fat."

She laughs, deep and hearty. It breaks the tension of what's in front of us today.

Yolanda, Greg, and Jerome walk out of the security office.

"Jim will meet us at Marci Peterson's office," Yolanda says.

I nod. As I step into the elevator, I look back at my apartment and hope I'm able to come home tonight. A part of me worries everything Claire and I have accomplished over the last five years, and finding Tinsley, was all a dream.

We ride the elevator down to the garage, and a large Suburban is waiting for us. As we exit the garage, moisture engulfs the vehicle. We make our way across town, and I watch the people scurrying around in their raincoats. It never rains in September in San Francisco, but it is today. It's one of those heavy mists that waivers between light rain and fog.

Miserable.

When we arrive. Jim is waiting with an umbrella, and

Jerome remains in the Suburban, ready to take us to the federal building in a little bit.

"You ready?" Jim holds the door open so I can exit.

I grasp Tinsley's hand. We walk into the building, and after an elevator ride to Marci's offices, a receptionist greets us. We're shown to a conference room.

After a moment Marci arrives, and she's a whirlwind of activity. "Did anyone give further thought to the connections we were talking about last night?"

Jim picks at an imaginary string on his suit pants. "I think there are more instances, and we should sit down and talk. Many of the people who were there when Cecelia went missing have had strange things happen since. It would be great to figure out why, and if they're related."

"I wasn't there," Tinsley quietly reminds Jim.

He nods. "That's true."

"Okay," Marci says. "I've spoken to Agent Gardner, and they're going to meet us at nine. We'll interview with him, a US Attorney Walker Clifton himself has chosen, and two other agents. Remember, this interview starts all over, and they only care that Heather McCoy is missing. They don't care about her not being pregnant. After that, we'll break for lunch. We can return here and have box lunches, if that works." She looks at Tinsley. "That way you can join us, as can Claire."

Tinsley nods. "That sounds good."

"This is good news," Marci assures us. "I need to find my earring. I'll be ready in ten minutes. Tinsley, I have this conference room reserved all day. Would you like to work from here? We have internet and unlimited drinks and crappy snacks—just what I'm sure you're used to with your startup background."

She grins and Tinsley's serious face cracks. "If it isn't an imposition, that would be great."

"Sure thing. I'll be right back." Marci runs out of the room.

Jim turns to us. "I know she seems a little flighty, but I think that's how she is when she's stressed. I promise you're in good hands."

I nod. "She's got this. I saw that last night. No big deal."

After one last hug, I follow Jim out, leaving Tinsley behind. Claire is waiting outside with a giant cup of coffee in a thermos. "You're going to kick ass today," she tells me. "Tinsley and I will be here waiting for you."

I nod and wave at her through the window as the car pulls away. We drive the few blocks to the federal building and pull up in front.

Inside, Marci knows the receptionist, and they chat while she takes down our information. We walk through the metal detectors and are led to an ugly room—even by my standards. It has a large metal table out of the 1970s and a chair that's a slight upgrade from a metal folding one. There's a flip-chart easel that probably hasn't had a pad of paper attached in some time. The wall to the hallway is dirty white, and the windows are covered with two-inch, yellowed, metal blinds.

We haven't waited long before the team walks in. We all stand as introductions are made, and I'm handed business cards from the three agents and the assistant US attorney.

We sit down. The assistant US attorney, Dhar Patel, looks at me. "I understand you know my boss."

I nod, but don't say anything since he didn't ask a question.

"They travel in the same social circles," Marci answers.

He seems surprised by that, and he looks at me to elaborate. I don't.

"Well, now that we've established that you know the US Attorney, tell me how you know Heather McCoy," he finally says.

"I don't," I reply.

"But you had sex with her." He cocks his head to the

side.

"No, I didn't."

"She claimed otherwise, didn't she?" he asks.

"Yes."

"Why should we believe you over her? She had a paternity test that said the child she was carrying was likely yours."

Here we go. The morning is peppered with the same questions I've answered a thousand times.

When we break for lunch, Marci hands Patel copies of all the affidavits, the jump drive, and CD.

We walk out, and Stan is waiting in the Suburban. We creep the few blocks to Marci's office, and when we arrive, she suggests we leave our federal visitor badges at reception on the way in.

Upstairs, Tinsley, Claire, and Mason are waiting with box lunches. Mason puts his down and comes over to shake my hand. "Hope you don't mind me crashing lunch. I wanted to be here for support."

"Thanks," I mutter.

"Marci, you look stunning as usual." Mason winks at her, and I'm not sure I've ever seen Mason flirt. I'm a bit taken aback.

"Mase, great to see you again. When was the last time? That's right, last week."

Now I get it. They know each other. I should have known better.

"How did it go?" Claire asks.

"I think well," I hedge.

"This guy here is a rock-star witness." Marci is all smiles as she kicks off her shoes. She takes a box lunch and sits down with her leg beneath her. "Man, the first question lobbed at him is asking if he knows Walker Clifton, this guy's boss's boss, and rather than tell him how tight they are, he nods." She snorts in laughter. "I knew we were going to be in great shape."

We talk about all sorts of things over lunch, not just business, and by the end I'm feeling much more at ease.

About twenty minutes before we have to return, Marci moves us to prep. "We know they have emails that are supposedly from you coming from Lewiston," she says, shuffling papers.

Jim removes a file from his messenger bag. "This is the research we did regarding those emails." He hands her the pile. "In the first one you can see the email address. Their copy doesn't capture the name, but if you look at it, you can see the email address is incorrect. It shows @disruptivetech.com when it's actually only @disruptive.com."

"That's good news," Marci says.

"Well, maybe," Claire replies meekly. "We do own @disruptivetech, as well as @disruptivetechnology, @disruptive, @disrupt, and @disruptivecommunications. We own all the .com and various country's versions of that, as we expect to grow internationally. But to confirm, right now our email is all @disruptive.com."

Jim nods. "The other thing is the geo-tag. It says Lewiston, but the ranch is Crow Nation."

Marci looks at me. "Do you have email capabilities on your smartphone?"

I nod.

"So, that's a tough one. What else can we expect?"

"They say my blood was in her apartment with her blood, but the second round of testing proved she wasn't pregnant." I look down at the table, and all the jubilance I felt after this morning has been replaced with dread. It doesn't matter that I didn't write them. Those emails provide a reliable link between me and Heather McCoy.

"The second blood test is a double-edged sword for them, so I don't expect they'll come back with that too hard. It proves you were correct about not being her baby's father, and that the first test was most likely tampered with." Marci searches through her file.

"What do we know about the lab where they did the original test?"

"Here's the information." Jim hands her another file. "My team was able to see that the lab had a hacker the evening of the test. We can't prove the hacker changed the test, but they've done additional checking, and there's no sign of the hacker before that day or since."

"I like that." Marci eyes his stack of files. "What else do you have?"

"These are the background checks on Heather McCoy, her boyfriend, both of their parents, a few friends, and Heather's brother." He hands her another batch of files.

Marci nods. "Okay, good. I'm going to keep these here. If I need them, I'll have them brought over. It's still our first date, so we're just feeling each other out." Marci winks at me, and I try to relax.

"I have a team in Illinois looking in to her parents and trying to see if Heather has shown up in town," Jim adds.

"We don't have a body, so there's a good chance she's in hiding because she attempted a scam and it backfired," Marci rationalizes. She begins to pack up her belongings. "We should be done about four — FBI are government employees, and they tend to work seven to four."

As we walk out, I ask, "Why did we leave our visitor badges at reception? Do you think they're bugged?"

"Oh, goodness no. I just wanted a nice lunch to celebrate a good morning without the reminder that we have to go back for a hard afternoon."

"Okay." I look back at Tinsley and Claire. "Do you think they're going to keep me overnight?"

"No. Not at all. But that doesn't mean you won't be under constant surveillance." Marci and I get in the Suburban and ride back to the federal building. "But, when the feds go to trial, they have a ninety-eight-percent conviction rate because they make sure everything lines up. And right now, we have enough to cast a lot of doubt. They have to fix some holes — including the email issue."

I breathe a little better.

"If you didn't know you owned all those domains, how did they know?" she asks me.

I shrug. "That's an excellent question. That part of the company is Claire's area. Plus, I hardly know my own email address because I mostly use texting or instant message. I don't email except from my laptop in the office."

She nods. "The geo-tag is Lewiston, Montana, but I'd also bet it's a laptop, not a smartphone that sent those messages. They'll have to disclose where in Lewiston, and I'll ask why someone would drive in to use public Wi-Fi when they have a network at home that works more than fine."

"I never worked in Lewiston, and they'll have a hard time coming up with anyone who knew me to say otherwise. Due to security issues, we only work on highly encrypted routers. We have memos out to all our staff about not using public Wi-Fi at this point."

Marci scribbles on her pad and taps her pen to her lower lip. "The biggest hole is where is Heather McCoy?"

"So, there's going to be a black cloud hanging over me for a while?"

"Maybe. I'm betting on Jim's team to find her. If she's alive and never had a baby, we know you're in the clear. If they find her body and she's not breathing, this is more than a black cloud."

We pull up to the federal building and head inside for the afternoon's round two.

CHAPTER 37

Tinsley

When Marci and Landon return shortly after four, I'm instantly relieved. I didn't realize how worried I was until I saw him. His tie is askew, and his shirt is opened. His hair is disheveled, and he looks exhausted. I race into his arms.

"I bet you're disappointed to not get my apartment to yourself for a few nights," he teases.

"Not in the least," I counter.

Claire squeezes his arm. "How did it go?"

"He was spot on," Marci assures us. "We discussed most of the issues they asked about over lunch, and he answered everything as he was supposed to. He did great."

We stand around and chat for a few minutes, and Marci takes off her shoes and stretches her toes. "I hate these shoes," she says in apology. "I should know better, but walking all over the federal building does me in."

A little while later, Landon is clearly ready to go, so we wander downstairs with Greg and Yolanda nearby. Claire gives us both hugs and is on her way, and I climb into the back of the car with Landon.

"What happened this afternoon?" I ask. "Did it really go okay?"

"They're convinced I paid someone to do it."

"Why would her accusation matter?" I muse. "We were involved, and you told me what was going on. I wasn't upset. I didn't leave you over it."

Landon puts his head back on the seat and rubs his eyes. "I know. But there are emails from the faulty email address—a lot of them and all full of threats."

I lay my head on his chest, and I can hear his heartbeat as he puts his arm around me.

"I swear I didn't touch her. Sure, I've been upset about the impact of the situation on my company and my relationships, but I never once considered harming her. All communications went through Fiona. I figured we'd face this when she had the baby."

"I've seen how you react to stress," I tell him. "This was an irritant. I know I sound like a broken record, but we've managed this. I don't believe you have a violent bone in your body."

When we get back to the apartment building, we shuffle out of the car and into the elevator. "What should we have for dinner?" I ask. "I want something decadent. How about pizza or maybe Mexican?"

Landon shrugs. "I'm fine with whatever you want."

"Okay." I look at Yolanda and Greg. "What do you guys feel like? I'm buying."

We decide on Mexican. San Francisco isn't known for good Mexican food, but I know a little place, and they'll deliver, so we're in for a treat.

While we wait, Landon sorts through the mail, still in his suit with his crooked tie. He picks up a package and looks at it funny. "Did you order anything from a company called Acme?"

"No. Isn't that the Roadrunner's company?"

"Maybe." He shakes it. "I'm nervous about opening this. What if someone sent me something like Heather's finger?"

"Let's get Yolanda and Greg in here before you open it. We can film it, just in case."

"That sounds like a good idea."

Yolanda brings her cell phone in and has Jim on the screen, watching. I'm recording, and we all agree to start.

With a knife, Landon slowly slits the tape around the box. His hands are shaking. He clears away bubble wrap and pulls out a black rubber ring. His brow furrows.

Suddenly I know what the box is. "This is personal," I announce. "Put it away."

But Landon has already reached into the box again. This time he pulls out a vibrator designed to go vaginally and anally at the same time.

Yolanda and Greg smirk.

Landon gets a funny look on his face as he realizes this is the box of toys he ordered ages ago.

I stuff my phone in my back pocket and reach for everything, hoping to put it back in the box. I must be as red as a tomato.

"I forgot I ordered these," Landon muses. He opens the cock ring and begins playing with it. "I'm not sure this is going to fit?"

I hear Jim choking back a laugh through the phone.

"You're right. It's probably too big," I say, more and more embarrassed by the second. I know lots of people have toys, but I don't want to know what they look like or what they are.

The house phone rings. The disruption is welcome, and Dee lets us know dinner has arrived and is on its way up. I yank the toys away from Landon and stuff them back in the box. I hide it in the kitchen as Neil arrives with our food.

I excuse myself and head for the guest room. I need a moment. I don't know why this is a big deal for me, but it is.

It's private.

It takes a while for me to return, and I realize everyone has waited to eat. "I'm sorry."

Yolanda and Greg pick up their meals. "We're under strict nondisclosure agreements," she says. "People often forget we're here, and we see all sorts of things. I promise, nothing we saw today will be discussed with anyone."

I nod.

Yolanda and Greg take their dinner to the security room, leaving us to eat alone. Once the door closes behind them, I look at Landon. "How did you forget you ordered these?"

"You know how long ago that was. I'm sorry. I've had a lot on my mind. I also didn't pay attention to what they said would be the return address."

I rub my temples. "Jim was on a video call."

"We have a healthy sex life. Think about all the fun we can have tonight."

I shake my head. "Oh no. Absolutely not. Those are going in the trash. I want nothing to do with them."

"No way. I want to see what that cock ring does. And, I'm starting to get hard just thinking of you on all fours using that double-penetration dildo."

He's made me smile. "I can't believe you bought that."

"That was one of the surprises."

"What else is in there?"

He gives me a look.

"Never mind. I don't want to know." I pick up my food. "Eat your dinner." I look at the bar. "I was going to make a margarita."

"Good, because I made one while you hid in the bathroom."

"I didn't hide," I say defensively.

Landon smirks. "Were you getting yourself off thinking of what we can do with the toys? I thought about doing that."

I roll my eyes and shove his shoulder. "No, I was trying

to figure out how I could tunnel out of the apartment and never show my face to Yolanda, Greg, or Jim again."

"Pah-leeze. These guys have seen so much worse. I bet they own worse. Can't you imagine Yolanda in a dominatrix outfit?"

"No! I don't want to know what anyone does in private."

Landon pulls me in. "Sex is healthy and normal. We're starting our exploration. We've got lots of time to show off for them."

I push back. "There will be no showing off."

He nods. "You're right. It's better if they don't watch. I wouldn't want them getting jealous."

"It's amazing that your ego fits into even this giant apartment."

"Thank you." Landon nuzzles my neck, and I realize he's strategically hitting all the points that make my panties wet.

"For what?" I breathe.

"For being here. After dinner, I'm going to show you my appreciation at least three times. Maybe more."

CHAPTER 38

Landon

Over the last month, since my interview with the FBI, I've been getting updates from Jim's team on what they've learned about Heather McCoy. They now have a credit card receipt from Idaho, on the other side of Yellowstone, shortly after the threatening emails were sent, and we—Jim's team, Fiona, and me—all think she sent those emails to herself. Marci sent our updates off to Dhar Patel at the US Attorney's office and was sure to copy Walker Clifton. But unfortunately, we still have to wonder where Heather's hiding.

In the meantime, I'm finally cast free and at work we've made incredible strides with the Translations software. Today is a demo for potential buyers. We're covering our bases and inviting a few other companies, just in case PeopleMover falls through. Claire and Tinsley are a bit of a mess. We have a room at the Westin on Union Square, and we're expecting over two hundred people, including the press. Mason has invited several of his client companies, and we're ready to share what we've created.

Backstage, Tinsley is pacing back and forth. Danica will give today's presentation in flawless Spanish, and our prototype will translate it to English for those who attend.

"You've got this," I tell Tinsley.

She nods. "It's make or break."

I don't know about break, but we'll be fine.

The lights dim, and the classical music that has been playing fades to the background. An announcer welcomes everyone, and to a round of roaring applause, Tinsley, Claire, and I are announced.

I welcome everyone and walk them through the satellite part of our communication product, which offers connectivity that puts 5G tech to shame. We show a highly glamorous video featuring people using the technology deep in canyons and far above tree lines. This gets a favorable buzz.

When I hand the event off to Tinsley, she moves to the center of the stage. The entire auditorium is silent. This is what people are here for. She starts a video that shows what the earpiece will look like and offers examples of people having a conversation in two different languages. As the lights come up, Danica takes over the presentation, speaking exclusively in Spanish. Those in the first few rows can hear her, but coming over the speaker is a woman's voice speaking in English, translating what she's saying in nearly real time, including the pauses.

When the demonstration concludes, Tinsley opens the floor up for questions.

The first person asks, "What is the actual translation delay?"

I repeat the question for the audience to hear. Danica responds in Spanish, and there is a three-second delay before the voice in English broadcasts to the audience. The crowd goes crazy.

We ask someone to ask a question using regional idioms. A woman in the front row raises her hand. "Like, you know, when I was a girl growing up in, like, the Valley," everyone I knew talked like this," she says in her best Valley Girl accent. "Can you manage that?"

There's a collective laugh through the auditorium. The system repeats the question to Danica in Spanish.

"Nice Valley Girl accent," Danica replies in Spanish, and the English is broadcast to the crowd.

Tinsley then asks for another volunteer to use some slang. She admits this is the hardest part of the software because some words have different meanings, so the programming had to be designed to make assumptions.

A gentleman stands. "Beyoncé's outfits always slay the game," he says. "Your favorite could never."

Tinsley closes her eyes and probably says a silent prayer. Danica listens to the translation and responds in Spanish, which is translated into English. "Beyoncé's outfits are elegant, but Seattle grunge is more my style."

The crowd erupts, and camera bulbs pop like firecrackers. I pull Claire and Tinsley to my side, and the three of us stand together.

Greer Ford, SHN's public relations expert, helps us manage reporters' questions. She also directs inquiries to Mason and his team. We stand together and watch.

"We did it," Claire says.

"Yes, we did," I confirm.

It takes over three hours before everyone has left the auditorium. By the end we're hiding behind the stage in a dressing room, drinking champagne with our teams, and we're all a bit nervous.

Greer and Mason join us.

Mason is grinning from ear to ear. "You guys blew it out of the water."

"The press was expecting a translator, but to know you could be wandering the Amazon and have the ability to talk to someone you came across knocked everyone's socks off." Greer is jubilant.

Mason's nodding. "I think you'll have some major competition among buyers for your software. You're going to be able to name your price, and I don't think anything will be too high."

We all look at each other and grin. I already have more than enough money for my grandchildren's grandchildren. Now it's about doing something for others.

"Tom Sutterland has already said he'll beat anyone else who wants it," Mason says.

Mason is preening, and it's great. We all love something that's genuinely a game-changer, and Claire was absolutely right when she insisted on Tinsley joining us.

Now for the tough ask. I clear my throat. "About that… We were wondering if we could license the use instead of selling it to a single provider."

Mason's brow creases. This is a huge shift in our thinking, with enormous potential. I like it because it means we'll own the translation market, and Morgan Bennett can eat our shorts.

"What we mean is that PeopleMover and other companies can pay to *use* the software," I explain. "Claire and I will put up the satellites needed with the help of SpaceX, and then 'rent' the usage space. We can charge a lot of money, and over the long term, we'll make more money, but we also want to provide small and disadvantaged countries with free or almost-free access."

Mason doesn't say anything for a moment.

I know if he still wants to sell outright, we'll have to. He invested, so he calls the shots. But I hope he'll see this our way. I think we can come up with a business plan for companies like PeopleMover and others to customize and lease the technology, which will subsidize it for those who can't afford it. I hope opening the world up to others and helping to save languages only used by small groups will have some appeal for him.

Finally, Mason's eyes light up. "Let's pull together a

business plan. I think I see what you're trying to do, and I like it."

"This would also mean that competing companies, like Morgan Bennett's, will be so far behind the curve with their own version that it'll be too late," Claire adds. "Everyone will already be leasing our software."

He nods. "That is absolutely brilliant. Truly."

Mason's brain is calculating, and I love it.

"I guess we'll also need to figure out how we're going to go public," I add.

"That's the easy part," Mason says. "I think the next step is getting you three out in front of the media — starting with all the morning shows in New York."

My stomach drops. "That could be a problem. With Heather McCoy still missing, we want them to focus on the software and not the fiasco with me."

"I get what you're saying…" Mason is staring off and already planning. "We'll figure it out. You guys just celebrate tonight. Let's get together in the next few days and work out the business plan. We can do that in our office."

"Sounds great," Tinsley replies.

I turn to look at her, and she's clearly exhausted. All the adrenaline has worn off, and she's wiped. "Do you think you can make it out to the car, or do you want to stay here in the hotel?"

"I want our bed, and I'm going to sleep for the rest of the week."

Yolanda helps us get to the car through the back of the hotel. "You have a huge crowd of people hoping to see you," she says. "It's crazy out there."

When the car pulls around the front, the crowd spills into Union Square.

"All of this is for us?" Tinsley asks.

Then I spot the signs that worry me.

Landon Walsh is a murderer and baby killer.

Give Heather's parents some closure. Tell them where her

body is.

Where is Heather McCoy?

I sit back and turn away from the windows. I don't want people to see me. Yolanda speaks into a radio. I think the crowd is making her nervous.

Suddenly there are police cars in front of us and behind us.

Tinsley relaxes in her seat. "Wow, that was intense."

"I hope this is going to ease up a bit," I fret as we drive back to The Adams.

"Jim and Fiona will be meeting you at your apartment," Yolanda says.

I nod.

The police cars flank us to my building, where the press is camped at the garage door. We make it past them to get inside, and I see two of Jim's men move in behind the Range Rover to prevent anyone from entering the garage. The horrible signs and crazy crowds are behind me. Immediately I feel better.

"Let's get you guys in quickly," Yolanda says.

My phone is ringing. It's my mother. I'm sure she watched the live stream of the presentation and has sent it to all her friends. If we had a fan club, she'd be president.

I answer. "Hey, Mom."

"Landon, you did fantastic today. Your dad and I are so proud of you, Claire, and Tinsley."

"Thanks, Mom." I get out of the car, and we're walking to the elevator.

It's hard to understand her underground. I'm getting every other syllable.

"We...jury...out...love..."

Aaannnd, I've lost the call. I'll call her back in a bit.

Ultimately, I'm feeling good. After Jim and Fiona give us their speeches about crowd control, I'm going to ravish Tinsley and put her to bed for the next week. We're only going to wake up for sex and sustenance. We can hide in our apartment until the press loses interest.

When we exit the elevator, there are a lot more people from Clear Security in my apartment than I was expecting. I guess this thing is serious.

"Did you see how well it went?"

Jim shakes my hand. "It was a great afternoon. I'm so happy for you both."

"Thanks. We're excited, too," Tinsley replies with a yawn.

"Were those crowds just for today, or can we expect them for a while?" I ask.

Jim looks over at Fiona, and immediately I know there's something coming I'm not going to like.

"Let's sit down," Fiona says. She walks over to the living room and pours a glass of my favorite bourbon. She hands it to me. The room has fallen silent.

"What's going on?" The tension crackles in the air.

"The FBI has convened a grand jury about Heather McCoy's disappearance," Fiona announces.

I look at her. *Why would they do that?* Then it hits me like a ton of bricks. "To convict me?"

Tinsley immediately interlaces her fingers with mine.

Jim leans forward on his elbows. "I'm afraid so."

"What does Marci know?" I demand.

"Nothing yet," Fiona replies softly.

"*Shit*. She told me they don't move forward unless they're certain they can convict."

I'm trying to reason how I could be convicted of a crime I didn't commit. Does this mean I'll be deported? What about my company? What about Tinsley? Is Claire going to be dragged into this? This must be a ploy to take our company away.

"Marci will be by in the morning," Fiona says. "I don't want you to worry about this."

Is she crazy? I didn't do anything, and I'm being framed. Of course I'm going to worry about this.

CHAPTER 39

Tinsley

I watch Landon sink into a giant, black hole. His shoulders round, his brilliant, milk chocolate eyes darken, and the lines around his eyes and mouth deepen.

I don't blame him, but we've come off an incredible day. We've announced to the world that we're changing the way we communicate, and it's a big deal.

I look at Jim. I've been around enough attorneys to know how they talk. "How can they move forward without a body? Has your team found Heather's body, and you haven't told us?"

Jim shakes his head. "No, we haven't found her, but we believe she's alive. We're trying to piece together where."

"Who's putting pressure on them to go to the grand jury?" I ask. "Because if it's Walker Clifton, I'll march right down to his office and get in his face."

Jim smiles. "We can't tell who's pushing for this, but we know it's not coming from Walker. Marci was on her way over to figure out what's going on."

Jim steps away to take a brief call and returns. "If anyone can get to Walker Clifton, Marci can. She seems to be the only attorney in San Francisco who isn't scared of him."

"That's because they all have political aspirations, and she doesn't," Fiona says.

Landon looks around the room at the half-dozen people gathered in his apartment. He lowers his voice. "I can have the jet fueled up and ready to go in less than an hour. I can be over the Canadian border in three hours, and I can hop from there to anywhere in the world."

My pulse increases. If he runs, he looks guilty, and there isn't a bone in my body that tells me he's guilty. This is a frame.

Fiona's eyes grow wide. "I don't recommend that. I know it seems easy to run right now, but I have to believe that with Jim's team and Marci, we're going to be fine."

That may be true, but I know Landon must feel everything he's worked for slipping through his fingers.

We talk for a short time longer, and they continue asking Landon to be patient and not run. He agrees, but once they've gone, he turns to me.

"What do you think?"

I take a deep breath. I need to be strong for him, but if he's going to run, I won't hesitate to go with him. "Let's see how the next few days shake out. Marci is a miracle worker, and Jim's team is motivated. And ultimately, we have the truth on our side."

He pours himself half a tumbler of bourbon and sinks into the plush couch. "I understand if you want to get far away from all of this."

"Get far away?" I shake my head, and then my blood pressure goes through the roof. I stand and take his glass from his hand, pointing my finger in his face. "When have I ever led you to believe I would walk out the door? We're both exhausted, and you're talking out your ass." I need to de-escalate this crap about running away.

We stare at each other. Reaching for his hand, I attempt to pull Landon up, but he doesn't budge, so I crawl over his lap and steady my knees at his hips. "Let's give some of those toys a test drive."

He perks up. "You'll let me use the double-penetration vibrator?"

I shake my head. "No way. But I think you'll like the cock ring."

He grins, and I know I've distracted him. "Where did you put the box?"

I'm already halfway into the kitchen. "I hid it."

I dig into a cabinet behind some pots and pans I'm sure have never been used. *Bingo*. Here's the box. I rummage through and pull out the cock ring, holding it up as if I've found gold. I study the packaging, and I need to download an app.

Landon watches as I figure this out. I keep my distance, because if I'm too close, we'll throw it aside, and I want to distract him from the freight train coming our way.

It's surprisingly easy to sync the Bluetooth, and the ring vibrates in my palm.

Wow. I like this.

Landon is nursing his drink and working his way back to the black hole.

"Let's see if this fits and what it does." I grab him by the hand and lead him back to our bedroom. We're hardly in the room before I push him against the wall and kiss him. I pull at his shirt, and his hard stomach tenses. He smells like pine and orange and tastes like good Kentucky bourbon. I push my tongue past his lips, and his meets it, stroke for stroke. He's eager, too.

I fall to my knees and release his buckle, in one movement unbuttoning and unzipping his pants, which pool at his feet. I push his boxer briefs to the floor and free his cock. It's deliciously hard and waves in my face. I look at the small ring and how big Landon already is. "I don't know if this will work. You're already hard."

Maybe if it's wet? Taking him in my mouth, I lick him thoroughly, and he only gets bigger. I try the lube, liberally coating his cock, and I begin to slide the ring down.

He grimaces. "I can't break my favorite toy."

I roll back on my heels and lead him to the bed. "You're always ready."

"It's a gift." Landon winks at me.

"What did your mom say earlier?"

His grin disappears. "Bringing my mom into our bedroom is definitely a mood killer."

I lift my eyebrow and purse my lips. I want to try this, and if he's too hard, it won't work. "What did she say?" I push.

"She was proud of the three of us."

"She mentioned me?"

He nods, as if of course she'd be proud of me. I glance in the mirror next to the bed, and he's still solid steel.

"Should we call Claire and see if she talked to your mom? Maybe we can invite her over?"

"Don't you dare," he growls.

He finally becomes flaccid enough that I can begin. This new toy focuses the sensations on those spots that feel good — the bottom and sides. I coat my hand and the ring, watching him twitch in anticipation.

The bed shifts as I lift myself above him, holding there and watching his expressions. I run my hand through his hair and scratch my nails down his torso.

Moving the cock ring down to the base, I nestle a nub underneath so it will vibrate his balls. I carefully move the app to its lowest setting. The pulsing on his hardness intensifies then fades a little.

He reaches to stroke himself.

"Not yet," I warn.

"You're cruel." Landon reaches for me. "And you're

still dressed."

I stand. "Alexa, please play 'Lady Marmalade.'"

"Here's 'Lady Marmalade' from the *Moulin Rouge* soundtrack, playing now," Alexa, the digital assistant, announces.

The music begins, and I turn around, swaying my hips back and forth. I inch my black pants over my ass. I'm wearing a skimpy thong, and I lean over so Landon has a good view of my ass as I kick my pants away.

He gasps.

Pulling my top over my head, I continue to move my hips to the music. I'm not going to be hired by a strip club anytime soon. I struggle to undress seductively *and* keep with the rhythm of the music.

I turn around in my black lace bra and mouth the French from the song. I shimmy toward him, and his eyes are glued to my breasts.

He's hard. Now it's time for some fun. With my phone, I increase the vibration on his cock.

Landon whistles between his teeth. "Get over here." He points to his hard cock.

"You like that?" I purr.

"I think you'd like it if you took it for a ride."

I continue to shimmy. "You think so? I think it's three socks, and I'm not sure it'll fit."

"Show me your tits," Landon growls.

Reaching behind my back, I unclasp my bra and let it fall to the floor, twirling to give him a complete view. "Better?"

"Mmmmm. Yes, some..." He begins to stroke himself, and it turns me on to see him lost in his satisfaction.

I step out of my panties, turning my back to him and giving him another view of my backside. I turn and look over my shoulder. "Like what you see?"

"Mmmm... Yes. Very much."

I lick my lips as I dance. He stands and throws me on

the bed, burying his head between my breasts.

I roll him on his back and increase the stimulation of the cock ring. My caresses are gentle, a fleeting counterpoint to the steady, deep growl of the vibrator.

His eyes plead with me to start, but I raise my eyebrows, waiting for an invitation.

"Are you going to make me beg?" he asks.

"I don't want to hurt you."

"If you don't get that tight cunt on my tool, I'm going to explode and waste all this great cum."

I smile. "Gee, you have such a way with words."

I straddle him, and he places his cock at my entrance. Slowly I lower myself. The pulsing from the ring can be felt through his dick, and it's like my own vibrator. He seems bigger than usual, and it takes a few minutes for me to adjust to his size. The vibration radiates, and it hits me just right.

His thumb reaches my aching nub and strums it. "Holy shit," I breathe. He doesn't stop. "Right there..."

He grabs my hips and pushes me down, over and over, on his hard rod.

He grunts and keeps going. After a tweak to my nipples, my second orgasm has me shaking.

I roll off of him, gasping for air. "Wow…"

Lying in bed, we're both breathing hard.

"That was fun," Landon says.

"Might be worth using again," I manage.

CHAPTER 40

Landon

I fell asleep for a short time, but my phone rings now, bringing me out of my haze. I glance at the time as I answer. It's shortly after four. I don't feel rested in the least.

"Landon, it's Jim. I'm on my way over with Bash and Levi. Marci is meeting us at your place."

"Okay, I'll let them know they can send you up. Is it only the four of you?"

"I think so."

I disconnect the call and let the night receptionist know I'm expecting Jim, his team, and Marci shortly.

"I hope they're coming with good news and not to tell me the FBI will be here in a few hours," I tell Tinsley, rubbing her arm.

She jumps out of bed and rushes into the shower.

I watch her leave. "You're showering for them?"

"I can't walk out smelling like sex."

Women. Like anyone would notice.

She steps out five minutes later. "Your turn."

"I don't need —" I look at her and know it's not worth the argument, so I strip off the clothes I'd put on, and climb into the shower. I don't want to upset her more than she already is.

When I get out, I hear her talking to Marci about drinks as I head for the living room. I pull my T-shirt over my head and pad out as Jim and his team arrive.

We gather around Jim as he places multiple pictures on the kitchen counter. I don't recognize their subject, though it's all the same woman. She has mousy brown hair and a big floppy hat in one. A baseball cap in another. Sunglasses in another. And a platinum bob in the other. In photos taken from a distance, we see her walking a dog.

It finally occurs to me. It's Heather McCoy. A flood of relief rushes through me.

"Is that who I think it is?" I ask.

Jim nods.

"We did some dumpster diving and have proved by DNA that it's her," Bash reports.

My legs almost buckle beneath me. I look up at the ceiling and pump my fists in the air. "Oh, thank God."

"These were obviously taken over several days. Why are we just learning this now?" Tinsley presses.

"We weren't sure," Jim says. "We put her through facial recognition once we got the right shot, and then we ran the DNA verification. At any time, it could have turned out to be a false positive."

"We didn't want to get Landon's hopes up, just in case," Levi explains.

"I wish you would have told him you had more than the credit card usage," Tinsley mutters.

Marci nods. "This is fantastic news. I'll take this over to Walker Clifton immediately."

Jim gives Marci the address where Heather has been staying. "She's been here in the city probably the whole time, hiding at her boyfriend's."

"Why didn't we check his home?" I ask.

"The police and FBI did," Jim answers.

Marci stops. "We have a leak somewhere. They have to have been tipped off in advance if there was no evidence there."

Jim nods. "And that leak is the person pushing for the investigation. Did you learn who's behind the push?"

"US Attorney Clifton didn't have much for me last night. He just told me to hold tight." As Marci begins to gather the pictures, she looks at them carefully. "Jim, what do you suggest?"

"Levi, Bash, and you go to Walker directly. We need to have them plan another raid on the boyfriend's house."

I like that Jim doesn't hesitate. I couldn't be happier that he's on my team.

Marci looks at her watch. "It's only four thirty. He'll be up in a half-hour."

"You know the man well," Tinsley remarks.

"It's my job. It's well known that he's a man of habits, and working out each morning is one of them. He worked out at the Y for years, but once he was appointed head of the Northern District of California, he moved to what we suspect is a home gym."

"We need him to see this without tipping off the mole," Marci muses.

"Do you think he'll be able to keep a raid quiet?" I ask.

"I do." She pushes the pictures into a pile and slides them into a file folder. "He's incredibly principled. Rumor has it, the president is looking at the governor for a position on his cabinet, and he's told several he'll appoint Walker to replace him."

"The governor's mansion sounds like an incredible place to have a poker game," I note.

Marci grins. "I'd love to see that."

We make some small talk over coffee, and Marci and

Jim's team leave shortly before five for Walker Clifton's home. I stare into my mug. "Now, we wait."

An hour later, we still haven't heard anything. Tinsley gets in the pool, and I watch her swim lap after lap for a full sixty minutes. I have the local news on, waiting and hoping for something. Anything.

I eventually get on my Peloton and put in a hard ride, half listening to my workout and half to the news.

When Dee calls from downstairs to tell me Marci has arrived, I'm nervous.

Tinsley holds my hand as we watch the elevators open. Unlike this morning, Marci now looks like the high-priced attorney she is, dressed in a robin's egg blue pencil skirt and an off-white silk blouse.

"I have good news." Marci puts her bag down. "Shortly after seven this morning, the FBI arrested Heather Marie McCoy, Patricia Jean Cooper, and Earl James Fort for fraud and blackmail."

Tinsley jumps up and down and leaps into a hug with Marci. "That's awesome."

Marci nods. "It should make the news, which means you'll be swarmed with paparazzi today, so if you want to get out of town, go now. Just tell me where I can find you. Otherwise, you'll be in here for a few weeks."

"I can't tell you how happy I am," I gush.

"I don't blame you. I'm pretty happy myself," Marci agrees.

"Who is the Patricia person?" I ask.

"She calls herself Patty, and she's married to Heather's brother. She was a paralegal in the DA's office and seems to be the person behind pushing to investigate Heather's disappearance. And, since the case started with the SFPD and the DA's office, she had access to pieces of information, and people were keeping her apprised as a courtesy. She was the mole." Marci smiles.

"That's fantastic. I can't believe in two hours they put all that together." I pull Tinsley into a hug.

"They didn't know she was Heather's sister-in-law. But we figured out she was pushing for the investigation. She was also behind the first faulty blood test at the lab. Through her work at the DA's office, she met a black hat hacker and hired him to make the switch. As soon as Heather was arrested, she threw Patty under the bus, along with her boyfriend, Earl. She said it was their idea. The crazy thing we learned was that Earl has been involved with both of them."

Tinsley's face scrunches up in disgust. "What's next?"

"You may have to testify against Heather and gang if they don't take a plea. But I'd suggest we pull in a PR team to celebrate not only this being a hoax, but also your good news about Disruptive."

Marci gives us hugs goodbye with a promise to keep us up to date.

When the elevator doors close, I turn to Tinsley. "What did you do with the box from the sex shop? I say we hang around here the next few days, stay naked, and celebrate by playing with our new toys."

CHAPTER 41

Tinsley

It's been over a week since I've been to work to see my team, and I'm ready to get out. Yolanda says the paparazzi are still hanging around, but I've been missing my ladies. I've been hesitant to go in to the office, or out with them in public, fearing Tomas will appear.

After long discussions with Jim and Yolanda, we've set a plan. I'm going out with my team, and if Tomas shows, we know something's up. If he doesn't, the girls and I will have a fun night hanging out.

I craft a text message to them, asking if they're up for happy hour tonight.

Me: I've been in hiding from the paparazzi, but how about Bourbon & Branch tonight? It's upscale, and they don't even have a sign, so it can be easy to miss if you don't know where you're going.

Danica: Sounds excellent. Bourbon is a man's drink, so there will be lots of men there.

Vanessa: Down, Danica. I think it sounds perfect.

Me: Do you mind if Landon joins us?

Ginger: Only if he brings single hot friends.

That makes me smile.

Me: I'll have him put the word out.

I turn to Landon. "Do you want to join my team and me for drinks at Bourbon & Branch tonight after work?"

"Oh, that sounds good. I can never find it, so maybe between you and Jim's team, I'll get there."

I shake my head. "According to Ginger, you must invite single friends if you're going to come."

He nods. "I can invite a few guys. But no guarantee they're good guys to date or have a lot of money in the bank."

I shrug. "That's fine."

With that settled, I get to work and trade Slack messages with the team. The pressure is on.

When the end of the day arrives, Landon has a call and says he'll join us when he's done, so I head out with my bodyguards.

The girls are already waiting for me when I arrive.

"We ordered your first drink," Danica informs me.

"Great. What am I having?"

"Bourbon." She grins.

To novices like me, all bourbons taste about the same. Some have more of a pepper or maybe a caramel taste, but nevertheless, I enjoy the drink.

We're laughing and catching up when I feel a hand on my back. I look up, and I'm disappointed to see Tomas.

"Hey. I haven't seen you in a while." He paints a smile on his face that doesn't reach his eyes. I spot Bridget, Tomas' camera woman from the Y, standing off in the shadows, pointing her phone in our direction, but trying not to be obvious.

"What are you doing here?" I ask.

"If I didn't know any better, I'd think you were stalking me," Tomas responds. He wiggles his eyebrows as if he's flirting, but I don't see it that way at all.

"How did you know we were here?" I ask, trying hard to keep my cool.

"Total luck to find you. I didn't know you'd be here."

I look at Yolanda, and she's on the phone. I watch as four guys descend on Tomas and Bridget without them realizing it.

I look over at Bridget and crook my finger. "Bridget, why don't you join us? The FBI will be here in a few minutes, so you might as well share what you have to say."

She looks around as three big burly men and a woman, all wearing FBI windbreakers, arrive at the bar.

Tomas starts to move away, but my team doesn't let him leave. "What the hell?"

"Tomas, we've been watching the Stanford Octagon PeopleMover page. You've been running a 'Where is Tinsley Pratt' thread where you and your loser friends stalk me, say horrible things about me, and tell lies. And while that is what jealous losers do, the truth is, you would never have been able to find me tonight unless you had a tracker on one of my team member's phones. That's illegal in California, and the best part is, because your little friend here recorded it all, we have proof of a conspiracy. And with the PeopleMover page, we have proof you've done this multiple times."

"You have nothing on me." Tomas holds his hands up as if he's innocent.

I shrug. "Let me introduce you to Cora Perry from the FBI. She'll be taking your cell phone." I lean in close. "I dare you to fight it. I hear the FBI only prosecutes when they know they can win."

Landon arrives as Tomas is being walked out. He looks crestfallen. "I missed it?"

I nod. "We weren't even here a half hour before Tomas and Bridget arrived."

Kissing me on the cheek, Landon nods to the girls. "I invited some friends." A wall of shoulders stands next to the table. "Ginger, I understand you requested some single men. Please meet Dash Meyers, Grey Merriman, Darren Porter, and Hunter Stillman."

Ginger's eyes grow large. "All for me?"

The whole table laughs.

CHAPTER 42

Landon

When we get home, it's almost midnight. Tomas' arrest was merely a blip in the evening. That won't be the end of him, and I still have to wonder what exactly he was up to, but it does mean he'll be out of Tinsley's life for a while, and I'm perfectly fine with that. I'm sure we'll be using Marci's services again when the time comes.

I think Darren and Ginger hit it off, and Danica liked Hunter. It was a fun night. Vanessa's wife showed up, and she was a ton of fun, too. We'll have to do more together with the teams.

I have a bit of a buzz, but I'm going to bed, and I plan on sleeping in tomorrow. It's the weekend, and I need a break from running the public relations gauntlet.

In between various FBI-related messes, Claire, Tinsley and I have answered unending questions—both on and off camera—about what our technology can do, what the implications are, and our future plans.

Mason tells us if we went public right now, we'd open at twenty-eight dollars a share. He believes with the current buzz, we'd split three times before we closed on the first day, and our shares would be worth over five hundred dollars each. That's a lot of money for the three of us. Claire and I already have more money than we could ever spend, and Tinsley doesn't seem particularly money motivated, as long as she can make her bills. I'd like us to do some angel funding. There are food banks across the US and Canada that need support. And maybe we should sit down with Jim's fiancée, Kate, to talk about the best way to build a foundation. Kate is building an incredible program with Bullseye.

Life is good.

Tinsley shuffles through the mail and stops at a thick envelope, hand calligraphed with our names. "Someone's getting married," she says as she slices it open.

After a moment, a grin breaks out on her face. "We're invited to a party at Caroline Arnault's. Do you think she and Mason are going to elope in front of friends?"

"She's been planning something for the spring in Italy," I say. I'm too tired to think about it. "I'm going to bed. Come with me." I hold my hand out for her, but Tinsley has been sucked in by her email on her phone.

"I'll be right there. My mom has a question about our schedule."

Tinsley told me not long ago that her mom had said she'd never marry again, but her boyfriend of something like sixteen years has told her she either needs to marry him or he's moving on. I know exactly how he feels. I would prefer to have Tinsley make some sort of an official commitment to me. Then maybe once we have some kids, I'll be able to get her to marry me. But we'll make it work however she wants to. I'm crazy about her.

I walk back to the master, and I smell vanilla and something burning. We better not have left a candle going all night. That could have started a huge fire. I swing the door open, and our bedroom is swathed with burning candles. Tiffany is lying provocatively on the bed with some kind of fur blanket. She's naked.

"What the hell?" I yell.

"Hey, handsome." Tiffany plays with her nipples, which she seems to have had pierced. "I thought after all the work you've been doing, you might want a break."

"How the hell did you get into my apartment?"

Tiffany opens her legs and begins to play with herself. I can't help but gape as I stare at her.

"Oh, I miss your big cock," she says. "My pussy is so wet, and it needs you."

"Get your fucking clothes on. You can't be here." I back up to the door, shaking my head. "You need to get the fuck out of my apartment."

Suddenly I see Tinsley running in with Greg and Yolanda on her heels. This can break two ways, and I'm not sure I'll come out ahead in either.

"But baby, you love me. I make you feel all good inside."

Tinsley looks at her in disgust. I'm ready to defend myself about how she got here, but instead, Yolanda steps forward and pulls Tiffany out of the room, binding her with zip ties.

"Oh baby, I like it rough. You should see how wet I am. We're going to make your night."

Greg is on the phone with 911.

As Yolanda leads her away from me, Tiffany's seduction moves from nasty to angry. "I can't believe you'd do this to me," she yells. "I've been patient, but I'm ready to finish what we started."

I'm so stunned I don't know what to do. I still can't figure out how the hell she got into my apartment.

Tinsley grabs Tiffany's clothes and throws them at Yolanda as they step into the hall. "She'll need these."

Yolanda catches them with one hand as she pushes the

trespasser out the door.

"That's it! She has to get out of the building," I fume. "How the fuck did she get into my apartment?" I call the only person who has any access to my place.

"Do you know what time it is?" Mike rumbles into the phone.

"I know it's fucking late. Tiffany Reynolds was in my bed when we got home tonight. What the fuck?"

"Yeah, how did that go? Did you get a ménage with Tinsley out of it? Tiffany is a freak in the sheets, man."

"Did you give her access to my apartment?" I'm blind with rage.

"Sure. I knew you had fun with her, and she's been pestering me about you, so with all the stress you've been under, I played a bit of matchmaker. Tell me it was fucking awesome."

"You thought it would be funny for me to find a woman naked in my bedroom when you know I'm in love with Tinsley? How fucking immature are you?"

"You don't need to be so hostile. I was only trying to help."

"Mike, Fiona McPhee will be sending you notice. I'm calling in the loan for the building. I want you out, and I want you out of my life. I can't fucking believe you thought this was acceptable. I have no patience for this kind of immature shit."

I disconnect the call and throw my phone across the room. I hear a crack. I blanch. That's my life on there.

"Feel better?" Tinsley asks.

"No! Can you believe he thought it would be funny for us to come home to Tiffany in our bed? I can't even tell you what he thought he was doing."

"You might have found it fun before you met me."

"No way. I may have picked up women, but there was a reason I didn't invite them into my apartment."

Tinsley stands on her tiptoes and kisses me. "It's kind of hot to see you so worked up."

"She was naked on our sheets. I can't sleep in those sheets."

Tinsley looks at the bed, which is a mess of rumpled sheets and that nasty fur blanket thing. "I'm good with that. We can change the sheets."

"I'm going to tell the housekeeper to burn these sheets," I tell her as we yank them off.

Tinsley is laughing. I can't believe it. She's not nearly as upset as I am.

I pick up my phone, and the screen is broken, but I can still use it. I text Fiona.

Me: I need a restraining order for Tiffany Reynolds. She was in our apartment and in our bed when we got home tonight.

Fiona: No problem. Has she been arrested?

Me: Yolanda and Greg escorted her downstairs.

Fiona: I'll follow up with Jim on the details in the morning. I hope you're burning those sheets.

Me: Trust me, I am.

Me: I also want to call in the loan with Mike. He thought it would be funny to give Tiffany access to my apartment. I want him out, and I can absorb the debt.

Fiona: I'll get that done for you on Monday. I'll need to get a few bits of information from you for that.

Me: Thanks, Fee.

Fiona: No problem. Have a good night.

I look over at Tinsley. She's made the bed with fresh

sheets. "I guess I'll need to get over to the Apple store tomorrow," I tell her.

"I understand from Mason that we can call them and they'll send someone here," she replies with a grin.

"That's a good idea. We have been on TV a lot recently."

She nods. "Is Fiona going to help with Tiffany?"

"Yes, and I'm calling in the construction loan on the building."

"What does that mean?"

"If Mike can't come up with the cash in less than two weeks, I'll own half the building — roughly eight apartments. We've been selling it off slowly to build desirability and, of course, the value."

"Does that mean he'll have to sell a bunch of apartments?"

I know she's trying to decide if she wants to buy one. But I want her living here with me. Getting down on my knees, I pull her close, and with my head on her belly, I close my eyes. "Tinsley, I know these past five months have been a whirlwind. My life was complete chaos before I met you. You center me and are the sun in my universe. I love you and want to spend the rest of my life with you. I know you don't want to get married, but can we make a commitment to be together for the rest of our lives?"

I look up into her big brown eyes. She nods and smiles. "I will commit to you. And if you want a big ceremony in front of friends and family in a church, I might be willing to do that."

I look at her, puzzled. "Did you propose to me?"

She grins. "I think I expanded on your proposal."

"Does this mean you want to get married? I didn't think you wanted that."

She lets out a deep breath. "I talked to my mom about it when she told me *she* was getting married again. She reminded me that a marriage is more than a piece of paper.

It's a commitment that goes beyond an agreement and sharing powers of attorney. It's an expression of our love. Is it okay that I changed my mind?"

I pick her up and twirl her in my arms. "We're going shopping for a ring." I know exactly what I want. I saw it at Cartier shortly after we met and knew it was perfect for her.

"A gold band is more than enough."

"Are you kidding? No way. You need a big rock that's a beacon, telling all men you're not available."

"We'll see." She bends down, and our lips meet in a soft, lingering kiss.

"I don't want what happened tonight to happen again."

"I know, but I also know that it might." Tinsley steps back so I can stand, and then she presses up against me. "You're a good-looking guy who stuffs his pants with two socks."

I pick her up and toss her on the bed. "You're going to be so sorry you said that."

"Do you promise?"

CHAPTER 43

Tinsley

Claire and I have talked several times over the last week about this party at Caroline's, and we know something is up with it. When I ask Caroline what I should bring, she says, "Totally not necessary."

Claire tried to get details from a few other friends, but everyone seems to be in the dark. All we know is that it's supposed to be a press-free event. It's hit the gossip pages, and I know it's going to be huge. I feel wholly unprepared.

I look down at my left hand. Landon picked the perfect ring for me—a very large, princess cut diamond and an eternity band of sapphires, all set in platinum. When he presented it to me, I rewarded him with an intense night of therapy with the cock ring.

To prepare for the party, Claire, Chrissy, and I schedule a girl's day to go shopping and end with a massage. Claire introduces me to her personal shopper at Nordstrom, Jennifer. It took almost three hours, and it seems like I've tried on three hundred dresses, but we finally found one. It's blue and silver and hugs all my curves. I would prefer that it not be so revealing, but Chrissy, Claire, and Jennifer swear it's perfect.

Claire also talks Jennifer into picking out a whole new wardrobe for me that isn't primarily jeans, Chuckies, and retro T-shirts.

"Where am I ever going to wear this stuff?" I bemoan.

"To start with, you'll wear it when we ring the opening bell on the Nasdaq. We also have a few events coming up, and I'm sure we'll find some other reasons for you," Claire replies.

"If you can get her out of her uniform of jeans and a T-shirt, I'll help you burn them all," Chrissy says.

"No ganging up on me." I try to sound annoyed, but I'm not.

Claire starts clapping and bouncing up and down. "Wait until we go shopping for a wedding dress."

I shake my head. I'm not ready for that. "And it would be a commitment dress," I correct with a raised eyebrow.

Before we leave, Jennifer comes in with an ivory-colored gown and a sexy pair of sandals. "I know you're not shopping for this occasion yet, but I thought you might want to keep this in mind."

She holds up the dress. It's sleeveless with a sweetheart neckline. The bodice is covered in hand-sewn Swarovski crystals, and the skirt is a simple A-line. I stop and stare.

"It's you," Chrissy breathes.

"Would you like to try it on?" Jennifer asks.

I nod. The ladies help me into the dress, but I'm too nervous to look in the mirror. When Claire gasps and covers her mouth with her hands, I finally do. It's a little longer in the back, so that it has a subtle train.

"It's perfect," I whisper.

The dress costs more than ten thousand dollars, but Chrissy and Claire talk me into it. "We haven't even decided where, let alone when, we'll have a ceremony," I protest.

"You said it would be in a church," Claire counters.

"It'll work."

Each of us spends more money than we expected to, and we send the packages back home while we get massages and have our hair blown out, plus mani/pedis — all in preparation for tonight.

I wish Chrissy could join us at the party. I need to find a good friend of Landon's to introduce her to. She's smart, funny, and sensitive. She deserves a guy who's not going to be intimidated by her job and will treat her like the queen she is.

At the end of our day, I'm relaxed and not sure I want to do anything beyond cuddling up with Landon for the evening. Before the driver delves into the garage below the building, Yolanda tells me, "I put the packages in your room. Jennifer will hold on to the white dress until you're ready, so Landon doesn't spot it. But she also told me to let you know you should look at other dresses, to make sure this is the one." She pauses. "I know it's not my place, but you looked beautiful in that dress."

I smile at her. "Thank you. That means a lot."

As Yolanda and I enter the apartment, I stop short. Landon is in his tuxedo. "Wow. You look good enough to eat."

He grins. "I saw a few packages arrive from Nordstrom; I have a feeling Claire has corrupted you."

"We picked out a couple new things for me. But I'll never be the shopper she is."

"We need to leave in a little over an hour." He looks at me suggestively.

"I'll be ready in time."

I walk past him and pull out the dress for tonight. Jennifer included sexy lingerie for each outfit. Today's dress calls for no bra, but she added petals, so if I'm cold, the high beams won't be garnering all the attention.

I lean over the dress on the bed, but I sense the moment Landon enters the room. He pulls something out of the drawer as I'm struggling with the tag. I don't want to pull it and risk a hole in my new dress. Suddenly, I feel his hands on me, plus a small vibration that he smooths over my skin.

I lean into him and moan. He reaches around to my mound.

"You're so wet."

"We can't be late," I breathe as I push into his hard cock, bound by his pants. He takes me by the hand into the bathroom, puts me on the counter, and inserts the egg-shaped vibe. My breath catches.

"God, you're beautiful."

He licks me from bottom to top, and between the vibe, his fingers, and his tongue, I'm over the edge quickly. He makes sure the vibrator stays in place.

"Are you going to make me wear this all night?" I stand, not sure what to do.

He picks up his phone and increases the speed.

I turn and grasp the counter to steady myself.

"I bet I could get you to do just about anything right now." Landon licks the base of my neck.

I hold my breath as he reaches around me, applying a bit of pressure to my clit, and I moan his name so loud, I wouldn't be surprised if the entire building heard me.

"You're so sexy when you come."

It takes a few minutes, but I finally come down from my bliss.

I turn and step into him. "I'm going to more than return the favor later tonight."

He winks at me and swats my ass. "Get dressed and leave the egg vibe where it is. We need to go."

My eyes go wide, but I pull my dress on, and we take the elevator to the garage with our team close at hand.

The traffic down Broadway is slow. There's a long line of cars, and we all seem to be headed the same place.

"I thought this was supposed to be a quiet party," I muse.

"It's Caroline Arnault. I'm not sure she does quiet."

When we pull up, Yolanda jumps out of the passenger side and opens the door. There's a covered walkway, and we exit the vehicle and walk in.

Caroline greets us at the door, looking stunning in a navy blue, full-length sequined dress. "Welcome. Please come in. There are bars throughout, and appetizers being passed. Festivities should start soon."

"Any spoilers about what's going on?" I press.

She grins and shakes her head.

We walk in and find Claire talking to Viviana. I join them as Landon heads for the bar. Viviana reaches for my hand and evaluates my engagement ring. "That's stunning."

I smile. "Landon did good."

"He's a great guy. Now we need to find me a good guy." She winks.

"Me, too," Claire adds.

I feel a sudden vibration from the egg, and I hold my breath, waiting for the sensation to pass. "Anyone know what's going on?" I manage.

Claire and Viviana shake their heads.

I smile and adjust my hips as the speed increases, deep inside me. I don't know whether to kill Landon or thank him. My breathing becomes quietly labored as my orgasm hits.

"Are we taking bets?" Walker Clifton walks up and hands drinks to Claire and Viviana. Landon is just behind him with my drink and a devilish look. The vibe stops as suddenly as it started.

"This might throw off the paparazzi if Caroline and Mason are getting married tonight," Viviana offers.

"How did everything shake out?" I hear Walker ask Landon in a low voice.

"Thanks for your help, man. I appreciate the stall until Jim's team was able to find her."

"No problem. Patel wasn't pushing the grand jury very hard. I don't think he would have gotten the green light to prosecute."

It isn't long before we're moved into a large room. Mason stands in front of the group and addresses everyone. "We're coming up on a year since the unfortunate event that took our beloved Cecelia Lancaster from us," he says.

I never met Cecelia, but goosebumps cover my arms.

"Eight and a half weeks ago, my good friend Nathan Lancaster was arrested for his wife's murder."

The crowd shuffles, and it's obvious no one here agrees with that turn of events.

"Well, I'd like to introduce you to the recently not-charged-and-released Nate Lancaster, who's come out of hiding to be here tonight."

The crowd breaks into applause as the ever-handsome Nate appears next to Mason. "Thank you all so much for your support. The last year has been tough, but the phone calls, emails, texts, and visits have not gone unnoticed. I appreciate all of you, and I know if my Cecelia were here, she'd be much more eloquent and giving you all hugs of gratitude."

The crowd claps as Nate raises his glass and grins. "I'd like to toast all of you for what you've done for my girls and me."

Everyone takes a drink.

"I'd also like to thank my best friend in the whole world, James Adelson, and his fiancée, Katherine Monroe, who put their nuptials on hold because of everything that's been happening. So, I've been ordained by the State of California and the Church of Every God, and Jim and Kate have agreed to let me marry them here tonight."

The crowd goes crazy.

"I wish Cecelia could be with us, but I'm so happy all of you are here to join me."

After the short ceremony, everyone toasts Jim and Kate, and they deserve it. It's wonderful to see them together and happy.

Landon holds me in his arms. "This was one fantastic party, eh?"

"It was a lovely evening," I agree.

"Seemed like you were particularly enjoying yourself right after we arrived," he adds with a raised eyebrow.

"I'm sure I don't know what you mean," I counter, suppressing a laugh. "I'm proud of myself for remaining upright, and I'm also happy you quit while you were ahead."

"I prefer to think of it as more of a pause in the action." He smiles and kisses my lips. After a moment, he squeezes me tight and sighs. "This year has had its ups and certainly its downs. Without you, I don't know how I would have managed."

I smile up at him, and my heart swells.

"I never thought I would feel so centered and complete," he adds. "I love you."

Running Hot

Tech Billionaires book 4

A Preview

by:
Ainsley St Claire

CHAPTER 1

Marcella

"Do we have any other options?" I stare down at Raven Stewart, my associate, and she shakes her head.

"Elena was all over Chirp last night, and the stock has bottomed out," she says. "The US Attorney's office wants her bad for stock manipulation."

"Who's assigned to the case?" I ask for the third time, hoping the answer has changed.

"Miguel Garcia."

"The man I beat out in law school for Order of the Coif. Great. Going over his head is going to have him gunning for my clients." I stare up at my *I love me* wall—an array of accomplishments that mean I've worked hard and I'm good at my job but mean nothing when you have to go see your arch enemy and grovel. "Call Walker Clifton's office and find out where he's going for lunch today. I'll stop by and sell a bit of my soul to him."

Raven slides a piece of paper across the desk. "He's at

the Union Club."

"Fuck. Really?"

Raven Stewart is one of the best associates I've ever had. She is a master chess player and always thinking four steps ahead.

"Is he there now?"

She looks at her watch and nods.

"Call me a rideshare. I'll be back in twenty minutes."

I sling my coat over my shoulders and grab my couture bag. Elena is going to pay for this.

When I step out on the sidewalk a few minute later, I look up at the concrete building and its giant columns. It's close to the capitol building, and the architecture looks the same, but there's one major distinction: no women are allowed inside the hallowed halls of this all-men's private gathering place called the Union Club.

The man I'm about to ask for a favor may very well end up president of the United States one day, but today he's the United States Attorney for the Northern District of California, and his minion wants to screw one of my clients for having a heated moment on Chirp last night with a senior member of her team.

I open the door, and the dark, wood paneled walls and low lighting scream debauchery. It always smells like Pledge to me, but that would be too mundane a product for the employees to use at such a highly regarded club.

The man behind the podium looks down in his tailored suit. "How may I help you?" he asks in such a monotone and distasteful way that I feel like gum stuck on the bottom of his shoe.

I paint a smile on my face. "I'd like to see Walker Clifton, please."

"We don't allow women on our premises."

I bet if I was a hooker, they'd allow me, but I'm not going to argue that with this guy who's only doing his job — despite the fact that he's condescending as hell.

"Can you let him know Marci Peterson would like a moment of his time?" I hand him a copy of my engraved business card. It at least alerts him that I'm of moderate importance and most likely not a woman threatening to sue Walker for paternity.

He lifts the card and hands it to a large gentleman with an earpiece who takes it and disappears.

A group of men enter behind me, and I step aside. Walker will make me wait. He always does. This is the little power game he plays. I pull my cell phone from my pocket and lean against the wall, my legs crossed at the ankles. I play a few rounds of Candy Crush.

I'd love to take these hideous shoes off. Stilettos are the brainchild of a man. I wish comfortable shoes were in style.

Groups of men continue to come through the entry, and the man at the front knows them all by name. It's impressive as he clicks on his computer and checks them in. Most of them assess me as they walk by. I'm not interested in any man who belongs to an all-men's club. It's too sexist for me.

They're probably all missionary-type guys anyway — *boring*.

"Well, well, well, look who's darkened our doorstep."

I stand up and slip my phone into my coat pocket. "Good to see you, Walker. Do you have a moment?"

He looks me up and down, and I'd swear his eyes become hooded, but I know better. He likes his women so thin they look like they'd break in half. I've got child-bearing hips, breasts that are more than a handful and have pointed down since I was twelve, not to mention wild, curly, blond hair that has a mind of its own.

"Of course." He looks over his shoulder. "Geoffrey, may we step into the parlor for a few moments?"

"Of course, sir."

Walker opens his arms, and I step three paces into a room I hadn't noticed. "Thank you."

The room smells like old cigar smoke, and two leather chairs are turned toward a billiard table. Walker points to the chairs.

"No, thank you. I only want to ask a favor." I push my hands into my pockets and bite the inside of my cheek. I hate this man, but I need to control myself.

"You are always asking for favors," he says slowly.

I shrug. "Your little minions are always gunning for my clients, who we both know are your future donors."

"What do you need?"

"Assistant US Attorney Miguel Garcia to step back from Elena Tuskan."

"Her stockholders are furious with her." Walker knows precisely why I'm here.

"That's the only reason they're selling off this morning," I explain. "She's the major stockholder and can take the financial hit."

Walker steps toward me, and I don't realize I'm backing up until the billiard table hits my thighs. "Why are you the only one who seems to get favors from me?" He's so close his breath warms my neck.

It takes me a moment to collect myself. "Because I did *you* a favor and put your dick in my mouth." I wince internally. That's a bit of a low blow. If I'm honest, he broke my heart, and the favors are all payback.

Walker smiles. "That's true. Why are Elena and her head of manufacturing fighting on Chirp?"

"Because he broke up with her, and her feelings are hurt." I glance down at his long fingers and remember what he's done to me with them. I clear my throat. "She'll take a hit financially, but she's stressed. Everything will be back to normal in a few days."

"And if they aren't?"

"Then she'll be without money, and no one will fund her again since she's too emotional."

He takes a few steps around the table and picks up one

of the balls. "You know, you'll owe me — again."

I nod and purse my lips, waiting for the day I'm the one he calls to cover his ass when he fucks up.

He rolls the ball around in his hand and then sends it across the table. "I will call in that favor one of these days."

"I'd expect nothing less."

He stares at me, and if it was anyone else, I'd swear he was thinking about my lips on his dick again. But he made it clear when we were fifteen that there would never be a repeat, and he always keeps his word.

"I'll talk to Mr. Garcia."

"Thank you." I turn to leave, and he reaches around me to open the door.

"One of these days I'm going to make you pay up," he reminds me.

"My checkbook will be ready."

My phone rings that evening, and I roll my eyes. It's almost eight thirty, but I have a few more hours of work before I can go home and start all over again tomorrow. Elena has been a mess all day. Sometimes I'm part lawyer, part therapist for her. I also have another client dealing with an ex who bugged his phone and harassed him and his wife. I have a small list of clients, but when it rains, it always pours, and these days I'm drinking from a firehose.

I reach for the phone, and the caller ID tells me it's my mother. If I don't answer, I know she'll keep calling.

"Hello, Mamma." I run my hands through my hair. It only makes the curls frizz, but it's a habit.

"Sweetheart, are you coming on Saturday to my party?" my mother asks in her rich Italian accent.

"Yes, Mamma. I told you I'd be there." She's going to call every day to make sure. That's probably three more calls.

"I think you should wear that pretty pink dress that brings out the pink in your cheeks."

I'm not sure it fits right now. I haven't been good about working out recently, and I order takeout three meals a day.

I roll my eyes. "Mamma, that's a summer dress. I'll be cold."

"Nonsense. You have beautiful shoulders. It's a great dress."

It has a full skirt and makes my waist look tiny, but my boobs fall out of the top. My mother is up to something. Someone is coming to the party, and she's playing matchmaker.

"Mamma? Who have you invited to the party?"

"Family. Friends. You know, the usual suspects."

She's trying to brush it off, but I know she's up to something. For all I know, it could be her gynecologist. She does that.

"Why do I think you're forgetting someone?"

"I promise you, there's no set-up going on. Just come and look gorgeous."

"I may have a date. Can I bring a plus one?" I don't, but this will temper her expectations.

"Of course, but warn him that your brothers will put him through the wringer."

I sigh. I have three brothers, and they're all hyper-protective. They're the reason I'm almost thirty-two years old and have no social life that isn't a family event. When I graduated from Michigan Law School, I should have found a job in New York or someplace far away from my family. But no. I moved home, where my brothers still try to run my personal life. No one is good enough.

It doesn't matter. I spend all my time working anyway.

"I'll warn him," I tell her. "He's not easily intimidated."

In her eyes, I'm an old maid. By my age, she had all four of us and was a widow. She's never remarried because my father was the love of her life.

She tells me all about her party plans, and I'm a good daughter and make the appropriate noises as she explains. My three sisters-in-law have been busy planning, and because I'm so screaming busy, I've just written a lot of checks, which doesn't bother me at all.

Just a few more days, and this will be behind me.

On Saturday, as promised, I arrive at my mother's sixtieth birthday party in my brother's backyard in the Sunset neighborhood of San Francisco. He's two blocks from Golden Gate Park and twenty blocks from the beach. In most parts of California, that would spell expensive real estate, and it is expensive, relatively speaking, but Sunset is in the avenues and is the working-class part of San Francisco, because it sits under clouds of dense fog for more than ten months of the year.

I've worn the pink dress, but covered up my overflowing chest with a sweater. I also wear a pair of heels that kill my feet. They look so good in the store when I try them on. They make my legs look longer and stick my butt out a bit, but if I stand in them too long, my toes cramp and my back hurts. I promise myself I won't be a slave to fashion forever.

As soon as I'm able, I kick my shoes off and enjoy the grass between my toes. I walk up and down, evaluating all the great food — antipasto, salami and fig crostini from the figs in my mother's backyard, rosemary-potato focaccia, bruschetta, meatballs that have simmered in my mother's homemade sauce, cannelloni, and thousands of fried foods. I want to indulge, but I know if I do, I'll have to spend hours I don't have right now on the elliptical in my apartment.

Breath warms my neck. "It's so sexy when you're barefoot."

I turn around. "Walker Clifton? Why are you here?"

"Your mother was a second mother to me. She invited me."

He's been handsome his whole life. His dark hair is short, but expensively cut, and if I had to bet, highlighted. He's wearing a rolled-neck wool sweater that sets off his emerald green eyes and naturally tanned skin, jeans that hug his perfect ass, and a pair of leather half-boots that I'm sure cost more than my brothers make in a year.

I roll my eyes. "You know, it's bad enough that I have to deal with you at work all week and pretend I don't know what an asshole you are, but this is my family time. You should leave."

"Hey, look who's here!" my oldest brother, Tommy, announces, bringing Walker into a side hug. "If it isn't the future governor of California gracing us with his presence."

My mother comes rushing over. "The whole family is here." She hugs Walker and kisses both of his cheeks, not so subtly winking at me.

My family loves Walker Clifton. They wouldn't if they knew he'd deflowered me when we were fifteen years old and then dumped me. If I were to tell Tommy his precious Walker popped my cherry, he'd probably cut off his dick. The thought makes me smile.

"You're beautiful when you smile," Walker whispers to me.

"I was thinking about what would happen if I told my brothers what you did to me when we were fifteen."

"They'd still love me." He smiles.

"Shall we find out?"

"I can take it, but can you?"

I wish I could haul off and kick him in the balls. He knows my brothers and me well enough that he's probably right. Damn it.

Walker's a pain in my ass.

I take my overflowing plate to one of the plastic tables

adorned with red and white checkered tablecloths, and Walker follows right behind and sits next to me.

"Just because my family likes you doesn't mean I have to," I remind him.

"This isn't what you said when you came to beg me to ask one of my — what did you call him? Minion? — to leave your precious, broken-hearted client alone."

I shake my head. It's none of his business that her employee got her pregnant and broke up with her because of it. I hate men. But I just smile and eat my dinner while my family files past to catch up with him.

Walker is our family celebrity. As the night wears on, he talks to everyone like the politician he is. He dances with my mom, and she laughs and blushes. He's good to her when he doesn't have to be. He does have some — albeit minimal — redeeming qualities.

I want to sneak out, but I'll never hear the end of it if I don't say goodbye, so I'm stuck until every last dish is washed and put away. Tomorrow morning will come early, but there's nothing I can do. I need to work. I'll sleep when I die.

As the party begins to die down, I'm sitting with my sister-in-law Francie and my nine-month-old nephew, Tommy Junior, who's eying my breasts like they might hold dessert.

Suddenly a warm hand touches my shoulder, which sends an electric jolt to my core. "I need to go, princess." The owner of the hand, Walker, nuzzles my neck and plants a kiss below my ear. "Can we have lunch this week?"

My mother overhears and answers for me. "She'd be delighted."

Oh, I'd rather put a salad fork through his eye — or mine. To say I hate this man would be an understatement. There's no way I'm going to share a meal with him.

I nod, but we both know he has no intention of meeting me for lunch. It's all for my mother's benefit.

"See you soon." He winks at me and walks off.

My mother sits down. "That man has been crazy about

you since you were in elementary school."

Hmph. If she only knew. "Mamma, I know you think Walker and I belong together, but let's be realistic." I dig out my phone and Google him. "Look at the women he dates." I show her picture after picture of socialites. "These women are waifs, with pedigrees and rich families. He needs *that* for his political aspirations, not his housekeeper's daughter and childhood friend."

"Oh sweetheart, those women are all window dressing." She pats my hand. "He loves you."

"Not only does he *not* love me, but if we didn't work together, he wouldn't look at me twice. Mamma, I hate that man. He's everything that's wrong with our society."

"Hate is just the opposite of love," she says calmly. "And we all know opposites attract."

PreOrder *Running Hot* on Amazon

Are you wondering where it all started?

Read Emerson & Dillon's steamy story.

Forbidden Love

Billionaire Venture Capitalists book 1

A Preview

by:
Ainsley St Claire

CHAPTER ONE

Emerson

I wasn't supposed to fall in love with him. I wasn't supposed to need him. I wasn't supposed to want him. But I did fall in love with him, I do need him, and I most certainly want him.

In the beginning....

I can't believe that today of all days I'm running late. I'm usually never late. I live the mantra that late is if you aren't at your destination fifteen minutes before scheduled time. Ugh!

Running into the new office in downtown San Francisco, I am greeted by a well put-together receptionist at Sullivan Healy Newhouse, often referred to as SHN. We're the preeminent venture capital firm in the Bay Area. As of last Friday afternoon, they purchased my company, Clear Professional Services, and I'm now joining the firm as a partner to manage the professional services of all their investment start-ups. It's a way to have a steady paycheck and work with some of the brightest people in San Francisco and the Bay Area.

The offices are bright and open with sparkling clear glass walls, leather office chairs in bright colors, white shellacked desks and tables, and bamboo wooden floors helping to give the space a clean and sharp look. Exiting the elevators, I introduce myself to the receptionist. "Hi. My name is Emerson Winthrop. I'm supposed to meet Sara White."

Smiling, she stands from behind her desk in a soft blue skirt suit that meets just above her knees, a black patterned silk blouse and a soft blue matching jacket. Her highlighted blonde hair is up in a tight chignon, and her jewelry is tasteful yet expensive. Reaching out, she shakes my hand and says, "Welcome, Emerson. I'm Annabelle Ryan. We're happy to have you here at SHN. I'll let Sara know you're here." She makes the call and alerts Sara of my arrival, then tells her she's going to bring me back to her office with a detour by the company break room. "Emerson, follow me. We'll grab coffee and breakfast, and I'll walk you back to Sara's office."

I saw the break room during the process of SHN buying my company; it was impressive then and even more so now. Located in the center of the office, it hosts coffee machines that make coffees, teas, different cocoas, and ciders, an espresso machine where you can make your own, and also a Nespresso machine. Lined atop white Caesarstone counters, there doesn't seem to be any escape from caffeine should anyone desire it. Next to the sink is a glass-fronted Sub-Zero refrigerator stuffed with sodas, juices, waters, fresh fruit and vegetables. Open shelving on the walls gives the kitchen a giant pantry feel with each floor-to-ceiling shelf containing unending rows of almost every snack you can imagine.

In the center, an island which stores all the various plates, silverware, chopsticks, napkins and a food buffet. This morning's breakfast food selection includes various fruit salad selections, bagels, pastries, a cheese plate and a warming plate with eggs and bacon. I'm awestruck. "Is this the spread every day?"

"Unfortunately for my waistline, yes. The guys can eat like crazy, though most of us girls here don't have the metabolism to eat like this. I usually bring in my own coffee so I'm not tempted. Lunch is catered every day and arrives about noon. There is a menu on the fridge so you'll know if you want to bring something in from home. And for those working late, there's a light dinner brought in most evenings." She reminds me of Vanna White as she points out the various amenities. "In the fridge is an assortment of sodas and beers. If we don't carry your favorite, let me know and we'll stock it."

I fill my cup with pure black coffee and an artificial sweetener and follow Annabelle to meet with Sara. She's the corporate counsel and currently runs all the operations at SHN. I'll be taking all the human resources and talent pieces off her plate. She's my peer and the only other female partner. During the purchase, we bonded, part of the reason I chose to sell to SHN.

Sara stands and approaches me with open arms. "Emerson! I'm so thrilled you're here." We make polite chitchat, and then she hands me a calendar for the day. It tells me I'll spend the morning with her going through paperwork, have lunch with the partners, and then I'll be with one of the partners in the afternoon—Dillon Healy.

Before I know it, the morning is gone, even though the real part of my onboarding paperwork was taken care of last week in the lawyer's offices when I sold my company for three times its value. All ten of my employees are transitioning this morning, too, but they all work remotely. Honestly, my business was small potatoes compared to the deals SHN works, but it was a lot to me.

Over the past five years, I grew Clear Professional Services into a dominating provider of all the back-office things small- and mid-sized businesses need, but may not want to do here in Silicon Valley and beyond. We handle billing and accounts receivable, accounts payable, manage the HR function which includes recruitment, and our goal is to never say no when a client asks for something for their business.

Sara and I walk over to lunch to stretch our legs and enjoy a bit of the rare sunshine. "I love this area, but I sure do miss the sunshine," Sara admits.

"It's getting hot out in the desert. It'll bring the fog in, and summer will be gone. Tell me how things are going with your new boyfriend… Henry, was it?"

Blushing, she shares, "He's great. It's still new, but it was unprofessional of me to tell you about him. Please don't let the guys know I said anything. They are very particular that our personal lives should remain personal."

"I understand. It will be our secret. But tell me about Henry. I have no social life, so I need to live vicariously through you."

"He's positively wonderful. I've never been able to be so free and open with anyone like I am with him. He works for a start-up down in Palo Alto."

"Sara! I don't want his stats, I want his *stats*! Is he a good kisser? Does he make you feel all gooey inside?"

Sara blushes a deep shade of pink, which turns even her ears. "He does. He has this way of making me feel good about myself but also seems to want to hear my opinions and ideas. We're moving fast, but we both agree this is pretty great."

I squeeze her arm. "That sounds amazing. I'll admit, I am a bit jealous, but it gives me some hope that there are still some decent guys out there."

We arrive at the trendy waterfront restaurant and are shown to a private room, where the three other partners are waiting for us.

CHAPTER TWO

Dillon

Sara and Emerson walk into the meeting, the girls both look amazing. I played with Sara before she joined the firm, but she wanted more from me than that. It had been a mistake, and thankfully only Mason, one of the other partners, figured it out; however, we almost lost Sara and her partnership because of it, which would have been devastating. Though looking at the two women now, I can't help but briefly fantasize about the three of us together.

Emerson is beautiful. She's tall and also wears a significant heel, which puts her over six feet. I love her blonde hair cascading down her back below her shoulder blades. The slit in her black pencil skirt is demure enough, work appropriate, but at the same time it makes me want to peek underneath to see what she's wearing. Her silk cream blouse with a black velvet trim is sexy in a librarian way.

"Ladies, welcome. Please have a seat." We put Emerson at the head of the table and order a bottle of 1992 Screaming

Eagle Cabernet Sauvignon. It's expensive, but we're excited to have Emerson as part of our team. We toast to her joining us.

It wasn't an easy sell at the beginning. Emerson had put together an interesting concept, and she didn't need us. Her company would do all the business management for various hot start-ups across the bay area and a few other tech hubs across the country — pay bills, recruit, stock option management, manage building issues and anything else that keeps the start-up from doing what they're supposed to be doing.

Before meeting Emerson, I remember someone talking at a party about the business management concept, and I didn't understand the value. Now I know that all those things are part of running a business, and it's certainly beneficial for someone else to deal with it.

In the last three years, we became the most sought-after venture capital firm in the Bay Area. Mason has an MBA from Harvard with an uncanny ability to understand the business side and positioning for sale or going public, Cameron brings a strong technology background to the table, and I bring the knowledge of the numbers. All three of us met at Stanford as undergrads. We were recruited by various start-ups out of school, and we lucked out with all three going huge, making us extremely wealthy very young.

We began our funding of start-ups together as a hobby and a way to share some of our luck, giving seed money to projects we liked as a side gig to our jobs. When four of our investments were bought for millions of dollars each, we were addicted to the gamble and the high of identifying a winner when investing in an exciting idea. Don't get me wrong, not everything we invested in has been successful, but our hit rate has been pretty high, and we like to get in early.

Sara was our company attorney at a law firm we used. We hung our shingle as Sullivan Healy Newhouse, or SHN, about three years ago and hired Sara out of the law firm, offering her partnership. Now we have close to fifty employees helping with the various start-ups and investigating up-and-coming trends. However, we knew something was missing, though we couldn't figure out what it was.

Then we watched a few of our start-ups not make it because they seemed to get bogged down in the operations side of the business and were no longer doing what they were supposed to be doing. It was then that I understood why a professional services company appeared to be a solution.

We're regulars at the Venture Capital Silicon Valley Summit. It offers concepts and start-ups an opportunity to present their ideas and business plans to venture capital firms and individuals. Each is looking at various kinds of funding and are hoping some will invest in their ideas and help make them realities — and the owners very wealthy.

During the conference, we usually sat in private rooms and met with potential investments. I'd never paid attention to nor attended any of the breakout sessions. Randomly, Emerson's talk on "How to Do What You Do Best Without Complications" caught my eye. It seemed to call to me, so I decided to hear what she had to say. I arrived a few minutes late and sat in the back with no expectations.

She was not only a knockout in her conservative black suit with a soft pink blouse and high-heeled black pumps, but she was smart. And not just smart — she was brilliant. Emerson gave an insightful presentation and answered question after question. She could speak to managing accounts receivable and multiple human resources issues, and her pet saying, "How to see the forest for the trees," hit home for me. I knew she was someone I could work with, so I collected all the marketing materials she had and brought them back to the team. They could hear my enthusiasm for what she could bring to our investments to make them stronger and better.

We put our research team on her and her company, and it seemed to be a no-brainer. At least for us.

I reached out to her with a request for coffee, and she politely brushed me off. She ducked my calls and emails for two months. I felt like a dog in heat when she finally agreed to meet me. Apparently, she had four other VC firms looking at her. I knew it was going to be tricky, mostly because she had no interest in selling. It took constant calls before she finally agreed to talk over the phone. My team shared our feelings that we would all benefit by working together. Sure, we could create it, but she had already worked out the kinks, and she was magnetic and would be a great asset to our team.

We went into full buy-mode with her. We invited her to the offices, and again she put us off. We sent her flowers and still no response. Before we could give up, our marketing team suggested we send a crate of oranges to her office with a note written by Mason, as the managing partner, asking "Can you squeeze us in?" She sent back a photo of her and a few members of her team drinking orange juice with a time and their address. The meeting was finally going to happen.

She impressed us all with her negotiation skills. When we got a look at her profit and loss statements, we were pleasantly surprised. She was extremely profitable and would be bringing a significant amount of business as well as ten employees across the Bay Area, plus one in San Antonio. She wasn't negotiating for herself, but we liked that she wanted to look out for her team. It took six months, but finally she and her team joined SHN.

Conversation during today's lunch was fun. We all laughed as Cameron shared a story about his weekend, getting stranded in a biker bar in Sacramento and being hit on by one of the biker's girlfriends. Apparently it was a mess, but he now has new fans in Sac.

We talked about a partner retreat, some business issues, and what we have pending. The two-and-a-half-hour lunch was an excellent start to our working relationship.

San Francisco is my favorite city. The City, as it's

referred to by the locals, is simply urban. Tall concrete buildings in an exact grid pattern, the grass saved for parks and the occasional backyard. Ever-present skyscrapers are smudged by the haze-filled sky, offering no direct sunlight and few birds. Cars race between red traffic lights, stubbornly flickering in their gray surroundings.

Sara decides she can't walk the eight blocks again in her shoes and chooses to ride back with Cameron and Mason to the office, who extend the offer to Emerson. Peering between the buildings at the cloudless skies and taking a deep breath, she says, "It's such a beautiful day. Dillon, we don't meet for another half hour. I think I'd like to walk back. Do you mind if I meet you back at the office?"

Surprised at her passing up a ride, I tell her, "I would be happy to walk with you."

Despite the three-inch heels, she's confident in herself. I can tell by her powerful stride, the way she holds her head up and her shoulders back.

As we walk, we make idle chitchat. "Where are you from originally?" she asks.

With my hands in my pockets, I walk and turn to her at the same time. "Just outside Detroit. What about you?"

"Denver. It's probably why I miss the sun so much. We tend to have more sunshine than San Diego."

"Summers are brutal here. The hot desert valley brings fog, gray and cold to San Francisco. How long have you lived here?"

"I moved to Palo Alto for undergrad and then went east to law school. After graduating almost eight years ago, I came back. And you?"

"I moved here when I was eighteen — which was a long time ago — to attend Stanford and never left."

There were people everywhere. Panhandlers, business suits, the workout-clad and tons of tourist with cameras. We dodged them all like salmon running upstream.

"Do you have any brothers or sisters?" she asks.

"I have a younger sister. How about you?"

"I have four brothers. I'm the baby."

"Four? Wow! That must have been crazy growing up."

"Any guy who looked at me would get the evil eye, and if he talked to me, they might take him out. Made me undesirable to boys while growing up."

"Are they all still in Denver?"

"Yes. All married with at least three kids. What about your sister?"

"She lives in Texas and is married but no kids yet. I'm expecting a call anytime now. She's a teacher, and my brother-in-law works for a big insurance company. They live to focus on their family."

"I suppose that's the way it should be."

We enter the building and I hold the door to the elevator. "You're probably right. Meet you in my office in fifteen minutes?"

To purchase or borrow from KU, please go to Amazon

ALSO BY AINSLEY ST CLAIRE

The Venture Capitalist Series

Forbidden Love (Venture Capitalist Book 1) **Available on Amazon**
(Emerson and Dillon's story) He's an eligible billionaire. She's off limits. Is a relationship worth the risk?

Promise (Venture Capitalist Book 2) **Available on Amazon**
(Sara and Trey's story) She's reclaiming her past. He's a billionaire dodging the spotlight. Can a romance of high achievers succeed in a world hungry for scandal?

Desire (Venture Capitalist Book 3) **Available on Amazon**
(Cameron and Hadlee's story) She used to be in the 1%. He's a self-made billionaire. Will one hot night fuel love's startup?

Temptation (Venture Capitalist Book 4) **Available on Amazon**
(Greer and Andy's story) She helps her clients become millionaires and billionaires. He transforms grapes into wine. Can they find more than love at the bottom of a glass?

Obsession (Venture Capitalist Book 5) **Available on Amazon**
(Cynthia and Todd's story) With hitmen hot on their heels, can Cynthia and Todd keep their love alive before the mob bankrupts their future?

Flawless (Venture Capitalist Book 6) **Available on Amazon**
(Constance and Parker's story) A woman with a secret. A tech wizard on the trail of hackers. A tycoon's dying revelation threatens everything.

Longing (Venture Capitalist Book 7) **Available on Amazon**
(Bella and Christopher's story) She's a biotech researcher in

race with time for a cure. If she pauses to have a life, will she lose the race? He needs a deal to keep his job. Can they find a path to love?

Enchanted (Venture Capitalist Book 8) **Available on Amazon** (Quinn and William's story) Women don't hold his interest past a week, until she accidentally leaves me a voice mail so hot it melts his phone. I need a fake fiancée for one week. What can a week hurt?

Fascination (Venture Capitalist Book 9) **Available on Amazon** (CeCe and Mason's story) It started when my boyfriend was caught in public with a girls lips on his you know what. People think my life is easy - they couldn't be more wrong. As my life falls apart, can we make the transition from friends to more?

Clear Security Holiday Heartbreakers
Gifted **Available on Amazon** (Kate and Jim's story) Forty kids are not going have a Christmas and I don't know how to fix it. I send out a call for help and my prince appears and that's when the wheels really fall off this wagon. Can he help me or am I doomed to fail all these deserving kids?

Tech Billionaires
House of Cards (Tech Billionaires Book 1) **Available on Amazon** (Maggie & Jonnie) Would you agree to a marriage to avoid going to jail? Maggie is the heiress to the Reinhardt Department Store fortune. Her father died and the board of the company expect Alex to run the company but they've never had a nonfamily member run the company. The board has a simple solution—she needs to put the family first and

marry Alex. Forget the fact that she isn't his type and she loves someone else.

Royally Flushed (Tech Billionaires Book 2) **Available on Amazon**
(Corrine & Jackson) Staying with him will be dangerous...They call him Billionaire, Environmentalist, and Playboy. I call him Boss. I try to keep it professional, I want to resist him, but the pull is too strong. A bomb threat, a ransacked apartment, mysterious warnings, all telling me to leave him alone. Yes, staying will be dangerous, but leaving him will destroy me.

Sleight of Hand (Tech Billionaires Book 3) **Available on Amazon**
The night was magical, the morning after wasn't. I was celebrating selling my company when I noticed him enter the bar. Landon knew just what to say and one thing led to another. It was supposed to be a onetime thing, but reality slapped me in the face the next morning. He arrived to sign the purchase papers, and now I was committed to work for him for an entire decade. When I can't make my code work, his patience runs thin. Someone is sabotaging us, and if we can't figure it out, I'll have no company, no money, and no future.

Coming Soon

September 2020

Running Hot (Tech Billionaires Book 4) **Available for Preorder On Amazon**
He must marry. She's the only one he wants he can't have. Can he convince her in time? Becoming Governor is the next step toward my destiny. But, my history will be a problem. The voters always favor a family man. I've done Marcella favors for years and now it's time to collect. She'll make the perfect Governor's wife. It's all for show, and she knows that. With this union, she'll be able to write her own ticket. Danger lurks around every corner, and I may be the only one who can protect her.

Follow Ainsley

Don't miss out on New Releases, Exclusive Giveaways and much more!

www.ainsleystclaire.com

Join Ainsley's **newsletter**
And get a FREE copy of GIFTED!
https://dl.bookfunnel.com/zi378x4ybx

Follow me on **Bookbub**
https://www.bookbub.com/profile/ainsley-st-claire

Like Ainsley St Claire on **Facebook**
https://www.facebook.com/ainsleystclaire/

Follow me on **Instagram**
https://www.instagram.com/authorhainsleystclaire/

Follow Ainsley St Claire on **Twitter**
@AinsleyStClaire

Follow Ainsley St Claire on **Goodreads**
https://www.goodreads.com/author/show/16752271.
Ainsley_St_Claire

Visit Ainsley's website for her current booklist

I love to hear from you directly, too. Please feel free to email me at **ainsley@ainsleystclaire.com** or check out my website

www.ainsleystclaire.com for updates.

Made in the USA
Columbia, SC
30 January 2021